THE
KING
OF
WARSAW

THE
KING
OF
WARSAW

SZCZEPAN TWARDOCH

TRANSLATED FROM THE POLISH BY **SEAN GASPER BYE**

 AMAZON **CROSSING**

Text copyright © 2016 by Szczepan Twardoch
Translation copyright © 2020 by Sean Gasper Bye
All rights reserved.

Previously published as *Król* by Wydawnictwo Literackie in Poland in 2016. Translated from Polish by Sean Gasper Bye. First published in English by Amazon Crossing in 2020.

Published by Amazon Crossing, Seattle

www.apub.com

Amazon, the Amazon logo, and Amazon Crossing are trademarks of Amazon.com, Inc., or its affiliates.

ISBN-13: 9781542044462 (hardcover)
ISBN-10: 1542044464 (hardcover)
ISBN-13: 9781542044448 (paperback)
ISBN-10: 1542044448 (paperback)

Cover design by Patrick Barry / Laserghost

Printed in the United States of America

First edition

Who ain't a slave?

—*Herman Melville, Moby-Dick*

א

ALEF

My father was killed by a tall, handsome Jew with the broad shoulders and strong back of a Maccabi boxer.

Now that boxer stands in the ring. It's the last fight of the evening and the last round of the fight, and I'm watching him from the first row. My name is Mojżesz Bernsztajn, I am seventeen, and I don't exist.

My name is Mojżesz Bernsztajn, I am seventeen, and I am not a person, I am no one, there is no me, I do not exist, I'm the skinny, impoverished son of nobody, and I am looking at the man who killed my father. I see him standing in the ring, handsome and strong.

My name is Mojżesz Inbar, I am sixty-seven. I've changed my name. I'm sitting at a typewriter, writing. I am not a person. I have no name.

The boxer in the ring is named Jakub Szapiro. The boxer has two beautiful sons, Dawid and Daniel, I likely didn't know that back then, but I do now. His black hair glistens with thick Brilliantine.

The boxer killed my father. But now he's fighting.

He's fighting in the final round of this match.

The match for the capital's team championship, League versus Maccabi, began with the flyweights, and so far there have been two sensations. The first was that Baśkiewicz and Doroba fought in higher weight classes. The second was a dispute among the referees. I suppose I wasn't very knowledgeable back then, so it didn't concern me much, but I could hear what the people next to me were saying. They were worked up. Over the fight and the sensations.

I took a seat in the front row, in the auditorium of the Miejskie Cinema on the corner of Długa and Hipoteczna Streets. The owners used to gladly rent it out. I think that must have been my very first time watching a fight.

Two Warsaws were gathered around the ring, alien to one another. I sat among them, right by the platform, but it felt as though I was sitting everywhere, in every chair where a Jew sat, and I was seeing the ring simultaneously from near and from far. No one saw me.

Those two Warsaws were gathered around the ring, speaking two languages, living in separate worlds, reading different newspapers, showing one another indifference at best, hatred at worst, but usually just remote disdain, as though they lived not on neighboring streets but an ocean apart. I was a pale, skinny youth, born somewhere or other, I don't remember where, it must have been seventeen years before, so let's say in 1920, and given the first name Mojżesz. My last name, Bernsztajn, I'd inherited the usual way from my father Naum, and my mother Miriam shared it as well. We were all of the Jewish faith, and I was born a citizen of the recently reborn Polish Republic, and I was sitting, a citizen of a somewhat lower class than the Poles, in the auditorium of the Miejskie Cinema in a building on the corner of Długa and Hipoteczna Streets that had formerly been the Nowość Theater and then housed the Bogusławski Theater before finally hosting movies and boxing.

The slim flyweight boxers were first to go and Jewish Warsaw wept with joy when the referee held up Rudstein's arm at the end of the fight. Kamiński, a bony League boxer, had given up after the first round, completely covered in blood.

Next up—the bantamweights. Our boxer won the first round, which I could tell thanks to the Jewish audience's cheers. He was named Jakubowicz. The Polish referee was clearly favoring his opponent from the League, reducing Jakubowicz's lead with a string of one-sided penalties. There were three rounds, after the third the referee unfairly gave the win to Baśkiewicz from the League, and then all hell broke loose. A fat Jewish man in glasses flung a paper bag full of cherries at the ref, shouting that everyone there knew how to count. A Polish hooligan threw himself on the fat man, but he gave as good as he got and they were quickly pulled apart, but the match broke off for a few minutes.

Once the auditorium had settled down, the featherweights entered the ring and very slow Szpiegelman lost easily on points to Teddy, a.k.a. Tadeusz Pietrzykowski, Warsaw city champion, the same who would later, in another world, fight as a prisoner in Auschwitz and Neuengamme.

In the lightweights, Rozenblum managed to thump tough and resilient Bareja.

In the welterweights, Niedobier absolutely dominated Przewódzki, but even so the ref called a draw. The Jewish audience booed, the Polish one cheered.

Next, the middleweights. Doroba from the League sent our Szlaz sprawling in the first moment of the first round. Everyone could see Szlaz had caught one of Doroba's explosive right crosses, which was all it took to finish him off. The Jewish audience sat grimly silent, the Polish one burst into triumphant applause.

In the light heavyweights, our luck turned: Neuding sent Włostowski to the canvas, and even though he did stand up on the ten, the judges declared it a technical knockout.

Then the heavyweights entered the ring.

"In the right corner, the competitor from Warsaw League, Andrzej Ziembiński!" the announcer's voice rang out. Applause.

He was unquestionably the handsomest of them all and looked nothing like a boxer, more like a track-and-field athlete. Very tall, he had long—though muscular—limbs and the extended torso of a swimmer. His hair was very light, almost white, shaved on the sides and longer on top with a part, and he had pale-blue eyes and an angular, art deco jaw.

For a moment I thought he looked like a movie star, but I soon realized it was something else, that he looked like the pictures and drawings of the German sportsmen, Aryan demigods, sometimes reprinted in illustrated magazines. At the same time there was something delicate in his face, almost childlike, cosseted, something I couldn't name but today I know is simply a trait of the upper crust, who are pampered their entire lives.

"In the left corner, ladies and gentlemen . . ." The announcer paused.

A murmur went through the Jewish stands.

"In the left corner in the colors of Maccabi Warsaw . . ." One more pause.

The crowd was buzzing. The announcer looked over the stands with satisfaction. More than twenty-five hundred spectators had come to the match.

"Jakub Szapiro!" he finally roared.

The Jewish fans jumped up and down, clapped, shouted, chanted his name, the Polish fans applauded reservedly. The boxers stood facing one another. The bell sounded and the auditorium went quiet.

He was beautiful, but his beauty was different from Ziembiński's, sulky. He was also a bit shorter—though certainly at least six feet—and not as slender, obviously heavier.

He had hard, vulgar features, his nose bore traces of a long-ago break, but he was handsome even in ridiculous shiny shorts, an athletic jersey with MACCABI across the chest, and socklike boxing boots that probed the brightly lit ring as though testing thin ice, gently, left-right, left-right, so gently, as though he were anything but a burly heavyweight boxer, 203 pounds of packed muscle, strong bones, and, protruding over the wide belt of his boxing shorts, a hard gut that filled out his vest when he swapped his sports gear for a suit.

Ziembiński weighed 196 pounds but he looked lighter, less than an ounce of fat under his skin, all his muscles sculpted by hard work, like a Greek statue.

I could clearly feel Szapiro's calm and confidence. I could also feel him shiver with pleasure when the crowd shouted his name. I could feel it, an almost sexual thrill moving throughout his body as they chanted: "Sza-pi-ro, Sza-pi-ro, Sza-pi-ro!"

I saw the calm he carried himself with, how sure he was of his body, how he wielded it. His body—drilled, beaten brutally in training—submitted to him, as though stretched on internal springs, he worked his head and shoulders freely, as though slipping under the beams of a low ceiling.

And how he hit.

Power comes from the legs. The soles of the feet, their inner edges, knees pulled in, everything very springy, the right glove protects the jaw from the right side, the left shoulder, elbow tucked in, protects it from the left. And when he strikes, his whole body snaps together in a single burst of energy.

His left hip and shoulder twist, pulled by the stomach and back muscles. These contracting muscles seize the diaphragm, the ribs, so that when he strikes a hiss of air squeezes out of his lungs.

He also pivots his left foot, as though putting out a cigarette, and suddenly throws his left arm outward, as though casting a stone. As it flies, his fist turns and strikes in a brief crack, like a whip, and immediately springs back.

Sometimes, though, his fist is not wrapped in a bandage or tucked inside a glove. Sometimes his fist does not hit a punching bag. Sometimes bare knuckles strike jawbones and teeth come spilling out.

Sometimes that's how it goes. Sometimes that's how it has to be.

But now he approaches Ziembiński light as a dancer, flowing around the ring, switching his legs, a little like Charlie Chaplin in a movie, he's getting closer, delicately jabbing the air with his left fist, as though seeking a hole in the cocoon around his opponent.

Ziembiński responds. He's fighting well, he's a great boxer, I know that now, because I don't think I did back then, I don't think I knew boxing well, I watched and didn't know what I was seeing, but now I remember watching them that evening and I think I was watching with an understanding eye, an analytic eye, an eye picking out all the things only a skillful eye could catch, one that knew what it was looking at. Maybe that's the eye I have today, not the one I had back then.

They fight at a faster pace than heavyweight boxers usually do. Facing a few of Ziembiński's lefts, Szapiro swerves out of the way, swift as a Luxtorpeda train (as they wrote in the next day's paper), but not on his leading left leg, instead on his right and for a moment he assumes a left-hander's stance, with his right hand in front, then throws two quick rights into Ziembiński's surprised face, splitting open his left eyebrow. The League boxer doesn't even know what hit him, but Szapiro eases up, hops back, loosens up, even though now he could press Ziembiński onto the ropes, rain hooks into his head and ribs.

"Finish him now, finish him!" shouts his second.

Szapiro could end it now. But he eases up. He's confident, too confident. He ignores his second's cries. He wants to keep punching.

He's thirty-seven. He isn't young anymore. He was born a subject of the Russian czar Nicholas II, at 23 Nowolipki Street, apartment 31, just over a mile from the place where he's fighting now. His birth certificate bore the Russian name Iakov, his wife (although they're not married, she's still his wife) calls him the Polish name Jakub, or sometimes, like his mother, the Yiddish name Yankyev. His last name remained unchanged but to me he was always Jakub, once he was no longer Mr. Szapiro, of course.

That evening I was eyeing him with hatred, though I didn't yet know he'd killed my father. I only knew he'd taken him away. I learned the whole story later, and later I also fell in love with Jakub Szapiro, and wanted to become Jakub Szapiro, and maybe in some way I have. And maybe now I know. Maybe now I know all of it.

◆ ◆ ◆

Two days earlier, I saw Szapiro drag my father Naum Bernsztajn out of our apartment in a tenement on the corner of Nalewki and Franciszkańska Streets, number 26, apartment 6, pulling him by his long beard and swearing under his breath.

"Biz' aleyn shildig, di shoyte ayno', di narisho' frayo'!"[1] Szapiro said as he jerked my father by the beard. Downstairs, escorted by gargantuan Pantaleon Karpiński and rat-faced Munja Weber, whom I'll write about later, Szapiro threw my father into the trunk of his Buick and drove off.

When Szapiro came I was standing in the kitchen, my mother whispered for me not to budge an inch, so I didn't. My father was hiding in the wardrobe, they found him right away and hauled him out, and when I saw them dragging him out of the building by his beard, I suddenly and unconsciously released the contents of my bladder and a splotch of urine quickly spread on my woolen pants.

Then Szapiro stopped near me, not releasing his grip on my father's beard.

"Hey now, don't be scared, kid," he said very gently.

I hadn't expected such gentleness. From up close, I could see tattooed on his right hand in pale, dark-blue lines a two-edged sword and four Hebrew letters: מוות, reading from right to left: *mem, vav, vav,* and *tav—mavet,* which means *death.*

---

1   It's your own fault you idiot, you stupid sucker!

Then I threw myself on him, straining to hit him. I'd had no problem throwing punches before, we'd had great battles on Broń Square, with Jewish and Christian children punching and throwing stones, heder versus heder, school versus school, until the police would chase us away. Just like everyone.

Szapiro was no teenage kid, though. He dodged my childish attack, rolled his eyes, didn't even hit me, just shoved me away. Mama cried out, I fell to the floor between the table and the sideboard, crying. The whole time I could see the sword and death tattooed on the back of the hand that clutched my father's beard.

I resolved then that I would never have a beard. All that followed from that decision went without saying. I decided to be like him.

As I eyed Szapiro at the boxing match in the Miejskie Cinema, I couldn't see his tattoo—it was hidden by the glove, plus the bandage underneath. Besides, I didn't know Hebrew well, sometimes even today I think I don't know Hebrew well. I don't know if I'd have guessed what מוות meant.

Despite the fact that I was probably seeing boxing for the first time in my life, I watched with fascination. Even as a boy I'd liked fistfights, to me they meant being a new, different Jew, a Jew from a world my father and mother had denied me, and which attracted me, although I knew little about it, a world that didn't fear the drafts and fresh air that so terrified the melamed from our heder, a world without peyos or taleisim. So I watch.

Szapiro, though he's heavy, is remarkably agile. He moves around Ziembiński on his bent legs as though looking for an opening in the taller boxer's impenetrable defenses, he keeps his guard low, right fist by the right side of his chest, the left at the same height in front of it.

I don't think boxers started holding their arms higher until after the war.

Szapiro keeps moving mechanically, left, right, using his elbows to block Ziembiński's few blows to his torso, dodging those to his head by feinting nimbly and springlike, as if he weren't fighting heavyweight but bantamweight, and he keeps backing away from his opponent, letting Ziembiński push him back to the ropes.

Ziembiński, despite the blood flowing from his broken eyebrow, has the clear advantage. He keeps attacking, Szapiro is only defending himself, with feints, with his guard, sometimes returning a quick left.

It looks like he's about to lose, and I wish hard that he would.

But he's completely calm. He's dodging, jumping back, faking with his left, having fun. As though working on a punching bag, not fighting an important match. He's enjoying himself, relaxed, and he can tell that Ziembiński, an experienced boxer all in all, is really frightened by his calm.

There is no more frightening opponent in the ring than a calm and confident one. The most terrifying expression a boxer can wear is a smile.

I keep thinking it's impossible for this Jew who took my father from our house to defeat this slender blond with Warsaw League's black, white, and green emblem embroidered on his jersey. Ziembiński seems to tower over him not only physically, not only by the reach of his arms and his height, but also because Ziembiński is at home here, he belongs to the class of this country's owners and rulers.

He might even be a worker, poorer than the now-late Naum Bernsztajn—though looking back I know he wasn't the least bit poor— yet as a light-haired giant with the League emblem on his chest, he would always be better than a Jewish boxer in a Maccabi shirt.

Back then I couldn't imagine a Jew beating a Christian in the ring, although we'd had fistfights with the Christian boys on Broń Square. That was different, though. I was seventeen then, I knew only the world of the heder, the yeshiva, the synagogue, and home.

Ziembiński pushes Szapiro back as far as the ropes. The Polish audience thinks he's through, but the Jewish boxer suddenly flies backward as though meaning to fall on his back. The ropes pull taut, supporting the weight of his body, and then launch him like a stone from a rubber slingshot—in a perfect rotation, Szapiro slips under Ziembiński's sweeping right hook and strikes him from below with a mighty left uppercut, powering that punch with the spring of the ropes, plus a twist of his shoulders and hips and a straightening of the spine; struck on the chin, Ziembiński immediately goes limp and falls to the mat with a thud, as though Szapiro flicked a switch in his jaw to turn him off just like you turn off an electric light.

Szapiro leaps over his opponent on the mat and goes to his corner, Ziembiński is lying quiet and unconscious, except he trembles like he's having a seizure, eyes rolled back in his head, legs and shoulders jolting like an animal being slaughtered.

The audience cheers, rises from their seats in the as-yet-undirected emotion flowing from the very surprise, the excitement at a fight that hasn't even lasted two minutes; a second later, that enthusiasm gains its bearings, everyone now realizes what's happened. The Jewish fans explode with joy as though they themselves had just brought down every Pole who'd ever looked down their noses at them, the Christians boo, outraged that the proper order of things has been disturbed.

The referee throws himself in Ziembiński's direction, starts to count him out, simultaneously checking his pulse; Szapiro doesn't even deign to look at them, the referee or his unconscious, fallen opponent.

Not waiting for the referee to pronounce the final "ten" and wave his arms, Szapiro spits out his mouth guard and nods to his second, who is in a navy-blue pullover with the word MACCABI spelled out in Latin letters on the chest.

A doctor hops into the ring and feels around on the skull of the Polish boxer, who is still unconscious but now lies peacefully on the floor.

Jakub's second pulls a case of cigarettes from his pocket, lights one, and places it straight in the boxer's mouth. Szapiro takes a couple of drags, then leans out over the ropes; his second takes the cigarette out of his mouth and extinguishes it.

Today I know no other boxer would allow himself such behavior, not then and not now, but I knew and I could see there was something arrogantly grand in Szapiro smoking without taking off his gloves and I liked it very much, because I had never seen a Jew who could afford to be so arrogantly grand. I knew Jews like that existed, but I'd never seen them.

I was seventeen then.

When I was ten, my mother and I went on vacation to a summer resort in Świder, outside Warsaw. Our belongings and my dad, who was looking after them, traveled in a cart, while Mama and I rode third class along what we called "di linye," the train line through the prosperous Jewish suburbs of Miedzeszyn, Falenica, and Michalin, then on to Świder itself. It was my first summer resort and my very first time in the countryside and I was enjoying everything, especially the sun—which was different from in town—and I came to adore the sun's burning glow, an adoration I haven't lost even here, amid white buildings, under a completely different sky, under the blazing sun of Eretz Yisrael.

Mama and I took a walk through the pine forest before she finally unrolled a blanket and from our basket took out some sandwiches and a bottle of lemonade with a patented bottle cap. I ran around the forest, careful never to lose sight of her. I was gathering pine cones. When I looked up, I saw a blond-haired little girl, older than me, Christian, with a blue dress and pigtails, standing over me.

"Hello," I said.

She snorted, rolled her eyes, turned her back, and ran off.

I understood then why she'd left. She didn't want to hear a "hello" from some snotty little Jew with peyos.

Later I came to see she might have left for any number of reasons, she might have been scared of me, she might have felt nothing, and maybe I just added in all the rest.

That day, in Świder, gathering pine cones among the trees and being ten years old, there was something I felt and knew: I didn't want anyone to look at me like that, but I had no idea what I could do about it and I considered it inherent to my being Jewish. It seemed this was how I'd be, this was how I'd stay. I didn't want to be this way, I didn't want to be Jewish, though not being Jewish seemed just as likely as becoming Tom Mix, whose silent horseback adventures we used to watch in the dark tunnels of the traveling movie theaters that in my youth still came to the courtyards of our world, our separate Warsaw.

In any case maybe none of this really happened to me at all, maybe it was Szapiro who told me this story? Our lives blur into one.

Sitting in the former Nowość Theater at the age of seventeen, I realized it wasn't true. I didn't have to be that boy gathering pine cones. A Jew doesn't have to be that kind of Jew, a Jew can be a different Jew, just as good as the Christian masters.

I saw how women, both Jewish and Christian, looked at Szapiro, and they looked at him completely differently from how that blond girl looked at me in the pine forest at the summer resort in Świder.

I see too, how Jakub Szapiro cranes his neck, taking a drag on the cigarette held firmly in his mouth, and he leans toward his second, who obediently removes the cigarette. Szapiro exhales a great cloud of blue smoke, which in the glare of the lights turns arabesques like some alphabet of manly strength, while Szapiro, shaking his shoulders, loosening his muscles, approaches the referee, as though awaiting the verdict, though everyone knows that not only did Ziembiński not get to his feet during the countdown, he's still lying there.

His seconds try to revive him and they finally succeed. The referee seizes the competitors' hands and raises Szapiro's high; Ziembiński sways on his feet and his blank stare wanders the room. The announcer declares the end of the last bout of the evening and the victory of the competitor from Maccabi Warsaw. We applaud. I applaud too.

Ziembiński, still addled, offers Szapiro his hand in the glove and Szapiro bumps it in a gesture which, in the morning edition of the *Warsaw Courier*, the Polish reporter Witold Sokoliński—no fan of Szapiro's—will call symbolic of the Jewish boxer's unsurprising lack of sportsmanship, stating clearly that Szapiro did not shake his opponent's hand.

A friendly Jewish reporter will write in *Our Review* that Szapiro shook Ziembiński's hand disdainfully.

Meanwhile, dazed Andrzej Ziembiński doesn't see the gesture at all. The referee leads him back to his corner where his seconds now wait.

The Christian audience sees the Jewish boxer's gesture and someone whistles, then in the front row of seats a small-statured man stands up, turns around to the audience, and looks, just looks, seemingly trying to spot whoever was whistling. The whistles immediately fall silent and I still don't know who was making them.

The announcer declares an overall victory for the League, nine bouts to seven.

Jakub Szapiro doesn't care about the result of the whole match. Jakub Szapiro is the winner. Jakub Szapiro is like David after defeating the Philistines and the Jebusites, Jakub is the king, and his sons, who of course are not present, are princes.

His second is waiting for him with a freshly lit cigarette. Szapiro takes a drag for a moment, looking at the audience in defiance and triumph, and under the weight of his gaze the last boos fall silent, then he lifts up the ropes, slips between them, and gracefully hops down. Now there's no more whistling. He keeps smoking as one second dries him off with a towel, and the other, the one who lit him the cigarette, unties and removes the gloves and bandages from his hands.

There are no more fights. The auditorium resounds with the murmur of voices and the shuffling of feet. The audience is still coming back down to earth, getting out of their chairs, collecting themselves, tomorrow's a workday, the boxing has come and gone, the world has returned.

The day I saw all this, something happened inside me. As if I'd been the one standing and fighting in the ring against that blond Goliath, as if I'd been in there myself.

As if everything yet to come in my life had its beginning, its origin in that less than two minutes in the ring. Once the seconds freed his hands and draped him in his dressing gown, Szapiro went up to the short, corpulent man sitting in the first row, the one who'd silenced the audience's whistles after Jakub's arrogant gesture.

The man's impressively domed head was completely devoid of hair. He made up for it with a large mustache, pomaded and curled up under his eyes, looking very old-fashioned but suited to his expensive, conservative, and quite tightly fitting navy-blue pinstripe suit.

Gold fobs and chains from his watch and key ring glistened on the vest hugging his round belly, his fingers were thrust in his vest pockets, and he had one leg crossed over the other. His legs were short and plump and it looked like someone trying to cross their middle finger and index finger—he barely managed to get his right calf over his left knee. This caused his pants legs to ride up high, revealing men's garters and an expanse of white flesh between a black silk sock and the hem of his pants. The toe of his patent leather shoe, tipped underneath with glistening tin, moved rhythmically as the man laughed so loudly he shook, and even from a distance, over the cheers of the audience, I could hear his high-pitched guffaw.

"What a pounding, Kuba, what a pounding!" he cried and clapped his fat hands.

I didn't know his real name then, though I knew perfectly well who he was. Everyone the length and breadth of the Jewish Northern District—from Kercelak to Tłomackie, from Broń Square to Mirowska Market, on Nalewki, Gęsia, Miła, and Leszno Streets—knew this short, jolly, frightening goy.

"Here comes Buddy Kaplica," they'd whisper, as, waddling on his bandy legs, he'd promenade down the sidewalk at a leisurely pace, jacket unbuttoned, thumbs in his vest pockets, a horn cigarette holder clenched between his teeth. Following him at a respectful distance were usually his bodyguards, the grips of their seven-shooters and Brownings always visible, unconcealed under their vests—even as they passed police officers, who looked the other way.

Back then I didn't know why Buddy was called Buddy. He was really called Jan Kaplica, but he became Buddy because whoever wanted his friendship was his friend, though his friendship came with a large price tag.

I didn't know how he'd started out. All anyone knew was he was in the Polish Socialist Party and even in czarist days he was running around with a pistol and doing expropriations for the socialist paramilitaries, then during the Great War he'd supposedly served directly under Józef Piłsudski—the hero of Polish independence—in his elite intelligence brigade. After that no one knew, but what they did know was once, when the police arrested Kaplica, the station got a phone call from the president of Poland himself, or some prime minister or deputy prime minister, and then some inspector or commissioner, or even maybe a minister, personally took him home in his own car, drove him to his house, opened the car door for him like a chauffeur, bowed, and to top it all off, apologized.

Nor did I know that it was on Buddy Kaplica's orders that Jakub Szapiro had killed my father. I couldn't even imagine a real big shot like Buddy Kaplica being aware that my father—a modest administrative clerk in the Jewish Clinic and a failed shopkeeper—even existed.

Yet to my father's misfortune, Buddy Kaplica knew perfectly well he existed.

On the day my father shuffled off his mortal coil at the hands of Jakub Szapiro and his men, Buddy Kaplica had been sitting, since seven in the morning, at his table in Sobenski's little snack bar at 22 Leszno Street, next to the Protestant church, as he did every day.

No one except Kaplica would ever consider sitting at that table. Sobenski—a firmly assimilated Jew who didn't go to synagogue at all, and if he did, only to the Great Synagogue, where the cantor dared to praise the Lord in Polish—would personally rush to work every day before six, so that by the time Kaplica arrived, the stuffed pastries and coffee were ready and hot. If Kaplica wished, Sobenski would run to the snack bar even on Shabbos.

Kaplica would arrive punctually at seven, hang up his bowler hat, and if it was autumn, his coat and scarf as well, or his fur coat if it was winter, and then—if he'd put galoshes over his shoes for rain or bad weather—take off the galoshes and place them under the coat stand.

Next he would greet Sobenski effusively, sit down, open up the *Warsaw Courier*, and read, simultaneously moving his lips and running his fat finger along the text. Sobenski would personally serve him a large coffee, black and hot, and some kosher stuffed pastries. Until seven thirty, no one had the right to bother Kaplica.

"That's my time, the only thirty minutes of the whole day that belongs to me alone!" he would say, and diligently study the classifieds and ads, and laugh at the cartoons and funny poems on the back page.

At half past seven, Dr. Radziwiłek would arrive, order a coffee, pick up *Our Review*, and join Kaplica at the little round table; they would read the paper together and confer for a long time. I'll tell of Radziwiłek later, he'll be an important person in this story, but not right now. At any rate he was Kaplica's closest accomplice and deputy.

Usually Kaplica would also invite Szapiro to come at seven thirty and allow him to listen in on those conversations with Radziwiłek, the sole one of his men allowed to do so, anointing him, as it were, the first among his soldiers.

At eight, the rest of Kaplica's gang would arrive, packing tightly into the little snack bar. They would eat and drink, trade gossip, shout over one another in Polish, Yiddish, and Russian, report on their early-morning duties, and present Kaplica the wads of banknotes he was due, while Kaplica, without rising from the table, would assign them their tasks for the coming day and night.

The day my father died began the same way.

On July 9, 1937, it was warm in Warsaw but not hot, in the high sixties, all day the sky was slightly cloudy with occasional rain.

At seven, Kaplica took his seat at Sobenski's, drank his coffee, and ate four pastries stuffed with chopped mutton and raisins. Sobenski turned on the radio and Kaplica listened to the morning news, then, when the radio started playing recorded music, he studied an article in the *Courier* about the situation in Spain.

"General Franco's really got our boys by the short and curlies," said Kaplica, worried, and on cue, Sobenski nodded and worried as well, though he couldn't have given less of a damn about Spain, the civil war, General Franco, or anything beyond the state of his snack bar's cash register.

Kaplica gave up on Spain and plunged into the ninety-ninth episode of Juliusz German's novel *The Amaranths*, in which Prince Poniatowski delivered a speech in a Warsaw theater. It was a boring episode and didn't interest him until the last paragraph, in which a "young, enchantingly lissome lady" appeared. He sighed and snapped his fingers for Sobenski, who refilled his coffee.

Radziwiłek didn't come because he had business in Łódź. At seven thirty, Szapiro, in a gray double-breasted suit and soft hat, drove up in his Buick. He greeted Kaplica and Sobenski, ordered a coffee, and picked up the still-unread *Our Review*—taking advantage of Radziwiłek's absence, since he found newspapers crumpled from other people's browsing somewhat distasteful—then he sat down next to his boss, without opening the paper.

"They caught those guys from Grochów district yesterday," he announced.

"That so?" Buddy wasn't too interested.

"Yep. At that whore of theirs, Jadźka's. Had a shoot-up with the cops."

"So what?"

"The cops shot Gac. The rest surrendered."

"Gac, that Eighth Infantry deserter?"

"That's him."

"Good for them," said Kaplica cheerfully. "Them hicks from Rembertów and Miłosna thought they could come to Warsaw and play with the big boys."

Szapiro opened his paper and settled into reading.

Before long, Buddy interrupted him. "Say, what they got in there about this Josyk Pędrak?"

"The same. Life sentence." The boxer shrugged.

"It's never the same."

"Well, if Baran had been Szmul instead of Stanisław, and Pędrak had been called Józef not Josyk, he could have pleaded self-defense, but as is, it's murder." Szapiro shrugged again.

Buddy thought for a moment, then agreed. He never made a judgment without thinking.

"Yeah, you got it. If it'd been a Pole against a Jew, there'd be a defense. But it's murder, it's the other way around."

He lit a cigarette. Szapiro noticed Kaplica's lighter had a revenue stamp from the state tobacco company.

"How much are those?" he asked.

"A złoty apiece."

"And Buddy Kaplica just civic-mindedly went to the tax office to buy a stamp for his lighter?" said Szapiro, surprised.

"I sure did. Civic duty. I owe it to the homeland. You ain't bought any?"

"Well no . . ."

"Well if they book you for an illegal lighter, you'll have no one to blame but yourself."

They both laughed and went on reading for a while, legs crossed, drinking coffee and smoking. The radio was playing waltzes; the program would continue until eight, then the station was off the air until midday.

"You know, Kuba, there's this little Jew who lives on Nalewki Street—Bernsztajn, Naum Bernsztajn. Ring any bells?" asked Kaplica after a moment, folding his paper to show the classifieds page.

"Sure does, Mr. Kaplica," answered Szapiro and also folded up his paper, understanding that the time to relax had come to an end and now he had to get down to business.

"All right. And this little Jew thinks he don't have to pay me," Kaplica continued, not taking his eye off the classifieds in the *Courier*.

"Dumb little Jew, if that's what he thinks."

"Dumb," agreed Kaplica, "but he's right. He ain't gonna pay me a grosz because he ain't got one. Munja checked. This Bernsztajn hasn't got a grosz to his name. Ain't no squeezing nothing out of him. You get no water from a dry rag unless you wring it tight."

Szapiro nodded solemnly, as though sorry to agree that this story didn't have a happy ending.

I had no idea that Naum Bernsztajn, a modest clerk in the Jewish Clinic, was in debt to Kaplica. Naum not only didn't tell me—kid that I was, that went without saying—but for a long time he didn't even tell my mother. He was in debt because he didn't want to stay a modest clerk and he'd stumbled upon a business to take over: a rubber goods store on Gęsia Street he could lease. He'd borrowed money from his family for the compensation and taken over the business. He was alone in the store from morning until closing. He bent over backward to pay the debt, turning almost no profit, even though business was good.

One day Kaplica came in. He bought a pair of PPG rubber galoshes, chatted amicably with Bernsztajn, then told him he had to pay fifty złotys by Shabbos. By this Shabbos and every following Shabbos, for as long as my father was in that store, because that was the price of a store on Gęsia Street, fifty złotys for Buddy every week.

On the first Shabbos, Naum paid. On the second as well. On the third, he didn't pay because he didn't have it. He came running to beg forgiveness. Szapiro, to stress the gravity of the situation, smashed Bernsztajn's nose in, and with a broken nose Bernsztajn had to solemnly swear that for the week's delay he'd bring not only a new fifty plus the fifty he owed, but another twenty-five as penalty.

He didn't. He had nowhere to get it. He gave up the store without compensation, everyone knew the situation he was in and no one had any intention of covering that cost for him. He hid, he didn't go out during the day. Buddy sent a boy to tell him the interest on the 125 złotys he owed was 25 percent a week.

I didn't know anything about this. Naum Bernsztajn told his family he was sick, he went to bed, and waited.

"Lomer antlofn," pleaded my mother, "lomer antlofn tsinersht tsi maa shvesto' ka Lodz in shpeyto' kan Erets Yisruel ode kan Amerikye. Lomer antlofn, Nukhim, vaal nish ka zakh of de velt vet indz kyene fataydign fan kas finim purits."[2]

My mother was a pious Jew, but life had taught her the Lord rarely protected pious Jews from the wrath of gentiles.

My father only shrugged her off and turned his face to the wall. He waited. He didn't run away to Łódź, or the Holy Land, or America, or anywhere else.

And finally, they came. They knocked. My mother opened the door, figuring correctly she might as well save the locks since there was no saving my father.

---

2   Let's run away. (. . .) Let's run away first to my sister's in Łódź, then to the Holy Land or America. Let's run away, Naum, because no power, human or divine, will protect us from the wrath of that rich man.

They took him away. I threw myself on Szapiro and he brushed me off.

Many times afterward I thought about that moment, when I threw myself on Szapiro, who was twice my weight, and hung on his forearm, screaming something in Yiddish, but who was screaming?

Szapiro dragged my father out of the apartment by his beard. My father was hunched over like a calf being led to slaughter.

I will never have a beard, I resolved then, hearing my mother's screams and watching clean-shaven Szapiro taking away my one and only father's beard. My own was barely sprouting but that very day I went to the market. I stole a little money from my mother. She saw me take it, but, sobbing, she didn't have the strength to protest. I wasn't crying. So I went to the market. I got rid of my raggedy coat and shirt and used my stolen money to buy short clothes. Rags, really, but not Jewish rags. Next I went to a Christian barber. I had him cut off my peyos and I asked for a shave. The barber laughed that there was nothing to shave, barely five hairs, but I stood my ground and was paying, so he put a warm towel on my face, then rubbed it with oil, mixed the cream with his brush, applied it, shaved me with a couple of sweeps of his hand, rinsed with cold water—I left and saw reflected in the store window the new me, a new, better Jew, hair short, in short clothes, with no peyos.

"Yakh vintsh diyo' alts dus gits Bernsztajn," I said to my reflection in the voice of Jakub Szapiro. "Daa nesiye zol zaan mit mazl!"[3]

Meanwhile my father was in the trunk of a Buick and going on his way, the same way we all go, until we reach our destination, after which we go nowhere.

Two days later, the evening of Sunday, July 11, after the fight in the Miejskie Cinema, Szapiro walked up to Kaplica, who warmly embraced him.

---

3   Good luck, Bernsztajn. (. . .) Safe travels!

"You sure fixed up that son of a bitch, Kuba," he said cheerfully. "You showed that fascist!"

I didn't hear those words but I know that's exactly what he said.

People were slowly making their way out. Kaplica stood up and set off for the dressing room with Szapiro. As they passed my seat, Szapiro, in his boxer's dressing gown, stopped and pointed me out with a gesture of his head.

"That's him," he said to Kaplica.

"Who?"

"Young Bernsztajn, Buddy."

Kaplica gave Szapiro a long look.

Then he turned to me. I lowered my eyes. Kaplica seized my jaw between his pudgy thumb and index finger and pulled my head up, his beady black eyes drilling into me. He wasn't smiling.

Suddenly he released my chin, pinched my cheek, and roared with laughter, as though with that look he had learned everything about me. Maybe he had.

"Fine kid we got here. Too bad for him."

He shrugged and forgot about me, walking away without looking back. Szapiro nodded to me, the same silent gesture my mother sometimes made behind my father's back when she wanted to wordlessly tell me: *For your own good, do what your father says, right now.*

I got up and followed them.

I was curious whether people would watch me. Before, for the whole of my brief life, I had been invisible. This ordinary, skinny little Jewish boy from Nalewki Street. One of a thousand skinny little Jewish boys from Nalewki Street.

And now a woman in a small hat was leaning over to her male companion in a light-colored suit, staring at me the whole time and whispering something in his ear. I remember the way she was looking at me.

But maybe she was looking at Szapiro and Buddy, at them walking, walking, striding, two big shots in handsome suits, striding through the city like they owned it.

We went through to the dressing room, previously for actors, now for boxers. With a look, Szapiro directed me to a chair. I sat down. Kaplica, excited and happy, was talking nonstop about the match.

"'Cause look here, Kuba, I saw him fighting Finn and I was a little worried he'd beat you on stamina, 'cause you're an offensive fighter, ain't ya, and he does great on defense, and seems like he runs on steam or electric, 'cause he never runs low, but you beat him good, Kuba, you knocked him on his ass!"

"We had a couple of those guys in the stands," noted Szapiro, taking a seat.

The adrenaline-fueled excitement had subsided and suddenly he could feel every muscle, joint, and tendon, as was usual after a fight where there was no possibility of respecting your body. His thighs were trembling.

"A couple of what guys?" Kaplica asked, not understanding.

"The Phalanx, Bolo Piasecki's men, the National Radicals, I can't tell which faction is which, but those fascist bastards, you know the type. I saw them. A couple even wore their fucking uniforms."

"Them baby Hitlers must be shitting themselves!" said Buddy delightedly. "Fantastic!"

He snapped his fingers, called out, and a big, grim bruiser entered the room. He was a head taller than Szapiro, and half a Kaplica taller than Kaplica.

"Pantaleon, bring some cognac, I got a bottle in the car, we're gonna celebrate," he ordered, as he put a record on the portable turntable.

The bruiser didn't say anything or even nod, just turned around and left. Kaplica wound the crank, set the needle, and the first, soft sounds of a tango trickled from the speaker.

"In the car? So you already picked up that Chrysler, Mr. Kaplica?" asked Szapiro, attempting to massage his trembling thighs.

"I did!" The question obviously delighted Kaplica as he lit a cigarette and slipped it into the long holder. "You better believe it! You'll see in a sec."

Szapiro stood with difficulty, removed his sweat-soaked boxing jersey, soft boots, and athletic shorts—under which he wore nothing—and stood naked. He didn't seem the slightest bit uncomfortable. I was embarrassed, but even more scared than embarrassed, so I didn't budge an inch.

He wasn't very hairy, only really around the groin, his circumcised penis wasn't too long, it even seemed shorter than mine, though it was very thick.

The boxer stretched his muscles, back, shoulders, and thighs in slow exercises, then poured hot water into a washtub, splashed it over himself, reached for the soap, lathered himself up completely, then rinsed himself off, and dried himself thoroughly, rubbing his skin with a towel. He looked in the mirror, reached for his shaving gear, glanced out of the corner of his eye at Kaplica, who was whistling along to the music, and although the man was showing no sign of impatience, Szapiro laid down the brush and soap without shaving. He sprayed on some cologne, took fresh underclothes and a white button-down shirt from a hanger, and put them on, hissing slightly with pain. Then he put on a dark-blue tie with a geometric brown pattern and a handsome gray two-piece suit, which even I could tell was not only just as expensive as Kaplica's but also fashionable, because the pants had a high waist, they buttoned over the navel, while the legs were very wide, which perfectly suited a man of Szapiro's sturdy build. The jacket, pulled in at the waist, had wide lapels and generously padded shoulders, which further emphasized Szapiro's athletic, yet heavyset figure. Next to him, Kaplica, in his old-fashioned clothes, looked like an old man, a provincial official, an accountant, or an auditor alongside a real movie heartthrob.

The boxer slipped on and tied an elegant pair of shoes, opened a drawer, and pulled out a wristwatch—a Glashütte as I later noticed—his wallet, and a switchblade, as well as two handkerchiefs—a checkered one and a white silk one—and placed all these accessories in their usual places: respectively, on his left wrist, in the inside pocket of his jacket, in his sock, in his pants pocket, and in his jacket's breast pocket, which much later I learned was a style called a besom pocket. I learned everything later. My whole life was later.

Meanwhile Szapiro drew a white carnation from a vase on the dressing table, took out the knife he had just hidden in his sock, flicked open the blade, trimmed the stem, and placed the flower in his buttonhole.

He reached for a brush and a box of pomade, which he rubbed in, then combed down his long hair and inspected himself in the mirror, full of masculine vanity, handsome, strong, everything I wasn't.

But which I somehow later became.

Or maybe only what I wanted to become, my whole life I wanted to be Szapiro pomading his hair in front of the mirror, yet I became something else.

"You got a lot more preening to do?" asked Kaplica, rolling his eyes, but without spite.

"Gotta be presentable. You know how it is."

Then he knelt carefully, wary of his aching muscles, and reached behind the dressing table, which was topped with a light-bulb-ringed mirror. He retrieved a small, flat, engraved pistol, with a pearl-inlaid grip. He didn't remove the magazine, didn't unlock the safety, he just put the gun in his pants pocket.

I knew nothing about guns back then, I could barely tell a pistol from a revolver, figuring if something looked like Tom Mix's gun, it had to be a revolver. Later I learned a lot about guns, much more than I'd have cared to, and today I know that flat pistol was a Colt 1903 pocket model, a seven-shooter with a clever internal hammer so it wouldn't catch on anything if you had to suddenly pull the pistol out of your pocket. Later, much later, and in a completely different place, when I started carrying a gun all the time, my first was a seven-shooter. A friend from my unit got me a small German Walther, and that seven-shooter almost got me killed: an Arab I'd shot three times in the chest was pumped full of opium and even though his wounds were fatal he kept running at me, knife in hand, screaming and spitting up blood, but I was out of ammunition. While I struggled with the magazine, the guy caught me and plunged his knife in, luckily the blade deflected off my ribs, and a second later my commander shot him in the head with a rifle.

When I got out of the hospital, the first chance I had, I swapped the Walther for an American .45. I've got it to this day. Heavily worn from years of carrying it in a leather holster, it sits in a drawer of the desk where I'm writing, I tap the soft keys of an electric typewriter whose type ball has Latin letters with no Polish accents—those I have to add by hand, with a pencil, on every page of the manuscript.

Above my desk, a plastic model of a 1936 Lockheed Model 10 Electra hangs on a fishing line. I like looking at it. I don't know if I made it or someone else did. I'm glad it's here. Whoever glued it together and painted it set the landing gear in the retracted position, so it can't stand up, it has to hang.

Sometimes I look out the window, down onto the street. An Arab boy pushes a small cart, which he's loaded with a huge pile of furniture, old or styled to look old, the bentwood legs and the striped upholstery of armchairs and sofas stacked on top of one another.

Cars drive past him—Fiats, Peugeots, Subarus, Volkswagens—and honk, regardless of their country of origin. An Orthodox man in a black frock coat is standing by a newsstand, smoking a cigarette, waiting for something. A girl walks past him in a green uniform with a black rifle on her back. I don't know if she's beautiful, I can't tell from this distance, but I don't feel like putting my glasses on.

It's very quiet in the apartment. The windows don't let any sound in.

I miss her fussing, her grouching, her constant nagging, which I'd tried to escape our whole life here, escape her sorrow, her despair, her grief for those who'd stayed and, because they'd stayed, perished—grief I had no intention of feeling because I was disgusted by their martyrdom and death; but then, with age, my feelings changed and I started thinking of their martyrdom like an annoying acquaintance you still put up with because you've gotten used to them.

I fled her stubborn yammering in Polish because I didn't want to hear that language, and I already spoke to her at home in Yiddish, while she answered me in Polish.

We didn't speak Hebrew at home. And we always had the same fight: I'd ask why she was talking to me in Polish, since after all she was the one who'd wanted to leave; she'd hated Poland more than I had, but she kept on speaking Polish, stubborn as a mule, as always. She'd shrug and then we'd argue, both of us yelling, the apartment empty.

Later we stopped yelling at one another, we lost the desire, we didn't care, then even later, not long ago now, the kids moved out, but I feel like they were never here, neither she nor the kids, as if I'd spent my whole life in this apartment alone, just the ghosts and me.

The Arab boy is pushing his cart full of antiques.

I used to see boys like him on the streets where I grew up, poor Jewish sons of poor Jewish cart drivers and porters, whose paths in life began with a cart, ready to take anything that fit and haul it over cobblestones that remembered the czar, and later, after they'd laid asphalt on top of those, over the asphalt and into the mud of Northern District courtyards, into the poor courtyards of rented tenements plastered with signs for every conceivable kind of business, not one of them worth a damn.

I feel much older than I am.

Fifty years ago, with no glasses, I watched Szapiro get dressed. I sat in silence. Kaplica kept on jabbering, analyzing the fight and having one smoke after another. Pantaleon, whom Kaplica called Leoś, brought a bottle of cognac and poured two glasses; Szapiro and Kaplica drank them, Pantaleon didn't drink.

I didn't yet know the part Pantaleon played in my father's miserable end.

After draining his glass of cognac, Kaplica wiped his mouth with the back of his hand, pulled out some smokes, and offered them to Szapiro and Pantaleon. We left the building that had once been the Bogusławski Theater, exiting onto Hipoteczna Street. It was nighttime, very mild and warm, and we could see the stars beautifully, because the frail light of the gas streetlamps couldn't hope to outshine them. In front of the theater stood the most beautiful car I had ever seen.

"Well?" asked Kaplica blissfully, looking at Szapiro.

"Well, Mr. Kaplica . . ."

The limousine was huge and red as a fire engine. The paint glistened, while the soft, aerodynamic lines of the body looked nothing like the cars on the streets I used to walk in those days, fifty years ago. The back wheels were almost invisible, hidden under closed, teardrop-shaped fenders, and chrome glistened against the red paint. Inside sat rat-faced Munja Weber, acting as chauffeur. At the sight of Kaplica he hopped out and bowed as he opened the back door.

To understand what that car looked like in Warsaw in those days, you have to remember that Buddy didn't just drive it on the few asphalt-paved main roads—on Nowy Świat, Mazowiecka, or Marszałkowska, the parts of Warsaw we want to reminisce about nowadays. Buddy's natural environment was the cobblestone or dirt roads and side streets of the City Center, north of Jerozolimskie Avenue. He would park his red Chrysler in front of the decaying tenements of Muranów district and the rented apartment houses of Wola district, where rotting wood ceilings sagged under the weight of their tenants.

It was the shoeless poor who ran their fingers over the red paint, not ladies at the races. Muddy puddles were reflected in its chrome bumpers.

"A Chrysler, Kuba," said Kaplica, pronouncing the word *Chrysler* with a strong Polish accent, and I immediately thought it must be a Christian car. Chrysler like Christ. "A Chrysler Imperial. Brand-new. Lilpop imported it for me. I gave him twenty-eight thousand! Ain't nobody in Poland got another one like it! Not the president, not Marshal Rydz-fuckin'-Śmigły, nobody. Come on, hop in!"

Twenty-eight thousand złotys. My father Naum Bernsztajn earned around a hundred złotys a month, in a good month. Which makes twelve hundred a year. Meaning Buddy's car was worth over twenty-three years of my father's labor. Word on the street was the mayor of Warsaw, Stefan Starzyński, earned thirty-five hundred a month. Poor men would sit by a wall or on the sidewalk and philosophize about what you could do with thirty-five hundred a month. These fantasies usually revolved around buying large amounts of food and throwing a gigantic party for the whole district. You could set up tables on the square, book a band, order a keg of beer and a few cases of vodka, get a whole pig from the best butchers on Marszałkowska Street, and celebrate for three days, like at a wedding. That's what you could do if you had thirty-five hundred like Mayor Starzyński. But even Starzyński couldn't afford Buddy's car. Buddy had more.

And Buddy sometimes threw parties like that on the squares; we'd all sit at makeshift tables made of boards on sawhorses, his gang would keep order, there'd be a pig and a kosher calf, there'd be vodka, a band, socialist songs, and kissing babies in neighborhood courtyard entrances. And cries of "Long live Kaplica!" raised joyfully and noisily by those for whom Buddy's generosity was the only source of relief and pleasure in the grim, proletarian, or lumpenproletarian lives of the poor and down-and-out.

We got into the Chrysler. I had been in a car a few times by then, but never one like this. The interior was spacious as a streetcar and upholstered in tan leather. Kaplica and Szapiro took the back seat; Munja, now in a real chauffeur's cap, indicated a fold-down, rear-facing seat for me. Kaplica was talking about the car, its eight-cylinder engine, its automatic clutch, and its overdrive, all of which naturally went over my head. All I understood was I'd found myself in a different world. A completely different world.

"And here, look," said Buddy excitedly, "I've got a Dictaphone!"

He pronounced this word with a Polish accent too, which of course didn't offend me at all, since back then I knew neither French nor English, only Polish and Yiddish, plus a little Hebrew.

"Let's roll!" shouted Kaplica before returning to showing off the Dictaphone.

From a box mounted between the seats, he pulled out a tube with a black, Bakelite funnel on one end. Munja started the engine without getting out of the car, the starter motor cranked the main engine, there was a jerk and the engine rumbled, growled, and started running, the powerful crankshaft turning eight light aluminum pistons.

"Now picture this, Kuba, I talk in here, and whatever I say gets recorded in there, on a wax cylinder, then I can give it to my secretary and she'll listen to it and type it out, get it?"

The chauffeur slowed and turned right at Centralniak jail on Daniłowiczowska Street.

Szapiro reached for the funnel, Kaplica pressed the steel button on the wooden Dictaphone box, and switched it from LISTEN to DICTATE.

"Now talk!" he ordered, then reached into his jacket pocket and pulled out a little box of mustache wax.

"But what am I supposed to say?" Szapiro was suddenly distressed and confused.

"Whatever you want. Just don't forget, it'll stay there, recorded," said Buddy, laughing.

He opened the little box, swept with his finger, rubbed the wax between the thumb, forefinger, and middle finger of each hand, and twirled up his old-fashioned mustache, one side after the other, the right side with the left hand, the left with the right. It smelled like sandalwood, it was a gorgeous smell, oriental and strong.

"Nobody's ever recorded me before," said Szapiro into the microphone. He hesitated for a moment, but then went on. "Nobody's ever recorded me before but now I'm gonna talk and I'll be recorded on this machine. My name is Jakub Szapiro, I'm a boxer in Warsaw, I'm thirty-seven, I was born on May 12, 1900, in Warsaw, and I've lived here my whole life. My mother's name was Dora, my father was called Yankyev, and I'm named after him, though I prefer the Polish version, Jakub. I just beat the League boxer Andrzej Ziembiński, a well-known fascist from the Phalanx, my whole body hurts from the fight, but he was the one who ended up on the mat, shaking like a slaughtered calf."

He was speaking almost jokingly, smiling, but focused, as though something depended on what he said into the black Bakelite funnel of the Dictaphone. I observed this in silence.

"For fifteen years I've fought in the colors of Maccabi Warsaw, though I prefer training in the Stars' gym. This was my last boxing match. I'm done going into the ring. You have to know when to make way for younger men. I work for Mr. Kaplica. Now we're driving through Warsaw in his beautiful new car. We're just passing the jail on Daniłowiczowska, here's hoping we never end up inside it. Mr. Kaplica's in the car, Munja's driving, I'm . . ."

Kaplica's car turned left, toward Teatralny Square, while Kaplica peered at me. I averted my eyes, embarrassed. I got embarrassed easily in those days. And now I'm embarrassed to think of my embarrassment. But I no longer avert my eyes.

"So we've still got young Bernsztajn."

Szapiro handed me the funnel of the machine that recorded voices. "Now you. Talk," he said.

I held the funnel in my hand like an idiot. I didn't know what I was supposed to say or what I could say, what was appropriate to say. I was searching for the words, searching for them desperately, and finally I latched on to what Szapiro had said.

"Nobody's ever recorded me before. My voice," I whispered.

"Louder!" yelled Szapiro, making me jump.

Kaplica was ignoring me. He opened an ashtray that held no ashes. He took a tiny paper bundle from inside it. He carefully unwrapped the paper and snorted some white powder.

"Nobody's ever recorded me," I repeated. "My voice. My name is Mojżesz Bernsztajn and I'm the son of Naum Bernsztajn, an observant Jew, I live at twenty-six Nalewki Street, apartment six."

At the sound of my father's name, Kaplica smiled to himself while Szapiro made an odd grimace, seemingly of disgust, but I knew nothing yet, I didn't know what had happened to my father, and I didn't find out for another few days. Then I did.

But I hadn't yet.

But maybe I'm remembering all this wrong. Maybe I didn't record anything on the Dictaphone.

"Where we headed, boss?" asked the driver.

Kaplica looked inquiringly at Szapiro, who shrugged.

"How 'bout we go to Ryfka's," decided Kaplica.

"I'd just like to sort out something at the Metropol first," said Szapiro suddenly, as though just remembering something. "Quick bit of business, won't take a minute."

"All right, so first to Tłomackie, then to Ryfka's. Mr. Szapiro the boxer's in charge here," ordered Kaplica and took the microphone from me. Unless I wasn't holding it, then he didn't.

The driver made a two-point turn and we set off up Bielańska Street, passing the Bank of Poland and the Jewish theaters at 5 Bielańska, where I used to go, stealthily slipping out of the apartment to watch farces performed in Yiddish, which I loved almost as much as the movies.

I immediately thought of the girl I was meant to take there on a date the next day, and I wondered sadly if I'd get to see her again. I did. Not once, not twice. But we didn't see each other the next day.

From Bielańska we took a narrow side street to the square, rolling slowly past the Main Judaic Library and the Great Synagogue. I wondered what would happen if one of my classmates saw me riding through Tłomackie in a car. With Buddy Kaplica himself.

And I wondered what would happen if my father, the observant Jew Naum Bernsztajn, saw me in this car.

We parked at the White Eagle Building, 13 Tłomackie Street, the ground floor of which housed the Metropol, which was usually full of Jewish writers and journalists, because upstairs the same address held the headquarters of the Union of Jewish Writers and Journalists in Poland. That was an organization I didn't know at the time, but I did know it was the hangout of those who filled the columns of the Yiddish-language papers *Haynt* and *Undzer Ekspres*, which my father read every day, despising the Polish-language and modern, assimilationist—as he thought—*Our Review*, which—he said—he only bought for the children's supplement. As a child I did in fact read the *Review*, and even as a teenager I would occasionally, slightly bashfully, sneak a glance at it. My father also often read the *Yidishe Togblat*, published by the earnestly orthodox Aguda, whose members certainly wouldn't be found hanging out on Tłomackie.

But as I, Mojżesz Bernsztajn, son of Naum Bernsztajn, sat in that red Chrysler in front of the Metropol, my father wasn't reading anything anymore.

But I didn't know that. Besides, maybe I wasn't sitting in the Chrysler at all, maybe Szapiro told me this whole story?

"Can you give me a moment, Mr. Kaplica?" Szapiro asked, when the driver brought the limousine to a halt.

"Don't sweat it! I wouldn't mind a drink. But first . . ." He slid the unwrapped paper toward Szapiro—I could see the white powder inside but didn't know then it was cocaine, though I learned that later. Szapiro wet his finger, took a liberal swipe, then stuck the finger in his mouth. He rubbed the powder onto his gums, then ran his tongue over them and swallowed. Kaplica unceremoniously licked off the contents of the paper, crumpled it up, tossed it on the floor, sneezed, snorted, and rubbed his face with his chubby hands.

"Let's hit it!" he cried joyfully, continuing to snort.

"What about this shrimp?" Szapiro nodded in my direction. I think that's what happened anyway.

"Whaddaya mean? He's coming with us!" answered Kaplica.

So we went.

The Metropol was a small bar, run by Wolf Handszer, and the place was now officially called the New Metropol, since the old one, which had belonged to the Bund, had gone bankrupt in 1933. The Bundists had served treyf: in the middle of the Jewish district, they'd have a display of suckling pigs *mit tsimes*, ham and onions, or stuffed eel, until finally a boycott was declared and it turned out kosher food was necessary after all.

Handszer served kosher and the thought gave me some relief as we walked into the bar. Despite the late hour—it was already past eleven—the joint was full, music was playing, and the crowd was mixed. Of course, truly religious Jews wouldn't risk the sin of coming there, but at one table, two bearded men in long, expensive frock coats sat over a bottle, discussing their bearded, frock-coated business in hushed tones. Theoretically the bar closed at midnight, but somehow no one was in a hurry to leave, and waiters were circulating among the tables taking orders. The courts routinely fined Handszer for not closing on time. It obviously paid off. He was famous for always politely thanking the court for the fine, even when it came out to two thousand złotys.

When we entered—Kaplica, Szapiro, and I—everyone turned to look at us. Those who didn't look right away did so after a second, after receiving a nudge or a kick under the table. Someone said something in someone's ear, someone else hissed, and then everyone looked away, in case—God forbid—Kaplica took offense at their staring.

Then someone whispered something, first one, then another, then a third, and instead of Kaplica's name, everywhere we heard "Szapiro," "Szapiro," and suddenly someone started clapping, and before long it had turned into a round of applause, maybe a little too brief, and not the kind where everyone joined in, but otherwise distinct.

They were applauding him for knocking out Ziembiński. News got around fast. Szapiro laughed and gave an offhanded bow.

The band struck up a tune I didn't recognize at the time because I didn't go to the movies; today I know it was a song from the musical comedy *One Floor Up*.

No, I can't keep writing.

◆　◆　◆

I rise from my typewriter and look out onto the street, out there it's calm. The boy with the cart full of furniture. The girl with the rifle. I can't stand the quiet anymore. I switch on the radio. In the old days, the radio in Warsaw didn't broadcast nonstop, during the day it went silent from eight to noon, and at night as well, but now the radio talks and plays music all day and night. *Twenty-four seven*, as the Americans say. *Twenty-four seven*. The radio is talking in Polish. About what's happening in Israel.

At the Eretz checkpoint, one of our tank transports drove into a Palestinian car. Four dead.

"Oh shit," I say out loud, in Polish. "Oh shit."

I feel very, very old, much older than my sixty-seven years.

It'll all kick off now, I think. I turn off the radio. I don't want to hear about it. I take a record from the shelf. Eugeniusz Bodo and Hanka Ordonówna, the most famous singers from before the war. I put it on the turntable and search for that very song I first heard fifty years ago, when we walked into the Metropol.

It plays.

"What're we on the lookout for?" Buddy asked fifty years ago, looking around the bar.

"Bernard Singer," replied Szapiro.

"The journalist?" said the mustachioed gangster, surprised.

Szapiro nodded.

A tall, thin man wearing a brown suit and round wire-rim glasses rushed out from behind the bar and jogged up to Kaplica, greeting him with the requisite humility of one who lives to serve others, and assured him he'd find us a table right away.

"No need for a table, Mr. Handszer," Szapiro replied, which to me seemed insensitive to Kaplica. But Kaplica didn't share my opinion.

"But I insist, even just for a quick one on the house," said Handszer.

"We'll sit," said Kaplica, making up his mind.

Handszer immediately threw out two slightly drunk young men who were wobbling over a single cup of tea at a table right next to the two bearded Jews, then personally wiped down the tabletop and pulled up two chairs.

"We're gonna need three," murmured Kaplica and a third chair immediately appeared. Although maybe he didn't say that at all, maybe Handszer simply pulled up another chair for me, unasked. Or maybe I stood alongside? I don't remember.

The bearded Jews finished their vodka and then made an unpardonable error: they stayed at their table, rather than hastily making themselves scarce.

I, meanwhile, was invisible. Nearly perceptible, because I'd come with Kaplica, but invisible—I was a shabbily dressed, skinny Jewish youngster with short-cropped hair and clumsy arms and legs. It was as though I wasn't there at all.

A waiter ran up to the table holding a bottle and a tray with small glasses and a plate of bread, pickles, and gefilte fish. He peered inquiringly at Kaplica.

"Come on, the kid'll have a drop too," said Kaplica.

So the waiter put the glasses on the table, poured the vodka, bowed, and ran off. Szapiro didn't sit down. He looked around the room, finally noticing someone at the bar.

He passed easily through the crowd, which parted before him like the Red Sea before Moses's staff.

At the bar stood Bernard Singer, short, slim, dark-haired, in an elegant suit. It's no exaggeration to say he was likely the best-known Jewish journalist. Even I had heard of him. My mother adored his columns in *Our Review*.

"Mr. Singer?" asked Szapiro.

Singer eyed Szapiro up and down disdainfully, gave no answer, turned back to the bar, and kept drinking his beer.

"We need to talk, Mr. Singer," said Szapiro.

Singer didn't react.

"Well if that's how it's gonna be . . . ," said Jakub sadly. He gave a helpless shrug and slammed Singer's head onto the bar.

The band stopped playing. The customers went silent. Singer slid to the floor, unconscious, blood gushing from his broken nose. Szapiro made his way back toward our table, rubbing his right shoulder.

"Seems to me Mr. Szapiro just didn't care for Mr. Singer's article in the latest *Review*, and here's what happens when a boxer turns literary critic," said Kaplica loudly, smiling under his mustache. "And next time any of you hacks gets the bright idea to call Mr. Szapiro 'a thug posing as a sportsman,' I'm quoting from memory there, you better think twice."

Horrified, Handszer ran up to Singer, wailing and trying to revive him. The customers in the bar stood stock-still, silent. Apparently one gawker was gawking the most rudely, because as Szapiro was walking past him, he suddenly turned as though to give him a hook punch, but just said "Boo!" and kept going. Terrified, the man spilled his beer all over himself.

Szapiro sat down at our table.

"I pulled my damn shoulder," he said grimly. "Let's drink."

I'd never drunk vodka before. My hands were trembling.

"Drink up, *malchik*," Kaplica ordered.

I reached for the glass.

"Like this," he said, demonstrating by plunging his mustache into the vodka and tossing his head back in a sudden motion, taking the glass with it.

I brought the glass to my mouth—it smelled foul. I took a sip—it burned.

"Drink!" snarled Szapiro.

I drank. Or I only really dumped the vodka into my mouth. It was so disgusting I spluttered, choked, and nearly threw up.

Kaplica and Szapiro both roared with laughter.

Meanwhile Singer had been revived and was being led out of the restaurant.

"Maybe he'll run crying to the cops," laughed Szapiro.

"Then he'll get a fine too, for disturbing the peace," replied Kaplica.

I couldn't see it then, but they were showing off in front of me. These two fully grown, powerful big shots, showing off in front of a little squirt like me. Everybody needs an audience.

Suddenly, one of the bearded men in the frock coats said, "Dos past nisht!"[4] As soon as I heard his Yiddish I could tell he wasn't from Warsaw.

---

4   You can't do that!

"You can't do that, gentlemen. You can't. For shame. And no one does anything?" added the other in Polish, looking around the room.

Kaplica chuckled under his breath, as though laughing at his own thoughts. He snapped his fingers for the waiter, who came running with the bottle and poured. Kaplica knocked back his glass and slowly turned to the protesting men.

"Well now, my friends," he said in a sweet voice, "you don't take to that sort of literary criticism?"

Both men looked at one another.

"What artistic discipline have you fellows mastered, may I ask?" he continued. "Singing? Painting? Dancing, maybe?"

"Nothing to do with art, sir," one of the religious Jews started to say—the younger one, with a thick, dark beard. He wore an expensive, stiff-brimmed silk hat.

"Then I think you guys should dance for us. Everybody'll watch."

"Now, look here . . . ," said the second, older one, rising from the table.

He was about fifty, sturdily built, broad-shouldered, a head taller than Kaplica. He wore an expensive wool frock coat with velvet-covered lapels. I could see an expensive gold watch on his left wrist.

Kaplica grinned. "You're gonna dance a tango," he said.

"Dance it yourself, meshugener."

"Feter . . . ,"[5] said the younger one, moving to hold him back.

At that moment a terrified Wolf Handszer came running up to them.

"Please go on your way, gentlemen, no need to pay the bill, it's on the house, but please go now, please go."

"The gentlemen ain't going nowhere," snarled Kaplica, his tone changed. "The gentlemen are gonna dance a tango. Strike up the band!"

---

5   Uncle . . .

The musicians looked at one another and Handszer, jittering nervously, nodded—so they started to play. A tango.

"Dance, dammit!" roared Kaplica. "Now!"

The Jews in frock coats lost what remained of their prior confidence. The other customers hurriedly, albeit stealthily, fled the restaurant.

"Gentlemen, let's maybe not anger Mr. Kaplica any more, why don't you dance and get out of here," whispered Handszer frantically.

Kaplica rose. He walked up to the older Jew, craned his neck, and looked him right in the eye. I saw the other man hesitate for a moment, but right behind Kaplica, Szapiro rose as well.

"Dance, Yid," growled Kaplica. "You'll be the lady, your pal will be the man. Now."

The younger man's hands were trembling.

"Feter libinker . . . Lomir tantsn, ikh bet aykh . . . ,"[6] he hissed.

He held the older man around the waist, took his right hand in his left, and stretched his arm up in a comical and terrifying parody of a dancing pose. Kaplica started clapping and jiggling his way around the two Jews, who were hopping from one foot to another.

"Them Jews sure dance beautiful, beautiful!" he shouted through his laughter.

The dancing Jews' beards were touching. The older one had tears in his eyes. Szapiro stood with a hand in his pocket, it even occurred to me he had it wrapped around the grip of the pistol. He was looking around, not laughing at all, not enjoying the torment of those being humiliated or protesting against it. He remained indifferent to their torment with the indifference of a man used to suffering, whether his own or his neighbors'. So Szapiro simply did what he was supposed to. He made sure nothing happened to Kaplica.

I was frightened and embarrassed right then, but more embarrassed than frightened. I was embarrassed that I was sitting at a table with

---

6   Uncle . . . Let's dance, please . . .

someone who took pleasure in humiliating other people, but I was even more embarrassed that I was a hundred times happier sitting with him than dancing that awful Jewish tango with those two.

I hadn't thought about that scene for many years, but I remembered it all a little over a decade ago, when Ben-Gal was defending the Valley of Tears from the Syrians and I hadn't slept for four nights straight. I was stooped over documents, reports, and maps, living only on coffee and cigarettes because there was no time for anything else, and then I remembered those two religious Jews in the Metropol, and I remembered their beards touching in the tango Kaplica made them dance, and I remembered Szapiro watching over Kaplica with his hand on his pistol-grip, and Kaplica, most terrible of all, gaily jiggling his way around the dancers on his stubby little legs, and since then I haven't forgotten them for a single moment.

Neither Kaplica, nor Szapiro, nor the dancing Jews.

As they were dancing, a tall, slim man with black, woolly hair burst into the Metropol. I could see a Browning in his hand and a resemblance to Jakub Szapiro, the man who'd killed my father, in his face.

"Day, iz sho' gyenig!"[7] he snarled, pressing his way through the crowd.

His name was Moryc Szapiro, he was Jakub's younger brother and a Zionist labor activist in the Left Poale Zion Party. Which I didn't know at the time. To me that night, he was only a man holding a Browning, wearing a white shirt with the sleeves rolled up and no collar, in tall boots with his pants tucked into them, yet at the same time I had the feeling I already knew everything about him in a way that was as obvious as day following night.

The band once again stopped playing.

---

7   Enough of this!

"Antlofts yidn, giyekh,"[8] whispered Mr. Handszer to the dancing Jews, then made a run for it himself, hiding behind the bar.

"I'm warning you, Mr. Kaplica," growled Moryc.

Kaplica turned to the younger Szapiro and glared at him. The Jews fled, along with the musicians from the band, while the two men sized one another up for a while longer, and there were four of us left: Kaplica, the two Szapiros, and terrified and invisible me.

"Moryc, gay sho' ahaym."[9]

"Famakh'n pisk, Yankyev. Yakh reyd nish' mi diyo',"[10] said Moryc. "I'm warning you, Mr. Kaplica," he continued in Polish, "I won't let you torment these people anymore. You don't wanna have us to deal with."

"Well done. All right, enough," replied Kaplica, placing his hand in his pocket. "We're just horsing around. Everything's fine and dandy now, my friend. Let's go, Kuba!"

And he left. Szapiro followed him. I followed them, invisible little nobody.

I climbed back into the red Imperial.

We set off.

Two days earlier my father hadn't climbed into, but rather had been thrown into the trunk of a brown Buick Model 48—a two-door touring coupe, as described in a Buick brochure I dug up many years later to identify the car seventeen-year-old me had seen. But was it me that saw it? Is the me that saw it the same as the me that remembers it?

So I used a brochure to identify the car seventeen-year-old Mojżesz Bernsztajn remembered. Jakub Szapiro's car.

Its trunk was modest by modern standards, but roomy in those days; it was a so-called integrated trunk, built into the body of the automobile, which at that time wasn't at all obvious, because there were

---

8 Get out of here, guys, right now.
9 Go home, Moryc.
10 Shut your trap, Jakub. I'm not talking to you.

still plenty of cars around with boxes for trunks, attached to the back with leather straps.

It would have been tough to throw my father into one of those boxes. An integrated trunk was much easier, even if it wasn't very big. But my father was a small man and he somehow fit.

Szapiro got in the driver's seat and his two companions who I met later—Pantaleon Karpiński and the other, Munja Weber, who often chauffeured for Kaplica—got into the back seat and the passenger seat, respectively. They drove out of the city on a beat-up road, through Koło district, past the Ulrich Gardens, through Górce and Blizne, and beyond Blizne, but before getting as far as Latchorzew they turned off the main road and, rattling over the potholes, came to a clay-pit pond.

Szapiro must have told me about this afterward, he definitely told me, that's how I know where they drove. But why would he tell me this story?

That I don't know.

At the pond, Szapiro, Pantaleon, and Munja got out and my father was hauled out of the trunk. He screamed and protested, which only led Pantaleon, the enormous psychopath whom I'll maybe talk about later, to kick him in the teeth with his hobnail boot.

Pantaleon had a strange haircut—long, thick hair combed back from the crown of his head to his neck. No one combed their hair that way back then. Later I learned why Pantaleon wore his hair long. I'll tell you about that later. It's just that his strange haircut came back to me now.

Munja told my father to undress. Rat-faced, skinny little Munja who'd come to Warsaw from who-knows-where.

He was swarthy and dark-haired with a black mustache. Most people took him for a Gypsy and he had slightly Asian features, although Munja himself said he was a Jew, a little Polonized and assimilated, but a Jew. He was born in Harbin, he came to Poland in 1925, and supposedly he knew Chinese.

Yet for all that, he didn't know Yiddish, he didn't follow the traditions, and was notorious for pulling out a knife in a fistfight, and shooting a pistol in a knife fight. That's how he was. No one respected him, but everyone was afraid of him because Munja made up for his diminutive build with zeal and aggression. He smoked like a chimney and had an ugly mustachioed wife who frightened him more than Kaplica, so he showed up at home no more than once a week.

This Munja ordered my father to undress. My father refused, so Munja knocked out my father's two front teeth with his brass knuckles. My father, crying and wailing with pain, stripped naked and stood before his executioners, slim and pale on crooked, skinny legs. Then Szapiro took a large, seven-pound mallet out of the car and swung it into my father's head, cracking his skull, knocking him unconscious, and causing a brain hemorrhage, though not yet killing him.

Pantaleon and Munja took off their jackets and put on butchers' aprons. Pantaleon took a doctor's bag containing two meat cleavers, a butcher's knife, and a surgical saw for amputations. Next Pantaleon bound my unconscious father's feet with the belt from his pants and effortlessly hung him from a tree branch, and my papa hung naked, his arms, his peyos, and his circumcised penis hanging according to the law of gravity, exactly the opposite of how they'd usually hung on my papa's body his whole boring life long.

Szapiro approached, flicked open his switchblade, and slit my father's throat, standing behind him so the blood from his still-living body didn't splatter over his shoes and pants.

I often think I was the one who slit his throat, not some Warsaw thug, that I am the guilty one, I made them slaughter my father like a beast, stringing him up with blood gushing from his throat.

They had to wait for my father to bleed to death. So Pantaleon ate the sandwich his wife had made him, grumbling about it not having enough lunch meat; Munja sharpened the cleaver; Szapiro wandered a little way off, sat by the water, took Sholem Asch's novel *Dos Shtetl* from his pocket, then removed his jacket, set it down carefully, lit a cigarette, and read.

"I hear you're meant to fight Ziembiński?" asked Munja, nosy as always.

Szapiro muttered a confirmation, not taking his eyes off the book.

"He's that fascist, right?" Munja Weber went on. "Supposedly he was in that big job where they shot up the Bund offices."

"I don't give a shit. He's just a boxer," said Jakub with a shrug.

My father had drained out of his body along with his blood, just like a pig draining out of its piggy body, so Pantaleon and Munja went to work.

This Szapiro didn't participate in.

First, they removed his head from his torso, Pantaleon expertly slipping the blade between the vertebrae. They didn't use the saw. They removed my father's arms and legs from his body, cutting carefully around the hip and shoulder joints, then preparing and cutting through the joint tendons and capsules. The bones, stripped of these bonds, were easy to jerk and twist out of the joints, rending my father's body into pieces.

When everything was ready, they called Szapiro, though it seemed like they were calling me.

Szapiro ordered them to wrap the head of Naum Bernsztajn, my father, in his own frock coat along with his wallet, which held a little money and his documents. Meanwhile, within Naum Bernsztajn's head sat Naum Bernsztajn's now-lifeless brain, and I think today I can say Naum Bernsztajn's head was Naum Bernsztajn's true home, that this head and this brain were where Naum Bernsztajn was when he lived and existed, because what was Naum Bernsztajn? Naum Bernsztajn was not Naum Bernsztajn's body, which now lay hacked to pieces on the ground. Naum Bernsztajn was Naum Bernsztajn's thoughts about Naum Bernsztajn, he was Naum Bernsztajn's memory, he was what took place in Naum Bernsztajn's brain as Naum Bernsztajn's body released substances into his bloodstream that were the source of Naum Bernsztajn's emotions, and he was therefore Naum Bernsztajn's endorphins, adrenaline, and cortisol, and the other substances that form the source of human emotions and which made up Naum Bernsztajn when, for instance, he made love to my mother—which he usually did on Shabbos, as befitted an observant Jew—and when her body's influence caused everything to happen in his body that made intercourse with her possible, or when he was afraid—and he was very afraid, and rightly afraid—as Jakub Szapiro dragged him by the beard out of our apartment at 26 Nalewki Street. What was going on inside him when, deprived of blood—and therefore of oxygen—his brain, Naum's home, expired?

First the space where Naum Bernsztajn was—made up of Naum Bernsztajn's thoughts about Naum Bernsztajn, his memories and fears—shrank and then vanished. And once the space where Naum Bernsztajn was had shrunk and vanished, Naum Bernsztajn vanished as well, and once he had, it was as if he'd never existed. All that remained was my memory of him, and maybe I'll be the last person on earth who remembers there was such a person as Naum Bernsztajn, an observant Jew who lived in Warsaw at 26 Nalewki Street, apartment number 6, but my memory of Naum Bernsztajn is not Naum Bernsztajn, it's me, a compulsorily retired *tat-aluf*—meaning a brigadier general—named Moshe Inbar, aged sixty-seven and sitting at an IBM Selectric II electric typewriter. General Moshe Inbar is listening to a record of songs by Eugeniusz Bodo and Hanka Ordonówna and thinking of his father, Naum Bernsztajn, and his death, and the later fate of his martyred body.

But does General Moshe Inbar have anything at all to do with Moyshe Bernsztajn?

Did Moyshe Bernsztajn, known as Mojżesz in Polish, exist? Did he exist to transform into the Hebrew Moshe Inbar?

Next, they laid out a tarp in the trunk of the Buick and threw in the hunks of meat that together had formed my father's body, though they were no longer my father.

They drove along dirt roads from Latchorzew to Paschalin and Babice, stopped at a clay pond, and threw in the legs on which Naum Bernsztajn had walked his whole life; then they went on to Chrzanów and Macierzysz, where in another pond they concealed the torso, arms, and hands Naum Bernsztajn used to stroke my hair; then finally the head, wrapped up in Naum Bernsztajn's clothes with documents identifying their owner as Naum Bernsztajn—a citizen of the Polish Republic, of the Jewish faith—which they sunk in a small lake in Odolany, indifferent to either the faith or the incompleteness of the now repeatedly sunken Naum Bernsztajn.

And then they returned to Warsaw.

Munja Weber went to Sobenski's snack bar to play cards; he had no reason to go home. Pantaleon Karpiński, naturally, walked home, bashed his wife in the face, lifted up her skirt, bent her over the kitchen table, and screwed her in a way he could be sure wouldn't get her pregnant, meaning in the backside. His wife didn't protest, because she knew if she did Pantaleon was prepared to kill her, just as he'd apparently killed his last wife. They already had five children, so she understood him not wanting to have another. So she bore the pain patiently, waiting for him to finish, which he did quickly. Then he demanded a cup of tea, which she hastily brewed him, knowing Pantaleon couldn't abide waiting.

"You're extremely lucky," her mother would tell her, "because he doesn't drink," and Pantaleon Karpiński's wife knew she was right. Pantaleon was a teetotaler. He thought vodka brought out the worst in people. He loathed drunks. So he drank his tea, had a slice of bread, and went to bed, setting his alarm for three thirty—his job at the slaughterhouse started at four.

Jakub Szapiro left his Buick in the parking garage in Dynasy, then took a droshky back to his apartment on Nalewki. He climbed the stairs to the fourth floor and found his family having supper. He said hello to Emilia Szapiro and kissed their twin sons, Dawid and Daniel, then took his seat at the family table.

Emilia smelled like home. Like calm. Like the comfort he craved and kept returning home for, a comfort I desired too.

She gave him a bowl of chicken noodle soup and two slices of bread, then sat down beside him and complained about Dawid. His teacher had accused him of acting out.

"Which teacher?" he asked.

"Polish class."

"She's an idiot. Don't worry, kiddo," he said to Dawid.

Emilia rolled her eyes.

"You know I'm right," said Jakub with a smile.

She did.

"I'll put the boys to bed. You go rest," he suggested.

She agreed, but she didn't rest or lie down, she cleaned up after supper. Jakub made sure his sons got ready for bed, read them five pages of Makuszyński's new book *Satan from the Seventh Grade*, and waited for the tired boys to fall asleep. Then he got undressed, washed up, went back one more time to kiss his sons—who were now asleep in their beds—and then lay down in his marriage bed, putting his pistol, knife, watch, and wallet away in the nightstand drawer.

When his wife came to him, he asked her to take off her nightgown. She did and allowed him to look at her. She had the strong body of an athlete. They'd met in the Maccabi sports club, she was a javelin thrower, but her strong body bore the traces of two pregnancies—loose skin marked with pearly stretch marks on her stomach and breasts, which were much heavier than they'd been when they first met.

She joined him under the covers.

"Let's go there, Jakub. Everything will be different there," she said afterward.

He lay lethargically, tasting her saliva in his mouth, smelling the strong odor of their bodies on the sheets. She was resting her head on his chest and he was stroking her hair.

"And what am I going to do there?" he asked. "I mean, I don't know five words of Hebrew."

"I've read in the *Review* the British want to create a Jewish state there. You hear that, Jakub? A Jewish state, can you imagine, Yankyev?"

"I read that too."

"So what's the problem?"

"A Jewish state and an Arab state too. Without Jerusalem."

"Yankyev, so what? Do you understand, having our own state . . . The boys will be in a country where they won't be a worse sort of person. They'll grow up in Tel Aviv, they'll live there like the Poles do in Warsaw, they'll be their own people in their own home. Not like us here."

"It's fine for me here, Emilia. I'm my own person in my own home. My city is enough for me."

"Warsaw?" she asked, although she knew it was Warsaw he had in mind.

"Of course. Warsaw."

"Yankyev, Warsaw belongs to the Poles."

He snorted.

"No, Emilia, Warsaw doesn't belong to the Poles. Warsaw belongs to Buddy. Warsaw belongs to me. It's Jakub Szapiro's, not some Yankyev's. Warsaw is ours. But we haven't got a religion or ethnicity either. Buddy isn't a Pole. I'm not a Jew. Buddy is Buddy, and I'm Szapiro. And Warsaw is our city, and we're Warsaw's."

"Sure, Yankyev, I know this routine by heart," she laughed. "You're not a Jew. Or a boxer from the Maccabi. Not even a little. Tell some goy you're not a Jew and he'll laugh till he drops."

"No, you mean I'll pound him till he drops," he said, laughing along with her.

"What do you want, all in all?"

He stopped laughing. He was silent for a while.

"I want to be king of this city," he answered slowly, after thinking it over, carefully separating out each word. "And I will be king of this city."

"I know, Yankyev. I know. And you will be, or they'll kill you first. But as I know you, and I know you better than anyone in the world, you'll be it, Yankyev. You'll be king. And then what will you do with it? With your kingdom? Are you going to guard it against the next young Jakub Szapiro?"

"I don't know, Emilia."

"Let's leave, Jakub."

"And what exactly am I supposed to do in Palestine, Emilia? Become a storekeeper? A farmer? The only thing I know how to do is beat people up, shoot, and chase bastards through the street."

She cuddled up to him. She smiled, a smile in the darkness.

"I bet our boys there really need people who can fight, shoot, and chase a bunch of dopes through the streets," she whispered, kissing him on the ear.

He kissed her back.

She was sure she'd finally convinced him, that they'd sell everything they had so they wouldn't be weighed down with baggage. She knew her Jakub had money, lots of money. He'd sell the car, sell the furniture, withdraw the savings he was definitely hiding somewhere, take the train to Romania, board a ship in the port of Constanța—after all, the *Polonia* sailed to Haifa—and once they were there, everything would be different.

"I have to take care of that young Bernsztajn somehow," he said then, and it was me he was thinking of.

Or maybe he didn't actually say that at all.

Emilia had some sense of why Jakub thought he had to look after young Bernsztajn. She knew Jakub so well she could even guess what she didn't know, reading his facial expressions, his eyes.

She merely said, sadly, "How can you look after that boy, Yankyev, how can you look after him?"

"I'll get him a ticket to my fight day after tomorrow."

She said nothing for a while. She stopped kissing him.

"You can get him a ticket. But then leave him in peace, you understand? Let him live far away from you. You won't help him. Not you. You can't."

"I get it."

"It's not okay, Yankyev," she said forcefully. "I love you, but it's not okay. What you did. I understand you had to. But you understand that I have to tell you this. You cannot take that boy."

He didn't answer. Emilia went back to kissing him. They made love again.

Meanwhile I was sitting with my younger brother in our shared room, neither of us speaking. We were hungry, our mother hadn't cooked anything since our father was taken, she stayed in the kitchen and cried with her mouth pressed shut, almost voicelessly, while we sat there with her crying and without our father. She saw me with my peyos gone and in short, Christian clothes. She didn't say a word.

Then two days later I was sitting in Buddy's red Chrysler, on the folding, backward-facing seat, and we were gliding through a Warsaw I didn't know, which I feared, which I hated and which, I knew then, I was becoming part of, riding in a car with Kaplica the gentile and Szapiro the Jew, high on drugs, alcohol, and violence.

And I felt the high too.

As the Imperial glides along Marszałkowska, following it in the air is a whale, a dark-gray, blunt-headed sperm whale. He passes an ad for the Baltic American Line, showing a dynamic art deco ocean liner, soars over the streetlamps, over the streetcar wires. The sperm whale opens and closes his jaws, moving his powerful, muscular bulk slowly, his mighty head brushing the roofs of the apartment houses, knocking off a few tiles. His tail fin brushes the tower of Wiedeński Station, the tin gutters tremble.

I only see him out of the corner of my eye, but I see him. His eyes burn and as he opens his mouth out comes a quiet, humming song. A very old one. He sees me too and in his song he whispers his name.

Litani. Litani. Litani.

I am Litani.

We cross Jerozolimskie, we are driving to Ryfka Kij's. I hunker down in the seat.

ב

BET

Szapiro, Pantaleon, and Munja killed my father on Friday, July 9, 1937.

Shabbos began the next Friday evening, but that Saturday, nothing in our home happened the way it should on Shabbos. My mother sat up all night at the kitchen table. By Friday evening she hadn't taken the cholent down to the bakery. We were hungry. Finally, my brother went over to our kindhearted neighbors and got some cholent from them, though it hadn't come out right, it was undercooked; they'd made two batches, they gave us the leftovers of the worse one, and it was hard to blame them. My mother didn't eat, my brother and I finished it.

Jakub Szapiro often said he didn't give a damn about traditions thought up three thousand years ago in the desert. He didn't keep Shabbos, he ate treyf, and said he enjoyed reading Marx, though his favorite thing to read was nothing but newspapers, preferably socialist ones, and in Yiddish, if you please.

On the Shabbos of July 10, he ate breakfast with his sons then phoned the offices of the *Warsaw Courier*, the most important Polish newspaper, and, putting on a voice and speaking through a handkerchief, informed them a man's body lay in the clay-pit pond near Latchorzew and that more information would come.

The editorial trainee on duty hurriedly passed on the message, and the story built up steam. Two hours later, Lieutenant Czerwiński from the penal division of the State Police Main Command and Witold Sokoliński, a reporter for the *Warsaw Courier*, were standing on the bank of a clay pond in Latchorzew, smoking and contemplating how the four officers looking for the body felt as they waded through waist-deep water. On the one hand, it was hot out and the water was cool. On the other, this was definitely corpse water. Disgusting.

Witold Sokoliński was a man of medium height, with a pointy, bald head and a slightly heavy build, ugly for being puffy and soft like a eunuch's. He was strangely awkward company, he had no way with women or men, he scared everyone off with his nervous, angry kobold-like sneer, which he used to mask the embarrassment that trailed him everywhere. It meant he wasn't the greatest reporter—his only passion was for money, which he never had, and he found nothing so fascinating as how much a colleague at his paper or a rival one earned or might earn. He suspected everyone made more than he did and took this as a personal slight. Though considering the low regard his own paper held him in, his suspicions were often correct.

Apart from that, he was petrified of microbes. He carried a tiny bottle of rectified spirit in his pocket, which he used to disinfect his hands whenever he was forced to touch something. Because, you see, there were microbes everywhere. He carried two handkerchiefs in the pockets of his unfashionable suits: one to mop his profusely sweaty brow and face, another to sprinkle with spirit and disinfect his palms whenever he had to shake someone's hand. That did not win him any friends. He opened door handles with his elbows. He had an ugly wife and three puny sons—not even they respected him.

"Ah, beat it, ya louse," hissed Officer Barlicki when he caught sight of the reporter.

It was Barlicki who'd found the limbless, headless body.

"Somebody had a score to settle," sighed Lieutenant Czerwiński at the macabre sight. He was a portly Warsaw bourgeois who looked more like an accountant than a policeman. But every thug who underestimated him because of his appearance soon regretted it.

"A Jew," said Officer Barlicki, pointing at my father's circumcised penis, which Pantaleon and Munja hadn't cut off.

"Bet he didn't pay," added Sokoliński.

"You see, boys, better pay Kaplica," summed up Czerwiński.

"You think it was him, Lieutenant?" asked Sokoliński warily.

"For sure. His modus operandi."

Sokoliński took out his notebook and pencil, jotted something down.

"Can I quote you?"

"You certainly cannot," said Czerwiński, bristling. "Don't you value your hide?"

That rattled Sokoliński. He was terrified of physical violence.

"If it was Kaplica," considered Sokoliński, "then that was just the point, wasn't it? To get it into the *Courier*. To scare folks."

Czerwiński eyed him carefully, but didn't respond.

"You know, Lieutenant," Sokoliński observed, "this has all got a scientific basis. A rational one. And the main thing is to be scientific, right? You can only get to the truth scientifically. I'm a chemist by training. And looking at it eugenically, the Jews are a lower race, you see? That's scientifically confirmed. Sci-en-tifically."

Czerwiński shook his head and started making his official notes. Sokoliński shook his head too and walked off. He thought Czerwiński was a simpleton with no respect for the power of reason.

"I bet he thinks some God sculpted man out of clay and the earth is flat too," he muttered under his breath.

Czerwiński overheard the remark and suddenly jerked his whole body in Sokoliński's direction like he was aiming a punch. Sokoliński was scared so badly he tried to jump away but tripped over his own feet and plopped onto his backside in the mud.

"Well there was no call for that," he said haughtily.

The officers loaded my father's remains into the back of a police van. Sokoliński got on his bike, hatless and with mud all over the seat of his pants, and pedaled laboriously back toward Warsaw. He wasn't much of a cyclist, and fairly obese besides.

Czerwiński pondered something as he watched him go.

"See there, Officer," he said to Barlicki pensively. "If you drilled a hole in the top of that bald head of his, he'd look just like . . ."

"Just like a prick, sir. We know. A prick with arms."

As this was going on, I was sitting at home. Some little urchin knocked at the door of our apartment—a barefoot, very poor boy, in a Jewish frock coat that was too big for him. He handed me an envelope. I gave him ten groszy and he ran off. The envelope held a ticket for a boxing match at the Miejskie Cinema. I should have burned it, but I didn't.

Now I ask myself—why did I go? I also asked myself yesterday and ten years ago, and thirty years ago, but I don't know.

Then, once the boy had run off, Magda arrived.

Magda Aszer.

She didn't knock, she just came in.

She was older than me, if only by a year. Her family was nothing like mine, they spoke Polish at home, her parents only spoke Yiddish when they wanted the kids not to understand, they rarely if ever went to synagogue, there were no mezuzahs on the doors, the kitchen wasn't kosher, and their newspaper was the Polish-language *Our Review*, never the Yiddish *Haynt*. The children learned Yiddish anyway, you couldn't live in and among us without speaking Yiddish, but Magda preferred Polish.

Furthermore, she didn't look Jewish. She had blond, curly hair, which she enthusiastically straightened, dark-blue eyes, and a broad, Slavic face with prominent cheekbones. She wasn't pretty, she wasn't ugly either—a little short, muscular, with strong shoulders and almost masculine biceps from swimming.

Later on, I often thought how Magda resembled Emilia Szapiro, Jakub's wife. They had something in common, and it wasn't just their broad, athletic shoulders. Magda swam, she swam passionately, three times a week she went to the Maccabi pool across the river in Saska Kępa district. She invited me along a few times, and I went and watched her swim in a white bathing suit and a swimming cap fastened under her chin, even though my father had enthusiastically told me stories about tzaddikim who'd cover their eyes at the sight of a woman and wouldn't dare approach a woman without another man there to protect them from sin. Today I know it wasn't only Magda and Emilia who looked alike, but their whole generation, that entire generation of Jewish girls who were the first to swim, run, and high jump, who learned to till the soil out in Grochów district, and later also learned to shoot, and used that skill both in Warsaw and in Palestine.

Meanwhile I, a scrawny Jewish boy in a kippah, my peyos pushed behind my ears and wearing a shabby frock coat that reached below my knees, would watch Magda swimming and getting out of the water, pulling off the cap that fastened under her chin and drying her hair, and through her white bathing suit I could make out the prominent nipples on her small breasts.

I knew it was a sin to look at her like that. I didn't care.

If my father had been born in Warsaw he wouldn't have cared either, but pious Naum Bernsztajn was born a hundred miles to the northeast, in Łomża, and died on the bank of a clay-pit pond near Latchorzew, but he came to Warsaw after World War I, a grown man, his wife's husband, a poor but devout Jew from a respected lineage, yet being from Łomża, Warsaw's Jews considered him a generation behind. Not everyone did, of course, but certainly those I spent my whole childhood eyeing enviously, the Jews dressed just like Christians, elegant, clean-shaven, European. My father, pious and quiet, was their opposite. If my father ever discovered my sinfulness!

But he never did.

The day after his death, the Shabbos of July 10, 1937, Magda came into our apartment, passed my mother sobbing voicelessly, and went into the bedroom I shared with my brother Emanuel.

"Emanuel, go to Mama," I said, because I was nasty and selfish. And he went.

Magda sat down beside me. She knew. Even more than I did.

And she's stayed for a long time since she sat down next to me like that. She's stayed to this day.

I can't bear the silence. But worse than the silence is what I might hear on the radio or TV. I get up from my typewriter, go to the fridge, and pour myself some cold water. Then I dial her number.

"Hello?"

I don't know what to say next. So I say nothing. I listen to her breathing heavily.

"Don't call me," she says after a moment, into the silence, in Polish. "You can't call me anymore." She hangs up.

She spoke to me in the same voice back then. It's impossible for a voice to have stayed completely the same. So maybe I'm remembering wrong. But I'm sure.

"Moyshe, I'm . . . ," she said quietly and gently, placing her hand on my knee, and right then I thought my father would never have allowed Magda to sit with me in my room. My mother wouldn't have allowed it either, had my father been alive.

Next she kissed me on the forehead and only then noticed I'd cut off my peyos. She ran her fingers over my shaved temples.

"Everything's going to be, somehow going to be . . . ," she whispered.

She kissed me again, again on the forehead. I tried to find her mouth, since I desired her the way one desires the first woman in one's life.

But she avoided my mouth. She moved away.

"I'm your friend, Moyshe, just a friend. You need a friend now. We can go see a show."

I didn't respond. Fifty years later, as she was moving out, final suitcase already in hand, she turned to me in the doorway, still straight-backed and strong, only her blond locks cut shorter, gray, and permed.

"My life would have been better if you'd ended up like all the others," she said very loudly.

"Magda . . . ," I wailed.

"Don't call me Magda!" she screamed and strode out, slamming the door.

I was left with that silly response and the bang of the door ringing in my ears, in an apartment where, once that slam had subsided, all that remained was silence.

But before, decades ago, my home had resounded with my sons' voices as they played on the floor, frolicking like puppies, squealing and shrieking. I don't know what happened to them.

Maybe they don't want to talk to me. Maybe they died in some war, one of many wars my country's had. I don't know what's happened to them.

I don't know why she doesn't want me to call her Magda.

But I return to Buddy Kaplica's red Chrysler Imperial, where I sat on the folding seat, a little drunk, for the first time in my life a little drunk.

"Moryc is getting too big for his boots," said Kaplica grimly once we'd set off. "You don't get your heater out of your pocket in front of me."

"Tough," said Szapiro, in a tone that even I found strangely staunch and arrogant.

Kaplica eyed him for a moment, stroking his mustache. He was thinking.

"Tough. All right, sure. He's your blood. Goes without saying, brother ain't gonna stand against brother. Wouldn't be right. Guess I gotta put up with it." Deciding the matter would remain closed, he suddenly declared, "We're going to Ryfka Kij's."

Moryc was an important figure in the Warsaw branch of Left Poale Zion, had studied law at Józef Piłsudski University, and was one of the young people of that era who needed a cause to dedicate their life to and did so the moment they found one, driven by the conviction that only a life dedicated to something greater than themselves was worth living. Back then none of these young people wanted to live life for its own sake. That's how they were, they all wanted to live for something more, all the young Bundists, Cominternists, folkists, fascists, Zionists, socialists, communists, nationalists. They all wanted to live for something. On some level it even made them respect one another, nationalists and Bundists, communists and Zionists could acknowledge if not one another's values, at least the quality of one another's character.

Jakub wasn't like that. He just wanted to live. Which Moryc couldn't understand.

The driver didn't ask the address, he just nodded. So we drove through Bankowy Square, down Żabia and Graniczna Streets, and then along the fence of the Saxon Gardens onto Marszałkowska Street, farther and farther south from my Warsaw, then finally the Chrysler Imperial turned right, onto Pius XI Street.

Until 1930, Pius XI Street had been called Piękna Street, but I didn't know that back then. I didn't know because I'd never ventured this far. This wasn't my city anymore; this was a Polish city.

This was a city of asphalt-paved, artificially lit streets, of clean sidewalks and elegant signs leading to elegant bars and restaurants. This wasn't my city, an invisible barrier like an ocean cut my city off from here, my city was filthier, poorer, and livelier; it smelled differently, or more often stank; the streets of my city spoke different tongues, even when speaking Polish, and celebrated different holidays, even when Christians celebrated them.

We parked in front of a slender apartment house at the sharp intersection of Pius XI and Koszykowa Streets. The building looked like a ship, its prow slicing through the two streets, and supporting a nearly church-like tower, crowned with a cupola. It was four stories high and the tower rose higher.

I didn't know then who Ryfka Kij was, of course. But that didn't worry me, as though the knowledge rested in an envelope I could open at any time. Buddy licked off the leftover cocaine wrapper, dusting his mustache with white powder.

"Let's go!" he ordered.

I was very afraid. I was afraid of Kaplica and afraid of Szapiro, yet though I was afraid I wanted to go with them, because I didn't want to be scrawny little Bernsztajn anymore, watching Szapiro drag my father out of our apartment by the beard.

I wanted to be Szapiro.

We went into number 49. I had never seen such a tidy entranceway in my life. A doorman, whose uniform looked more expensive than any of my father's clothes, opened the door before we could knock. He bowed deeply, removing his cap. Kaplica tossed him five złotys. We climbed a beautiful, winding staircase to the fourth floor, Szapiro knocked on the door, the judas hole scraped, then the door opened.

"Come in, gentlemen," a big, tuxedoed bruiser said, and bowed.

Kaplica walked inside, rubbing his hands with glee.

The apartment was dimly lit. We went from the hallway into the salon, where half-naked girls in see-through slips, short tulle capes, panties, and stockings sat on sofas and ottomans. Some even had bare breasts. I had theoretically never seen anything like this before, neither bare-breasted women nor such skimpy clothing, but it didn't seem the slightest bit unusual and even now I'm surprised—a boy of seventeen, first time laying eyes on that, and nothing. But that's exactly how I remember it. Nothing.

There were seven girls. Three blonds—two of them bleached—one redhead, three with black hair.

Three men sat among the girls, two in suits, one in a Polish uniform. In the corner, a still-handsome, though now fairly shaggy man in a white tuxedo jacket was quietly tinkling away on a white piano. There was a bar in the salon, tended by another white-jacketed man who was busy wiping glasses. Numerous colorful bottles of booze stood on a glistening shelf behind the bar. I had never seen so much alcohol at once, all in different colors.

Everything shimmered and shone, the bar was surfaced in glistening russet-toned brass, mirrors hung on the wall, a chandelier twinkled with crystals.

A slim, fully clothed woman sat on a stool at the bar. She was fully clothed by the standards of the joint, which I already knew to be a brothel, a place where women took the wrong path, as my recently deceased father would have put it.

By the standards of my family home—as defined by my mother in her wig and modest clothing—the woman at the bar was half-naked. Her gown, long and black but shining with hundreds of sequins, revealed her slim back and shoulders. Her hairstyle was already somewhat old-fashioned, a bob that had been popular in the twenties. She was even wearing a tiara headband in her hair that looked like something from more than a decade before.

Kaplica went up to her and she turned around.

She wasn't beautiful, but she wasn't ugly either, she looked average, her mouth narrow and seemingly determined, her face a little prematurely aged and mismatched to her youthful shoulders and neckline, yet her eyes were completely other, foreign to that average face: large, moist, very dark, hidden behind exceptionally long, black lashes, and topped with powerful, dark brows—eyes that could change from scorching to icy in an instant, but were never lukewarm.

"Good evening, madam," said Kaplica with a bow.

She proffered her gloved hand. Kaplica kissed it solemnly.

"Good evening, Mr. Kaplica. As ever it's an honor to have you here with us," she said with an enchanting smile.

"And will I be graced with the honor of your company this evening?" inquired the gangster, with a smile I might have called lighthearted if lightheartedness were not the last quality I'd associate with Kaplica.

"Mr. Kaplica, those days are long over. If you were twenty years younger and eight inches taller, it would be my pleasure to accept. But you're not," she replied, returning his smile.

I winced. *He'll kill her*, I thought.

"And what if I had an extra two thousand złotys to give you, Miss Ryfka?" he asked, twirling his mustache.

She laid a hand on his shoulder.

"Buddy, darling, I haven't been a whore for a long time," she said softly, but something dangerous lurked in her voice. Her voice held a threat, a memory of something just between her and Buddy, something that had happened long ago. Even I could hear it right then.

Or maybe not, I don't know, I don't remember, I don't know how much of this I knew back then and what I learned later, but today, here at my green typewriter, I know something dangerous lurked in her voice, because I have spent my whole life among people with danger lurking in their voices.

Kaplica kept toying with that danger.

"But, Miss Ryfka, to what kind of whore does a man offer two thousand złotys?" he ventured.

"An expensive one," she said icily, removing her hand from his shoulder.

That evening I thought she looked like someone infinitely wise and infinitely powerful, this slim, rather unpretty woman, overseeing hookers and ruined by life. She said nothing and looked him dead in the eye in a way that required no words.

"Then I plead for mercy, I beg forgiveness, Miss Ryfka," said Kaplica, backing off. "Please don't hold it against me if, when faced with a woman of your caliber and not being eight inches taller or twenty years younger, I resort to the single thing I possess . . . Except, that is, for a certain artistry unfitting to speak of even in this company, along with the tool it requires, which nature has endowed me with generously."

She laughed at his joke, seemingly in reconciliation. The hatchet was buried.

"I definitely remember that artistry of yours, Mr. Kaplica, and the tool too. I remember thinking it might tear me in half!"

Now they were laughing together. Buddy pulled himself onto a high barstool. His stubby little legs couldn't reach the step beneath the bar and dangled there instead.

"Now tell me, Ryfka, when was that?"

"In twenty-two."

"Fifteen years . . . Time flies faster than we can keep up with," said Buddy philosophically.

"Michał, pour these gentlemen some cognac," she said to the bartender. "Well, since I'm off-limits nowadays, what can I offer you, Buddy?"

"Is Magda here?" he asked.

I heard the name of my love and I went cold, though I certainly knew it wasn't her he meant. And yet.

"She's waiting for you, Mr. Kaplica." Ryfka smiled.

"Then call her out, please, we'll have a drink first," ordered Kaplica.

"Oh now, Mr. Kaplica, don't you know she's too young to drink alcohol?" teased Ryfka.

"Then have Michał warm her up some milk and honey!" Kaplica slapped his thighs with laughter.

Szapiro didn't sit down, he leaned against the wall and lit a cigarette. One of the girls got up, a plump blond with a tiny button nose and languid, sulky eyes that reminded me of the odalisques in sultans' seraglios I used to see in photo albums and books my father, now two days dead, didn't allow us to read.

She rose and approached us. I could see her breasts through the thin tulle of her nightgown, white and round with dark, flat nipples.

"Want me to take care of the kid, Mr. Szapiro?" she asked Jakub, then turned to me. "I'm Kasia."

Her voice was low, a little husky. I could feel myself getting hard at the sight of her breasts under the nightgown—suddenly, violently hard. I liked the sight of her breasts. At least I think I did.

Yet there was something in her eyes, her gaze, which told me to be careful, which put me off, warned me, portended the deepest depths of oceans of indifference, apathy, half death, warned me Kasia might pull me down too if I let her.

Szapiro glanced at me and saw a pale, terrified Jewish youth in ugly Christian rags, head covered, his mother crying in the kitchen for the second day straight, his father dismembered and laid to rest in the clay ponds outside Warsaw.

"No need," he replied. "Another time."

I thought the girl would be annoyed but naturally I was wrong. Annoyance was not among her professional duties.

"Then maybe there's something I can do for you, Mr. Szapiro?" she said more coquettishly, and sidling up to him, she touched his chest and groin.

Another girl approached us, taller and slimmer with her dark hair pinned up, looking as though she wanted to give the blond a run for her money.

"I'm new here. Name's Ola. I'll give it to you for free, Mr. Szapiro, often as you like," she said. "You're a hell of a guy, Mr. Szapiro, ain't nobody like you. Nobody!"

He considered for a moment.

"Not tonight, girls. Next time," he finally said, seemingly with a tinge of regret.

He took me by the arm and led me to the bar. Ola sat back down in her chair. Kasia sank back to the bottom of her ocean.

"Siddown. You hungry?"

I nodded. He sat next to me and took off his hat.

"Bartender, you got anything hot to eat?" he asked.

"Hot, we got boiled beef or pork knuckle. Have the pork knuckle, I recommend it, it's better."

"You gonna eat treyf?" asked Szapiro, peering at me searchingly.

I shook my head.

"Is the beef kosher?" he asked the bartender.

"Kosher, sure." The bartender grinned. "Tzaddiks the world over come to eat this beef, it's so kosher." He placed a bottle of chilled Baczewski vodka and two glasses in front of Szapiro and me.

Szapiro laughed loudly.

"Rabbi Michaelson ruled our boiled beef is so kosher, Mr. Szapiro, that you can chow down on pork with cream sauce to the end of your days and nothing'll ever be unkosher, that's how super-kosher we've kosherized this beef for you."

"I'm apikores here, give me the pork knuckle, and boiled beef for the boy," ordered Jakub, still chuckling. "But make it quick, we're starving."

Szapiro poured vodka into both glasses, his full, mine halfway. He passed me a cigarette. I'd smoked before, so I took it. He offered me a light too. I took a drag.

"Gitanes. French. The best," Szapiro informed me, so I took another drag. They were strong and flavorful, I had to admit. To this day I like

Gitanes, but they're hard to get here, so I mostly smoke whatever's at hand. Which is usually no good.

Or maybe I didn't smoke that night? I don't remember.

The uniformed officer left the salon arm in arm with the blond who'd approached us. The remaining two customers disappeared off somewhere. Meanwhile, a young girl emerged from behind a curtain and took a seat next to Kaplica. Szapiro caught me looking at her.

"Magda," he said.

Kaplica placed a hand on her thigh. She was wearing pigtails and a school uniform. She looked very young, her body had just begun to fill out. I thought maybe they'd picked a girl who looked young and dressed her up as a schoolgirl. I'd read in one of the books my father had forbidden me that sometimes people had strange sexual proclivities.

"Don't stare, Kaplica's ready to shoot you," hissed the boxer. "Nobody but him gets to touch her."

"How old is she?" I asked foolishly.

"Twelve. Shut up."

At that moment Buddy threw me a look, glaring with the evil eyes of a terrifying big shot. His eyes held a threat and a challenge. Kaplica was challenging a defenseless seventeen-year-old Jewish boy because he always challenged everyone everywhere, all over the world. That's what made him Kaplica. Or maybe he was looking at Szapiro, not me?

Szapiro didn't accept the challenge. I immediately looked away too. I took another drag. The bartender served our food. My plate held a thick hunk of beef, still steaming, two carrots, a slice of celery, and two potatoes, all boiled, everything drenched in horseradish sauce. I was sure the combination wasn't kosher—maybe the meat was beef but there was definitely dairy in the sauce. And a gentile had definitely cooked it, anyway.

Meanwhile on Szapiro's plate lay an enormous boiled pork knuckle, on the bone with bristly skin, so utterly piggish I could almost hear the disgusting beasts oinking. Szapiro sliced off a large, steaming hunk of meat with skin and fat, dipped it in a dish of mustard, placed it in his mouth, and chewed blissfully, like a real goy. I thought it should make me feel sick, but no, instead I thought it looked delicious.

"In 1917 I was in Czerwoniak prison in Łomża," he said after swallowing the first mouthful. He glanced at me and saw me dithering over my plate.

"Eat," he snapped.

I obediently sliced into the meat and, mentally apologizing to God and my father, I put it in my mouth and began to chew. Then I thought I'd never tasted anything so good. The creamy horseradish sauce, the meat dissolving delightfully into delicate fibers in my mouth . . . I chewed and all I felt was bliss.

"So I was in Czerwoniak prison in Łomża," continued Szapiro. "Seventeen years old, same as you are now. I got cell number two twenty-one. No cellmate. Inside was a raggedy straw mattress, a table, a bed. Nothing else. Whole prison was under German military control."

He was drunk now, but I listened to him very carefully.

"Running Czerwoniak was a commandant, name of Schramm, see? Schramm. That was his name." He took a sip of vodka. "But we called him something else, something else. We used to say he was Traitor. He always had his bullwhip with him and he killed plenty of guys with that bullwhip, and beat plenty more unconscious. I was an ordinary little nipper. I was in prison 'cause of a fuckup on a house job, the mark woke up, this big rugged fella, and I was a skinny little thing, just like you now, he cracked me on the nut and held me down, he sent his son for the police, and then they gave me two years. *Zwei Jahre Gefängnis für schweren Einbruchdiebstahl*, that was how they read out my sentence, it was a military court. Mornings they gave me coffee and nothing else, afternoons a quart of stinking sauerkraut, then potato soup at four, the kind that's more like potato water, and two and a half ounces of bread, this tiny little bite-size piece. And I'll tell you, Bernsztajn, hell's got nothing on a year in Czerwoniak under the German occupation. When

Poland was founded and they finally let me out I decided I'd never turn down any food out of fear of hell, because that was hell. And nobody was gonna thrash me and get away with it, no German, no Pole, no Jew. Commandant Schramm was the last one to hit me unpunished. You get me, Bernsztajn?"

I didn't get him, because I was eating and for the first time since my father's kidnapping I wasn't thinking about the kidnapping, just about the food and nothing else. But I nodded.

Kaplica finished his cognac, gave the girl a chocolate, then slipped his hand between her thighs under her skirt. He smiled warmly to himself. The girl was indifferent and withdrawn, she unwrapped the chocolate and put it in her mouth. Kaplica whispered something in her ear.

We were eating in silence. After a moment, Kaplica slid off the barstool and adjusted his jacket and tie, which was knotted around a stiff, unfashionable collar.

"Gonna head back with cutie-pie here." He bowed with a grin.

He took her hand and they left. The girl didn't protest.

"How'd she end up here?" I asked.

"She came on her own, begged Ryfka, so Ryfka took her in," replied Szapiro.

"A little kid like that?"

"A street kid is no little kid. Here she gets warmth, clothes, and food. Any wonder she'd rather be here than on the street, eating scraps and shivering in rags?" he said, washing down the pork knuckle with more vodka.

Ryfka went behind the bar and took a glass for herself. Jakub poured her some Baczewski and they drank a shot. Szapiro, clearly troubled, shrugged helplessly as though to say, *Nothing I can do about it*. Ryfka nodded sadly. They drank another shot.

"What's up with this one?" she asked, gesturing toward me with her head.

"Dunno. We'll see," replied Szapiro with a shrug.

"I might have something for him to do."

Today I feel guilty about all this. I feel guilty Kaplica was raping a twelve-year-old girl and I did nothing, didn't even lift a finger.

Now, tapping away on my typewriter, I tell myself I couldn't have done anything. I was a skinny seventeen-year-old little Jew, I couldn't have done anything.

But I'm not sure. Maybe I was someone else.

That night I didn't even dare look up from my plate, as though I might see the future in the swirls of sauce and boiled vegetables.

And what would I have seen? Aging General Moshe Inbar in an empty apartment on Dizengoff Street in Tel Aviv, banging away hopelessly on a typewriter and trying to work out how a man could have a life like his.

Or maybe I'd have seen someone else. Maybe Jakub Szapiro in some cheap apartment also in Tel Aviv, very old, but alive, insignificant, forgotten, scraping by on his pension, thinking back to his long-ago glory days?

Maybe even writing up his memoirs, just like me, on the same typewriter.

War is starting up again all around, but no one needs Moshe Inbar. Meanwhile Moshe Inbar isn't so old yet. Moshe Inbar has fifty years of experience.

The moment we arrived it was the Haganah, then the Palmach, and so on and on, my whole life. Everything Szapiro taught me came in very handy in my new country. For fifty whole years I did the same thing.

Forty years ago, my comrades and I in the Harel Brigade leveled Saris, and my hand didn't even tremble as I fired my gun and threw grenades. All my country's wars built up layers of knowledge inside me that no one needs anymore, and rather than sitting over documents and maps, General Moshe Inbar sits at a green IBM Selectric II, writing a story in Polish that no one needs, that no one can read, or ever will. I won't be sending this to Keter Publishing after all. I can't. For three months now, Moshe Inbar, who nobody needs, has been sitting, feeling sorry for himself, at his typewriter. He stares at the model Lockheed Model 10 Electra hanging over his desk.

And Magda Inbar doesn't want to be called Inbar anymore. Magda is Aszer again. Or something else. She doesn't even want me to call her Magda.

"I wasted my whole life on you," she said. "I wasted my youth, I wasted my adulthood, and now I'm wasting my old age on you."

If you'd died back then my life would have been better, that's what she meant.

I'd rather think about what I haven't thought about all these years.

So I'll go back to when I was eating treyf for the first time in my life, at the bar at Ryfka Kij's on the corner of Pius XI and Koszykowa.

"I might have a job for this kid," said Ryfka, eyeing me up.

Szapiro slammed his silverware down on the copper bar top.

"I'll make you cough up pus and blood if you say something like that again!"

"Oh, fine, what is he, a relative of yours? He's cute, fatten him up a little and he'd do great. But come on, I'm not gonna snatch him from you. Maybe he wants to. How 'bout it, kid?"

"Hands off the boy, Ryfka. He doesn't want to. As far as you're concerned, he's a relative. A close one."

At the time I didn't understand what he meant. But he was right, wasn't he? It was blood that connected us. The blood of Naum Bernsztajn, my father. But today that "he'd do great" of Ryfka's sort of sounds flattering—I'm not a homosexual, but that's how it sounds, flattering. Because she wasn't thinking about women, after all.

Anyway, maybe that conversation happened another time. Maybe they were talking about someone else, some little urchin bringing a package? I can't remember everything.

The phone rang behind the bar. A beautiful, modern black Bakelite Siemens. Ryfka answered. This I remember perfectly.

71

After an extended "Hellooo?" she was silent for a moment, listening. "Yes, they're here," she responded. "Naturally, you'd be more than welcome." She hung up. "The Doctor says he's coming by," she said, pouring herself and Szapiro yet another round. "I didn't know he was back from America already."

"Last week. Drunk already?" asked the boxer.

"Not yet."

"So much the better. He'll probably bring Pantaleon."

Ryfka nodded.

"Can you stay?" she asked. "They'll ruin my business."

"I'll stay."

There was something in her voice, something else, something I didn't expect to hear.

Ryfka took down a couple of bottles from the shelf behind the bar and put them in locked cabinets. I gathered she was hiding the more expensive ones.

"Kasia, Ola, you get the night off, now scram!" she shouted.

"Can I go too?" asked the piano player, his voice trembling.

"I need you here, Jacek. Play."

He sighed and kept playing. Suddenly jettisoning all their harem-girl indolence, Kasia and Ola got off the ottoman and fled the salon. The four prostitutes left in the room took out compacts from the recesses of the sofas and started powdering their noses like crazy. Szapiro lit a cigarette.

I looked at the tattoo on his right hand, the two-edged sword and death.

After fifteen minutes, which I spent sitting over my empty plate listening uncomprehendingly to Ryfka and Szapiro's laconic conversation, someone knocked on the door in the hall, so loudly we could hear it even in the salon.

Janusz Radziwiłek, PhD. At the time, I didn't know he was Jewish. He didn't look it. He was tall and slim with an aristocratically Aryan face and features that back then everyone called noble, though I don't know why. What could be noble about facial features? To me, Radziwiłek had upper-class features. He was also wearing a uniform, an officer's uniform of the paramilitary Rifleman's Association, which at the time I associated unambiguously with the upper classes.

It wasn't just any old uniform, it was military green with a standing collar and a red braid on that collar, topped off with a peaked cap with a Polish eagle. Under its brim he wore round, wire-rim glasses, like someone upper class—they gave him an intellectual look, despite the uniform. Even his forehead was high, patrician, noble. His thinning, dark hair was combed straight back and it glistened with Brilliantine once he removed his cap.

The tips of his black boots also glistened. They were knee-high—you could immediately tell they were made-to-measure—and laced all the way up at the front.

If not for those boots and the uniform he'd look like a professor. He also had a professor's hands: slender, with long fingers. He wore a signet ring on his little finger, like a count, and on second thought it occurred to me he looked more like a count than a professor. To my mind, an officer and a count went together better than an officer and a professor.

He hadn't come alone. Accompanying him was a small young man with a somber, handsome face. Like Radziwiłek, he wore a Rifleman's Association uniform, but instead of jodhpurs he wore trousers with a stripe down the sides, and ordinary shoes. His epaulettes bore a local chapter distinction.

His name was Eduard Tyutchev. He was the son of a Russian aristocrat who'd settled in Warsaw in 1919, fathered an illegitimate son, then died. He was apparently a distant relative of the poet Tyutchev. He loved literature, he was eighteen, and had already killed three people.

"Good evening to all people here," said Radziwiłek from the doorway in a squeaky voice completely mismatched to his professorial veneer, and additionally in peculiar, bad Polish. "Good evening, Miss Ryfka!"

Tyutchev sat down in the nearest armchair and lit a cigarette. From his shirt pocket he took out a small book of verse and lost himself in reading.

"Good evening, Mr. Szapiro!" squeaked Radziwiłek. He didn't have a Jewish accent, he just spoke oddly. Ryfka curtsied behind the bar.

My mother always feared bad Polish. My father had thought nothing of Polish whatsoever, although he spoke it reasonably well, but the Polish world didn't interest him. To my father, the Poles and Poland were just as foreign as, say, the Portuguese, except not as far away.

Still, he'd have lived the same in Lisbon as in Warsaw.

As for my mother, Poland interested her somewhat, even though she was religious. Not interested enough to read Polish newspapers, she never so much as touched the *Courier*, but a Jewish paper in Polish like *Our Review*, certainly—as long as my father didn't see. That was why, despite my father's protests, I went to Kryński High School on the corner of Miodowa and Senatorska Streets, and although it was a Jewish school, teaching was in Polish. I was the only boy there with peyos—short ones tucked behind my ears, but still. I caught hell for those. And at home for the uniform, too—my mother had to swear to my father he'd never set eyes on me in my uniform, so as soon as I got home I changed into normal, Jewish clothes.

I went to an eight-year secondary school, because I went in 1930, before the education reform. In September I was supposed to start my final year, then pass my exams the next year and go to college. Without consulting my father, my mother and I had decided I would become a doctor. After all, I was a good student, so I'd pass my exams (we didn't know just then they would be introducing anti-Jewish quotas) and in 1944 I would graduate as Dr. Mojżesz Bernsztajn, MD.

That was what my mother wanted. I wasn't as enthusiastic as she was, but "Dr. Mojżesz Bernsztajn, MD" sounded a lot better than "some Jewish kid from 26 Nalewki Street, apartment 6."

It even sounded better than "famously devout Naum Bernsztajn from 26 Nalewki Street, apartment 6," especially given my dear father Naum Bernsztajn hadn't paid Buddy Kaplica what he owed him and wound up in chunks in the clay ponds outside Warsaw, and by the time I was sitting at the bar at Ryfka Kij's in Christian clothes, I knew nothing would come of my final year of secondary school, my exams, or my medical studies.

And nothing did. And that is almost certainly why I am still alive today, Tat-Aluf Moshe Inbar, Brigadier General Moshe Inbar. Dr. Mojżesz Bernsztajn, MD, couldn't happen, but General Moshe Inbar did.

At Ryfka Kij's all I knew was there was no going back to school now, because there was no longer a Naum Bernsztajn to pay for it.

"Good day to kind lady especially!" Dr. Radziwiłek bowed to one of the prostitutes, a slim peroxide blond. He took out a fifty-złoty bill and ceremoniously presented it to her.

The girl rose gracefully. Radziwiłek offered her his arm, bowed to Ryfka and Szapiro, and without further ado headed to one of the bedrooms.

"When he gets back the fun'll start," muttered Ryfka, topping up the half-empty vodka bottle with water.

Szapiro swallowed the last bite of the pork knuckle, stretched, and emptied his glass.

"Know who that is?" he asked me.

I didn't.

"Exactly. Everyone knows Buddy. But nobody knows the Doctor unless they're supposed to."

All this was going completely over my head.

"Let me tell you a story about him," he said.

And he did, laconically and without embellishment. Or maybe he was just talking to himself.

Janusz Radziwiłek's name was not Janusz Radziwiłek and no one knew his real name. Probably something normal, Yiddish, like Chaim, Mordke, Shloyme, or Moyshe, but no one knew what. He was forty-four and the first thirteen years of his life he'd spent as a Hasidic boy, mainly in heder, where he studied the Torah, the Mishnah, and the Gemara, like every Hasidic boy. Then one day in 1905, a rebel fighter burst into the heder with a revolver in his hand and a scarf tied over his face.

The heder students could tell right away—he was a Christian.

The melamed thought: a pogrom.

The boys thought: a revolutionary.

The rebel with the revolver, a soldier of the Combat Organization of the Polish Socialist Party under Józef Piłsudski, was a hero in the imaginations of the thirteen-year-old Jewish boys, even those from Hasidic families.

"Is there a back door here?" bellowed the rebel.

"Antlof fin dane', du s'i nish' kan ort fa diyo'!"[11] cried the melamed, whom young not-yet-Doctor Janusz Radziwiłek thought was a coward for wanting to throw a hero out of their school. He thought of himself as an heir to the Maccabees.

"I show you the way," said not-yet-Radziwiłek.

They could already hear the gendarmes tramping up the stairway to the heder.

The rebel was named Jan Kaplica, though in those days he wasn't yet Buddy. To hold off his pursuers for a moment, he cracked the door open and fired his officer's seven-shooter twice down the stairs. All hell broke loose in the heder. The students screamed, the melamed hid under his desk. Not-yet-Radziwiłek led the rebel out and helped

---

11 Get out of here, this is no place for you!

Kaplica slip away from the czar's officers, thus saving his freedom and surely his neck as well.

"What's your name?" asked young, twenty-five-year-old Kaplica, once they were safe.

"Radziwiłł!" said not-yet-Radziwiłek, blurting out the name of one of Poland's most famous noble families, because it was the first Christian name that came to mind. "Please take me with you."

Kaplica burst into laughter at the thought this little Jew could be a Radziwiłł. Laboriously reloading his revolver, he told not-yet-Radziwiłek to run off back home.

"I don't want to go home. I hate my home. I love revolution. In my home ain't no revolution and won't be. I can't go back to there. I save your life. You gotta do what I ask," exclaimed not-yet-Radziwiłek in response, in other words he said it as Chaim, Meir, or Shloyme, and those were the most correct Polish sentences he'd strung together in his entire life.

And Kaplica, a simple man, accepted this argument and took not-yet-Radziwiłek with him.

Kaplica was a unit commander and later introduced the young Jew to Sosnkowski, the organization's leader in Warsaw. "He's too little for a Radziwiłł!" laughed Sosnowski. "More like a *Radziwiłek*. Janusz." And so he acquired his diminutive ending and became Radziwiłek. He didn't go back to heder. He went to a secular school. He was a courier for illegal pamphlets, he kept watch, he hid weapons, he was active, always under the wing and care of Kaplica.

He never went home. He was born that day in the heder. The day he showed Kaplica the way out, he was born anew.

In 1910, the organization paid for him to go abroad to study in Switzerland and he stayed there until 1918, returning with a doctorate in chemistry, exquisite manners, money, and terrible English, French, and German. He never learned good Polish, he'd nearly forgotten his Yiddish, and he never knew Hebrew. So he spoke five languages and none of them well. This made people underestimate the Doctor's intelligence, which suited him fine.

He never returned to political work, yet he did return to the Rifleman's Association, where he immediately became a district commander, and he also returned to Kaplica and his Socialist Party comrades. Building off the Association's structures, Radziwiłek assembled a powerful fighting squad that accepted any man who was good with a Browning, a truncheon, and his fists, and also took on the boxer and veteran of the Bolshevik War, Jakub Szapiro. Before Piłsudski returned to power in the coup of 1926, they'd had their work cut out for them on the streets, while on the margins he and Buddy were building up their little empire in the City Center.

Buddy was in charge of the protection money from Kercelak market and running things day-to-day, meaning the informal running of the Northern District, from Wola and Ochota districts in the west, up to the slums by Gdański Station in Żoliborz district—where they recruited boys as couriers—as well as the whole northern, Jewish part of the City Center.

Wherever poverty reigned on the left bank of the Vistula in Warsaw—and, aside from a few islands of Europe and prosperity, poverty reigned everywhere—there Buddy reigned too. His executive authority did not extend to the opposite bank of the river, but his notoriety did, and over there he also prompted respect. Songs about Buddy were sung in the slums of distant Annopol, and every hoodlum in Łódź, Sosnowiec, and Częstochowa had heard of him too.

Meanwhile Radziwiłek remained in the shadows. He lacked Buddy's charisma, he wasn't cut out to be a folk hero; he was too disdainful of anyone stupider and weaker than him, and too greedy. He tended to the political machinations and in addition to reinforcing Kaplica politically, he made sure no one on the street had any doubt who ruled there. Beyond the structures of the Rifleman's Association, whose uniform he usually wore, he was also an active member of the Polish Socialist Party.

In one way or another every socialist gang answered to Radziwiłek, the Bund recognized his authority, and the left-wing Zionists—willingly or unwillingly—accepted it too. The Doctor thought more broadly and boldly than Kaplica: he sought out new markets, new sources of capital, and won over new friends. They complemented one another, and while perhaps they didn't like one another, they realized they needed each other.

Szapiro summarized all this for me that night with drunken fluency, skipping over the details. The details I learned myself, later, but that night, listening to him at Ryfka's, I quickly saw he had a larger point. He wasn't just telling me this so I knew who I was dealing with.

As he was talking about Radziwiłek, Pantaleon Karpiński entered Ryfka's salon. He didn't even glance at the girls—he went up to the bar, but some distance from us. He did not say hello.

"Brew me some tea," he growled in a low, rumbling voice.

Even then he terrified me, this huge man, over six and a half feet tall, with a strangely shaped, square head, hair slicked back absurdly under an ordinary newsboy cap, dressed like any old workman, in pants that were far too short for him, suspenders, and a collarless shirt with the sleeves rolled up high, revealing bulging, powerful forearms and huge biceps.

"You got it, Mr. Karpiński," chirped Ryfka.

She feared him. The girls feared him too and were whispering something to one another. Michał the bartender feared him, so did the bruiser at the door, even though he was completely out of sight I was sure of it, and the pianist feared him, I was sure of that too.

Only Szapiro didn't, and that bravery of Szapiro's somehow infected me.

First to emerge from the lovemaking rooms was Kaplica, jacket in hand, shirt open, buttoning his fly.

"Ryfka, pour me a cognac," he commanded, dispensing with the "Miss," then climbed onto a stool next to Pantaleon. "And have a girl check up on my little angel back there, she's worn out."

Two prostitutes immediately leaped up and dashed out of the salon.

"What you doing sitting out here?" Kaplica said, taking a friendly interest in Pantaleon.

"I fucked this morning." Pantaleon pronounced the words slowly, with long pauses between them.

"So what if you did?" said Kaplica, surprised. "You can't do it twice?"

"Not allowed."

"Heh-heh, hear that, folks?" said Kaplica cheerfully, slapping his knees with delight. "Leoś says you're not allowed to fuck twice in one day."

"Not allowed," murmured Pantaleon again and swallowed the cup of boiling hot tea in one gulp. "Fuck once a day and heaven's on its way. Jesus said that."

Everyone laughed, Ryfka, Buddy, and Szapiro. Only Pantaleon didn't laugh. Pantaleon crossed himself.

"It's no laughing matter, brothers and sisters. You can't fuck more often than that. Lord Jesus will get mad and your pecker might shrivel up."

"Your pecker?" I asked.

They all looked at me, except Pantaleon. They started laughing. Now I understood, though I didn't get why it was so funny. Ryfka went up to me and leaned over the bar so that if I'd looked at her neckline I'd definitely see her breasts.

"You know, your pecker," she said in her silky alto. "Prick. Cock. Willy. Shlong. Shmeckel. Or the circumcised thing you've got in your pants, yingele. Your pecker will shrivel up, your balls will rot. If you fuck more than once a day. You gonna do that? You want to make Lord Jesus mad?"

I looked down, embarrassed. I don't know if I was more embarrassed at a woman talking about male genitals or a Jew talking about Jesus like that. Lord Jesus. Even pronouncing that name. In my house no one ever spoke that name out loud. An offense against God. A sin to say that name.

Szapiro slapped me on the back and poured me some more vodka.

"Drink up," he said loudly, then leaned over and added in a drunken whisper, "and don't ask dumb questions. Or smart ones either. If you don't understand something, keep your trap shut till you do. Nobody's gonna explain anything to you. Maybe you'll manage."

Kaplica pulled out some paper bundles of cocaine. He gave one to Pantaleon, who immediately licked off all the white powder, then chewed the paper thoroughly and spat it out behind him.

The paper landed on the toe of the black boots of the district commander of the Rifleman's Association, Doctor of Chemical Sciences Janusz Radziwiłek.

His uniform was just as impeccable as the moment he'd entered Ryfka Kij's salon. All the buttons done up, the belt, the diagonal chest strap, the round cap, the shooting badges, the distinction ribbons. But now a chewed-up spitball straight from Pantaleon's mouth rested on the toe of his right boot.

"You!" He pointed at the last of the girls still sitting in the salon.

She immediately ran up to him. With a glance, he indicated the tip of his boot. The girl gave Ryfka a look, it wasn't a long look, and Ryfka nervously nodded. The girl took the hem of her peignoir and wiped the saliva-soaked paper off Radziwiłek's boot. Ryfka gestured at the door with her eyes. The girl fled.

Radziwiłek approached the bar and, leaning on it, glared at Pantaleon.

Tyutchev, still sitting in the armchair by the door, his eyes glued to his book, used his left hand to undo the holster strap on the Luger he wore, German-style, on his left hip. But Radziwiłek stopped him with a brief wave of his hand.

Pantaleon said nothing. Radziwiłek waited. It was clear he wasn't going to let it go. He didn't fear Pantaleon.

"Well?"

"Leoś, you numbskull, apologize to the Doctor!" roared Kaplica, suddenly seeming alarmed this pleasant evening might descend into a brawl.

"In the name of God I beg forgiveness," said Pantaleon, only looking straight ahead and clenching his large fists.

"For what you apologize to me?" growled the Doctor in a threatening tone, as though demanding contrition from a misbehaving schoolboy.

Pantaleon said nothing and stared blankly ahead.

"For fucking what?" roared the Doctor, slamming his fist on the copper bar top. "For what you fucking apologize?"

Kaplica pointedly cleared his throat.

"For spitting on your boot. By accident," murmured Pantaleon, still staring ahead, and Radziwiłek immediately brightened up.

"Oh but is nothing, don't worry, Mr. Karpiński, it's trifle, mere trifle. *Kein Ding*," he replied grandly and generously. "Miss Ryfka, I humbly ask glass of cognac to start. Large glass of cognac."

She served it immediately, and he immediately drank it.

"Please, a second."

She served a second too. And he drank the second. In one gulp.

"Here we go," murmured Szapiro.

"Radziwiłek, my friend, what's the rush?" asked Kaplica.

"*Ars longa, vita brevis,*" replied Radziwiłek.

"Eh?" said Buddy, confused.

"Life short, art long," explained the Doctor.

"Ah, you're full of crap. Ryfka, pour me one too," said Kaplica.

And now they were drinking together, at a slower pace. Kaplica ordered some hot kiełbasa and mustard, Ryfka brought it, and they ate with their fingers, dipping the kiełbasas in a dish of brown mustard.

"Buddy, my friend, I saw in America a thing that make my eyes open now," began Radziwiłek.

"Mm-hmm," murmured Buddy, not really listening because he was busy sucking the fat out of the thick kiełbasas.

"There they have a thing they call *gangs*. Like our fighting squad."

"Mm-hmm." Buddy finished his cognac and reached for another kielbasa.

"But, Buddy, such order they have there. Division. Military discipline."

"We got that too. Ever since we fought under Piłsudski."

"We need sell drugs. Biggest margin."

"You mean to tell me the whores and Kercelak market ain't enough for us?" asked Kaplica.

"Enough or not enough," replied Radziwiłek philosophically, then he changed the subject. "I read *ABC* today."

"That anti-Semitic rag?" asked Szapiro, surprised.

"Anti-Semitic ain't the half of it, come on, they're the worst nationalist or, y'know, fascist cruds," said Kaplica, even more surprised, because for him, not being a socialist meant not even being human.

"I very well know what kind newspaper it is," continued the Doctor. "I read it because I must have knowledge how enemy think. You not think so?"

They agreed.

"Know about survey?"

"Sure, sure," replied Kaplica. "There was a thing in the *Courier* too. How to throw Jews out of the army."

"Exact. What we do with this?" asked the Doctor, taking a large swig of vodka from yet another glass filled to the brim.

"Let them throw us out. Why should we serve in their army?" Szapiro shrugged.

"Kuba! That's heresy," said Kaplica, outraged. "You, a veteran! And decorated! You should be ashamed, Kuba!"

"We need that army like we need a pain in the dick."

"What's this us-and-them stuff?" said Kaplica, getting hot under the collar. "Kuba, you fought the Bolsheviks for Poland and now you're giving me this?"

Szapiro waved his hand dismissively.

The Doctor pulled a newspaper clipping from the pocket of his uniform.

"Here some young retired officer write that for Jews should be work camp, lumber for barracks, and lotta barbed wire. This from Wednesday, July seventh. Are we some monkey, to have barbed wire? Or I am some Negro to keep me in camp? I wanna know who write such things."

"Jakub . . ." Kaplica nodded at the piece of paper. "Is *ABC* the same crowd as that Ziembiński you did a number on?"

Szapiro went up to the Doctor, took the clipping, and glanced over it.

"No. They're both nationalists, but Ziembiński hangs out with the Phalanx, and them and *ABC* don't get along. The Phalanx is too radical, even for *ABC*. But our fella here, won't take me long to work out who he is," he said and slipped the clipping into the inside pocket of his jacket. "Ryfka, gimme the phone."

She passed it to him, he pulled a slim notebook out of his pocket, found a number, and dialed.

"Give me Mr. Witold Sokoliński please. I'll wait. Yes."

Radziwiłek gave him an inquiring look. Szapiro reassured him with a gesture.

"Oh, good evening, Mr. Sokoliński. This is Jakub Szapiro. Jakub Szapiro. I know you saw me this evening at the Metropol, isn't that right?"

Kaplica grinned from ear to ear so the tips of his turned-up handlebar mustache almost reached his eyes. He was grinning at the thought of how terrified the journalist must be.

I didn't see this with my own eyes, I'd never been inside the *Courier*'s offices, though many times I'd walked past the building at 40 Krakowskie Przedmieście on the corner of Karowa Street, with a sign on the roof sporting the title of the largest newspaper in Warsaw, and Poland, which also appeared on the façade. Yet I could perfectly imagine Sokoliński sitting in the editorial office on the fourth floor, his bald pate white with fear at the thought someone like Jakub Szapiro was aware of his existence.

He'd seen firsthand what Jakub Szapiro could do to a journalist. As we know.

"Listen here," said Jakub. "Tell me who at *ABC* is in charge of this survey about throwing Jews out of the army. Uh-huh. Uh-huh. Yeah, I know what paper you work for, Mr. Sokoliński, and I know the *Courier* isn't *ABC*. Mr. Sokoliński, I don't give a damn if you disagree with the survey. I do agree, we need that army of yours like we need a soft cock."

Kaplica rolled his eyes. Szapiro was smirking to himself, like a schoolkid playing a prank on a classmate he didn't like.

"Listen, Sokoliński, quit fucking me around." He suddenly changed his tone. "You want me to come see you? Maybe at your office? Or should I visit you at home? Twenty-seven Mickiewicz Street. How 'bout it? Well if there's no need, who's in charge of it over there? Mr. Kazimierz Bobiński, you say. All right. What's the easiest place to find him, if not in his office? Don't give me that crap, Mr. Sokoliński . . . Art and Fashion Café. Now tell me what this Bobiński looks like. Uh-huh. Uh-huh. Fantastic. I had a feeling you and me'd get along."

He hung up the phone and gave a broad grin.

"Want me to head over?" he asked Radziwiłek.

The Doctor considered for a moment. I didn't know it then, but now I know he had to think about his long-term plans, in which politics played an important role.

"Not yet," he finally replied. "It must be done, but not yet now. I tell you when."

And they kept drinking.

They were on their fifth glass when yet another guest entered the salon. He was a portly, staid old gentleman who looked like a book-keeper at a prosperous firm, a little tipsy, a watch in his vest pocket and a walking stick in his hand, hair thinning, with the look of a man leading an uncomplicated, comfortable, and meaningless life.

Whistling to himself, he stepped inside, furrowed his brow when he saw there were no girls, then noticed the company at the bar, while the company noticed the gentleman.

"Oh, I beg your pardon," he squealed, terrified, and turned on his heel and headed for the exit.

"Stop, because shoot!" roared Radziwiłek, yanking his Browning out of the holster at his officer's belt. He fired over the man's head and plaster rained down from the ceiling.

It was the first time in my life hearing a gunshot at such close range, let alone in a closed room. I almost fell off the barstool. Kaplica was giggling to himself. My ears were ringing. Ryfka was polishing the glasses with a grim look on her face. Szapiro, his face equally grim, was smoking a cigarette. Pantaleon was staring straight ahead, fists clenched, as though still suffering through the humiliating apology. The pianist, a forty-five-year-old lounge lizard by the name of Jacek Bykow, bolted.

The portly bookkeeper threw himself to the floor, covering his head with his hands. The Doctor went up to him, gun in hand.

"What this mean? Why run away?" he asked.

"Please don't shoot! I have a wife, kids, please don't shoot," wailed the bookkeeper.

"Have wife? *Ehefrau?* And goes to brothel?" shouted the Doctor.

Ryfka snorted with laughter, Szapiro too, Kaplica got into the spirit of things and let out a cackle, even Tyutchev smiled. Only Pantaleon remained seemingly frozen in outrage.

The Doctor grabbed the bookkeeper by the collar and hauled him to his feet.

"I've done nothing, I've done nothing . . . ," the man sniveled.

"Nothing?" asked Radziwiłek threateningly, jabbing the barrel of the gun into his victim's chest.

"Nothing, have mercy, Officer, nothing . . . ," wept the bookkeeper.

The Doctor suddenly beamed.

"If nothing, then have fun with us! Drink! Now! Ryfka, pour cognac for gentleman!"

The old fellow didn't trust the sudden change of mood, yet Radziwiłek, oblivious, pulled him to the bar. Ryfka poured a cognac and the bookkeeper drank it.

By the third round he'd loosened up a little. It looked like he was still scared but was starting to believe he'd get out of this alive. The Doctor put an arm over his shoulders, not letting go of the Browning, kissed him on the cheek, and drank too, drank a large amount quickly.

"You name?" he asked, kissing the bookkeeper on the cheek.

"D-Darling," he stammered.

"What?" Radziwiłek hadn't heard.

"Darling," said Darling, embarrassed. "Tomasz Darling."

"Darling! *Ausgezeichnet!*" roared the Doctor. "Mr. Darling, you my friend. Forever."

Darling nodded nervously.

"I show you something, Mr. Darling. Look! Miss Ryfka, piano, play!"

Ryfka called the pianist back, who came in reluctantly and was literally trembling with fear.

"Mr. Bykow! Play '*Einzug der Gladiatoren*'!" ordered the Doctor. "Play! *Schnell!*"

Bykow started trembling even harder.

"I don't know it . . . I'm awfully sorry, but I don't know what to say, I don't know it . . . ," he moaned.

"*Dummkopf!*" snarled Radziwiłek and went up to the pianist, still clutching his pistol. "Easy! Music from circus! Play! *Eins, zwei, drei!*"

Hearing it was meant to be circus music, the pianist realized what the Doctor meant. He started playing and the moment he did, he forgot his fear.

Even I knew the tune, though I'd never been to the circus. The circus was a godless entertainment, sons of godly Jews didn't go to the circus. Sons of dead godly Jews were another matter. They apparently would even go to a brothel. Does godliness pass away when life does, is a dead Jew no longer godly? Even if he isn't, that godliness of my father's hung over me like the shadow of a thundercloud, huge and heavy.

The pianist played. And the moment I heard the first bars, I recognized it: this was the tune they played at the circus as the clowns entered the ring.

Radziwiłek waved his pistol rhythmically like a conductor's baton, ran up to the bar, and placed his hand on Pantaleon's shoulder.

"Well, now? Mr. Karpiński! Well! Well! Mr. Darling see baby face!"

Pantaleon didn't react. He stared straight ahead. His fists were no longer clenched and his hands lay flat on the copper bar top.

"Right now!" ordered the Doctor. "Baby face!"

Pantaleon turned slowly to Kaplica.

"Buddy, as God is my witness, I won't stand any more of this," he rumbled.

Kaplica knocked back a glass of cognac.

"You're gonna do what the Doctor says. That's an order. The organization demands it," he snarled, not breaking his smile.

Pantaleon turned away from Kaplica and fixed his gaze on the same spot he'd been staring at since the Doctor had come in. It looked like he was burning a hole in the paneling behind the bar with his eyes.

"Szapiro!" shouted Kaplica.

"Eat shit," swore Szapiro under his breath.

He swore, but got up. He wobbled, drunk, but only for a moment. He drew his pistol from his pocket. He went up to Pantaleon.

"Come on, pal, do what he says," he said gently, as though persuading a child to take his fish oil. "Do it. Else he'll throw a fit. Do it."

Pantaleon sniffed. He got up from the stool, took a few steps, and stopped in the middle of the salon. He sniffed again and slowly ran his hand up from the back of his neck to the top of his head. He covered the raised hair with his cap and let his hands drop.

"Now, look, Mr. Darling, look here! Will be circus!" cried Radziwiłek happily, pointing at the back of Pantaleon's head.

Pantaleon Karpiński stood facing me. I could only see his face, lips, and eyes squeezed tight into furious slits. Meanwhile Mr. Darling was peering at whatever Radziwiłek wanted to show him so badly.

"Sweet Jesus!" cried Mr. Darling, to Radziwiłek's delight, and bolted like he'd seen the devil. Radziwiłek fired a shot after him, the bullet winging the arm of Mr. Darling's jacket and hitting the wall. Mr. Darling escaped.

Radziwiłek looked at me as though he'd only just noticed me, and pointed his pistol at me.

"Who this?" he asked. "Who this shitting kike?"

"He's with me," said Szapiro calmly.

"Come here!" commanded Radziwiłek. "See!"

Pantaleon was standing motionless. I slid off the stool and went up to Radziwiłek.

"Here, here, come!" Radziwiłek pointed to a spot in front of him. "Look!"

I did. On the back of Pantaleon Karpiński's head, there was a face. Smaller than a full-grown one, with eyes closed and a sad, frowning mouth. On its upper lip and where its chin should be grew sparse black hair, like what had started to appear on my face a few years before.

I froze. I knew what was happening to me: I was staring into the abyss. I was touching the feet of God. Or maybe I'm remembering wrong. Maybe I was only scared right then, the abyss came later. I don't know.

I rise from my desk. I walk to the window. The street. Tel Aviv. I return to my desk, my green typewriter, and my cup of cold coffee.

Fifty years on, I need only close my eyes and I can see that face on the back of Pantaleon Karpiński's head, its drooping features, its twisted mouth with hairy lips and closed eyes. And most frightening of all: a barely perceptible resemblance to Pantaleon's first face.

"Freak! Make smile! Mr. Karpiński! Make it smile!" said Radziwiłek cheerfully.

"All right, that's enough, Doctor," said Szapiro, trying to calm him down.

"Smile!" cried the Doctor.

Pantaleon clenched his fists, smiled with his first face, and the second face smiled too, though its eyes remained closed.

A wave of heat came over me, then I felt light-headed, and then the world suddenly fell into darkness and everything went black. I fainted.

By the time Szapiro revived me, Pantaleon was gone.

"Let's get out of here," said Szapiro. "Come on."

The fun at Ryfka's was in full swing. Buddy and the Doctor were drinking at the bar. Between them, kneeling on a stool and sticking out her behind, was Kasia, the blond whose breasts I'd seen as soon as we came into the salon. Now she was laying those breasts and her face on the copper bar top. The Doctor was drinking with his right hand and his left was fiddling around between her thighs. I could tell it hurt her, she was grimacing and squeezing her eyes shut. Buddy didn't pay her any attention. Ryfka was writing something down in a large ledger laid out on the bar not far from the blond. Bykow was playing wistful tunes.

"Come on," repeated Szapiro.

In that moment I forgot he'd taken my father from our house. I didn't want to remember. He gave me his hand like a father to his child, I took that hand and he led me out, and we left.

I didn't know it then but today I think that was the moment I stopped believing in God. To this day I'm not a believer. Because of Pantaleon Karpiński's second face.

A taxi was already waiting downstairs, a black Chevrolet. We got in but the driver didn't start moving.

"Hold up for a second," said Szapiro to the driver, who shrugged and waited obediently.

Pantaleon Karpiński's second face had altered something in me, like flicking a switch. The sight of it made my certainty in God's existence seem absurd.

Either God, or the second face on the back of Pantaleon Karpiński's head.

Instead of God, I began to believe in monstrosity. Warsaw didn't have so much of that and later, when I came here, I didn't have time for such things, so monstrosities only made a serious appearance in my life after the war of '48.

Since the early 1950s I've subscribed to medical journals. I buy medical books. I flip through them and clip out the photos and sketches. I arrange them into one enormous whole. They're my proof there is no humanity. There is no such thing as a human being.

Since Siamese twins exist, there is no God. If one person has a different person growing out of them—if hanging off one adult man's rib cage is half of another, a pelvis and frail, tiny legs, like a toddler's—then what is a human being? How many people is that? What is the body? Why is the body?

In the bathroom, before getting in the shower, I often examine my body, which is nearly seventy, although it looks much older. I have an old man's body enveloped in pale skin, apart from my face and forearms, tanned from many years of wearing a uniform with rolled-up sleeves. The skin on my arms is flabby, creased, but I've still got muscles underneath. My belly is plump and round because I haven't left the house in nearly a month. I just sit at my typewriter and eat a lot, though I'm convinced if I just went back on the diet I made myself follow in the service, in three weeks I'd be back to looking wiry again. I'm sure I would. No trouble.

But what is this body, the one I see in the mirror? Am I hidden within this body, am I this body too?

And who is the half person growing out of the chest of another person? Since two conjoined twins—sharing one body, endowed with two heads—are two people, but a headless half twin is barely a parasite, does that mean a human being is a head? Or rather inside the head, hidden inside the head, just as I am hidden inside this little apartment where I've lived since the late 1940s and which was once ours, but now is mine, and since it's been mine I've barely left, I just hide like a hermit crab inside someone else's shell and am I hiding the same way inside the shell of my skull?

There is no God since a person can have two heads or, even worse, two faces, there is no God because there is no man. Is man not his own face? Since a baby can be born without a brain, with a bloody, open hollow of a skull ending above its eyes, who is born then? A human being? Meat?

There is no God. There are fetuses with anencephaly. People with anencephaly?

I'm not interested in deformities, in fingers growing like a lobster claw or elephantiasis, though after all they're often just as monstrous. Slim people with calves twice as thick as their torsos, unable to move. Or that same elephantiasis in the scrotum, swelling it to the size of a soccer ball. I'm not interested in horrible skin diseases, keloid horns growing out of the head, tumors that take up a person's whole face, all terrifying, but none of it proof there is no God. I examine these pictures with curiosity, but I don't clip them out of the medical journals,

I don't paste them into my scrapbook, my scrapbook devoted to the nonexistence of God.

No, the impossibility of defining the boundary between one human and another, that is the best proof there is no God, and I, Tat-Aluf Moshe Inbar, tell that to every rabbi, every imam, or priest who will listen: there is no God because there is no man. Something exists, some beings exist, but if it's impossible to define where one human ends and another begins, then a human as an individual—meaning something separate from the rest of the world and people—then humanity as we have come to understand it does not exist.

That's what my scrapbook is about. My scrapbook started with Pantaleon Karpiński's second face and its smile. I don't have his picture but I remember both faces, even today. And I ask myself, how many people were there in Pantaleon Karpiński's Janus head? Why did the second face smile when the first one did? Are there two people in there?

In my album I have a photo of babies with heads grown together at the crown—were there two people in that one baby? Or maybe none— maybe babies, being less intelligent than cats, aren't people at all, maybe they're born nonpeople and only later become people, I don't know when exactly, because I don't know anything about childhood development, I don't know when they start to talk or walk and which happens first, I don't know.

And the me of fifty years ago, the me in the old Chevrolet, am I the same person? Supposedly all the molecules in my body have been replaced. Maybe except for the enamel on my teeth and bones, now that I think about it, but after all, my bones and teeth aren't me. But is that all that's left of the me who went from Warsaw to Jaffa, everything has been replaced, only the enamel on my teeth remains?

That and my memory. Or rather a painstaking reconstruction of it. What do I remember at all?

And am I, retired Tat-Aluf Moshe Inbar, and that little skinny Jewish boy from Nalewki, Moyshe Bernsztajn, the same person? What links us? My memory of him?

He never thought he would be the man I've become. Only I know that. Moyshe Bernsztajn in 1937 knows nothing of it.

Moyshe Bernsztajn in 1937 sat in a taxi parked at the intersection of Koszykowa and Pius XI Streets, sat and had no idea why they were waiting. He found out a moment later, when Pantaleon, panting and heaving, climbed into the taxi.

"All right, let's go. Nalewki," said Szapiro laconically.

"You got it, boss," murmured the driver in his leather driving coat, which he wore because he was driving a taxi with an open cab, separated completely from the passengers. By then there were plenty of modern taxis with the driver sitting inside with the passengers as in a normal car, but this one was older, it must have been about ten years old.

Pantaleon sat across from Moyshe Bernsztajn, I mean across from me, Moshe Inbar, but more like across from Moyshe Bernsztajn. And across from Szapiro. His hands gripped his knees.

"Well you can't help it," said Szapiro sympathetically.

These days his sympathy surprises me. After all, Szapiro knew Pantaleon was a monster, a tormented one, but a monster nonetheless. I wasn't surprised at that moment, at that moment I, a newly born atheist, also felt within myself fear and disgust combined with sympathy.

The taxi set off.

"I sometimes hear the voices of that devilry in my head. It speaks to me. In many voices. Then I pray to Jesus, but it doesn't help," murmured Pantaleon, staring at the floor of the car.

Szapiro nodded.

"That's when you drink."

"I hate vodka. Vodka is death. But that's when I drink. Because it says awful things to me. Diabolic things. And I do them, those things, I do what my devil brother tells me. And I'm hungry."

"How about a frankfurter on a roll?" suggested Szapiro and, without waiting for Pantaleon's response, gave the driver the appropriate instructions in a tone that I later learned from him and which proved useful my whole life, though not now that I'm retired.

We stopped on the corner of Marszałkowska Street and Jerozolimskie Avenue, in front of Fuchs's flower store, where a cart stood all night with a pot of boiling water with frankfurters floating in it. I'd never seen a cart like this up close because I'd never ventured into this area, though a similar one stood on Krakowskie Przedmieście, at the intersection with Trębacka and Kozia Streets. But mainly I'd never eaten frankfurters before.

"Want one?" asked Szapiro.

My first instinct was to stupidly ask if they were kosher, but just as I found myself hoping they weren't treyf, it occurred to me—so what if they were? I ate treyf.

I wasn't hungry, I'd just eaten. But I'd never eaten frankfurters from a street cart in a taxi at night and this would be my first time doing so.

"Yes please," I whispered.

Szapiro got out, bought three frankfurters and three rolls on three paper trays, each topped with a generous glob of mustard, then handed them to us and we ate in silence. The taxi driver didn't dare protest us eating in his car.

Then we stopped on the corner of Miła and Lubecki Streets, where Pantaleon lived.

From the corner of Miła and Lubecki, Pantaleon Karpiński and his devil brother went into his apartment, where his devil brother told Pantaleon to take off his military belt—made of thick, old leather—wake up his wife, and drag her by the hair into the kitchen, where it told him to tear off her nightshirt, bend her over the kitchen table with her bottom sticking out, and lash her with the belt, lash her until she bled, with a zeal surpassing that of a certain Traitor when he used to lash Jakub Szapiro with a bullwhip in his years of imprisonment in Łomża.

The whipping wasn't remotely erotic. Pantaleon was not aroused, neither of the two Pantaleons was aroused.

It was pure violence, unadulterated by lust. Pantaleon lashed his wife because he wanted her to suffer and howl like the voices of his demon brother howling in his head, and Pantaleon Karpiński's wife did howl, until he pulled her nightcap off her head and jammed it in her mouth, afraid her howling would wake the neighbors, who'd report him to the watchman, and then Pantaleon would have to tangle with the watchman too, and break his arm or nose. Or kill him.

So he lashed her with the hard, heavy belt and panted, and lashed, and panted, while her fat bottom, back, and thighs flowed with blood and her skin broke open, and when she finally lost consciousness he simply picked her up effortlessly, in a nearly tender gesture, carried her to the bedroom, threw her onto the bed, then went back to the kitchen, took out the bottle of vodka they kept for guests, and drank until the voices went quiet.

It wasn't the first time they'd tormented him, but this was the first time he'd reached for the vodka in two years. All told, he'd been avoiding it since 1919, the year he escaped from the circus, where they'd plied him heavily with vodka. He only drank when his devil brother's voice grew so loud he couldn't stand it.

There were two people on Earth he was afraid of: Buddy and the Doctor, the Doctor and Buddy, no one other than them could force him to show his devil brother's face, but they could and Pantaleon went along with it because he thought everyone had to have a tormentor.

He even believed Buddy and the Doctor had their own tormentors, though they were hard to see.

The voices finally went silent, stifled by alcohol, and then Pantaleon rested his head, full of Pantaleon Karpiński and his devil brother, on his lumpy forearms and sank into alcoholic darkness. Pantaleon and his brother disappeared, at least until morning, only until morning, but it was always a relief.

Buddy Kaplica went home too, as he always did. He didn't like spending the night away from home. His Chrysler and driver were waiting outside Ryfka's. He got in, a little sloshed, pleased with life and himself, and rode home, falling asleep on the way as usual.

He lived far away, practically out of town, right on the city limits, in an unremarkable detached house on the corner of Domaniewska and Puławska Streets. The large house was surrounded by a garden, in the garden grew apple trees, and inside the house were three girls, Zuzanna, Janina, and Krystyna, to whom Buddy was the sweetest father, while his wife, Maria, was the best mother.

They had no servants; Kaplica didn't want strangers in the house.

"I got four girls at home, and what, I'm gonna pay extra for some skivvy I don't know?" he would ask.

Maria Kaplica was a simple working-class woman and couldn't imagine someone else serving her either. Only their eldest daughter, Krystyna, a graduate of the Nazarene Sisters' high school on Czerniakowska Street, occasionally grumbled that all her school friends had servants and cooks at home, and that they were the only ones who had to do everything themselves, and was Papa too poor to hire somebody?

Buddy didn't give her whining a second thought. He did have ambition and greed growing inside him, but the house—suitable for a higher rank of clerk or an officer, a major for instance—was not an ostentatious expression of that greed, not like his extremely ostentatious Chrysler, at any rate.

Maria Kaplica was heavyset and inconspicuous, she treated her husband like a king, sage, and high priest wrapped in one. He sometimes beat her, like all husbands did, but not very hard and, in his opinion, never without reason. She meekly agreed with that in principle, except when he beat her because he was drunk. Anyway, she rarely gave him cause to, she was a wonderful housekeeper and cook. So she didn't get a beating more than once a month.

When he was drunk it was a different story. Once he'd inebriatedly fired his pistol at her, but missed. That time the girls hadn't even dared come downstairs. They saw their father that drunk once a year, around May Day. Apart from May 1, he drank every day, but never to the point of losing control of himself. But on May Day he played a leading role in the workers' demonstration in the morning and then painted the town, well, red. It was well known that whoever came out partying on May Day would be in his good books. Radziwiłek and Szapiro always went along, but that wasn't a day to stop by the snack bar on Leszno or Ryfka's—Sobenski's and Ryfka Kij's were everyday places, while May Day demanded festive locales.

So they normally had lunch either at the Hotel Bristol or Simon & Stecki's. They ate the most expensive lobster, crayfish, and oysters, telling the waiters to demonstrate how to eat them elegantly and joking that here was the working class, enjoying the most exquisite luxuries through the mouths of its representatives. Then they'd implement this principle more broadly. After lunch they did the rounds of the city. They started with the cafés: the Zakopianka, the Szwajcarska, Lardelli's Bagatelle, the Ziemiańska, then it was time for the Adria, the Oaza, and the Cristal, where they no longer ate but only drank vodka, drank until they just about passed out, then snorted some cocaine and drank some more. They went to the Europejski Hotel for breakfast, where some suites and the best, most festive girls already awaited them. They unwound a little in the girls' company then hit the town yet again. Every year was the same, the faces and locations changed but the program never did.

He would roll home the evening of Constitution Day on May 3, sometimes alone, sometimes with hookers. He was always in nothing but his pants and an open shirt, because he'd have lost his coat and jacket somewhere along the way. His hands would be shaking and he'd stink of stale vodka, vomit, and cigarette smoke.

On the Constitution Day of 1935 he shot at his wife because she'd expressed her displeasure at the two girls of Jewish extraction he'd brought home with him, pointing out they both looked younger than his eldest daughter, Krystyna, then seventeen.

"You goddamned anti-Semite!" he roared, because all evening the topic of conversation between him and his comrades had been the rising anti-Semitism on the streets of Poland.

He missed, the bullet embedded itself in the wall, but Maria Kaplica got the message and fled upstairs, locking herself in the bedroom and preemptively bolting the girls' rooms shut—younger Zuzanna and Janina slept together in one room, Krystyna had her own.

At any rate, that was one of the happiest Constitution Days in the history of the Kaplicas' marriage—counting, of course, since 1919, because it wasn't celebrated before then—since it passed without any beatings. Kaplica fell asleep fifteen minutes later in a chair at the table, the hookers slipped off immediately, not daring to steal anything, and Kaplica slept for eighteen hours. The next day he ordered flowers for his wife and all was forgiven.

Another year he managed to break her forearm beating her with an iron poker, which hurt Maria Kaplica less than the words he was screaming as he did so, calling his faithful and devoted wife a fat pig who'd wasted the years of his youth and was robbing him of his hard-earned pennies.

Kaplica's daughters heard all this, but they didn't dare go downstairs this time either. Their mother had warned them it was today, today was the day Papa would come home drunk.

The next day they sat down to supper together as usual, Maria Kaplica had her arm in a cast, so her only role in preparing the food was managing her three daughters.

Buddy grilled his daughters about the goings-on at the Nazarene Sisters', if those damned nuns weren't putting too much churchy non-sense into their heads, and Maria Kaplica, fearful as ever of her husband's blasphemy, piously crossed herself, which only egged him on.

That July evening in 1937, after visiting Ryfka's, Buddy returned home to Mokotów in his Chrysler and ate the supper his wife had made. Maria Kaplica told him how her day had gone, which didn't interest him at all so he didn't listen. He browsed the evening edition of the *Courier*, asked about his daughters, didn't listen to the answer, then headed up to the bedroom to play solitaire.

He finished the game. Kaplica reflected on his life, as well as the situation of the working class and the socialist movement, then moved on to more serious considerations.

"I've nursed a viper at my bosom, that goddamn Jew," he muttered, thinking of Radziwiłek.

He got dressed for bed and looked in the mirror. He brushed his mustache, slapped his round belly, lifted it up to view his large endowment, whose proportions were a source of tremendous pride, scratched himself, and went to sleep.

Meanwhile I still didn't know where I'd sleep that night. I didn't want to go back home to my mother and brother. I was ashamed at that emotion, but it was how I truly felt. Anything not to go back to them. And I didn't.

"You can sleep at my place," said Szapiro, hearing my thoughts.

I often had that impression. That he could hear my thoughts.

I also thought about the theater, which I was supposed to go to the next day with Magda, and I already knew I wouldn't. Those thoughts he didn't hear.

We stopped on Nalewki Street, at number 40. Fourteen doors down, on the corner of Franciszkańska, was my family home. Five minutes and I'd be with my mother and brother.

But I never returned to them. I never saw them again.

I remember their faces, I remember the faces of my mother and my brother very well, but I only remember them from one moment, that awful moment when Szapiro took my father away. I don't remember, maybe I don't want to remember, them from other, better times.

I remember Emanuel's face and the fear in it, and my mother's stupefaction, and truth be told not much more.

Szapiro paid the driver, we got out, the Christian watchman opened the door for us, even here in the Jewish district the watchmen were usually Christian. Szapiro tossed him a couple of złotys and we went upstairs. Jakub opened the door for me, letting me go first, as a host would a guest.

The apartment, made up of three others joined together, took up the whole floor and was unlike anything in our district. Our place, the Bernsztajns', was actually large, because we had three rooms, never mind that we sublet one of them. We had no running water, there was a single outhouse in the courtyard, water for cleaning and cooking got brought in a bucket from the courtyard well, which was placed suspiciously close to the outhouse. We burned coal in freestanding potbellied stoves. Everyone on Nalewki lived like that.

It was different at the Szapiros'. Jakub had bought out the entire building, though he'd done it in Emilia's name, and the Szapiros lived there themselves, which was practically unheard-of in Warsaw apartment houses. The storefronts on the first floor and the tenants on the second paid cheap rent, well below market rate, because Jakub had money anyway and needed a reputation as a defender of the poor. So using his own money, he installed running water and heat in the apartments, and reserved a whole floor for himself and his family, where he joined up the already-existing apartments.

Of course, he could have simply moved out and settled in one of the beautiful, modern housing developments in other districts: Żoliborz, the good part of the City Center, Mokotów, or Saska Kępa, or in a villa outside the city like Buddy, but he didn't want to. The Northern District, with the stink of its street gutters, the smell of cholent on Friday, and its undoubted filth was the only homeland he had, and he was incapable of giving this homeland up. And since he was incapable, he didn't want to either. He didn't want to assimilate. On Warsaw's Nalewki Street he was at home, in Little Jerusalem. Settling in Mokotów district would mean settling in Poland, but Jakub didn't want to live in Poland, because he didn't like Poland, though he liked assimilators even less, he didn't like those upper-class Jews for whom Nalewki, Miła, or Smocza Streets stank worse than the worst-stinking Polish or Ruthenian villages, because to them the poverty and stench of the Polish peasant weren't poverty or stench, while the poverty and stench of Nalewki, its squalid shops, porters with bundles on their backs, this whole garlic-and-spice-scented antechamber of Asia, were their poverty and their stench, which they wanted to wash from themselves as quickly and thoroughly as possible.

Jakub didn't want to wash anything from himself. There was something ostentatious and insolent in the way he paraded along Nalewki Street in the most expensive suits from Zaremba's, how he hopped over puddles in shoes that shone brighter than a Polish colonel's boots, how he would drive around the Northern District in his Buick. People, our people, the Jewish poor, didn't look on him with the disdain they had for the haughty Poles, they didn't look at him with the hatred and fear they reserved for them, they felt no envy. Jakub Szapiro wore those suits and drove that Buick on their behalf, as it were, because Jakub Szapiro had remained one of them. He lived on Nalewki, in his own apartment building, but on Nalewki. He didn't talk in Polish to those who didn't like hearing Polish, and though he had no regard for God or tradition, he didn't flaunt his unbelief and disdain for custom in front of those who might find that hurtful.

On the street, he would reverently bow to the old men who were owed respect, and he bowed with the same respect to the Jewish journalists and writers spending long hours in the headquarters of the Association of Jewish Writers and Journalists at 13 Tłomackie Street, because he considered them the guardians of Jewish identity and distinctiveness and surrounded them in an invisible protection and care, invisible because they would doubtless have no wish for protection from a bandit. He even respected those who were actively hostile to him, like Singer. Even though he'd personally beaten him up, he wouldn't have wished any Pole to do him harm. And if one did—he would take revenge.

Szapiro's wife was waiting in the kitchen. They were not married, yet everyone considered Emilia his wife, and although her documents still featured her maiden name, Kahan, no one called her anything other than "Mrs. Szapiro." Daniel and Dawid were playing checkers on the rug in the modestly and elegantly furnished living room. They peered at me, fixed their eyes on me, they looked, curious, with a little distance, a little hope, they looked at someone between their world and the world of the grown-ups.

"This is young Bernsztajn," said Szapiro simply. "He's going to be with us now."

"Have you two eaten?" said Emilia Szapiro, née Kahan, concerned but not questioning the presence of this new member of her household.

"At Ryfka's and then franks from the cart. Where'll you make up the boy's bed?"

"In the guest room. You know they still haven't found that American lady pilot? I'm so frightened for her. I was reading about it in the paper today."

Jakub thought for a moment. His first instinct was to wonder what he cared about some American lady pilot. His second was that this news made him sad. He hoped they'd find her.

He showed me my room. Emilia brought in bedsheets.

I lay down, for the first time in my life so very not at home. Jakub put his sons to bed as usual, then the Szapiros closed themselves up in their bedroom, but I couldn't get to sleep. I got up and sat by the window.

Out the window, over Nalewki Street, floated a gray sperm whale. He was glowering at me with a burning eye, he knocked the chimneys with his huge head.

Litani, I am Litani. Your ashen hair, Shulamith—he sang, baring his toothy maw, and then curled up, dove between the apartment houses, and vanished from my sight.

ג

GIMEL

In Warsaw on Bankowy Square, in Ujazdowski Hospital, in Żoliborz Oficerski and Żoliborz Dziennikarski, in Mokotów, in Saska Kępa, at the racetracks, in the Belweder Palace, in the Ministry of War, on Hoża Street, and on Marszałkowska Street, Yom Kippur fell on Wednesday, September 15, in the Year of Our Lord 1937, and no one especially noticed. It passed unremarked. In the *Courier* of September 16, not a word was written about Yom Kippur.

In Jerusalem, the day of Yom Kippur passed peacefully. At the Wailing Wall, crowds gathered, offering up prayers. The police arrested a certain Ari Kaczer, a member of Betar, for blowing a shofar against regulations. A bomb was found in a synagogue in the Old City, which did not perform its designated purpose since it did not explode.

In Warsaw on Gęsia Street, on Smocza Street, on Nalewki Street, on Nowolipki Street, on Karmelicka Street, on Miła Street, on Leszno Street, and on all the other Jewish streets of the Northern District, and in the districts of Praga, Pelcowizna, and Powiśle, Yom Kippur fell on the tenth of Tishrei, 5698, years from the creation of the world. In *Our Review*, a whole column was dedicated to the Yom Kippur celebrations.

On Tuesday evening, the Jewish streets of Warsaw emptied of people completely; buses and streetcars ran empty, all the observant Jews had gone to synagogue for Kol Nidre, and I, Moyshe Bernsztajn, for the first time in my adult, conscious life, did not go to synagogue for Kol Nidre.

Ever since my Bar Mitzvah I had always gone with my father, like every Jewish boy. First my father would perform *kappores*: to atone for sins, he would swing a white rooster over his head and then kill the rooster, and my mother would pour boiling water over it, pluck the feathers, and gut it. I liked seeing the rooster's entrails. Next my mother would get a cleaver and divide the rooster into pieces to give to the poor. Its head already gone, my mother would first cut off its feet and neck for soup, then chop off its legs, chop off its wings, and then use the cleaver to divide the legless, wingless body in half, each with one dry rooster breast.

Then my father and I would go to synagogue.

Men would stand with Torah scrolls to the left and right of the cantor, who would sing in Aramaic about the vows we would make for the whole year between this Yom Kippur and the next. *Kol nidray, veesuray, ushviay, vakharumay, vikunoumay, vekinisay, vikhiniay.*

Consider all of our future prayers and promises null and void.

My father would explain to me this did not in the least mean a religious Jew could break his word. He would explain it was meant to indicate atonement for the promises we did not manage to keep despite the goodwill in which we made them.

Or maybe it was Szapiro who used to tell me about his father, maybe it was Szapiro's father who explained the meaning of Kol Nidre, not mine?

My father was chopped up like a rooster's body for kappores.

Witold Sokoliński reported in the *Courier* every time another piece of Naum Bernsztajn's body was found. Last was the head, wrapped in my father's frock coat along with his documents, and all was clear.

I didn't want to hear about this. For two months I had been living a new life. I had grabbed my father's scrawny body by the ankles, swung it three times around my head, and offered it as sacrifice.

Amid the apartment houses, the solid bulk of a sperm whale slowly slicing through the air, barnacles growing out of his thick skin, slowly opening his toothy maw.

Litani. Litani. Litani.

I never arranged my father's funeral. I didn't say Kaddish. I don't know if anyone did. I think so, but I don't know. He was there, he vanished, he was gone.

"Daa' mame in brido' zene' avek ka Lomzhe, tsi de shvesto' iyo'," said Emilia Szapiro at one of my first breakfasts in their apartment, with Emilia, Jakub, and the boys. "Yankyev 'ot zay gyegyebm s'gyelt."[12]

Her Yiddish bore an almost imperceptible, yet present, trace of speaking Polish alongside our own language ever since childhood.

Jakub threw her a glance over his plate.

I said nothing. I ate. It tasted good. Jakub gave them some money and they left. They were all right, somewhere far away. Or was it the boys they told that to?

Later we went to train at the Stars' gym on Leszno Street. Wearing ill-fitting exercise gear Szapiro had leant me, I wrapped up my hands.

Szapiro himself didn't practice anymore. He no longer thought of himself as a boxer. He was a coach now. He'd gotten noticeably heavier in the two months between his last fight and Yom Kippur, at least five or ten pounds, and he'd had to get his vests and jackets let out.

Now he was teaching the junior team how to wrap their hands.

The wrist's the main thing. I've seen so many boxers who weren't boxers anymore because they didn't take care of their wrists and now they can't hit anyone with those hands hanging off the ends of their

---

12 Your mother and brother have gone to Łomża, to her sister's. (. . .) Jakub gave them the money.

forearms like withered tulip heads. So I bandaged my hands carefully, sensing the sperm whale's eyes on me.

He was floating over Leszno Street and soaking up the aroma of sweat wafting off the boys, youths, and men jumping rope, hitting leather punching bags, shadowboxing, doing knee bends and push-ups. He was waiting. Singing a quiet hunting song.

Meanwhile Szapiro had started mitt drills with a young boy, more or less my age, but quite a bit taller and better developed physically. He trained with the ferocity of a rottweiler. I watched from one side, waiting for my turn.

"Left, rotate, go, go, hook, go!" cried Jakub.

The boy's gloves struck the mitts on Jakub's hands: *whap-whap-whap*, like applause, rapid, over and over. Jakub was shouting, working his feet like a true boxer, giving the boy the mitts straight on, to the side, down for an uppercut, against his own belly to call for a hit on the torso, and the young boxer kept hitting them with a *bang*, in unflinching, quick, loose punches.

"Rotate!" Szapiro called out and made a sweeping hook with the mitt.

The boy ducked the mitt aimed at his head, dropped low on his legs, but still controlling his hook, from the other side, hitting the mitt his coach already had prepared on his other hand with a pleasant-sounding *thwack*.

"Legs, more, more, more!"

He moved, his legs constantly in motion, as though the floor were red-hot steel.

"More, dammit, what is that, cream puff, what the hell is that, you trying to wipe your ass, more, more, left, left, what's this raggedy-ass stuff, more, left, left, left, make that left long, long arm, not so damn stubby! Extend! Rotate! More, dammit, one, feint, left, right, better, more, you're moving, dammit, left, right, more, why the hell you standing there, get outta your head, dammit, more, feint, right, more, uppercut, left hook, down, down dammit, better, long arm, longer, not stubby, uppercut, left, right, left hook, good, leg under me, come in, good, keep your distance. What the hell is that, what is that, you a gimp? Left, right, feint, come up to me, right up, leg, good, repeat, left, right, feint, right, hook, what is this, you hit like my grandma. Repeat, harder, left, right, feint, right, hook, guard up, cream puff, the hell is that? I'll get you next time, repeat, left, right, feint, right, hook, God fucking dammit, arm, guard up, what the hell is this, you call this boxing? You call this boxing? This shit? Get out of this club, gimp, left, leeeeeft, harder, guard, arm higher or I'll get you, arm, god fucking *dammit!*"

Jakub got him. He whacked the boy on the temple with his mitt, the boy spun and landed on his ass on the mat, looking around with unseeing eyes.

I had left my mother and brother. They were gone. They'd disappeared. They'd left for Łomża. Everybody was gone. There was nobody left. I'd left them all. Only I was left. Litani was soaking up the smell of sweat, feeling out my shape with his quiet song.

"All right now, all right, get up, great, that's progress!" shouted Szapiro, suddenly pleased with his student, as though he hadn't been hauling him over the coals just a moment before.

I had left my mother and my brother. Because I wanted to box. Because I wanted to watch Szapiro walk into the ring.

I was wrapping my hands. Wrist, an X across the palm, knuckles, around the thumb, wrist again. Then I stood by the wall, I observed.

"You've got long fingers, like me," Szapiro had once remarked, tightening up the bandage on my left hand. "They told me at the start these were a pianist's fingers, not a boxer's. Well they had another thing coming."

My father was chopped up and floating in a watery grave, and I was learning how to walk, hold my hands, guard my jaw behind my right fist and my left shoulder.

I was like a baby standing on his own feet for the first time, propping himself up on the wall.

In the Stars' gym I was reborn. I tucked my elbow in while Szapiro pummeled me with hooks and straights.

To this day I make steps I learned back then, to this day I walk the paths I discovered then, to this day I hear the words he spoke to me then.

I was seventeen. I had left my mother and brother and my father's body, chopped up for kappores.

◆　◆　◆

The days were all very similar, but at the same time so different from all the previous days of my previous life—each one was exciting as sin, and at night I'd fall asleep impatient for the next day.

I kept waking up at night screaming, then Emilia Szapiro would come to my room and stroke my head. I knew somewhere out there, amid the tenements, courtyards, over the Vistula River and over the bridges, hid Litani, the gray sperm whale with the burning eyes.

"Sleep now, kiddo, go to sleep," she would murmur to me in Polish. She would lay down beside me and enclose me in a motherly embrace, though she wasn't my mother, but she was warm, she smelled like a woman or Szapiro's cologne.

Sometimes I'd wake up and hear her and Jakub having sex, hear their moans, then in the morning I'd look at her in the kitchen and think of those moans.

Every morning a mechanic would bring the Buick from Dynasy garage. By then I'd be working on the breakfast Emilia had made me, which always included bread and butter, milk, and sometimes cheese or cold cuts. It was all treyf and tasted wonderful, cooked and served with a love I'd never experienced before.

She was warm, caring, never asked me for anything, expected nothing from me, asked nothing, demanded nothing. She often touched me. Back then I thought she was better than my real mother. These days I don't know. I don't remember. I don't remember my real mother. I remember Emilia Szapiro better.

No, that isn't true. I remember perfectly what my real mother was like. My darling Yiddishe mamele was no darling Yiddishe mamele. I remember her numbness as Szapiro took my father away to chop him into pieces.

Now I know, or rather I've realized: my Jewish mother must have loved me. But I never felt loved. Maybe I didn't have time to.

How funny, I think today, an old general writing on his typewriter about how his mother didn't love him. All the blood I have on my hands and I'm thinking about how my mother didn't love me, Tat-Aluf Moshe Inbar is writing on his typewriter about how his mother didn't love him.

She radiated a coldness that never went away, even when she hugged us. When she kissed us, her mouth remained cold, though her lips were warm with the usual warmth of a human body. Or maybe she didn't kiss us at all.

Emilia Szapiro was warm and soft like Shabbos challah dough, which she sometimes made herself, kneading it, and I would watch her, hypnotized, her slender fingers sinking into the dough, the dough between her fingers. I wanted to be that dough. I wanted her to press her hands into me.

I saw how she loved her sons, how she loved them with her body, her arms, her head. How she kissed them, how she sang them to sleep, how she fed them, how she cared for them.

I saw how Jakub loved his sons. He was a completely different father from mine, from all the fathers I'd known, and I think he was completely different from his own father.

Jakub's father hadn't hesitated to use his fists or a switch. Jakub had never hit a child.

Jakub shot at people, slit the throats of innocent old men, but he'd never hit a child. I don't know why. A child's suffering is worth just as much as an adult's or an old man's—that is, nothing. But that's just how Jakub was.

Jakub treated his sons seriously. He treated me seriously. Jakub talked to Daniel and Dawid like they were small people. Small, but people.

I can barely remember them. They've faded away in my memory. They were twins, fraternal ones, but even so very similar to one another, though lacking the inhuman similarity of identical twins. I guess Daniel was the more reflective, melancholy one, he preferred books and wood blocks, while Dawid was more mischievous.

I never went back home again. I passed my family's building hundreds of times and never even went into the courtyard. I never saw my mother or my brother again. I didn't say Kaddish for my father. I don't know where they buried his chopped-up body, to this day I don't know what happened to that body.

I'd eat breakfast and watch Emilia bustling around the kitchen. Back then I didn't know I'd never see my mother or my brother again, yet I knew I didn't want to go back to them. Szapiro wouldn't eat, because right after breakfast we'd be on our way to the snack bar on Leszno Street, where he'd eat breakfast at the table with Kaplica, Radziwiłek, and the newspapers.

They'd let me sit with them. Szapiro would order me a coffee. I could never hear their conversation because they always spoke in hushed tones, but I knew what they were talking about.

So I'd drink my coffee, then we'd walk a little ways to the Stars' gym, which was also on Leszno Street. Szapiro, when he was still boxing, had fought for Maccabi, but the Stars' gym was closer and the Star was where he preferred coaching the juniors. And because he was Jakub Szapiro, he could coach wherever he felt like and be well received everywhere.

The first day, Szapiro gave me navy-blue athletic shorts, a white tank top, soft white socks, and ankle-high black boxing shoes with white laces.

I put all this on. Szapiro wore an identical outfit. He showed me how to wrap my hands, so I wrapped them and started learning how to walk.

I'd left my mother. I'd left my brother. I'd left my father's body who knows where. As though I'd flung them all into the abyss.

Let them stay in the abyss. Forever.

After one of my first training sessions we drove to Kercelak market, as we did every Tuesday and Friday, which were the traditional market days. I'd rather remember this, I'd rather remember us doing the rounds of the marketplace than remember my father, brother, and mother. This was my first time going along with him.

At Kercelak, Jakub parked his Buick on the Okopowa Street side as usual and we walked the rest of the way, toward Wolska and Chłodna Streets, me following him like a shadow, through the tarp-covered structures where everyone was selling everything from booths, stands, stalls, and where a choir of greetings accompanied us, along with the bells of the T and Z streetcars.

"Good afternoon, Mr. Szapiro, sir. Respect, Mr. Szapiro. Mr. Szapiro, what a pleasure. Respec', Mr. Szapiro. A gitn tueg reb Szapiro, a gitn."[13]

He said hello to everyone: the woman selling potatoes and beets; the aspiring storekeeper; the stall owner with suits for twenty złotys; the Jewish junk dealer; and the beggar whose only items for sale were three pairs of women's stockings, almost new, which he hung over his forearm and shook as if he thought that might attract someone willing to give him a złoty; Szapiro said hello to the pigeon fancier standing by cages full of cooing birds; the mandolin and guitar seller whose stall

---

13　Hello, Mr. Szapiro.

reverberated with endless strumming; as well as a market tailor of the Jewish persuasion who was also a nonpracticing atheist, installed on a wooden platform resembling a stage, and using a clattering Singer sewing machine to perform express alterations on the spot.

At that moment the tailor wasn't sewing, he was waiting for customers. He stroked the shabby black paint of the machine, his only source of income, as though petting the back of a cow whose milk fed an entire family. His name was Józef Sztajgiec and all he wanted from life was to sew at Kercelak market.

We kept moving.

The crowd parted before us as people greeted Szapiro: women with checkered shawls covering their upper arms stepped aside; bearded Jewish men with poor and wealthy frock coats, though more often poor, made way; paupers in their shirtsleeves; the somewhat wealthier in jackets, sweaters, and light coats. We might occasionally see a dress or an elegant trench coat there, but rarely, very rarely; Kercelak was where proletarian Wola district outfitted itself, not exactly trench-coat territory.

On the men's heads were bowler hats, fedoras, newsboy caps, and yarmulkes, the women wore hats, but more often country headscarves.

Not everyone knew Jakub Szapiro. All the sellers did, but only some of the customers. And yet as he walked through the crowd like that, he didn't need to push through. The crowd parted on its own. There was something about Jakub that told them they needed to get out of the way, something like what had once made the waters part for Moses.

Szapiro had only one errand to run, he was in a hurry, so he didn't return the greetings.

In that regard he was able to be less strict with himself than Buddy.

Buddy was like a father. He couldn't ignore greetings, he had to good-naturedly return them, because only this would guarantee that if Buddy had to punish someone, no one would stand in their defense. If Buddy ignored a person's greeting, that meant trouble for whomever he'd ignored. Disfavor. And it was better not to earn Buddy's disfavor, everyone knew that.

Szapiro's errand was at the restaurant in Kercelak. It was a decrepit spot, located in a wooden shack with cast-iron pipes jutting out higgledy-piggledy from ovens for whipping up the simplest food: tripe, sauerkraut stew, the cheapest boiled kiełbasa, Warsaw schnitzel, and meatballs.

Inside was packed to bursting with tables. The practice here was of vacating your table without question the moment you were done—you came here to eat, not to hang out—but of course that didn't apply to Szapiro.

When we went in, the owner, a big fat fellow called Choromańczyk, whistled and with a glance of his eyes showed the door to two little *gavroches* just sopping up the tripe juice on their plates with some bread. They left immediately, passing Szapiro, hats in hand.

"Morning, Mr. Szapiro," they whispered in chorus.

Jakub hung up his hat, sat at a table, snapped his fingers for a waiter, ordered Warsaw-style tripe and a shot of vodka.

He received a double portion of tripe and a whole bottle of vodka. He withdrew the slim notebook and his eternal fountain pen from his pocket.

He didn't have to announce his presence. Everyone knew. And whoever was meant to come knew it perfectly well. And that Jakub Szapiro shouldn't be made to wait.

So Tolek the pigeon fancier came, owner of 120 cages of pigeons on the Leszno side—ordinary birds, racing birds, and fake racing birds. He left twenty złotys. A woman came who sold tin buckets in the part of the market with metal goods, between Okopowa and Chłodna Streets, she left twenty-three złotys. Szapiro noted it down.

Next came the proprietor of a solid, closed, and heated stall containing a numismatics store that sold everything: from czarist gold coins to Japanese currency, old czarist paper rubles to post-war Polish marks from the days of hyperinflation. He bowed, greeted Jakub in Yiddish, lay down fifty złotys, the fifty złotys went into Jakub's jacket pocket, and the appropriate entry went into his notebook.

The rakish mandolin seller came and he left twenty. Noted.

Borowski the cobbler came as well. Jakub glanced at him as he walked into the restaurant and could see right away there was trouble.

"Mr. Szapiro, wonderful Mr. Szapiro," began Borowski meekly.

Szapiro flipped back two pages. "You didn't pay me last week either," he said.

"Mr. Szapiro, it's 'cause my wife wants to marry my daughter off and we gotta throw a wedding party," said Borowski, on the verge of tears.

"So who you think is gonna hurt you more, your little wifey or Mr. Karpiński?"

"You don't know my wife, Mr. Szapiro." Borowski was not joking.

Szapiro guffawed in spite of himself. He pushed away the plate of tripe, poured himself some more vodka, and took a drink. He stood up and hit Borowski with a short, fast uppercut in his solar plexus, like a snakebite. Borowski crumpled to the ground. Szapiro placed his foot on his neck.

"Tomorrow. You come to Sobenski's snack bar with the forty złotys you owe plus twenty penalty, sixty altogether. Got it?"

Borowski only wailed.

"And don't let me down, Mr. Borowski. Because they'll pick you out of the clay ponds piece by piece and the only thing holding you together in the coffin will be your suit."

Jakub glanced at his watch. It wasn't even noon and already he'd beaten somebody up.

Borowski scampered out of the restaurant.

After him a few more came, then finally Choromańczyk paid. Jakub finished his tripe and asked him to pack some takeout provisions, which the fat proprietor did without hesitation, even throwing in a bottle of decent wine, far beyond what the restaurant usually offered.

This was how Mojżesz Bernsztajn's new life looked.

Practice at the Stars' gym. Kercelak. Sometimes a visit to Ryfka's.

Emilia at home. Playing with Jakub and Emilia's kids, Daniel and Dawid.

By Yom Kippur, more than two months since I'd moved into the Szapiros', I already had some idea how to walk like a boxer and I had my own gloves.

It was also known in the city, or at least in our part of it, that I was a member of the Szapiro household and I quickly perceived that when I walked down the street I was no longer Mojżesz Bernsztajn, son of Naum. I was Mojżesz, the kid who went around with Szapiro. A few religious Jews I knew from my previous life stopped responding to my polite greetings, of course. But how many religious Jews had there been before who noticed my existence? Now the shopkeepers would say first: "A gitn tueg, dem bukho', a gitn! Me 'ot akh du lang nish' gyezeyen, nemts zakh epes, nemts!"[14] and they would offer a sweet bun or an apple. The bullies I used to get in fights with or had to run away from would step out of my way.

I was Szapiro's boy. For the first time in my life I was somebody.

Or maybe there was no me at all.

❖ ❖ ❖

On the eve of Yom Kippur, instead of going to Kol Nidre, Magda and I went to see a play, Ruszkowski's *Widow Jadzia*, adapted by Poland's most famous Jewish author, Julian Tuwim. It was on at the Polski Theater. We'd planned to go to a play the day after my father died, but

---

14   Hello, young sir! We haven't seen you in a while, please, have something!

we didn't. We didn't go for more than two months, until the evening before Yom Kippur.

We agreed to meet on the little square in front of the General Mutual Insurance Company, on the corner of Copernicus and Sewerynów Streets, right next to the theater. I couldn't show my face at her house. Everyone knew I was Szapiro's boy. Magda lived nearby, at 33 Smocza Street, near the corner of Gęsia. I didn't want her to turn up at Szapiro's apartment either.

She was standing there waiting for me. I glanced at the watch, my first ever, on my left wrist: I was on time. She was the early one. She smiled at my gesture.

She wore a simple navy-blue dress with a white collar and black flats. She'd carefully arranged her blond curls.

"There you are," she said simply.

In those two months we'd only seen each other a few times, on the street. I'd take my hat off, say hello, she'd return the greeting. The first and second times I hadn't stopped because I was walking with Szapiro.

"You like that girl, huh?" he said the second time we passed her. It was a warm August evening. We were on our way back from the gym, I had a canvas bag with gloves, shoes, and my gym clothes slung over my shoulder.

"She's just a friend," I replied.

Szapiro started laughing and laughed the whole way back. At home he told Emilia the whole story.

I was embarrassed, especially in front of her.

Emilia didn't laugh. She pulled me in front of a large mirror, stood behind me, held me by the shoulders. She looked my reflection up and down.

"You've become a man. You're like my Jakub. Girls might like you," she whispered in my ear.

I was even more embarrassed. I didn't understand it at the time, because I didn't know the nature of this emotion, or the nature and complexity of other emotions, I didn't know what was happening in my heart and my body, yet I desired Jakub Szapiro's wife the same way I desired Magda Aszer, but at the same time, differently. More, and not as much.

"Jakub, come here!" she called to her husband.

He came into the room with a piece of kiełbasa in one hand and a newspaper in the other.

"You see how he looks?"

Jakub turned to look at me and I turned to look at myself. Now I was a different Moyshe. I was Szapiro's boy. A skinny Jewish boy in pants and a jacket that were too big, and an old checkered shirt. I had two shirts, one suit. Shaved temples, hair longer on top, with a part.

"We've got to dress him up some," said Emilia.

Szapiro looked at my reflection in the mirror and frowned as though he'd only just noticed my worn-out clothes.

Twelve hours later I was standing in the fitting room of a tailor shop.

"Mr. Szapiro!" said the tailor, pleased to see us.

It was a typical Warsaw August morning. On Nalewki it smelled of cholent, everywhere else it smelled of mignonettes. Tadeusz Zaremba's tailor shop was located at 52 Koszykowa Street, in one of the beautiful apartment houses on this stylish street that, indeed, smelled of mignonettes. In my previous life I'd never ventured this far, but by then I'd gotten to know it, driving with Szapiro and Buddy to stop by Ryfka Kij's, barely more than a dozen buildings along at number 68.

Mannequins stood in the crystal store windows on either side of the entrance, with combinations of shirts, jackets, ties, and bow ties pinned to them. I remember them well: on the left, brown checkered and herringbone tweeds, already prepared for autumn, and wool ties to match; beside them, umbrellas, checkered newsboy caps, and azure driving gloves; on the right, a tuxedo and tails, plus a glistening top hat, a walking stick, and white deerskin gloves.

We went inside.

"Mr. Szapiro!" said the tailor, pleased to see us, as I've just written, though the customer already in the shop was not pleased. He was a tall, slender, and gray-haired man with an English mustache and a navy-blue suit, also English by the look of it. He'd just been browsing samples of shirt material, then turned around instinctively as we came in and peered at us for two seconds too long, with obvious disgust.

Of course, Szapiro was very properly dressed, in an evidently, though not ostentatiously, expensive double-breasted gray flannel suit. Today I suspect his black-and-white saddle shoes crossed the line into ostentatiousness, just like the gold cuff links with red rubies that he had an eye to purchase just then.

The tall man with the English mustache frowned. He was reading Szapiro like a book, with the ease typical of people of his class, people with his handsome Aryan features, height, and pride, a pride I didn't yet know I hated, though hate it I did.

Their eyes met, Szapiro and the man browsing shirt material samples.

This tall, slim, older man with the English mustache knew at once who he was dealing with. A Jew. A thug. A crook. A gangster. He wanted nothing to do with some Jewish bandit from Nalewki. Seeing a Jewish bandit from Nalewki in Zaremba's luxury store offended this man's class—and, as it later turned out, ethnic—sensibilities.

The customer shot Zaremba a reproachful look. The tailor's confidence evaporated.

"Mr. Ziembiński, I'll be right back with you, meanwhile Piotr will see to Mr. Szapiro and our young guest," he said, with a nod to his apprentice.

The man with the English mustache was clearly outraged he'd been mentioned in the same sentence as Mr. Szapiro. He slammed shut the pattern book with samples of white and blue Egyptian cotton, snorted, and bristled his mustache.

"Good day, Mr. Zaremba," he said as coldly as if hereby declaring he was changing tailors, permanently.

He took his gray homburg from its hook and left, closing the door behind him with an ostentatiously offensive gentleness.

"I beg your pardon," murmured Zaremba.

"Ziembiński?" asked Szapiro, whose curiosity had clearly been piqued.

"Of course, Mr. Ziembiński, the prosecutor," replied Zaremba.

"Anything to do with the boxer Andrzej Ziembiński?"

"Only that he fathered him. Now how may I serve you, Mr. Szapiro?"

Serve you or your money? I thought, because I was young and foolish and didn't understand it amounted to the same thing. A moment later I stood in the middle of the shop, my arms raised to shoulder height as the apprentice took my measurements, noting down the numbers from the tape measure. My skinny body quantified and recorded on a tailor's order form.

Zaremba and Szapiro were picking out suit material. Finally, Szapiro showed me a sample of dark-gray flannel in delicate, almost invisible pinstripes.

"Like it?"

I nodded. I had never seen such beautiful material in my life.

"Three-button single-breasted, a vest, two pair of pants, two white shirts, ties—black, gray, navy blue, and navy-blue striped—and four pair of socks," ordered Szapiro.

Total 180 złotys, payable in cash. You could buy a cheapish suit from the Jews for twenty-five; the best one at Jabłkowski Brothers department store cost a hundred. Szapiro put up the full amount at once, counting out from a thick bundle of bills in his pocket, the way he might pay for some bread rolls.

"Would the young gentleman be so kind as to come in for a fitting next week?" asked Zaremba.

I did. By then we'd also gone to Kielman's to order shoes.

A month later, instead of going to synagogue for Kol Nidre, I went with Magda Aszer to see *Widow Jadzia* at the Polski Theater.

From the moment she looked at me I could tell she saw a different person.

As I walked down the street I examined my reflection in the store windows. I was a different person, my first time dressed this way, in a suit, glistening shoes, a white shirt, and a black tie, looking like a big shot, even with a white handkerchief in my breast pocket.

Before I left, Szapiro had looked me over carefully and happily, before unclipping the Glashütte watch from his wrist.

"Give me your hand," he said, and fastened the watch to my left hand. "It's automatic, you don't have to wind it. It winds itself from the motion of your arm."

"Then maybe he should wear it on his right," added Emilia's muffled voice from the kitchen. Szapiro let out a laugh.

She'd been spying on me while I masturbated. I didn't know it then. Or maybe they were talking about one of their sons?

Lying in my bed in one of the three bedrooms in the Szapiros' apartment, I slid the comforter down and, thinking of the body of Emilia Szapiro and the body of Magda Aszer, I masturbated slowly, taking care not to make any noise.

And then I saw her, through the crack in the door, barely visible in the dim glow of the streetlights. My hand raced for the comforter.

"Don't stop," she said in a way that meant I couldn't stop and I didn't.

She watched me and I felt violated, and therefore loved. I had never experienced anything so arousing in my life. She was watching me the way she watched Jakub.

Szapiro laughed, but in addition to the Glashütte watch he gave me twenty złotys for tickets and a coffee after the show. He'd never given me money before and I hadn't dared ask. I had fifty złotys of my own set aside, for a rainy day, for the moment Szapiro threw me out of the house, a moment I was convinced would definitely come, convinced too there was no going back to my family home after abandoning my mother and brother.

Magda was waiting in front of the General Mutual Insurance Company, in a modest dress with a white collar, and looking at me, at me in my new suit, my first real one, which fit me like a glove. In that dark-gray suit from Zaremba's, I was no longer a skinny little Jew from Nalewki, I was a slim, elegant young man with Semitic good looks.

There's a big difference between a skinny little Jew from Nalewki and a slim, elegant young man with Semitic good looks.

The day before, I'd read in the *Courier* that an averagely dressed woman had jumped from Poniatowski Bridge into the Vistula River, intending suicide. I remember to this day, because at the moment I was thinking of my new suit. The *Courier's* journalist noted specifically that the woman was averagely dressed. Just like that. Averagely.

She could have been dressed richly, she could have been dressed poorly, she could have been dressed averagely. Neither richly nor poorly. Averagely. And that averageness was significant for her suicidal leap. She'd jumped into the Vistula dressed averagely. So maybe she was a storekeeper's wife. Or a servant wearing hand-me-downs from her mistress. Or the wife of a modest clerk. Or a modest clerk herself. But that is exactly how she jumped into the Vistula River, dressed averagely.

She didn't jump unhappy, sick, despised, desperate, bored, apathetic; she didn't jump from a broken heart, from love, or even as a joke, or as a bet, or out of foolishness; she didn't stumble as she gave someone a scare pretending to jump, she jumped into the Vistula River dressed averagely.

And, dressed averagely, she was pulled out of the Vistula by a police patrol that happened to be nearby in a motorboat.

Whether the patrol pulled out the averagely dressed woman alive or dead, the *Courier* didn't say. Yet she was definitely dressed averagely.

Magda Aszer, waiting for me on the square in front of the General Mutual Insurance building, was dressed averagely. I was dressed well, that's what you'd say of me.

On a bridge over the Vistula, a well-dressed young man with Semitic good looks threw himself into the river.

The body of retired Tat-Aluf Moshe Inbar was found in an apartment on Dizengoff Street in Tel Aviv. The cause of death was likely suicide. In the course of the investigation, police were able to rule out foul play. Death must have occurred some weeks ago. Neighbors informed police after concerns were raised by the smell emanating from the apartment. It would sound a little different in Hebrew.

"You clean up nice," said Magda, surprised. She hadn't seen me in my new threads yet.

I smiled at her, proud of my new look.

"Did Szapiro dress you up like that?" she added with a cynicism I hadn't heard in her voice before, though I would go on to hear it for a long time, my whole life.

As though Szapiro was looming over me. I was always in his shadow.

And now I was no longer a well-dressed, slim young man with Semitic good looks. Once again I was a skinny little Jew from Nalewki whom Szapiro had dressed up. I bit my tongue and we walked to the theater. I paid for the tickets I'd reserved earlier over the phone in my name, which I'd pronounced with a hint of embarrassment. Or anyway I thought I'd heard the cashier sigh quietly when she heard me say "Mojżesz Bernsztajn." But it was probably just my impression.

We took our seats in the fourth row. It was the first time I'd been in a Polish theater, and it was the Polski Theater to boot. We didn't talk.

I don't remember the play, although I laughed in all the right places. I couldn't shake the feeling Szapiro and Emilia were sitting a couple of rows behind us, but maybe it was just a feeling?

Maria Modzelewska, a big star back then, was playing the lead. I looked at Magda beside me, at the skin of her forearms, I heard her laugh, and I tried to catch her scent but couldn't, because the woman in front of us with the beautiful hat blocking some of our view was so heavily perfumed, with Chanel N°5 no less, though of course in those days I didn't recognize the smell, since how could I recognize a perfume that cost fifty złotys for a tiny bottle?

As I said earlier, it felt like Szapiro and Emilia were sitting a few rows behind us, watching us, a few times I caught them out of the corner of my eye, I could hear their voices at intermission.

Magda had also sprinkled herself with perfume, a cheap one from the Warsaw Chemical Laboratory—I could only smell it later, when we went for a stroll in the Saxon Gardens, by the fountain. We sat down on a bench. We still weren't talking. It was dark and we were sitting close together, and that was the moment I caught the delicate scent of her perfume.

"Did you like the play?" I asked stupidly, and Magda kissed me.

It was my first. I was too stunned to respond the way I thought a man should. Especially since it was her who kissed me.

My father would have thought under no circumstances should a man find himself alone with a girl on a park bench at night. It was a terrible sin.

Szapiro would have gone further than kissing, to the activities kissing should lead to.

I'd seen him screwing his wife. I was on my way to the bathroom one night and they'd left the door ajar, and in the half-light, I saw his powerful back and buttocks, and I heard his hips smacking against Emilia's protruding backside, with her on all fours in front of him. She was moaning, whispering something, he was going at it in silence.

The sight aroused me and I stood there as though hypnotized.

Then Emilia glimpsed me over her shoulder.

"You want to join in?" she asked.

I ran off. Their laughter and moans pursued me. Though maybe she didn't ask that at all.

In the morning, at breakfast, they smiled knowingly, both of them, but didn't even hint at what had happened overnight.

I'd been scared and run off, but really I'd wanted to join in. Yet maybe I'd only dreamed it, maybe I hadn't seen Szapiro making love to his wife at all, maybe it would never occur to Emilia to invite me into their marriage bed?

Magda kissed me and I didn't even lay my hand on her breasts. She smiled.

"Szapiro's boy, that's what they call you, did you know that?" she asked.

I didn't answer.

"Szapiro's boy, and so shy. It's cute."

We walked back to Nalewki through now-deserted Bankowy Square, Tłomackie Street, Przejazd Street. We passed Simons Arcade. We didn't hold hands. She didn't want me to walk her all the way home and I didn't know how to insist.

We stood on the corner of Nalewki and Świętojerska Streets, by a children's goods store called Cytryna. The early evening was still warm, summery, so we just stood there together. In silence. We didn't want to go farther. Farther along was Gęsia Street, Magda would turn onto Gęsia and go home, and I would continue to 40 Nalewki Street, to the Szapiros'.

Farther on also stood the building where my mother and brother no longer were.

"Want a cigarette?" asked Magda.

"You smoke?" I responded, again idiotically.

"Well, sometimes. When I'm not training."

"You're not training?"

"It's too cold now," she explained to me, idiot.

She had a pack in her bag. She offered me one. I didn't have a light, idiot, so she lit it for me.

"It's Yom Kippur today," I said, to say something.

My whole life I've been afraid of silence.

"Are you going to the protest tomorrow?" she asked.

I shrugged. Of course I was going to the protest. I was Szapiro's boy. All Szapiro's boys were going to the protest.

She smiled. She kissed me on the cheek, turned, and ran off, and I went back to the Szapiros'.

They were sitting in the living room, both reading, the boys were already asleep. Emilia and Jakub looked as though they hadn't gone out anywhere. Jakub had on a silk smoking jacket that tied closed at the waist and had quilted lapels of a sort surely no one on Nalewki wore but him. Emilia was in an elegant silk paisley housecoat.

"Pour yourself some cognac and sit down with us, read a little," ordered Szapiro.

I poured myself a glass and sat down. I took one of the books from the shelf. It was in Yiddish. I took a sip of cognac. I didn't like the taste.

Then the phone rang.

"Answer it," ordered Jakub.

I did, announcing this was the Szapiro residence.

"I need speak to Jakub," said the Doctor.

I handed the receiver to Szapiro, who let me stay by the phone and listen in on their conversation.

"Time has come," declared Radziwiłek in an official tone, as though declaring the arrival of the Messiah. "We gotta finally deal with retired colonel who wanna lock up Jews in camps."

Szapiro immediately remembered what they had talked about two months before. Witold Sokoliński had named Kazimierz Bobiński from *ABC* as the one responsible for the survey. Szapiro sighed quietly.

"Don't sigh to me here. Sort it out?"

"Yeah, sort it out," replied Jakub.

Radziwiłek hung up without saying goodbye. Jakub reached for the telephone book and found the number for Art and Fashion Café. He called and asked if Mr. Bobiński happened to be there. He was.

"I gotta go," Jakub said to Emilia. "The boy's coming with me."

Emilia shrugged without looking up from her book. She had known him too long to put up a fight.

I was already dressed, so I had to wait a moment for Jakub to change, then we got in the Buick and pulled up in grand style in front of Art and Fashion Café at 11 Królewska Street.

Szapiro had put on a navy-blue, double-breasted suit, a white shirt, and a claret-colored silk tie, and swapped his slippers for Oxfords. When he entered the packed café, a dozen or so pairs of ladies' eyes immediately sized him up from head to toe.

I was completely invisible in his shadow, which was understandable—those eyes examining Szapiro were giving him straight A's. For the suit, of course, but above all for what filled it out—that massive boxer's body, now thicker at the waist—and for his confidence and calm, which in turn filled out that powerful bulk.

The bright interior of Art and Fashion Café was packed with small square tables surrounded by simple chairs with arms. Portraits hung on the wall—eighteenth-century Polish noblemen, some with mustaches and Sarmatian robes, others in powdered wigs and clean-shaven. At the tables sat a company of men and women, the artistic and literary, dressed to the nines for the evening.

I knew we two Jewish proletarians didn't really fit in here, and I felt I stuck out like a sore thumb; this wasn't the Metropol or our brothel at Ryfka's, this place was theirs.

Yet Szapiro seemed at home as he walked in, though he'd never been to Art and Fashion. His confidence and calm had strong foundations—in one inside pocket of his jacket, he had five thousand złotys in a thick wad held together with a rubber band, and in the other, five hundred dollars. His right coat pocket held a pistol. In his left pants pocket, he had two hundred złotys in small bills; in the right, a knuckle-duster; in his muscles, the strength to use it; in his heart, a willingness to do violence. These were his foundation, these determined his power and significance: strength, money, and bravery, the readiness to break the law at any moment, to go to prison if he had to.

And it was only somewhere deep inside Jakub Szapiro that something dark lay dormant. I didn't know it then, but now, fifty years later in another world, I do.

Jakub Szapiro was the strongest man I ever knew, and I knew many strong men. I knew Dayan. I knew men from Unit 101, like Ariel Sharon. They never invited me to join, I didn't serve in the 101 because they only accepted kibbutzniks—that was how they thought back then, that only someone born on a kibbutz or a moshav was fit to defend Israel; it hurt me they thought I wasn't fit, but I knew them all, all those slim, suntanned men with their uniform sleeves rolled up, as quick to fire a gun as to laugh.

I knew them all yet never, my whole life, did I meet someone like Szapiro, so inwardly strong, decisive, determined in everything he was doing.

I once saw the Soviet nuclear icebreaker *Arktika* on TV; it reached the North Pole in '77, smashing its way through ice thirteen feet thick. It had an armored double hull, reactors powering it, and could push through ice that would stop any other ship in the world. That's exactly the kind of man Szapiro was.

Or to put it another way: he was like a sperm whale, the largest actively hunting predator, seemingly lumbering, lazy, but when he had to be—quick and deadly.

And yet inside, somewhere beneath his solar plexus, lurking within Szapiro was a small, hard black ball, a grain, an atom of crystallization, and for years everything you couldn't see on Szapiro's outside built up in layers around it.

An awful childhood, the poorest of the poor, because they were the Jewish poor under the czar. His father's belt. Street brawls. Fear.

Then one decisive moment, when his father raised his hand to him with a switch and Jakub stopped that hand, seized it by the wrist, squeezed, and realized his father would never hit him again, because he was stronger than his father. That moment he tore the switch from his father's hand, threw him to the ground, and, ignoring his mother's screams, thrashed him with that switch until it broke, then took a fistful of paper rubles from his father's wallet, left the apartment, and never returned. Not long after, the First World War broke out.

A teenager growing up on his own in German-occupied Warsaw under the kaiser and Hans Beseler. Hunger and cold. Then everything he went through in the trenches, fighting the Bolsheviks. Again fear, again hunger, again cold, loneliness, abandonment.

And then the faces of all those he'd killed to conquer fear, hunger, cold, loneliness. I know those faces as though I'd seen them with my own eyes. He told me stories of them.

The face of Naum Bernsztajn, whose throat he slit. I, Moyshe Bernsztajn, the son of the man he had to murder, clinging to his sleeve.

Sometimes Szapiro's anger would come exploding out of that small, hard black ball. And sometimes other things would.

But that night, in Art and Fashion, even he'd forgotten his anger, which was buried deep inside. He was as the café ladies saw him— powerful, strong, with a boxer's good looks and the sex appeal typical of a man partial to violence. That's what they saw as they snuck glances at him, though they were too well-bred to leave their tables, where sickly intellectuals, pomaded actors, or penniless poets were amusing themselves in conversation; the ladies were too well-bred to leave their tables, approach him, and slip him a note with their telephone number. Or with an address, date, and time.

Yes, they were too well-bred for that, and maybe too smart as well. Yet somehow such notes did make their way to him, slipped under the door of his dressing room after fights, brought by courier to Sobenski's snack bar, or tossed his way by handsomely paid, discreet male waiters. I read somewhere that after Cardinal Richelieu's death, a box was found by his bed full of unopened letters from women pleading for a single hour of his night. Szapiro had no such box of notes from women because he usually just crumpled them up and threw them away. He much preferred honest whores, who didn't fool around with notes, to upper-class women.

Meanwhile he looked around for a man matching the description Witold Sokoliński had given him back in July when he identified who'd written the survey on removing Jews from the military.

He spotted him almost immediately.

Kazimierz Bobiński was average height, very slender, and wearing a gray three-piece English suit with a gentle pinstripe, crimson socks, a white shirt, an impeccable cornflower-blue tie, very expensive cuff links, and polished shoes. His hair was slicked with Brilliantine, his nails were manicured, and he had a pencil mustache clipped a sixteenth of an inch above the line dividing the carmine of his lips from the skin and an eighth of an inch below the line of his nose. He'd spotted Jakub Szapiro a second after he walked into Art and Fashion, and in the next second had fallen in love with him. He didn't notice me at all. I was hiding in Jakub's shadow, Jakub's charisma rendering me invisible.

He was expecting this visit. Sokoliński hadn't warned him, he'd been too afraid to, but he'd mentioned it to a few colleagues and news had gone around the journalism world that a certain Szapiro was on the lookout for Kazimierz Bobiński. Meanwhile Bobiński, unlike Witold Sokoliński of the *Courier*, wasn't afraid in the slightest. Bobiński was glad to meet him.

Now he was sitting at a table with Dr. Wojciech Zaleski, the head of *ABC* and the radical nationalists' leading economic theoretician, a man seeking a third way between capitalism and communism, who dreamed of a Catholic Greater Poland with no proletariat and no Jews, socialists, or degenerates.

Zaleski was pontificating about the need to exclude Jews from economic and public life and forcing them to emigrate, using all necessary sanctions and harassment. He did this as though reciting an article in his newspaper or practicing public speaking, mostly ignoring his interlocutor. By this time Bobiński had given up listening anyway.

"Wojtuś, my dear," he said, finally interrupting him, "these days there are a few more pressing issues than the exclusion of Jews from economic and social life. And besides, you're being awfully boring."

"What issues would those be?" fumed Zaleski.

"Korolec."

Korolec, an important activist in the *ABC* faction of radical nationalists, had been killed four days earlier by unknown perpetrators, yet whose affiliation with the rival Phalanx faction was known and obvious to anyone who might take an interest in Korolec's death.

"Are we going to let Piasecki's Phalanx do as they please?" continued Bobiński. "Tadzio Gluziński's just gotten out of the hospital. Five broken ribs, three missing teeth, a fractured skull!"

"Of course, of course." Zaleski grew decidedly more somber, then returned to his haranguing tone, declaring, "Interfactional struggles are worst of all. We should fight the Jew, the socialist, and the Bolshevik, yet we clash with Bolo Piasecki and his people, who share, after all . . ."

"Kwasieborski and Wasiutyński," replied Bobiński laconically. Those were the names of two key Phalanx operatives.

Zaleski considered for a moment.

"Are you sure?"

"Yes. Put them in the hospital for a month or so. But no worse than that. Now, Wojtuś, be a friend and shake a leg, will you? I've got an important matter to attend to," he replied in an imperious tone.

Zaleski gave him a surprised look, and in response Bobiński nodded toward Szapiro. Zaleski gave an offended harrumph, got up, and left without paying his bill.

Szapiro sat down in Zaleski's seat. He raised his hand and ordered a coffee, which the waitress brought quickly. Bobiński ordered champagne.

"Won't you have a drink?" he asked, indicating his glass.

Szapiro declined the alcohol. I stood alongside, leaning against the wall, my hands in my pockets in a gesture I'd picked up from Warsaw's street thugs, and stayed that way.

Jakub only glanced at me once, smiled to himself, and shook his head.

The two men said nothing.

"You are exceptionally beautiful, Mr. Szapiro," said Bobiński, breaking the silence.

"Beg pardon?" said Szapiro.

"Exceptionally beautiful. You have something in you of an antique statue, those arms of yours, your shoulders, Mr. Szapiro, your face, which need not be Semitic at all, it might just as well be Greek, might it not?"

"Uh, I'm not sure."

"I am. Looking at you, I feel my previously hardened conviction the Jews must be expelled to Madagascar softening somewhat. On the other hand I feel something else hardening."

Szapiro spluttered into his coffee.

"Come now, Mr. Szapiro, no need for prudery. You're no virgin after all, you're more of a man of the world than I. But tell me, Mr. Szapiro, what brings you to me?"

"That survey about chucking Jews out of the military," replied Jakub, forcing himself to act dignified.

"Ah, yes. Now I wouldn't want to offend you, but I'm not going to lie either, and, well, those are my views. Jews aren't fit for soldiering. And generally speaking, I believe you should all leave the country."

"My wife thinks the same, Mr. Bobiński."

"As a nationalist, Zionism is close to my heart. Madagascarism too. That being said, *you* I would rather keep here, Mr. Szapiro," said the journalist dreamily.

"I'm not going anywhere," Szapiro said, deciding to play along. "This is my city."

Bobiński fluttered his long eyelashes, saying, "And, as an inhabitant of this city, I could be yours too."

Szapiro's patience was running out and he waved his hand dismissively.

"Fine, fine," said Bobiński, "I'm flirting with you here, but you must want something concrete from me, am I right? Sadly I doubt you came to see me out of affection."

At that moment, Szapiro realized Bobiński didn't fear him in the slightest. He was shocked at the bravery hidden in this trim body, yet bravery it undeniably was.

Jakub considered for a moment in silence while Bobiński, smiling, sipped his champagne. Then Jakub said, "I want the name of the retired officer who answered your survey in the July seventh issue."

"Suddenly some article from back in July interests Mr. Szapiro. Now. Strange."

"Strange or not, I want that name. And address."

"But surely you understand I can't share that under any circumstances?"

Szapiro nodded. He understood.

"And I'm sure you intend to threaten me with violence if I don't tell you, isn't that right?"

Jakub gave a helpless shrug, indicating that if he was forced to that eventuality, then of course.

"My, how arousing! You're so manly, Mr. Szapiro. All around us here"—Bobiński gestured in a circle with his hand, as though encompassing everyone in the café—"nothing but lampreys. Leeches. No spine. Weaklings. Nematodes. Pussies. But you, Mr. Szapiro, well, you take my breath away."

Jakub smiled, genuinely embarrassed.

"But as far as violence goes, Mr. Szapiro, at this moment in my pocket, my right hand is gripping a small Browning .25 caliber, which I never part with. I'd prefer to be gripping something different, warmer than cold steel, something I can only imagine, but as you can see, I'm left with no choice. Twenty-five is no caliber at all, yet from this distance, under the table, into the stomach, into the groin, with a heavy heart, but, well, what can I say, you know how it is."

"I do," replied Szapiro, because he did.

"And if you felt like jumping me later on, starting today I won't go anywhere without bodyguards from the gang, even though they're stunningly dull, ugly Polish brats, earnest and potato-y. True believers. Atrocious. You have your own people, of course, maybe we'll have a shoot-up, but is it worth it over some reserve lieutenant or other? I don't think so."

"No, it's not," agreed Szapiro, because it wasn't.

"So I have another proposal." Bobiński lowered his voice. "Come to my place. Let me take care of you, undress you, I'll run a bath. I'll kiss you like no piece of skirt has ever kissed you before, and don't worry about anything, I wouldn't even dream of attempting to sully your virginity. But if you wanted me, then certainly, why not. And then I'll tell you the name of that unfortunate soul and his address too, I'll just have to check it at the office."

"Do I look like a whore to you, Mr. Bobiński?" asked Jakub, very quietly, but I could clearly hear the little black ball in his chest starting to pulse, ready at any second to explode with his terrible fury.

"Whatever do you mean? Though I myself am awfully whorish, Mr. Szapiro," replied Bobiński, disarming Jakub with his frankness. "And I've fallen awfully in love with you, at first sight."

"Well you're going to suffer for that love, I'm only into girls."

Bobiński nodded wordlessly. They sat in silence like that for a few minutes, each one waiting. Bobiński ordered another champagne. Jakub weighed his options. Something told him he couldn't just grab Bobiński by the collar and haul him out of the café, because the fascist wouldn't hesitate to shoot. This was a brave man he was dealing with, no question.

"Enough flirting. Let's talk like men. About politics. You know big changes are afoot?"

"How do you mean?" said Jakub, politely interested.

"At the so-called heights of power. It seems Marshal Rydz-Śmigły, with a certain Colonel Koc as middleman, is forging an alliance with the most radical elements of the nationalist movement—the Phalanx, led by a certain Bolo. Bolo Piasecki."

"I've heard of Bolesław Piasecki," replied Szapiro. "A sorta little Polish Hitler, but dumber."

"He's not dumb at all, this Piasecki. And he's highly ambitious and even more ruthless. Who knows, you might be right, under the proper circumstances he could become someone like Hitler."

"Don't forget who you're talking to."

Bobiński just smiled.

"I know you're acquainted with a certain Andrzej Ziembiński, correct?"

Jakub nodded, and just then I remembered the brown glove covering a hand tattooed with a sword and *death* in Hebrew striking Ziembiński with an uppercut to the chin, Ziembiński falling limply in the ring, his limbs quivering as he lay there.

"Well, Piasecki's his boss," continued Bobiński. "Ziembiński's his right-hand man. Apart from the boxing you know him from, he's also in law school and his father's a prosecutor."

"I've met him."

"The father? Bet he loved you. There's a real Jew hater, my friend! Anyway, Ziembiński's got ambition, but he's also not your usual wimpy college boy from a good home. Ziembiński likes the street, brass knuckles, likes feeling his blood pump faster. His boss Piasecki stays off the streets, he's the brains, not the brawn. And he makes extra sure not to go anywhere without his revolver. Now listen closely, Mr. Szapiro, since I've got a feeling this might concern you personally. Piasecki's got his eye on *ABC* too, since right now our faction and his Phalanx are headed for war. In fairness, we could join up with him at any moment, that's just not in the cards right now. But you're the ones who're worse off, you see? Our nationalist unity and alliance excludes you. The government's going to stop supporting pinkos like Kaplica. Once the marshal gets his deal and does what it looks like he might, nobody in Internal Affairs is going to care if Kaplica used to be one of Piłsudski's men. And then that will be that: you fall. But for Piasecki's Phalanx, with their shit-colored shirts and black jodhpurs, that will be that too: they rise. You see, Mr. Szapiro?"

"And what's your position in all this?" asked Jakub. "What's your relationship with this Piasecki?"

"Oh, he's a gorgeous boy, really gorgeous," said Bobiński dreamily.

"That's not what I'm asking," said Jakub, chuckling genuinely.

"I know. But first I must point out that pampered little boy can't hold a candle to your masculine, animal charm. My position is we at *ABC* consider Bolo's Phalanx venal troublemakers who'll do anything to cozy up to the men in power. Ah, but a moment . . . You were wondering about the response to the survey we published on July seventh?"

"Yes."

"With the retired officer proposing we lock up the Jews from the army in camps, that we just need some lumber and barbed wire?"

Szapiro nodded.

"In that case I'll tell you," said the journalist suddenly.

"In exchange for what?"

"For nothing. Out of sympathy. Or maybe admiration. Because I don't give a damn about that old man and you're gorgeous. He's called Jerzy Górski. I even remember his address, because it's simple. Eight Kobielska Street, apartment eight as well. In Grochów district. Maybe I'm telling you because I think this Górski sides with Bolo. I'm sure that must be it."

Szapiro wrote down the address in the small, slim notebook he always carried with him, then got up.

"Then why did you publish it in your paper?" he asked.

"He's a good writer," said Bobiński with a toothy grin. "Don't hold it against me, Mr. Szapiro."

"Mr. Bobiński . . . ," began Jakub and then stopped, as though searching for the words.

"Yes?"

"There's a protest tomorrow, Wolska Street at Bankowy Square. You heard?"

"I did."

"Don't go to the counterprotest. Some friendly advice. There's gonna be a punch-up. Why risk it?"

"If you say not to go, I won't."

"You're all right, Mr. Bobiński . . . for a fascist."

"Likewise, Mr. Szapiro."

They gave one another a polite bow. Jakub paid for his coffee and we left.

The next day, we were the last to arrive at the protest, in a column of three cars: first, Kaplica's Chrysler, then Szapiro's Buick with me inside, and finally Radziwiłek in his small rear-engine Mercedes 170 H, with Tyutchev driving. The weather was beautiful, perfect for a protest, warm, a clear sky, but not hot.

A crowd had gathered in front of the Metalworkers' Union headquarters at 44 Wolska Street.

"Looks like almost ten thousand people," murmured Pantaleon, staring out the window.

Szapiro nodded.

Many times I saw how good they were at measuring crowd size. From experience, I learned to as well. It often came in handy. Like when I was lining up for my daily ration of filthy drinking water during the siege of Jerusalem in 1948, and five thousand people were lined up with me, holding buckets and cans, waiting for their water.

I've always hated crowds. Crowds frighten me. Lots of people in one place, belly to back, shoulder to shoulder, mouth to mouth, breathing down your neck, pickpockets eager with their dexterous hands. Pushing my way through Kercelak market or Simons Arcade, and later all the crowds of all the years of my life.

"I hate crowds," muttered Szapiro and I felt he was very dear to me, very important.

The people gathered in front of the union headquarters were standing orderly, calm, silent. Placards rose above the crowds:

THE POLISH SOCIALIST PARTY CALLS

DOWN WITH EXPLOITATION

THE BLOOD OF THE WORKERS

DOWN WITH ANTI-SEMITISM

WORKERS OF THE WORLD UNITE

I was sitting in the back seat of the Buick, behind Pantaleon. I couldn't stop peering at the back of his head, couldn't get my mind off what his thick black hair concealed.

Pantaleon's devil brother was sleeping. I wondered if I could wake it up. If when it woke up it would see me. And what it might think of me. And if it would tell Pantaleon what it thought.

Was Pantaleon its master? Or did the devil brother rule Pantaleon? What did it whisper to him about me at night?

The Buick, the Chrysler, and the Mercedes pulled over, looking like a government convoy. Szapiro took a pistol from the glove compartment I'd never seen him with before: a large, thirteen-round Browning Hi-Power. A 9 mm, the same ammunition as the Luger.

A good pistol. Gaddhafi carries a gold-plated Hi-Power, Saddam too, Ali Ağca shot the pope with a Hi-Power. But I always preferred an American .45. A .45 puts better holes in people. And it's American, not European, like all the 9 mms. And I don't like Europe.

I prefer America, I prefer America by a lot.

I stopped liking Europe before I'd really gotten the hang of thinking it existed, and long before I thought I might be European myself.

How could I be European?

I'm Tat-Aluf Moshe Inbar, for forty-odd years I've been fighting Arabs in the Middle East, I tore around the desert in a Jeep, dodging Russian tanks with Syrian, Jordanian, and Egyptian crews, I burned those tanks. Not ten years after that protest on Wolska I could speak Arabic so well I could pretend I was Syrian to an Egyptian, or Egyptian to a Syrian; how does that make me European? How was I ever European?

I'm Tat-Aluf Moshe Inbar.

Retired, sadly, and Magda Aszer's got herself a lover boy she's living with and doesn't want me to call her Magda.

So back to when I was Mojżesz Bernsztajn, age seventeen, a skinny kid who'd never think for a second he was European, especially not when it came to the ammunition in a Browning Hi-Power.

Szapiro reloaded and put on the safety with the hammer cocked.

"You got a heater?" he asked Pantaleon.

Pantaleon nodded and showed the grip of his seven-shooter.

I, a little seventeen-year-old Jew, formerly from Nalewki Street and now from nowhere, sat in the back seat and trembled at the sight of their guns. With fear and excitement.

Szapiro took off his brimmed hat, reached back into the glove compartment, and pulled out a proletarian newsboy cap.

"Let's go."

We got out. Szapiro and Pantaleon cast their eyes over the streets and the rooftops. Szapiro took off his jacket, rolled up his sleeves, then, taking the grip of the Browning in his right hand, placed it in his right pants pocket, seemingly casually, but with his hand tensed.

Pantaleon reached into his own pocket and handed me a small blackjack: a heavy roll of thick leather, stuffed with lead pellets. I thought it looked like the penis of some heavy beast whose strength was now flowing into me.

The strength of large animals fascinated me. I'd never been to a zoo, but it was enough to see a large Percheron draft horse with shaggy hooves, its powerful muscles at work under its thick skin. I always used to watch them, enchanted, as they pulled carts full of coal. Then in a pasture at the summer resort in Świder I saw a black bull with a smooth, shining coat and imagined it defeating a bear in combat. There was no way that mass of coiled, bulging muscle could lose to a bear.

Now I possessed that strength, I, skinny Jewish Moyshe Bernsztajn, held in my hand the core of male, animal power, the beast's penis.

"Put it in your pants pocket," ordered Pantaleon hoarsely.

I did. Near my own, much punier, penis.

Szapiro raised a hand and snapped his fingers and a dozen or so young guys, proletarian types, broke off from the crowd. They kept their right hands in the pockets of their jackets or pants. I'd already learned that meant their hidden hands were gripping pistols.

They stopped by the cars.

Szapiro nodded to signal everything was okay, and only then did Kaplica and Radziwiłek emerge, the first heavily, the second nimbly. Kaplica was wearing one of his many unfashionable and expensive suits, while Radziwiłek and Tyutchev were in their Rifleman's Association uniforms.

They made for the crowd, I trotted after them, Moyshe Bernsztajn the little Jew in an expensive suit from Zaremba's, with a leather blackjack in my pocket.

Kaplica deftly climbed up to a podium cobbled together from boxes. Applause rang out.

"Long live Buddy!" they cried.

And then they started chanting:

"Kap-li-ca, Kap-li-ca, Kap-li-ca!"

"Shout along with everyone," murmured Pantaleon in my ear.

I yelled out. Kap-li-ca! Kap-li-ca! Kap-li-ca! I somehow understood that, all in all, I owed my new life, my new suit, Magda's kiss, and Emilia Szapiro's eyes to this short little bald guy in ugly clothes.

Jakub Szapiro didn't shout, Jakub Szapiro kept his eyes on the crowd.

Kaplica raised his hand and the crowd fell silent.

"What's the latest anti-Semitic malarkey these radical nationalist bozos are pulling? The jingoistic bastards!" cried out Buddy.

When they heard the word *bastards*, the crowd rumbled with joy like a giant dog, tickled by the vulgar description of their shared enemy.

"Whaddya they mean they want to throw Jews out of the army? Or stage boycotts? Don't they know all workers are brothers? Yesterday in Grochów district, they were smashing Jewish windows in! Yes! Concrete action, comrades, not just empty words."

Here he reached into his pocket, took out a piece of paper, held it far from his face, and read.

"At Zelik Aroch's apartment at thirty-two Osiecka Street. And at Icek Glaszmidt's apartment at twelve Tubiańska Street. Them nationalist punks! And where's the respect for the law? In Berlin they've brought the ghetto to the classroom, forcing Jews to sit on yellow-painted benches, are we gonna have the same here? That's not the Poland we fought the partitioners for, not the one we bled for in 1920 at war with the Bolsheviks!"

The workers applauded. On mention of the war of 1920, Szapiro smiled to himself.

"Like hell Buddy bled in the war. My ass," he muttered under his breath, as though to me.

"Yeah?"

"He spent the whole war hiding in Warsaw, didn't even stick his nose out, even with the Russians bearing down on the city," replied Jakub quietly. "He was fine getting some shots off around a corner at the czar's gendarmes, but the trenches were another story."

"We won't allow it!" cried Kaplica. "We'll show them Polish fascists what the workers' anger really means! Just like our boys fighting in Spain, we won't surrender!"

But I wasn't listening to him. I was observing Jakub Szapiro and trying to follow his eyes, which were slowly, deliberately working their way over our surroundings. I didn't know back then what it took to see like that, I didn't, though now I do: you remain tense, but completely calm, not tense like a bow but like a crossbow, which when cocked can be laid aside and even left for a long time. You're focused on looking, your whole being is looking and seeing. Every detail is important.

Jakub Szapiro was looking and analyzing, consciously or not, I don't know, but he was analyzing. I remember that, as if I were in his head.

Wasn't that pig-eyed blond guy with the bad skin acting too fidgety? Weren't those two whispering suspiciously?

There had to be a provocateur in the crowd, there definitely was a provocateur, they'd definitely sent one, could be a policeman, could be a nationalist, who was the provocateur, would the provocateur make a move today, or just give a report on this rabble when it was all over?

I've used my eyes that way many times. But not that day. That day I saw Jakub Szapiro. Yes, I knew he'd killed my father, but at the same time I didn't. I didn't know, though I must have known. I was grateful to him for it, although I'd truly loved Naum Bernsztajn, the observant Jew, my father, who wouldn't live to see all the cruelties everyone saw, because he'd had his own, personal cruelty, his throat slit, his body chopped up like a rooster's body for kappores.

If Jakub Szapiro hadn't killed my father on Buddy's orders, if he hadn't made a victim out of him, I would never have left Warsaw.

Jakub Szapiro was beautiful and I loved him.

A wind band struck up, the bearers raised banners in socialist red and placed the pole ends into the leather carrying pouches at their belts.

"The cruel tyrants of the nation," intoned Kaplica, raising his clenched left fist, happy, in his element, full of justified masculine pride at being leader of the pack.

"Have always shed the workers' blood. The people's wrath and indignation arises in a mighty flood!" responded the crowd, raising their left fists in proletarian fashion, happy there was someone to lead them, to guide them, who they could trust, a caregiver, a father, a leader.

We set off. Marching. I remember it so well, that uplifting, strengthening sense of belonging, but also, since I'm marching arm in arm with Szapiro, the sense of leading the crowd.

We're marching.

Gang first and the workers follow. So we were at the front.

Szapiro, Pantaleon, others, with military discipline, in groups of four. The first five groups—hands in their pants and jacket pockets, gripping their pistols, their heaters, keen gazes, lips pursed. I walked with Szapiro, seemingly breaking the order, like a subscript between two groups, out of formation.

The next five groups were heavy brawlers, banners in their right hands, the pole along their legs, nearly to the ground, like a saber in the hands of an officer in a color party, but proletarian. Then the reserve, with knuckle-dusters, knives, and blackjacks hidden in their pants. Among them I caught a glimpse of Moryc Szapiro, Jakub's brother. Only for a moment, but I noticed him and Jakub did too.

Then the banners. The band. Then the people.

We're singing.

> Far and wide spreads the tide of our wrath,
> We hoist the flag of revolution

It proclaims: workers' aims, rebels' path,
Tyrants' defeat, retribution
We raise our standard, freedom's banner,
Its color is the deepest red,
For on it workers' blood was shed!

I also sing.

Its color is the deepest red.
Its color is the deepest red, for it the workers' blood was shed.
Its color is the deepest re-e-ed, for on it workers' blood was shed!

The crowd is like a huge animal.

I am Jonah in the belly of the whale, devoured but not digested. The huge mass of a living, animal body, nearer to the divine than to man.

A whale's 180-ton body in the ocean, when placed beside a man, becomes divine, a heathen idol of fat and muscle—with a prophet living in its innards.

I live in the crowd. I am Jonah, I have a lead-filled blackjack in my pocket. The crowd weighs six hundred tons, as much as four fin whales, six hundred tons of human bulk, its color is the deepest red, for on it workers' blood was shed.

We march down Wolska Street toward the Old City, we're marching slowly and singing. At times someone waves a flag from a window, red or white and red, and cries: "Long live!"

On Chłodna Street, the Bund and Left Poale Zion join us, in temporary truce, the processions intermingling, I remember it so exactly, the moment of intermingling, the leaders' shouts, and the procession reforms again, Polish placards, Yiddish placards, and me right behind Szapiro, Szapiro relaxed and alert, and we march on. Behind our gang is the Bund's gang, solid, scrappy boys, then Poale Zion's gang; I see Moryc Szapiro among them.

We don't run into the police until the corner of Elektoralna and Solna Streets, in front of the low, sprawling Frybes building. A bored mounted patrol with navy-blue uniforms, sabers in scabbards and pistols in holsters, faces shaded by wide brims, straps buckled beneath their chins. They regard us without emotion. One seems less interested in us than a store window with a sign that says APPAREL.

As Kaplica passes them, they unapologetically salute him. Kaplica also raises two fingers to his hat.

There are a few more on Bankowy Square, over a dozen officers, an army of mounted police in loose formation in front of the Lesser Brothers trading house. They stand relaxed, waiting, not looking our way.

Our procession halts, only the head of it enters the square.

"Not so many *Polizei* come today," says Radziwiłek.

"They know there ain't no need," says Kaplica with a shrug.

Only then do we notice the counterprotest. It's smaller than ours. Most are wearing students' caps and civilian clothes. A few groups in light-colored uniform shirts with diagonal straps across the chest and dark berets. They're coming from the direction of Senatorska Street, from the square in front of the Polish Industrial Bank and Mniszech Palace.

"Whaddaya think?" asks Kaplica, nodding his head in their direction.

"Right-wing student groups, Piasecki's Phalanx men, just little pricks from the college. I don't see anybody serious over there," responds Szapiro, ever vigilant, tense. "But there could be some shooting."

"Them fascists not dare," declares Radziwiłek, pushing his stiff cap to the back of his head.

And I just stand there, stand in silence behind Szapiro and Kaplica and I listen, and watch, and stand there just like I'm sitting now at my green typewriter and writing down all I remember.

Pantaleon nods grimly and pulls his pistol from his pocket, opens it up, and one by one, checks all seven chambers in the cylinder. I think about his devil brother, what it's whispering, whispering, whispering to him.

Shoot shoot shoot punch stab kill shoot.

"Them fascists might dare," says Szapiro mockingly, though Radziwiłek doesn't even notice the joke. "In May they opened fire on a Bund march."

"They not dare," says Radziwiłek emphatically and pulls his right hand from his jacket pocket, clutching a pistol.

"Put your heaters away, put 'em away. Can always get 'em out again," Kaplica says soothingly, and they conceal their weapons, reluctantly. "Pick me up."

Szapiro and Pantaleon lift him.

"Band! 'The Warszawianka 1905'! Sing!" cries Kaplica.

So we sing.

March, march, O Warsaw, sacred and righteous, our struggle unites us! Warsaw, march on!

And we enter Bankowy Square. *March, march, O Warsaw.* A dozen thugs break ranks with the nationalist protest and rush toward us, stop, hurl stones and cobbles torn up from the road. Someone gets one in the head, blood gushes out, he falls.

"Let us pass!" screams Szapiro and our gang, armed with their pistols, fans out, a few men from our back ranks race out front and bottles and stones fly at the fascists. They don't retreat.

"They're not just college kids," murmurs Szapiro. "That's the National Workers' Party gang, they're real bruisers. Plus we got some college kids like Ziembiński."

He points out one of the fascist gangsters.

"There, you guys see him? There he is, that nasty blond son of a bitch. Standing there, with the NWP gang."

The NWP goons look normal, proletarian, like anybody in our protest or any other. Alongside them, Ziembiński is someone from another world, another species.

He towers a head over them, fed on different food as a kid and maybe formed from different genes, in a uniform shirt and black jodhpurs, holding his right hand in his pocket in an obvious gesture, not throwing stones or bottles, just giving orders.

"Let's move. Heaters stay in pockets. Munja, pipe," commands Kaplica and he rolls up his sleeves. Munja hands him a short steel pipe.

I understand his command is for me too, so we get moving.

I hold back, behind Szapiro, and it gives me great joy to watch him run nimbly up to the front-most fascist, a proletarian brawler from the NWP, who stupidly makes a wide swing. Szapiro ducks his sweeping sidewinder. I watch seemingly in slow motion as the fascist in the black beret is surprised, how on earth could this big Jew suddenly be so close and off to the side, and then this big Jew pounds a short brass-knuckled uppercut into his chin, shoves his chest, and the bold gangster plunges into darkness even before his limp body hits the pavement. More are already running to help, Szapiro takes down the first one with a short kick above the knee. To this day I can still hear the glorious crunch of the bone.

Then the next one, same again, a boxer's rotation under the punch, a knife appears in his opponent's hand, neutralize the knife, knuckleduster to the temple, shove the body away, next please.

Ziembiński has spotted Jakub now. He hesitates. He backs away, not itching for a confrontation.

Kaplica, small and mobile, is bashing his pipe into heads, forearms, and knees, breaking a few bones.

Pantaleon is roaring and smashing his fist into the face of a man he's holding under the arm, seemingly unaware he's beating the shit out of someone unconscious. But Pantaleon knows. Pantaleon wants the face of this man he's holding to be a completely different face from now on, so he's smashing his fist the way he'd smash with a stone; he breaks the man's nose, cheekbones, jaw, he knocks out his teeth, but he doesn't kill him, because if the man is alive his new face will be an eternal reminder of Pantaleon's wrath, fury, and darkness. He finally drops the limp body on the pavement, raises his arms high, spreads his hands, and howls, roars like a bull, then makes for the nationalists like he's hungry to devour them.

His right hand drips with his own blood mixed with his victim's.

The Phalanx is starting to fall back. They can see who they're up against, these aren't workers they're fighting. They haven't got anyone like Szapiro, Pantaleon, Munja, or Kaplica, anyone like us. The Phalanx men are true believers, even these toughs, these proletarians. We're professionals. So they retreat without panicking. Szapiro takes down two more, Pantaleon roars, furious he can't reach anyone.

Ziembiński calls the retreat.

Our band keeps playing, our workers keep singing.

Then the first shot rings out.

At least I think it's a shot, the others do too. Suddenly everyone is scattering in panic. The nationalists hide behind the low wall of the fountain, they on one side, we on the other, lying on the pavement.

"Don't shoot, it was a firecracker, a firecracker!" screams Szapiro, but it's already too late.

Pantaleon raises his seven-shooter over the fountain wall and fires blindly. A bullet strikes the elbow of a boy with a trident, but the boy's carved from stone and doesn't budge, continuing to hold up the large basin of the fountain. Kaplica squeezes off a shot from his Browning, into the air so he doesn't accidentally kill someone, since a dead fascist means problems. The nationalists return fire, also aiming high, over our heads, since a dead socialist means problems, and a dead gangster means enormous problems, probably having to get out of the city or find someplace to hide.

We'd rather not shoot someone like Ziembiński either.

Both marches, the workers and the nationalists, retreat in panic. The gangsters are left on the square. That means us on one side and the Phalanx and a couple of tough working boys from the NWP on the other.

Then I hear whistles. The gunshots stop. From the courtyard of the Treasury Ministry Palace emerges a previously unseen company of the State Police Reserve, in tight formation, menacing, wearing low German helmets and steel trench armor that covers their torsos and thighs, wielding oval-shaped shields and batons, as though from another era, like medieval knights.

Behind them, a gray-green water tank rolls out—an armored police car with a water cannon instead of a machine gun. Mounted police are on their way too. The tank picks up speed and without warning starts blasting water all over the nationalists and us.

"Well here comes the reserve," mutters Buddy to himself.

"Scatter!" shouts Szapiro.

Then Kaplica stands up, rising over the top of the fountain wall. He puts his pistol in his pocket.

"The hell we will! No goddamned scattering! The hell we will!" he roars. "I'm Kaplica, god fucking dammit, ain't nobody hosing me down, this is my city!"

He walks toward the police.

"They're gonna shoot him," whispers Szapiro.

But the blast of water bypasses the tiny bandit.

"Come on, you wanna piss all over old Buddy, huh!" shouts Kaplica, facing the armored policemen. He lifts his short arms wide, as if to invite them.

They stop. The cannon ceases pumping water.

Two uniformed men approach Buddy and salute. They speak briefly, but we can't hear what about. Buddy is smiling and happy, he's already on his way back, but then Lieutenant Czerwiński from the Penal Division of the State Police Main Command pushes through the cordon of armored police, in all of his bourgeois portliness.

"Nu, in ot iz du detsi de drayo',"[15] sighs Szapiro.

"Halt!" cries Czerwiński. "Halt! Arrest him!"

The men in uniform don't seem to hear his order. They turn their backs and look away. They know Kaplica's got every one of their addresses. So Czerwiński, who's known for being as brave as all the policemen in Warsaw combined, arrests Buddy himself. With a smile, Kaplica hands over his gun, using two fingers to pull it from his pocket so the policeman doesn't mistake him for wanting to shoot.

"Keep cool, Lieutenant, it'll all turn out fine."

"Silence!" roars Czerwiński, furious and at his wits' end.

They take Kaplica behind the cordon, load him into a car, and drive off.

"Disperse," says Szapiro and spins his hand over his head, sending a signal to the front of the procession. "The cops'll take care of 'em now."

The armored and mounted police head for the nationalists. The nationalists make a break for it, the mounted police whack them with the flats of their sabers, which we watch with great satisfaction. No policeman even glances at us.

That's exactly how I remember it.

I get up from my typewriter.

I look out the window. Nothing special, that same street, sunlight, white. I turn away. I want to put on my uniform. I open the wardrobe,

---

15 Well this weasel is just who we needed.

where bare hangers remain in the space left by Magda's clothes. I look for my uniform. Simple olive trousers with a short-sleeve button-down shirt, tucked in, with my numerous order ribbons over the left pocket and paratrooper's wings over the right. I look, too, for my red beret and brown paratrooper's boots to tuck my trousers into.

They're gone. I can't find my uniform anywhere. I turn the whole apartment upside down. Here are my civilian suits, shirts with long and short sleeves, ties, drawers scattered with dirty shoes, but no uniform.

Maybe she took it. Fine, tough luck, what do I need a uniform for anyway, I'm retired. The main thing is I've got my sidearm, my trusty old .45 with the rust scraped off. In my desk drawer, in a brown leather holster.

Struck with a sudden fear I go back to my desk and yank the drawer open. It's gone.

I phone Magda. It rings. I wait a long time, finally she answers.

"Hello?" says her voice, the voice of an old woman.

"Did you take my uniform and my gun?"

The response is silence. I can hear her breathing. She hasn't hung up, she's holding the receiver at her mouth and not speaking.

"Magda, did you take my uniform and my gun? Did he tell you to?"

"Don't call me Magda," she responds slowly, and I can hear in her voice she's very sad.

"Did you take them or not?"

"You need help," she says.

I hang up.

I go back to my typewriter. I recheck all the desk drawers. The gun is gone. For a moment I think maybe it was never here, but that would mean insanity, I don't want to fall into insanity.

I need to write.

After the demonstration we went to Ryfka's, where by now I was a regular, since I followed Jakub Szapiro everywhere, like a shadow.

By night I'd listen to him having sex with Emilia, by day we'd practice together at the Star gym, go collect money from market traders, and drink coffee, and vodka, and go for walks, and take trips in the car, and buy all sorts of things, me always in tow, Mojżesz Bernsztajn, the little shadow of great Jakub Szapiro.

Szapiro was hyped up from the fight, agitated, he wouldn't sit down, he kept fidgeting, hopping from one foot to the other like he was in the ring.

"Pour us some vodka," he commanded.

We were standing at the bar. Szapiro, Radziwiłek, Pantaleon, Munja, and me. Tyutchev, in his usual armchair by the door, was reading *Chuzhoe Nebo* by Nikolay Gumilyov. Radziwiłek, very calm, was sipping tea with Pantaleon.

Szapiro, Munja, and I were drinking vodka, Bykow was playing hits on the piano in his off-white tux jacket, though once everyone was really drunk he played whatever he felt like, he improvised, which was what I liked listening to most.

We'd already had three shots each, Szapiro ordered fried liver, which came promptly.

There were only three girls, since it was so early. Plump, blond Kasia with her ample, flat-nippled breasts, adrift in her ocean of indifference; Ola; and slim, dark Sonia, whom Jakub had a certain weakness for.

Moryc came as well, which surprised me, because I'd thought a man like him would have no desire to drink vodka in a brothel. Or even tea.

Now I'm surprised to think I knew so much about Moryc back then. Jakub never talked about him, not at all, I hadn't seen him since the single time at the Metropol, and yet I knew him, I knew him precisely.

Moryc wouldn't come drink vodka in a brothel.

Moryc wouldn't come to a brothel for the usual reason for coming to a brothel either.

Moryc had a conscience. Moryc had a goal in life. Moryc believed in the idea of a Jewish state in Palestine. Moryc did nothing he thought wouldn't at least indirectly advance the idea of a Jewish state in Palestine. When Moryc opened his eyes in the morning, he opened them for a Jewish state in Palestine. When he got out of bed, he got out for a Jewish state in Palestine. He ate, breathed, learned, laughed, worked, lived for a future Jewish state in Palestine.

It was a little hard to believe Moryc would drink vodka in Ryfka's brothel for a future Jewish state in Palestine.

But how was it Jakub and Moryc, born into a home like mine, a religious Jewish home, lived such different lives, since in the end they were so alike? Even physically, they were both powerful, seemingly heavyset, brawny, but also both decisive, spirited, powerful.

Ryfka poured everyone a shot. We drank them.

"Pass me the phone," said Szapiro.

Ryfka handed it to him. He dialed a number, waited.

"Quiet, Mr. Bykow," he snarled to the pianist, who stopped playing immediately. "Hello. This is Szapiro speaking. Good afternoon, miss. Yes. Szapiro, Jakub Szapiro. I wanted to speak to Mr. Litwińczuk. About Mr. Kaplica. Are you new there, miss? All right, tell Secretary Litwińczuk that it's about Mr. Kaplica. I'll wait."

He waited with the receiver to his ear, murmuring to me conspiratorially. Or to Ryfka. He was murmuring to someone anyway.

"Hello, yes, good afternoon, Szapiro here. Good afternoon, Mr. Secretary. Of course, about Kaplica. Yes, that's right, arrested. No sir, we won't wait until it's all cleared up. No. I understand."

He was silent for a moment, listening to some extended explanation through the receiver. Finally, ostentatiously rolling his eyes, he held it away from his ear.

"All right, listen here, Mr. Litwińczuk," he said, taking a different tone. Quieter, almost hissing, but in that different tone I could hear the same strength and decisiveness he showed when he stepped into the ring. "No, shut up and listen. Or hang up the phone, go to the prime minister, and tell him you just blew off Jakub Szapiro, Jan Kaplica's business partner. Yes, Buddy. Buddy Kaplica, yes. Yes, that Szapiro, uh-huh. No, Warsaw champion in 1935. Yes. But team champion."

When he heard the word *partner*, Dr. Radziwiłek, sitting next to us with some tea, shook so hard his cup rattled on the saucer he was holding up in front of him. I noticed the shaking and I'm sure Szapiro did too, but no one else did.

"Guess you don't know Mr. Kaplica and Prime Minister Składkowski have been close ever since they were fighting the czar with Piłsudski. You didn't? Well now you do. I bet the PM'll be thrilled. Yeah? Good. Good. Please, I don't know which station. Probably number twelve, on Daniłowiczowska. Well how am I supposed to know? Look, who's in charge of the police, me or Prime Minister Składkowski? Who oughta know? Right. I'll count on it. All right. We'll be waiting at this number. Goodbye, Mr. Litwińczuk."

He hung up.

"They'll call," said Jakub. "We wait. We gotta get Buddy back right away or he'll lose his shit. Gimme some more vodka."

She did.

"Question is, how long Mr. PM stays PM, to call PM about this," said Radziwiłek impassively, as though he were asking for more bread.

Jakub, still worked up from the fight and the boisterous phone conversation, jolted. He hopped to his feet at the bar.

"What's that you're saying, Doctor?" he said, cheerfully astonished, though after all he remembered his recent conversation with Bobiński in Art and Fashion Café.

"Different talk in city," responded Radziwiłek, not changing his tone. "Talk that Marshal Rydz-Śmigły planning something. *Mit diesem Oberst, wie heisst er?* United Poland?"

"You mean a colonel? From the National Unity party? Must be Koc."

"*Ja, ja. Oberst* Koc. Adam Koc. *Na*, so *dieser Oberst* and Marshal Rydz-Śmigły maybe want a coup as well? Koc make a deal with Phalanx? *Ja, ja.* Make alliance with *Nationalisten?*"

"The marshal and the Phalanx?" said Jakub, looking more surprised.

"Yes, yes. Overthrow prime minister. Overthrow president. Rydz-Śmigły become president himself. Yes, yes," said the Doctor, nodding.

Jakub shrugged.

"Does that affect us at all?"

"Affect, affect!" replied the Doctor. "They don't like Jews one bit."

Jakub turned away, deciding to change the subject to something more appealing, and gave his brother a jab, who so far had been standing in silence by the bar, focused, though relaxed.

"Hey, Moryc, Moryc, you come for a screw, yingele, a screw?" laughed Jakub, tipsy, and somehow I could tell his joviality was a cover for something, if not a certain fear of Moryc, then definitely respect.

Munja and Pantaleon were drinking grimly in silence.

"Kh'bi' gyekime' ousreydn a vort mit diyo'," Moryc responded, finally. "Zakh ibebeten."[16]

"Okay, let's talk, but we're in mixed company here, how 'bout in Polish?"

"Dus zene' yidishe inyunim, iz lome' reydn yidish. Rivkye, gis mi' araa', a glezele!"[17]

She poured. He drank.

"Yankyev, di miz' avekfurn mit miyo' kan Erets Yisruel. Dortn iz indzo' tsikinft. Du zene' nur di shmokes fin Falangye. Nish' ka gite tsaatn kime' far indz in Poyln."[18]

---

16   I came to talk. (. . .) To make up.

17   These are Jewish matters so let's talk Yiddish. Ryfka, pour me one!

18   You have to leave with me for Eretz Yisrael, Jakub. Our future is there. Here there's just those Phalanx bastards. There's nothing good coming for us in Poland.

"'Cause everybody over there loves Jews, right? They can't wait to head for the goddamn desert to make room for our state. Or why not Madagascar, huh?" snarled Jakub back at him, stubbornly speaking Polish.

Moryc hesitated for a moment. He indicated his glass to Ryfka. She poured, he drank.

"You're needed there, Yankyev. In the organization. There'll be tickets, everything paid for. For you, Emilia, and the boys. The train to Constanţa, by ship from there. The organization will pay for first class, because after all we know the great Mr. Jakub Szapiro requires comforts."

"I'm not going to some kibbutz," Jakub growled and took a drink.

"You wouldn't have to. Come on, no one wants to make you a farmer, Yankyev. You'd live however you liked. We need you in the Haganah. The Haganah needs people like you, soldiers. Powerful, strong people. We've got enough farmers."

Jakub understood how much it cost Moryc to swallow his pride and say something like that to him, to Jakub, whose life he scorned and whose immorality disgusted him. And he understood why Moryc was paying that price. Anything was worth it for the cause.

"I'm not a soldier, I'm a bandit and a boxer."

"You are, you are. Yankyev, war could break out again over there any day, full force, like last year, you get it?"

"But there's meant to be a truce, they're gonna make a Jewish state supposedly. Emilia said so. What's his name, Peel?"

"Peel. So it takes Emilia to tell you all this? You don't read the papers? What kind of man are you?" said Moryc heatedly.

"I read what I care about and I care about what affects me. Sports and the crime columns, and local news. What do I care about Arabs in some country a long way off?" said Jakub provocatively.

Moryc bridled, perhaps too theatrically, as though he wanted to start an argument, but suddenly let it slide.

"S'vet gurnisht zaan fin deym itsto', Yankyev,"[19] he said earnestly.

"Fin vues?"[20] Jakub also grew earnest and only now switched into Yiddish, as if it were the language designated for serious talk.

"Fin de yidisho' medine in Erets. Kh'mayn itsto'. Bald vet men arestirn al-Husseini in sho'. Alts vet zakh un'aybn fin s'nay. Di Hagana da'f hubm zelno'. Mentshn vi di, Yankyev."[21]

"Kh'bi' nish' ka zelno',"[22] Jakub said again and took a drink.

"Du devart indz nish' ka gits."[23]

We watched him: Moryc, Ryfka behind the bar, and I. We could see Jakub was thinking. That he was hesitating.

I get up from my typewriter. I think about that moment back then, I remember everything so exactly. The bar, the bored hookers in armchairs by the wall, I remember their names and faces so well, Ola, Sonia, plump Kasia, Bykow playing the piano, Ryfka Kij behind the bar.

Moryc is silent, there's nothing more to say.

Jakub lights a cigarette, takes a long drag, and releases the smoke through his nose.

Jakub's life is at a fork in the road. Jakub faces a decision.

Jakub thinks of some generic palm trees, sand, and oases he knows only from poor-quality photos reproduced in the newspapers. Of Arabs with white scarves around their heads. Of Haganah fighters in tropical uniforms with shorts and Turkish fezzes.

He thinks of the streets he loves and knows, where he is known and loved. On these streets, every hat is taken off to him. Girls in cafés ask for his autograph and blush when he asks if they'd join him for a

---

19 None of that's going to happen now, Jakub.
20 None of what?
21 Of the Jewish state in Eretz Yisrael. Not now, I mean. Any moment they're going to arrest al-Husseini and that's it, it'll start all over again. The Haganah needs soldiers, Jakub. People like you.
22 I'm no soldier.
23 Nothing good awaits us here.

walk—and never say no. The butcher sets aside the best cuts for him. The policemen salute him, because here comes the great boxer Jakub Szapiro, on foot or in his beautiful car with his beautiful wife and beautiful sons.

But out there, what will he have? Sand. Rifles. Commands. Palm trees.

Jakub smokes a cigarette and suddenly stands motionless, in reality or just in my memory I don't know, but he stands motionless, in his gray, double-breasted suit, white shirt, navy-blue tie, and black-and-white oxfords, he stands, resting his elbow on the bar, and decides.

"Go to hell, Moryc," he says in Polish, very loudly and distinctly. "Go to hell."

Radziwiłek smiles to himself, sipping his tea in silence. Pantaleon and Munja's conversation doesn't interest the Szapiro brothers.

I stand behind him, hidden, and inscribe everything on my memory.

Moryc shakes his head.

Sometimes a man gives a loud "no" and that "no" gnaws at him for the rest of his life. Even if he ought to take it back, he wouldn't. He's proud of that great "no." But for his whole life, it gnaws at him.

I remember that moment well, very well. And I want to describe it.

Jakub was resting his elbow on the bar. He was smoking a cigarette.

"Go to hell, Moryc," he said. "Go to hell."

Moryc shook his head, shrugged, had another shot, went up to Jakub, and swung to hit him with a hook to the jaw. Jakub leaned out of the way with no difficulty, pushed his brother back, and stood in position.

"Okay, come on, squirt," he snarled, and Moryc went for him, but before he could reach, Radziwiłek stepped between them and separated the brothers.

"*Nu*, enough. *Konets. Nicht schlagen* here, clear?" he said.

Moryc put his hands up.

"Iz faan! Gayts in dr'erd!"[24] he snarled and left.

"I could use a screw," said Szapiro.

The girls leaped up as if on command, all three approached him, including Kasia, the one I remembered best from my first visit to Ryfka's and from the visits after that as well. She sometimes turned her eyes my way, but more toward Szapiro.

Szapiro picked out Ola and Sonia. Kasia returned to the bottom of her ocean. Szapiro gave Ryfka a look.

I remember exactly the way they looked at one another, Jakub and Ryfka.

They loved each other once, that was clear. And she still loved him, that was also clear. But he'd chosen Emilia, it went without saying. He had children with Emilia.

Ryfka had no children. And suddenly I knew: Ryfka couldn't have children. I also knew Ryfka wasn't a prostitute.

I don't know if it would have changed anything if she were.

"Take good care of him, girls. Just how he likes it," said Ryfka, her voice flat.

He put his arms around them. They went off to a room. I stayed behind, no way I was going with them. I sipped my vodka at the bar and no one noticed me, I was a little, invisible Jew from Nalewki Street, Moyshe Bernsztajn, seventeen years of age.

But I know perfectly well what went on back there, in the best of Ryfka's rooms. What Szapiro would get up to with the girls. First, he'd watch a little, because he liked watching them kiss and undress one another, then he'd fuck them one after the other and in various configurations, brutally, wheezing and shouting as he did so, but he wouldn't come.

By the end the two girls would lie there completely exhausted, their crotches sore, while he paced the room with an erect cock, drinking,

---

24 Fine! You can all drop dead.

putting a record on the brown plate of the portable HMV turntable, turning the crank, and playing American music, Bing Crosby, Benny Goodman, Count Basie; they'd listen together, he'd lie down on the bed, drinking, they'd work his privates with their mouths and hands, without result; the girls would finally fall asleep while he'd go soft, not achieving what he'd set out to achieve, so he'd keep drinking; when he couldn't do that anymore, he'd snort cocaine and then drink some more, the girls would be already asleep in the big bed but he wouldn't be able to fall asleep, he'd tremble, lying between them, he wouldn't be able to drink anymore, so he'd only lay there trembling, and then he'd scream, howl, cry, curled up like a giant human embryo, naked, filthy, sweaty.

Once all this was over, Ryfka came in. She woke up the working girls, sent them on their way, and lay down beside him, hugged him, covered him up, stroked his hair.

"Emilia," he whispered, and she let it slide.

"Sho', Yankyev, sho'. Dus bin akh. Sho', sho' . . . zay riyik, Yankl, riyik . . . ,"[25] she whispered.

She only wanted him to calm down, but he was trembling in her arms, he didn't know where he was, he didn't know what was happening to him, he was only pain, fear, despair—everything he couldn't be and was not in the light of day. He cried.

I can't remember what I was up to then. Maybe I was gingerly sipping vodka at the bar, with everyone else?

Maybe I went off with some girl? I don't know. Everyone at Ryfka's was waiting for one phone call, that was the procedure.

Radziwiłek finished his tea and demanded a girl.

"Kasia will go," said Ryfka from behind the bar. "Just please don't wreck her like you've been doing lately, all right, Doctor? She couldn't work for a week."

---

25   It's over, Jakub, it's over. I'm here. It's over, it's over . . . Hush, Jakub, hush . . .

"I not prefer Kasia," replied the Doctor coldly. "Ryfka calls for another."

"But no one else wants to go with you anymore, Doctor." She lowered her eyes.

"Either Miss Ryfka find some girl or I take myself Miss Ryfka," said Radziwiłek.

"Then you'll have Jakub to deal with," she suddenly snarled, changing her tone completely.

Radziwiłek gaped at her with his cold, fishlike eyes. Right then I saw the threat was a serious one and that the Doctor genuinely feared Jakub Szapiro.

"In the name of the Father, the Son, and the Holy Ghost, amen," said Pantaleon, because he'd finished his third cup of tea. "I'd like to go home, Doctor. May I have permission?"

Radziwiłek nodded. Apart from us, Munja also remained at the bar.

"Let us have Kasia therefore," said the Doctor, finally. Ryfka nodded.

Pantaleon went home. Bykow closed the piano and followed him. Munja finished his quart bottle, which given his puny stature seemed like plenty, then made himself comfortable on the sofa in the brothel salon and fell asleep, snoring.

Kasia rose from her ottoman, though without leaving the bottom of her ocean of indifference. Radziwiłek headed for the rooms and she followed him.

Ryfka went to Szapiro.

"Keep an eye on the phone, yingele. And don't fall asleep on me," she ordered.

The cook and the kitchen assistant left too. I was alone. After a moment, the two sleepy girls Jakub had taken for the night walked past. They put on light coats then left to sleep off their work—and once again, I was alone.

What did I do that night as I waited? I don't remember. I could hear cries through the wall and realized they were Kasia's cries—and they weren't cries of pleasure. I felt sorry for her, Kasia seemed like a nice girl. I liked her. Then the cries fell silent.

I paced the salon, looked out the window. The curtains gave off the musty smell of dust, so I drew them apart, opened the french windows, and went out on the balcony on the narrow façade of the building slicing through Pius XI and Koszykowa Streets like the prow of a ship. And I stood at that prow like the captain of a stone ship, peering down Koszykowa Street, toward Warsaw Polytechnic and the Jerozolimskie barracks.

The night was warm, still summery. It was quiet, the streetlamps were still burning. A car drove past once, droshkies twice, a night street-car once, crossing Koszykowa from Chałubiński Street. I glanced at the grandfather clock in the salon, four o'clock, so nearly two hours until dawn. I went back out on the balcony and saw him again.

He was floating over the Polytechnic and looking at me. His eyes were burning, he was singing, calling me.

I am Jonah, I thought.

I am Jonah. I called out of mine affliction unto the Lord.

Suddenly the phone rang. I turned away from the sperm whale. I ran to pick up the receiver, but Jakub was already there, appearing as if out of nowhere, freshly shaved, smelling of cologne, in a suit and an elegantly knotted tie.

He picked it up. I hadn't made it in time.

"Hello? Yes. Fantastic. We're on our way."

Ryfka followed him into the salon, in a wrinkled dress and with mussed hair.

"They letting him out?" she asked.

"Sure are. Same as always."

"Where were they keeping him?"

"Like I said, station twelve. On Daniłowiczowska."

Radziwiłek stepped into the salon and sat elegantly on a tall stool by the bar. He was wearing only his uniform trousers and an open shirt. He scratched his belly through the shirt.

"Scrambled eggs with coffee!" he suddenly roared, as though speaking these words in a normal voice would be unacceptable before dawn.

"They're letting Buddy out. We gotta go," said Szapiro.

"They can even let out emperor of Japan. I breakfast first," replied the Doctor.

It seemed to me Jakub was trying to read more into Radziwiłek's tone.

"How 'bout we all eat?" said Ryfka, ending the dispute. "It won't take long. And how's Kasia feeling, Doctor?"

"She sleep," he said.

"Let's eat, then," said Szapiro, but I knew to an extent his acceptance was for want of other options, only making sure he didn't lose face in this little spat with the Doctor.

There was nobody in the kitchen, so Ryfka went back herself to put together coffee and the food.

"Go check on Kasia," Szapiro ordered me.

I got up, I went, still seemingly unnoticed, overlooked, imperceptible. I don't remember if Szapiro went with me. I have the feeling we went together, of course. I turned on the light in the room. Or Jakub did.

Kasia was lying on bloody sheets, faceup, naked, and also bloody herself.

The blood had caked in a thick crust on her plump thighs. Her face was smashed, her snub nose broken, with two black eyes and eyelids filled with blood as though she'd just come out of the ring, so swollen she definitely couldn't open them.

Szapiro touched her neck.

"She's alive," he murmured. "But barely."

I saw the anger gathering within him, birthing in his stomach, beneath the solar plexus, the small, hard black ball, slowly growing only to abruptly explode, fill up his whole body, strike his head, his glands, squeeze his diaphragm.

"I'll kill that son of a bitch," he snarled, turned on his heel, and headed for the salon. He burst in like a bull into the arena and threw himself at Radziwiłek, punching the Doctor in the head. The Doctor fell off his barstool, and Szapiro landed on top of him on the floor. The Doctor quickly realized what was happening, he pushed the boxer back, they rolled together, pounding their fists into one another, then suddenly both froze motionless, as though petrified.

"*Nu, molodets*, one move and Eduard shoot you through head," gasped out the Doctor, pinned to the floor.

The barrel of a gun was pressed to the back of Jakub's head. The barrel led to a Luger pistol. The Luger was in Eduard Tyutchev's hand. In his other hand, Tyutchev still held the book of Gumilyov's poetry, with a finger in the spot where he'd interrupted his reading. He intended to return to it shortly. Tyutchev's heart held nothing, not fear, not lust for murder, not anger, nothing at all. Tyutchev's heart was empty.

Pressed to the other side of Szapiro's neck was a razor blade, its handle in Radziwiłek's manicured hand. It had already nicked Szapiro's skin, a drop of blood was rolling down the blade.

"Calm, calm?" asked the Doctor.

"Calm," said Szapiro finally, releasing his grip and slowly climbing off the Doctor. He got up and backed away. Tyutchev backed away too, though he didn't return his gun to its holster.

The Doctor also got to his feet. He wiped off the razor on a napkin, folded it up, and placed it in his pocket.

"Be glad I not kill," he said calmly. "And apologize. Immediately."

"Go to hell, Radziwiłek," replied Szapiro.

"I very not like that. If I killed, I not have to hear filthy words. Be glad I not kill," declared the Doctor. He waved Tyutchev away, brushed some imagined dust off himself, then turned back to the bar, to his coffee. "When that scrambled eggs get here?"

Szapiro stood at the bar, next to Radziwiłek. The aromas of frying bacon and coffee were already wafting in from the kitchen.

"I'll make you regret that, you piece of shit," Jakub whispered.

Radziwiłek shrugged. Ryfka returned with scrambled eggs, bacon, and coffee and placed the food on the bar.

"Go to Kasia," Szapiro whispered to her, lowering his eyes. "Call for an ambulance first. We've got to take her to the hospital."

"The hospital just called."

"What?"

"Maryla. A john. She was about to leave, I just found out."

"Dammit to hell!" said Jakub, furious. "What is this, a plague?"

"It's always the way," replied Ryfka. "Maybe they slip something in at the water plants, bromide or something, and all at once nobody in Warsaw can get a hard-on, and if they can't get a hard-on, they beat up the girls. How about it, Doctor? Couldn't get a hard-on? You had to smash up your little doll?"

The Doctor shrugged and kept heartily eating his scrambled eggs, sucking on the bacon fat before he swallowed it. We didn't eat. Szapiro just had a cup of coffee, got his coat, and also took a camera—a small, elegant Leica—from a cabinet behind the bar.

Ryfka spat on the floor.

"I hope your prick shrivels up, you pig, I hope you get fucked in the ass," Ryfka swore quietly at Radziwiłek. The Doctor heard her curse but didn't react.

"Let's get out of here," said Szapiro.

We passed Tyutchev by the door. He was reading. He looked up from his book and peered at Szapiro with his sad eyes, without anger, more like with curiosity.

We went downstairs. In the darkness of the hour before dawn, the traffic was starting up. Christian workers were heading for factories. A policeman was strolling down Koszykowa Street. We got in the Buick and drove to Daniłowiczowska Street, through the slowly awakening city.

Sperm whales' eyes can retract into their bodies and bulge outward, changing the animal's field of vision. Even when they burn. I saw him as we drove up Marszałkowska Street, he floated over us, then stopped above the Saxon Gardens as we turned onto Królewska Street, and I lost sight of him in the glare of the rising sun.

I could still faintly make him out over the top of the jail as we drove onto Daniłowiczowska Street, and I could see the shadow of his powerful bulk on the chimneys of the Puls soap works, and the slow, dancing rhythm of his tail fin.

We parked in front of Police Station 12, housed in a former synagogue.

Szapiro took his pistol out of his pocket and hid it under the seat. We got out. The sperm whale was gone, only his fiery stare remained, his gaze fixed on me.

We entered the station. Buddy was waiting for us in the lobby, sitting in a chair, legs crossed, reading a newspaper.

I wondered why he hadn't left on his own, since he was free now. After all, he could have stepped out of the station, hailed a droshky or a cab, and gone wherever he liked.

He could have, but he didn't want to. And that was when I began, in a way, to understand. Kaplica was royalty and he required royal treatment.

"My friends!" he cried joyfully at the sight of us, rising from his chair.

The policeman saluted as we walked out, we all got into Jakub's Buick and drove out to Buddy's villa, at the corner of Puławska and Domaniewska Streets. We drove in silence, Buddy was tired, he said nothing as he observed the streets of the awakening city.

"I've got the address of that retired officer," said Szapiro once we'd arrived.

"The one with the throwing Jews outta the army? The one the Doctor wanted?"

"That's him. Number eight Kobielska Street, apartment eight. Bobiński gave it to me, because the *ABC* crowd and Piasecki aren't getting along right now, and it turns out this pip-squeak of an officer is on Piasecki's side, even though they were publishing him in *ABC*."

"Well you're gonna have to pay him a visit, Kuba."

"Will do. Today. First I gotta sort something out in Żoliborz district, then I'll head over to Grochów for this officer. Meanwhile, Dr. Radziwiłek beat the hell out of Kasia. They had to send her to the hospital. She's sharing a room with Maryla."

Buddy shrugged helplessly.

"If he does that again I'll kill him," growled Szapiro. "Tell him that, Buddy. I'll shoot him like a damn dog. He won't even know what hit him."

"You ain't gonna shoot him, Jakub, you ain't," murmured Kaplica as he got out of the car. "Unless you get an order. Then you will. Meanwhile have a good day, son, I gotta rest up now, I ain't gonna be in town today."

Szapiro shook his head, I could see the anger boiling inside him, somewhere in his stomach, under his ribs, steaming up into his head. But he didn't do anything.

Nor did I. I just sat in the back of the Buick, invisible little Moyshe Bernsztajn, little old me, little old nobody.

Jakub threw the car into gear, turned around, and headed for Żoliborz.

ד

DALET

I remember, I remember so well, us standing at the door of that white-collar Żoliborz apartment. Szapiro pushes the electric doorbell button. The Leica is hanging around his neck. After a moment a boy who looks about ten, in a handsome sailor's outfit, opens the door a crack, only as much as the chain allows. Jakub hesitates for a second, but only a second.

"Your papa here?"

"He's having breakfast," answers the boy.

"Outta the way," commands Jakub.

The boy doesn't understand, but he does get out of the way, Jakub gives the door a kick, the chain snaps, the boy screams, and we dash into the apartment, me trailing him, like always, like a shadow.

The apartment looks affluent but not wealthy, modern, a living room, two bedrooms, a kitchen—we head straight for the kitchen, where we can hear a female and a male voice shouting at their son what all this noise is.

They're sitting at the table, a man in a tie but no jacket, tall, fairly handsome, a prematurely aged woman, and a daughter with braids. They haven't had time to get their wits about them, Jakub's holding his switchblade, he runs up to the man, takes a large backswing behind his head, and plunges the knife into the man's hand, pinning it to the table.

Everyone screams. Then Jakub gets out his pistol.

"Shut your faces, intelligentsia scum," he says quietly and there's something in his voice, a terrible threat, that silences them. The man with the hand pinned to the table is trembling, he grasps his immobilized wrist with his other hand and feels a warm, dark splotch growing on the crotch of his pants.

"Bring that little squirt in here," Jakub orders the woman. "If you make a run for it you won't see your daughter alive."

The woman is back in less than twenty seconds. She wraps her arms around her children and squeezes into the corner of the bright, modern kitchen with them. The children don't cry, they press their faces into her withered breasts, they almost don't breathe.

I get the sense this woman is someone accustomed to violence. The kids too. I had friends like that in heder, whose fathers beat them more and harder than the others. You could tell them by the way they accepted whippings from the melamed, without protest, without screaming, their eyes empty, as though they'd left their bodies.

"What have you done?" the woman asks quietly and right away I can tell she's asking her husband.

The husband says nothing, Jakub also ignores her question.

His left hand seizes the husband by the pomaded hair on the crown of his head, he puts away the pistol, slips his right hand into a set of brass knuckles, and hits him.

The first blow breaks the man's nose. The second knocks out his front teeth. They're not knockout punches, Jakub wants him to feel them. The third blow on the nose again, his already-broken bone is smashed, crushed, it changes shape completely, bending into a *C*, his eyes swell up. Two streams of blood flow quickly down, onto his tie, onto his white shirt, and onto his fried eggs.

The fourth blow doesn't come, it doesn't have to. The man falls facedown on the table, unconscious.

"Last night your husband, and your dad, kiddos, went to a brothel under our protection, Ryfka Kij's. It was probably his first time, and definitely his last. He was unhappy with our girl's services, since she didn't want to get fucked in the ass, so he hit her multiple times in the face, knocking out her teeth and breaking her nose. I figured I'd give him a lesson in proper behavior. You well-bred Poles value proper behavior, right?

"Snap a picture," he orders me, lifting the master of the house's battered head up by the hair.

I don't know anything about photography, but I take one. Or Jakub does it himself. I don't remember. Jakub lets go of his still-unconscious victim's head and pulls the knife out of his hand.

"You got a phone?"

The woman, her mouth clenched, nods.

"In the living room," she whispers.

Jakub goes to the living room and dials a number.

"Gimme Ryfka," he says into the receiver.

"Ryfka, the son of a bitch got what was coming to him. Tell Maryla. She'll get a picture too. Yeah, Ryfka, I know. I know you haven't got any girls left. I know he deserved it too. Yeah. Ryfka, beating everybody up and castrating 'em isn't an option, unfortunately."

He hangs up, then tears the cord out of the phone.

"Let's beat it," he says to me and we go out the door, run down the stairs, and hop into the Buick.

"We're going on a picnic, kid," he says cheerfully, but somewhere under the surface of that cheerfulness, somewhere very deep, I can hear trembling. Jakub is afraid. It's not a physical fear, Jakub Szapiro doesn't physically fear anyone or anything on this earth, Jakub Szapiro doesn't fear Hitler who's fighting the Republic in Spain with his Condor Legion. Jakub Szapiro doesn't fear Franco, Stalin, or Marshal Rydz-Śmigły. He doesn't fear sharks or bears, not even polar ones. He doesn't fear bullets, knives, or cudgels, or the people wielding them.

Yet Jakub Szapiro is afraid of something.

He's smiling and talking about going on a picnic, but at the same time he's thinking of his sons.

He's thinking of Moryc, his brother. Of Emilia, his wife. He's thinking of the innocent.

The next thin layer of black substance spreads over the black pearl in Jakub's stomach. This layer holds the crunch of bones in a man's face from an apartment in Żoliborz district, his fear, his wife and children's terror, and that same layer holds the hookers Maryla and Kasia, beaten, battered.

Jakub has avenged Maryla, but Kasia he couldn't.

"Gyevalt fa' gyevalt. Andesh kyen dus nish' zaan,"[26] Jakub says to himself, once we're in the car and on our way to pick up Emilia and the boys. He says this as if trying to convince himself of the laws he's led his whole life by.

Maryla gets the pictures a few days later. She lies on the white, starched sheets of the Warsaw Jewish Hospital, standing at her bed are Ryfka and Jakub and myself, Maryla is holding the photographs with decoratively trimmed edges, the pictures show the man who beat her up, and he's worse off than she is. Maryla nods her bandaged head and hands the photos back.

"Thank you," she whispers.

And suddenly I realize this has taken away her pain. I understand and at the same time I don't, but I know it, I knew, I witnessed. The photos lessened her suffering, though admittedly not the physical kind. But some kind.

This happens a few days later. But the same day we avenge Maryla we have to force our way into yet another apartment, keep moving around that vicious circle, bring violence and accept violence, like in boxing, you take a blow, you return it, you eat, then something eats

---

26 Violence for violence. There's no other way.

you, you come from God and you return to God, you come from dust and to dust you shall return, when the microbes eat you that's violence, and when you squash a spider that's violence, everything is violence— so we go to visit one more apartment, from Żoliborz over the river to Grochów district, picking up Munja from the snack bar on the way, and before long we stand at the fairly filthy door of number 8, on the third floor of an apartment house on Kobielska Street. This isn't our turf. We have to be careful.

Munja, who arrived with us, stands guard by the car, his hand placed in an obvious gesture on the grip of the heater in his pocket; I can see him through the window of the staircase, a small, sharp-eyed rat, ready to bite. Szapiro and I are at the door. Szapiro with a briefcase, in a new suit from Zaremba's and a light English raincoat tied at the waist, and I'm elegantly dressed too.

Despite the early hour, a few shady characters look us over cautiously as they stroll by, and now they're standing in a courtyard entrance, but they know a bruiser when they see one, so no one even thinks to approach the Buick parked on Kobielska Street, since Munja is standing guard, ostentatiously armed.

Szapiro lays the briefcase aside for a moment and pulls on thin black leather gloves to hide the Hebrew tattoo with the sword on his right hand, then knocks. After a moment the door opens a crack, but still on the chain. Through the gap, the unshaven, sleepy face of a man in an undershirt peers out.

"Are you Lieutenant Górski?" asks Szapiro.

"Who's asking?" answers the sleepy face.

"My name is Mróz, Lieutenant, I'm a journalist from *ABC*. In July we published your letter responding to our survey about excluding Jews from the military, it met with a very enthusiastic response, and we'd like to talk to you about further collaboration."

"Mróz, from *ABC*, eh? Not sure I recall . . ." Lieutenant Górski is now alert, he peers at us suspiciously.

"From *ABC*. I haven't been in Warsaw long, I used to be based in Lwów. Dr. Zaleski sent us. We've also got that outstanding fee for you. In cash." Szapiro pulls an envelope from his pocket and I'm impressed by his foresight. "May we come in?"

"Ah, there was meant to be a fee?"

"Yes, naturally, this unfortunate delay is simply an oversight. That's why I've come to bring it personally, and also to apologize."

The lieutenant hesitates another moment, he looks Jakub over, probably struck by his Semitic good looks, but he unfastens the chain.

"Come in. Just it's an awful mess here, I'm an old bachelor, you'll have to forgive me."

We go in. The apartment is tiny, one room, a table, two chairs, a filthy bed, a sink. A shared bathroom in the stairwell.

Only now do I notice Lieutenant Górski is moving on crutches. He's about forty, very thin and disheveled. His right pant leg is wrapped up and safety-pinned four inches below the knee. And I suddenly see hesitation in Szapiro's eyes. Even though I can't see his eyes at all. I just know that seeing that wrapped-up empty pant leg, Jakub hesitates. He's already closed his fist around the brass knuckles concealed in his pocket, but now he loosens his fingers, releases the brass.

"Please have a seat." He indicates to Jakub a seat by the table.

Jakub sits, I stand by the window, appropriately modest.

"I won't offer you anything because I haven't got anything," says Górski. "Since you've got a fee for me, I can buy myself something to eat, some tea, a little vodka. So good thing you came. I was surprised you folks published me, since I'm more of a Piasecki man, and you're *ABC* . . . And I'm even more surprised you're paying, but every penny helps."

"There's no love lost between us recently, but isn't the national issue more important than factional disputes?" Szapiro is playing it by ear, like a born actor. "Small gestures like this make a big difference, when the unity of the nationalist movement needs to be rebuilt. But why did you send it to us, to *ABC*?"

"Because at least somebody reads *ABC*, but the Phalanx papers we've got, forget it."

"Your leg?" asks Szapiro. "We didn't know."

"I wrote I'm a war invalid. Battle of Komarów, gunshot, small wound, gangrene, had to amputate."

"Where did you serve?" asks Szapiro.

"Forty-Fifth Borderlands Rifles," replies Górski. "You a vet too?"

"Twenty-First Infantry. Platoon leader."

"The Children of Warsaw," says Górski, nodding.

"Uh-huh. Gave me the Cross of Valor."

"Maybe they thought you looked right for it," laughs Górski.

"How's that?"

"Well, you've got a sort of Semitic complexion, haven't you? Pardon me for saying so, but you could pass for a Yid. No offense, I know you're a good Pole, you've done a lot for Poland with the stuff you write in *ABC*, I just mean how you look," explains Górski, somewhat nervously.

Szapiro stops talking. He stares silently at the retired lieutenant.

"So how about that fee?" says Górski, suddenly interested. "'Cause, you know, there's no living off the kinda pension they give me. Not enough for food. I don't eat my fill. A war invalid, a veteran, and I can't eat my fill, that's the Jewish order we got in Poland."

"I'm not from *ABC*," says Szapiro suddenly, looking Górski in the eye.

"What?" says the lieutenant, surprised.

"My name is Jakub Szapiro."

"Szapiro . . ." Górski suddenly starts to understand.

Jakub gets up. He takes the brass knuckles from his pocket and carefully places them on his right hand without removing his thin gloves.

Górski is no fool. He quickly connects the dots. Just as quickly he realizes he has no chance in a physical confrontation with this two-hundred-pound Jew. Even on two legs he wouldn't have a chance, to say nothing of the obvious protrusion he's just spotted in Jakub's coat pocket.

So he doesn't budge from his stool, he sits still and eyes Szapiro. I can guess how furious he must be with himself. Led on by the sight of the envelope, he had no trouble believing this brawny guy who clearly looked both Jewish and thuggish might be a journalist from *ABC*.

"You gonna beat up a war invalid? 'Cause you sure are a soldier, I can tell," he said.

Szapiro stands before him and I can see him hesitating.

He didn't hesitate when he slit Naum Bernsztajn's throat. He didn't hesitate even for a moment. But today he hesitates. Though he hasn't come here to kill. He hesitates about hitting Lieutenant Górski.

He places his left hand, the one without the brass knuckles, into his pocket and pulls out a newspaper clipping.

"*ABC Daily News* from July seventh. 'We must simultaneously deprive Jews of full civil rights and impose a poll tax, with obligatory forced labor for the state in the event of evading the poll tax, in place of military service.'"

Górski swallows hard.

"If you don't agree with what I wrote there, you send an article to one of those newspapers of yours, not come after the author with brass knuckles, right? Or is this how you Jews do things?"

"Assigning Jews to hard labor is intended to achieve maximum benefit at minimum cost. All that is needed to organize hard labor are shovels and picks, a few old pots, lumber for barracks, and a large amount of barbed wire," continues Szapiro, and I suddenly understand why he's doing this.

He's reading that to work up enough rage in himself to do to Górski what he thinks he should.

But he didn't have to work up anything in himself to slit Naum Bernsztajn's throat. He killed Naum Bernsztajn, my father, like flood, fire, wind, or lightning kills a man. Like מוות, which he has tattooed on his right hand. Like death.

"'A large amount of barbed wire,' you sick fuck?" asks Szapiro, clenching his fingers around the brass knuckles.

Rage is gathering in him the way waves of pleasure gather as he moves inside a woman's body.

"You need a large amount of barbed wire, motherfucker?" he repeats, slowly building up his fury.

He hands Górski the clipping.

"Read," he commands. "The last section. 'Organization of Labor Camps.' Read, you little shit."

The officer reads out, his voice trembling: "I propose handing over the organization of forced labor camps for Jews to young Armed Forces retirees, commissioned as well as noncommissioned officers. We must use former noncommissioned officers to oversee the Jews' work. This will guarantee the Yids work hard, without excuses."

Szapiro takes a step toward him.

"So now, you wanna lock me up in a camp? Like some Hottentot?" he asks. "You want to keep an eye on me yourself? Put me to work?"

"Do what you have to, kike, just spare me this bullshit," replies Górski, raising his head. "You'll still live to see the day we lock you all up behind barbed wire."

Szapiro hits him. Just once, a short right hook to the left temple. Górski flies off his chair and falls unconscious to the floor with a *thud*.

"We're taking him," Szapiro says to me.

And we did. Or Szapiro took him himself, I don't remember, Górski was skinny as a rail, plus he was missing a leg, which made him a few pounds less to carry.

With Górski over Szapiro's shoulder, we went downstairs.

"Open the trunk," Jakub ordered Munja, walking out onto the street.

Munja was surprised, but he didn't dawdle opening the trunk, and got his Browning out just in case. Jakub flung Górski into the trunk that not so long ago had held my father Naum Bernsztajn on the way to his journey's end, then reached in and pulled out a coil of barbed wire he'd placed there in advance, and used it to bind the hands of the retired Polish Armed Forces officer behind his back.

"There's barbed wire for you, you son of a bitch," he said, and slammed the lid shut.

We got in the Buick, but as we pulled out, one of the shady characters hanging out in the courtyard entrance set off after us on a bike that was too big for him.

He followed us around the corner onto Rębkowska Street, still keeping pace, then a right off Rębkowska onto Grochowska Street, where Szapiro stepped on the gas and we pulled away from him without any trouble.

"They'll find us anyway," murmured Munja.

"We'll take the scenic route," replied Jakub and turned off Grochowska onto Zieleniecka, going straight from there onto the Poniatowski Bridge.

As we crossed the Vistula, I glanced upriver and spotted him again. He was floating in the air over Czerniakowski Port, nearly vertical, his tail hanging loosely, large as a bus, gray. He was sleeping.

Szapiro opened the throttle, the Buick's eight cylinders roared, and at that moment Litani opened one eye, and that eye burst into flame.

The sperm whale gazed down at us and saw us, saw us as we were, Munja, Szapiro, and me. Szapiro glanced over his left shoulder and suddenly slammed the brakes as hard as he could, so hard Munja smashed his face into the clock on the lid of the glove compartment, while Górski helplessly banged into the divider between the trunk and the passenger compartment. I managed to brace myself against the passenger seat and made it through without a scratch.

The tires squealed, the Buick danced for a moment, and came to a halt.

Szapiro put the car in neutral, stepped on the brake pedal, and stared openmouthed out the window.

That was when I realized he could see it too.

Litani peered at us with one eye and opened his maw, and sang.

The words I couldn't understand, but I knew what this ancient song was about and Szapiro knew too.

Litani sang of his power and his might from the depths. Will someone skewer me on a hook, will someone wrap a cord around my tongue? Will they drive a spike through my nose, will someone make me their slave?

All under heaven is mine, no man will fit a bit to my mouth.

"Cocksucking motherfucker!" Munja screamed, his eyes watering. His nose was bleeding.

"Don't be such a crybaby," snarled Szapiro and without even looking at him, tossed him a handkerchief from his jacket pocket.

"Why in almighty fuck didn't you tell us you were gonna brake?"

Litani drew his eyes into his body, rolled over on his right side, swung his huge tail, and swam upriver through the air, toward Saska Kępa and Gocław.

"My nose is fucking broken, you shithead, I broke my goddamn nose on this cocksucking dashboard clock!" screamed Munja.

Szapiro slowly turned in his seat, and then suddenly, before Munja could realize what was happening, pressed the barrel of his pistol—the small Colt 1903 with the pearl inlays on the grip glistening between his fingers—to Munja's head.

"If I hear one more squeak out of you, rat, you're gonna end up in the trunk with that bastard," said Jakub, his voice a terrifying whisper.

Once again I could see, I could sense the black ball of rage pressing outward, pulsing beneath his diaphragm. I knew it could explode at any moment.

Munja put his hands up.

"Easy, chief, calm down . . ."

Szapiro turned back, slipped the pistol into his pocket, and placed his hands on the steering wheel.

Blaring its horn, a small Opel truck passed us, and I saw Jakub consider for a second whether to race after it, chase it down, drive it off the road, haul the driver out of his seat, and batter him, kick him to death. But he didn't.

He took a deep breath, engaged the clutch, pulled the gearshift toward him, and slowly headed across the bridge, driving and breathing hard, doing his best to regain his calm.

He turned off the bridge onto Solec Street, from Solec past the church onto Wilanowska, and parked in front of the residential building for Bank of Poland employees, at the intersection of Wilanowska, Czerniakowska, and Okrąg Streets.

Munja looked at him questioningly, still pressing the handkerchief to his nose.

"I used to live here. On Wilanowska. Back with Ryfka. In this beautiful, bright apartment, looking out on the street and the church. No one's ever loved me like she loved me back then in that apartment," he said to himself, unexpectedly quietly, and yet to us.

"What'd we come here for, boss? For nostalgia?"

"I gotta make a call. Look after the car," explained Jakub, suddenly snapping out of his memories.

He nodded to me, we got out. There was a public phone booth in the apartment building, which I didn't know about but Szapiro did. He dug around in his pocket, found twenty groszy, slid it into the phone, and made a call.

"Tell Buddy we'll be there in ten minutes with the goods. He's alive. Make room in the back to hold him," he said into the receiver without saying hello or introducing himself, and he hung up without saying goodbye.

We went back to the car.

Munja handed the bloodied handkerchief back to Szapiro.

"Shove it up your ass," was Jakub's friendly advice, and we set off up Czerniakowska to Książęca Street, then farther, along Nowy Świat and Krakowskie Przedmieście, to Tłomackie, and then Leszno Street.

Szapiro parked at Sobenski's snack bar. He and Munja seized the now-conscious Lieutenant Górski under the arms and dragged him into the restaurant.

Inside, Kaplica and Radziwiłek were sitting at a table, Pantaleon was nearby, drinking tea standing up.

"Boy, this is some idea you had, Kuba, bringing him here," Buddy said and stood up to get a look at the crippled man.

"Didn't wanna decide on my own."

Górski lay on his side on the floor. The pant leg that had been pinned under his stump had come undone and lay empty on the floor, limp as a sausage skin.

"Well how you feeling now, ya fascist scum?" asked Buddy cheerfully, going up to Górski. "Fine and dandy, eh?"

"I'm not scared of you bastards," Górski replied haughtily. "Go ahead and kill me, my life's shit, I got nothing in this world to miss. I got nothing. I got no leg, I got no girl, I got no friends, can't afford a whore, and anyway I can't get my dick hard since I dunno when, can't afford vodka, can barely afford some dry bread. Just enough so I don't starve, no more than that. You've taken everything from me already, you Jewish cabal, you bloodsuckers, everything. I gave my leg for Poland, but turns out it was your Poland, Piłsudski and the frock-coaters' Jew Poland, and your Poland shit all over me. I got nothing. My life isn't worth a goddamn. I'd have killed myself a ways back, but that's a sin. Go ahead and kill me yourselves. I don't care. I'm not scared. You filthy kikes'll get what's coming to you. We'll finally find a Polish Hitler for you and he'll lock you in camps like the Brits did with the Negroes in Africa, just you wait and see."

Szapiro looked at him with a certain astonishment. It took a lot of courage to talk like that when you were lying on the floor missing a leg and with your hands tied behind your back with barbed wire.

"Fucking shit-eating Yids," added Górski and spat on the ground at their feet.

"Now you got that wrong, 'cause I'm a Pole," Buddy said cheerfully and kicked their prisoner in the mouth. "A Pole, a socialist, and anti-Semitism repulses me. So do little baby Hitlers like you, scum."

Górski spat a stream of blood and knocked-out teeth.

"All you motherfuckerth can thuck my cock," he gibbered through his crushed mouth. "Jewth, thocialistth, Bolshevikth, the thame fucking traitorth."

Radziwiłek finished his stuffed pastry, washed it down with coffee, rose from his chair, and approached Górski.

"I very no like listen to fascist when he talk disgusting, I no like," he declared.

"Lock him up in the back," ordered Buddy. "Mr. Sobenski, clear out some space there."

Pantaleon and Munja seized Górski, now bleeding profusely, by his bound arms and dragged him to the back room.

I remember it very clearly: one shoe dragging on the floor, the loose pant leg, blood.

"So what do we do with him now, Buddy? The clay ponds? Let him go? What's all this about?" asked Szapiro.

"Don't ask me, ask the Doctor, the Doctor wanted him," said Buddy with a shrug.

Szapiro turned to Radziwiłek.

"What're we doing with him, Doctor?"

"I take care, no worry," answered Radziwiłek. "For now leave him here, Tyutchev later take him somewhere, so we no trouble Mr. Sobenski. No worry."

"Great, 'cause today I'm meeting my wife, my brother, and my sister-in-law out of town for a picnic," said Jakub, with something of a challenge in his voice and perhaps also the triviality of this information, a challenge so clear even Buddy noticed it, giving Jakub an unhappy frown and a reproachful glance.

Radziwiłek reacted by finishing his coffee and leaving.

The phone behind the counter rang and Sobenski answered.

"Mr. Szapiro, Miss Ryfka for you."

Szapiro went to the phone, reaching behind the counter for the receiver.

"Thank you, Jakub," said Ryfka.

"Ne za shto," responded Jakub and hung up.

I've had enough writing. I get up from my typewriter. I walk to the window.

The same view as ever. The Arab boy pushing a cart loaded with a huge stack of furniture, old or styled to look old, bentwood legs and striped upholstery on chairs and sofas piled high. I've already seen him here. I have the feeling even the furniture is arranged the same as before.

Cars pass him. Next to the newsstand, an Orthodox man smokes a cigarette, waiting for something. A girl in a uniform passes him, a black rifle on her back, barrel pointing down.

Silence. The window lets no sound through.

And suddenly the doorbell shatters the silence. I go up to the door, look through the peephole, it's Magda. I open the door.

She comes in.

"How are you doing?" she asks.

I shrug.

She goes into the living room, touches the leather of my punching bag.

"You're training, huh?"

Again, I shrug.

"Just so I don't get completely out of shape."

That's not true, I'm not training at all.

I stopped training when Magda left. She never let me hang a punching bag in the house and for even the simplest, most routine technique I had to go to the gym. So when she left I went to the sporting goods store and bought a punching bag—leather, blue, large, 175 pounds—and I hung it in the living room, right in the middle. I had to ask a friend to help me mount the hook on the ceiling, I couldn't do it myself. He installed the hook. He hung the bag.

Since then I've walked past that punching bag in our cramped living room every day and never once touched it, but today I will. Soon as Magda goes.

She nods.

"Enjoy the holidays?"

I don't understand what she means, so I don't answer.

"Did you take my pistol? My uniform?" I ask.

She gives me a long, alert look, but doesn't answer. She goes up to the radio receiver, turns it on, switches it to shortwave, and searches for a frequency.

"You used to like listening to Radio Free Europe, and since January first they've stopped jamming it, did you hear?" she asks.

I go up to her and switch off the radio.

"How are the boys?" I ask.

She gives me another look. She sighs. Very, very deeply.

"I can't take this anymore, all right?" she says. "This pretending. I played along with your game a bit, but I don't want to play anymore."

I shrug. Magda takes her bag and leaves.

By the time the door closes behind her, I've gotten my bandages from the drawer and wrapped up my hands.

Fifty years ago, Szapiro showed me how to wrap my hands and I still wrap them exactly as I did back then in the Stars' gym.

I wrap my hands. I've boxed my whole life. Other people played tennis or soccer, but I boxed. I trained kids a little too, and I used to yell at them like a trainer yelling at some young whippersnapper at the Stars' half a century ago.

I warm up—shoulder rolls forward, backward, left forward, right backward, and reverse, jump up and down. Then jump rope.

When I jump, the old man's fat on my stomach and chest bounces up and down. It looks funny.

I practice my technique in front of the mirror, still bare-handed, so I have no trouble seeing the position of my fists: straights, steps, hooks, uppercuts, blocks, parries, rotations, dodges, then combinations and series, everything. It takes forty-five minutes and sweat's already pouring off me, and I get winded, but when you get winded like that you've got to stick it out, so I stick it out, I pull on my gloves, lace them up, use my teeth for assistance. Now they've got Velcro gloves, but I prefer laces.

And I have a good workout on the bag. For the first time since she left. I pound my gloves into the bag until plaster pours down from the ceiling. My neighbors don't dare to complain.

Well, maybe I wasn't actually punching as hard as it seemed.

And then I wake up. My hands aren't wrapped. I only dreamed the workout. And I'm too tired to do it awake.

But I think Magda really was here.

It's so hard to get out of bed.

◆ ◆ ◆

We drove to 40 Nalewki Street, Jakub honked, a moment later Emilia and the boys came down and all three of them climbed into the back seat with me, Dawid sat on his mom's lap and Daniel sat next to me.

"I'm not sure this is a good idea," said Jakub. "We didn't part on friendly terms."

"Which is why it's a good idea," Emilia replied, as confident as women are when they are clearly outpacing men in understanding emotional subtleties.

From Nalewki we drove to Gęsia Street, where Moryc lived right beside the Jewish cemetery, in a single room with his fiancée. Unmarried. I ran to get them and they came down a moment later. Moryc was wearing sporty clothes: knickerbockers, checkered socks, a light jacket, and a peaked cap; his fiancée, a secular, Jewish, ethereal, and raven-haired woman named Zosia, was in a floral dress. She squeezed in with us on the back seat, Moryc got in next to Jakub. He offered him a handshake, to be friendly.

"Zaa nish' bayz of miyo' fa' de avanture,"[27] Moryc said first, apparently somewhat humble, though Jakub immediately could tell Moryc was actually demonstrating his moral superiority, as always, by letting it go and not nursing a grudge.

"Kh'vel trakhtn vegn daan Erets Yisruel,"[28] he therefore replied, so his brother didn't get too comfortable thinking that a man of ideas held a morally superior position over a street bandit living for himself alone.

We took Okopowa Street to Kercelak market, where Jakub had some business to attend to.

We all got out. Emilia, Moryc, and Zosia took the boys for fried dough cakes, bought from the hand of a head-scarfed country granny on the very edge of the square.

Jakub went to Choromańczyk's restaurant to pick up the money he was owed, everything went smoothly, the requisite annotations went into his notebook, the cash made its way to his inside coat pocket, and we returned to the car, where everyone else was already waiting.

"How 'bout I drive?" asked Moryc.

Jakub stopped for a moment, for a moment he felt the burden of the cash in his coat pocket, gangster cash, and he saw Moryc's request was an absolution from that burden. Moryc, by offering him a ride, was really asking for peace. Without a word, yet with a smile, Jakub handed

---

27 Don't hold that argument against me, brother.
28 I'll think about your Eretz Yisrael.

him the keys and for a moment they were like brothers separated by nothing.

"Only Dad can drive the car!" shrieked Daniel, or maybe Dawid, I don't remember which.

Jakub chuckled and got into the passenger seat, Moryc sat behind the wheel, and we all once again squeezed into the back. We took Towarowa Street, passing the Jerozolimskie tollhouses on Zawisza Square, and continued on Grójecka Avenue.

Moryc wasn't a good driver, he was inexperienced, he kept jerking the car back and forth, but Szapiro went on patiently explaining.

If not peace, this was at least a truce.

On the way out of Ochota district, the road surface deteriorated, cobblestones drowned in mud, instead of apartment houses the road was lined with cottages, and a smattering of electrical wires was the only sign of modernity.

Moryc finally turned left off Krakowska Highway and we drove to a spot near the airport, then laid ourselves out on the grass with food and drinks.

Moryc and Zosia had brought sandwiches and white wine, Jakub had a takeout lunch from Choromańczyk's, Emilia brought gefilte fish. We all ate and drank.

"We're going away next year," Zosia said suddenly.

I looked at her. She was beautiful, younger and slimmer than Emilia and, objectively speaking, definitely prettier than her, though I liked Emilia more.

"Where you going away to? For long?" asked Jakub, curious.

"For good. To Palestine. In February."

"Well, I still want to get my last semester done anyway," added Moryc.

"Even with the segregated classrooms?" asked Emilia. "After what happened last year, when those bastards blockaded the university for a whole month?"

Moryc shrugged helplessly. Jakub took a large swig of wine from the bottle.

"The right-wing student groups are forcing their hand. And the Mutual Aid can't get a handle on them. Three-quarters of the Christian students read *ABC*. That's the other reason you gotta leave, Kuba. In the end the nationalists will make a deal with the regime."

"I know," said Jakub grimly. "A guy from *ABC* was telling me as much."

"Some friends you got, brother," said Moryc, shaking his head. "Anyway, give it a few years and they'll be in bed together. Nothing here for us. You could all come with us. Take the ship from Constanţa."

"Apparently they're plotting a coup," said Zosia, looking up from her basket.

"Who?" said Jakub, intrigued.

"Marshal Rydz-Śmigły, Colonel Koc," she explained. "You know, them."

"What do they need a coup for when they've got all the power, they're on the inside," said Jakub with a laugh. "At most they'll make a deal with the fascists, co-opt them into the government, and that'll be that."

Moryc concealed his smile. He knew what would come next and he was enjoying this—putting his brother in his place a little.

"Rydz-Śmigły and Koc want to strike at the whole left faction of the regime. All Piłsudski's orphans," Zosia explained patiently, with the tone of a good teacher. "They want to have a sort of Polish night of the long knives. Eliminate the old Piłsudski men and the president, and even the rest of them too."

"And who'll be doing the eliminating?"

"The Phalanx. Apparently they made a deal with Piasecki. They've already got a proscription list. That's what Koc's National Unity party is about, it's part of their power grab. The whole city's talking about it."

Jakub was listening carefully and Moryc was very pleasantly surprised Jakub didn't think it beneath him to have a woman ten years his junior explaining political complexities to him. Maybe his brother wasn't such a backward-thinking lout as he sometimes thought.

"And where do we fit in?" asked Emilia.

"Who do you mean 'we'?" said Moryc, provocatively.

"I don't know. Us. The Jews," she replied.

"But which ones? The Bund? Us? Those bastards from Betar? The Orthodox dimwits from the Aguda?" said Moryc—by "us" clearly having in mind his own party, Left Poale Zion.

"Well probably in different ways," replied Zosia. "Betar wants the same as these damn fascists: all the Jews in Poland better leave for Palestine."

"Well, more like Piasecki and friends don't give a damn where to stick the Jews, as long as they drive us out of Poland, ideally with one suitcase apiece," protested Moryc. "I mean, they're after our money, our wealth, right?"

"Yeah, especially yours," laughed Jakub.

"Betar wants a Jewish Palestine," Moryc continued, ignoring him. "Except just like Jabotinsky, they've got no idea about social and economic issues."

"I don't give a shit about Palestine or social and economic issues."

"Yeah, well," said Moryc, dismissively.

A plane emerged from a hangar, midsize, exceptionally modern for those days, with two engines on the wings and a twin tail. The engines were already running in low gear as it taxied toward the runway. Beneath a row of four windows it said LOT POLISH AIRLINES.

"What type of plane is that?" Jakub asked Moryc, who, all his friends knew, held a deep affection for aviation, with that unique love every progressive mind used to harbor for technology in those days. A love rooted in the hope technology could transform the human condition.

"A Lockheed Model 10 Electra," said Daniel. "Uncle Moryc taught me! I know all of them, Lockheed, Junkers, Douglas, all of them!"

"So is that a good plane?" Jakub decided to placate his brother by giving him the pleasure of enthusing about his passion.

"Very. Speed a hundred and seventy-five knots, range seven hundred miles, ten passengers. That American pilot Amelia Earhart flew one just like it on her trans-Pacific flight."

"Not exactly the best advertisement for the plane. She went missing, didn't she? I read it in the paper. And there's been no word."

"They'll find her yet, just you wait!" said Emilia.

"You could take one of those to Greece. There's a regular connection," said Moryc. "If you've got the money. Snap your fingers and you're there. Then from Greece, from Thessaloniki, by ship to Jaffa."

"But isn't it true the Brits aren't letting anyone in now?" said Jakub doubtfully.

"That's right. But the organization can help," Moryc assured him. "You guys'll see."

We were happy that day, I remember. Even I, a silent and almost invisible witness to all this, little Bernsztajn in an elegant suit, Jakub's shadow, the shadow of a man, the trace of a man, even I was happy as we sat on that warm September day on the grass near the airport, watching the planes take off until sunset.

The Lockheed was followed by a large DC-2, then a three-engine Junkers, both with LOT markings. I liked the DC-2 the most, the Junkers looked funny to me with its propeller on the nose next to the propellers on the wings.

And then over the airport terminal, over its tower, I saw the huge sperm whale, his body not slicing through the air like the slender cigars of the airplane fuselages but rolling up and down, as if the air were thick.

And he looked at me. Or at Jakub. And his eyes burned with red fire. He opened his toothy maw and spoke words that were words, but which I don't know how to, I can't, write down.

Jakub saw him too, we were both looking. The rest of our group seemed not to notice the whale, but I'm sure he was there, over the air traffic control tower, floating in the air, and I know he'd followed us there, followed me and Jakub, he had his eyes on us.

He snapped his jaw, said something again and again, then turned on his side, waved his huge tail, and dove, disappearing behind the building, and swam away.

Litani.

"So you're going back to school, huh?" Jakub asked, once night had begun to fall and we were loading the blankets, silverware, and leftover food into the trunk, which a few unlucky souls had traveled in before, including my father.

My father, Naum Bernsztajn, his body chopped up like a rooster for kappores. His head separated from his torso, his arms separated, his legs separated. The color of slashed and bloodless meat, like meat at a butcher's shop. My father's blood soaked into the ground, the blood of Naum Bernsztajn, who didn't have the money to pay Kaplica, and didn't want to run away, didn't know how to defend himself.

"That's right," replied Moryc.

"And you're going to sit in the Jewish ghetto seats, like some Negro? Maybe they'll paint them yellow for you, like Hitler did with the park benches. Or they'll blockade the university for a month, like last year?"

"Supposedly our seats will be marked with student record numbers. At the School of Economics and the Polytechnic they'll have letters. But I've just got one semester to go. Then we'll be out of here. You guys should come with us, Jakub. Our place is there."

Jakub reflected for a moment, then smiled to himself and shook his head in disbelief.

"And when do you guys start classes?" he asked.

"October seventh."

"We'll be there."

"I don't want you to be there."

"Moryc, do you want to be on your own against Ziembiński and his gang?"

Moryc Szapiro didn't answer.

"We'll be there whether you like it or not. This is our city. No baby Hitler in jodhpurs is going to tell us where to sit in lectures in our city."

"'Us'? Jakub, when have you even spent fifteen minutes at a lecture?"

Moryc was ten years younger than Jakub. When he was three, back before the war, his parents passed him over to a wealthy relative from Częstochowa to raise him, before passing away themselves. When Jakub returned from the war, he took his brother back from their cousins and raised him himself. At the time his own life was fairly turbulent, so he often left his brother in the care of some friendly aunts, but he never neglected his brother and was never out of his life for more than a few weeks. First he sent him to kindergarten at the Bundist Central Yiddish School Organization on Krochmalna Street, where the teaching was bilingual, in Polish and Yiddish, and Moryc was beautifully fluent in both languages, with no accent.

His third and fourth languages, Hebrew and French, he learned at the La'or Boys' Grammar School on Nalewki, not far from Simons Arcade, where Jakub paid fifty złotys a month tuition, and for that fifty złotys a month Moryc quickly outgrew his brother intellectually, and his brother was no dunce himself. Moryc also became a left-wing Zionist, in keeping with his school's profile. He wasn't such a bookworm or a pushover either—he wasn't scared of a fight and was quick with his fists. He was feared on the street, and not only because everyone knew who Jakub was.

Even so, Moryc quickly found Jakub's reputation a burden he did his utmost to free himself from. He didn't apply to college after graduating, against his brother's wishes. He moved out of Jakub's and rented a tiny room in a tumbledown building in Muranów district, got a badly paid office job, and spent the rest of his time organizing for Left Poale Zion.

A couple of years on he finally went to school, studying none too diligently and dreaming, dreaming of Palestine. He spoke Hebrew as fluently as if he'd been born under the palm trees on a kibbutz, not under the mold-covered ceiling of apartment 31 at 23 Nowolipki Street.

"We've got to go to Palestine, Jakub," he said.

And then we parted ways and each returned to his business, Moryc to his meetings and speeches, Jakub to his protection money at Kercelak and training young boys at the Stars'.

At night he made love to Emilia, and I listened to their lovemaking.

In the morning he had breakfast with his sons and I listened to their conversations.

A few times a week we drove to Ryfka's, sometimes he took a girl for himself, sometimes he drank and then he wept and howled in the night, and Ryfka hugged him and kissed him, and he was only ever completely defenseless with her, soft, as though crawling out of his boxer's armor.

He didn't cry with Emilia, he commanded himself to be a pillar of strength for her.

He also started getting money together and converting it into gold. And he started talking to Moryc.

About kibbutzim and moshavim.

About the politics of the Mandates Commission. About Foreign Secretary Anthony Eden and his eight thousand people for eight months. About Orde Wingate's eccentric exploits. About the special Haganah units, where someone like Jakub Szapiro would have no problem standing on his own feet again.

Jakub listened and daydreamed.

Meanwhile there was a lot going on in the city.

At the end of September Bobiński from *ABC* was on his way home from dinner at the Hotel Bristol bar, pleasantly tipsy and in the charming company of a certain young man. The young man apparently lived on Dobra Street, that's what he'd told Bobiński, and the watchman was meant to be very friendly and wouldn't get in the way; the young man invited Mr. Bobiński up for a glass of wine and a chat about the prospects of Italian fascism and the superiority of conceptualizing the nation as a cultural-historical community, rather than defining it in the racist German fashion, on the principle of blood.

When they took Karowa Street down the embankment, and the hour was late, they passed a courtyard entrance. From it, six men emerged.

They were wearing Phalanx uniforms, light-colored shirts and black jodhpurs. Bobiński immediately understood there would be no discussing the prospects of Italian fascism with the young man now running as fast as his legs could carry him toward the Vistula, nor would he taste his mouth, nor run his hand through his blond hair, nor feel the sweet weight of his muscular body.

So he reached into his pocket for his .25 caliber, drew it, aimed.

"Back off, you bastards," he growled.

They didn't back off. He fired the instant they leaped at him. They must have been betting he wouldn't pull the trigger. He hit one in the shoulder and a second later was on the ground, then two seconds later lost consciousness when they kicked him in the temple with a steel-toed boot.

They threw him unconscious into the back of a Ford truck.

He woke up forty-five minutes later when a bucket of water was thrown on him. He was naked and his hands were tied behind his back, pulled toward the ceiling by a rope thrown over a rafter, painfully twisting his shoulders.

On a chair nearby sat Andrzej Ziembiński in a handsome suit, smoking a cigarette. Once he'd finished it, he stubbed it out on Bobiński's forehead, then kicked him in the groin and asked if he was the one who'd revealed Lieutenant Górski's identity, then Andrzej Ziembiński's men pulled on the rope, and Bobiński's shoulders popped out of their sockets, and he felt like his dislocated shoulders were tearing him in half and he howled, and in that howl he managed to get across that he'd tell them everything.

He told them about Szapiro.

Ziembiński trembled with excitement to hear his enemy's name.

"Shove a bottle up this traitor pederast's ass then put a bullet in his head, stick him in a sack, weigh it down, and throw it in the Vistula," Ziembiński ordered.

Kazimierz Bobiński began to focus intensely on the taste of the mouth of a certain boy he'd spent a heady two weeks with in Rome the previous year, the taste of wine and pasta in a trattoria in Trastevere, the sight of the Alps out the window of the plane, and the soft hands of his mother, Aurelia Bobińska, née Rataj; then he suffered much, and then he died, and then his body settled in the Vistula, and remained there.

That evening Andrzej Ziembiński didn't feel like working anymore and didn't check in with his boss, Bolesław Piasecki, until morning.

They met for breakfast in the Bristol bar, the very place Bobiński had left the evening before with the double-crossing young man.

Ziembiński informed his superior that the retired war invalid Lieutenant Jerzy Górski had most likely been kidnapped by Jakub Szapiro, boxer, thug, and right-hand man to the well-known gangster Buddy Kaplica, and they'd have to think up a solid plan to get their hands on Jakub Szapiro, because he wouldn't be as simple to surprise as Bobiński.

Bolesław Piasecki, a twenty-two-year-old blond with his hair arranged in careful waves and a sandy mustache, swallowed a large mouthful of scrambled eggs and replied this wasn't news to him, since he'd been contacted yesterday evening by a certain Dr. Janusz Radziwiłek, a high-ranking officer in the Rifleman's Association, and simultaneously a collaborator of Kaplica's and an important figure in the labor and socialist movement in the districts of Wola, Ochota, and the northwestern City Center. Radziwiłek had asserted Lieutenant Jerzy Górski was in his power and he was open to a discussion. This gave Piasecki a wonderful idea to resolve a certain small, yet key, technical problem that had emerged after an all-night conference with Colonel Koc yesterday, namely the problem of one Buddy Kaplica's influence and his ability to mobilize the street, plus his connections in left-wing circles of the regime and the equally great respect he enjoyed from the dregs of society on Warsaw's Left Bank.

It occurred to Ziembiński that Kazimierz Bobiński had suffered and died for nothing, that all in all it was a waste of a man and an activist, though he didn't reveal this knowledge to his boss.

Meanwhile, Piasecki said he had a special plan for Radziwiłek and was meeting with him shortly, and if Ziembiński had his gun on him, then why not come along with him a short distance to Powiśle district, where the meeting was, since better safe than sorry.

Ziembiński had his gun, so they went.

Radziwiłek, who had a powerful sweet tooth, was sitting in Jankowski's little patisserie in Powiśle, at 19 Radna Street, one building down from the corner of Browarna Street. The patisserie was suitably small and modest for the neighborhood's underprivileged clientele: five marble-topped tables at one wall, a counter at the other with a display case full of sweets, and a kitchen in the back.

Radziwiłek was eating a pączki and drinking coffee, wearing his Rifleman's Association dress uniform, with a strap across the chest, jodhpurs, and glistening boots, since he felt the authority of the uniform would help him greatly to settle this issue. Tyutchev sat at a table in the opposite corner of the cramped room, turned to one side, as though he hadn't come with Radziwiłek at all. He wasn't eating or drinking, just wondering if there'd be a shoot-up.

When Piasecki and Ziembiński came in, Radziwiłek didn't get up, instead impolitely gesturing to a chair for Piasecki. Tyutchev waited.

"I'm Bolesław Piasecki," his guest began. "But I won't shake your hand." He sat down.

Radziwiłek bridled. "Have a seat, Mr. Piasecki, I have no need of a handshake from you," he said in completely correct Polish—so different from the broken Polish he used in our company. At least, I think he did.

Piasecki only ordered a coffee. He looked with disdain as Radziwiłek ordered a third pączki with rose hip jelly filling, eating it with gusto and no manners whatsoever.

"Well?" he finally asked.

The Doctor blew some crumbs off the sleeve of his uniform.

"I've got that bastard," he replied. "And I can punish him for the filth he's been writing in that newspaper of yours, or I can give him back to you."

"We don't want him back. That alcoholic cripple is no use to our cause. Human ballast."

Radziwiłek thought for a moment and looked at this fascist with the respect reserved for an adversary who is as repugnant as he is sophisticated.

"And yet you're meeting with me," Radziwiłek finally said.

Piasecki grinned broadly. Radziwiłek peered at him and slowly began to see he shouldn't underestimate this jumped-up kid.

"Go ahead and punish him," Piasecki said. "Brutally. But so the blame falls on Kaplica."

Radziwiłek turned his eyes to heaven, where it would seem this young fascist had fallen from.

"And what will I get in return, Mr. Piasecki?"

"A lot's going to change in Poland before long. And you'll take Kaplica's place and you'll have our sympathy once things have changed a lot in Poland, and I do mean a lot. And you know, Doctor, those who've protected Kaplica so far, all the old Piłsudski men, they won't protect him anymore."

"But you know I'm a Jew, don't you?" asked Radziwiłek seriously, brushing crumbs from the breast of his uniform.

"In the new Poland, my friend, it may transpire that I am the one who determines who is a Jew and who isn't," said Piasecki, smiling with a confidence so impudent it even impressed Radziwiłek.

"When?" asked the Doctor simply, ignoring the offensive "my friend."

"In a few days. October eighth."

"What guarantee are you giving me?" Radziwiłek pressed him further.

"My word. Well I guess that's everything then, isn't it?" asked Piasecki, rising from his chair.

"No, not yet," said the Doctor, and Piasecki sat down again. "There are plenty of ways you could try to hit Kaplica. Even without committing one of your men."

Piasecki thought for a moment, stroking his mustache. He saw it wasn't worth lying.

"My organization has important business to carry out. Maybe the most important in the history of our nation," he said, suddenly growing impassioned. "Poland must be great or perish. Only we, I, my organization can give her that greatness, no one else. Our empire will rise and it will rise even if it has to rise from our blood, understand? You don't, because you people think differently, but it's true. Yet my organization seems to be wavering. We have enemies inside our movement and, naturally, among our opponents. We need a sacrifice, a sacrifice that will strengthen and unite us."

"You're looking for your own Horst Wessel, *ja*? Or Gustloff?" asked Radziwiłek, disappointed by Piasecki's passion. He'd taken him for someone more intelligent, but he rightly viewed all enthusiasm as a sign of stupidity.

Piasecki smiled to himself.

"Sure, why not. We're looking for our own Horst Wessel or Gustloff."

"And here we have a war hero, but a one-legged alcoholic is no loss as far as the organization is concerned. It's all clear."

"As day. Now why don't you tell me what's in it for you? This Górski. I get it, he's an anti-Semite, but there's no shortage of those. I'm an anti-Semite too."

Radziwiłek stared at him, fiddling with his rifleman's cap on the tabletop.

"He wrote about lumber and barbed wire. To lock us up in camps," he said finally.

"And that's why you kidnapped him? Because he wrote about lumber?"

Radziwiłek shrugged and smiled to himself.

"Dr. Radziwiłek. I'll make a call from here to a certain prosecutor who can help us with this. I think he'll come quickly. He's the father of one of my people, of my right-hand man. Will you wait?"

"I'll wait. As long as I don't have to talk to you anymore," he said.

So he sat, eating pączkis, and waited.

Prosecutor Ziembiński arrived fifteen minutes later. Radziwiłek got up and offered him his hand, then Ziembiński greeted Piasecki, they sat down, ordered coffee, and the Doctor and the young fascist lay out everything there was to lay out. The prosecutor responded, offering his suggestions to resolve this matter, which by now they had established lay in their mutual interests.

"And one more thing," the prosecutor added finally. "I want Szapiro behind bars."

"Out of the question," said the Doctor. "First of all, he's the key to all of this holding together. I need him."

"Goddamn it, that murderer goes to my tailor! I can't get my clothes made in the same store as a murderer!"

"Please don't yell," said Radziwiłek calmly, fixing his expressionless, dead-fish gaze on Ziembiński.

Ziembiński found that gaze terrifying. He feared almost nothing, but that gaze he found terrifying.

"You'll have to make do with Kaplica, Prosecutor. Szapiro is a street hero, the people love him. Me they don't. It should be the other way around, but I can't do anything about that. If I let you take Szapiro away from them, in the end some little shit will put a knife or a bullet in my back. I won't give him to you, Prosecutor."

"I have no desire to rub shoulders with gangsters at my tailor!"

"Then get a new tailor," said Radziwiłek, just as Marie Antoinette, with regal coolness, had advised the poor to eat cake rather than bread.

The prosecutor harrumphed and stroked his English mustache. For a moment he couldn't accept defeat, yet the longer he resisted internally, the clearer it became. He finally got up, coldly said goodbye, and left with Piasecki.

Radziwiłek ordered another pączki with rose hip jelly.

It must have gone something like that. That's how I imagine it, that's how I reconstruct it based on what was once told to me, what I've interpreted, it must have gone something like that.

❖ ❖ ❖

I haven't written for a few months. Or longer. I don't know. I'm not sure. I haven't written in a long time, but today I'm sitting down at my typewriter again and writing.

In spite of it all, those were beautiful times, in their way. Back then.

A few days after the picnic, Jakub gave me my first pistol, a Spanish .25 caliber, and taught me how to shoot, our bullets shattering bottles in the woods of Bielany district, far behind the Central Institute of Physical Education. We stood shoulder to shoulder, shooting, pistols held high in our right hands, our elbows slightly bent, like in shooting competitions, the empty beer bottles we'd lined up on a wooden cross-bar burst so beautifully, bang, bang, bang, bang.

I guess that's how it was, it seems that way. Or maybe it was only Jakub shooting. But we were living.

But today, now, there's no living anymore.

This morning I saw on TV they killed Abu Jihad. In Tunis.

Our commandos killed him. We won't admit it. And I find out from TV and I can only guess it was our commandos, I don't even know what unit, though of course I have my suspicions. Only suspicions. But I should be one of the ones advising the whole operation. And two or three years from now I should be someone who'd plan the whole thing. But now I never will.

No hunching over military papers. And no more crawling over the sand all night with a rifle in my hand, or plunging a knife into a guard's neck, all that's behind me now.

I'm out of cigarettes. But I won't leave the apartment anymore, not at all.

I feel like I've forgotten Hebrew. Now I only think in Polish. I forgot Yiddish a long, long time ago.

I haven't written for a long while. And I wasn't planning to write today either. The typewriter stayed under its cover. I ate a little dry bread, two tomatoes, drank a Coke, turned on the TV. They were showing a rebroadcast of Holyfield's bout with de León last week, so I watched the whole thing.

In the first round, de León danced bravely around Holyfield, guard low. The same way Jakub fought with one of the Doroba brothers. He kept changing the rhythm of his steps, throwing hooks at his torso, Holyfield barely got in a couple of straight punches, one hit its target.

In the second round he went on offense, pushed de León up against the ropes and started bashing away, in contact, with uppercuts all over his torso. Bam, bam, bam, impassive and implacable, as though tender-izing meat for a cutlet, like Polish women did, I remember they'd pound pork to make cutlets once in a blue moon, pork was expensive. Emilia, gorgeous Emilia, Szapiro's wife, also pounded pork for cutlets, like the Polish women, like Holyfield arduously and implacably bashing away on de León's torso.

Even here I sometimes hear the blows of mallets on meat, pounding, wham, wham, wham, but maybe it just seems that way, maybe it's some distant afterimage.

But I can hear, upstairs, downstairs, mallets pounding meat.

I don't know.

I left my brother. I left my mother. For good. I didn't want to leave them for good. Once I was in Palestine, I wrote them a letter, then another, they never wrote back to me; they would have had time, I wrote in January 1939, months before the invasion. They could have written back. They didn't. Maybe they changed their address? They didn't write back. Maybe they came to Palestine? My whole life I told myself that. Maybe they went to New York. Maybe to Palestine. Maybe anything. I didn't try to look for them, though I'm just the sort of person who could have found them, after all. I've found others, when ordered to, when asked.

Holyfield was pounding de León's torso, constantly pressing him to the ropes, then he moved the pummeling up to de León's head; de León tried a few times to fight back, but his punches were weak, very weak. After the second round, a commentator asked Mike Tyson, who was sitting in the audience, about the fight and he babbled something, I don't know, I don't speak English. Tyson was in a beige suit and had a part shaved into his frizzy hair. I don't like Tyson.

After Tyson's statement there was a cut in the rebroadcast, and suddenly it jumped to the seventh round. Holyfield hit de León a few times in the head, so he was barely staying on his feet. By the eighth it was a bloodbath: de León was only standing because he was leaning on the ropes, Holyfield bashing him in the head, finally the ref cut the fight short.

I was full of admiration for the loser, de León. To take a beating like that and stay on your feet, that was something. Then came the news and they reported on the death of Abu Jihad. Then I took a shower and called Magda.

"Hello?" a man's voice answered. In Polish.

I also responded in Polish. In Polish I asked this jerk who he was, what he was doing in my wife's apartment, what right he had to pick up the phone, and if he knew who I was, and if he really wanted to cross me. Someone like me.

"Hey, it's him calling again . . ." He kept speaking Polish, loudly, but not into the receiver.

I heard some answer from the depths of her new apartment, but her voice was so muffled I couldn't make out what. And I heard nothing more, because after her answer he hung up.

So she probably told him to hang up.

I guess I'll get back to writing now. I'll just eat something first. And maybe work out a little. I don't know who's bringing me food, because there's always something in the fridge. Something modest, but always something. Maybe Magda, my love, my darling Magda Aszer, who's been with me my whole life, from Warsaw to Tel Aviv, maybe it's her bringing me food, when I'm asleep, she's got keys after all.

Or one of my sons, Aviram or Yo'av, my sons, who can both call themselves *sabras* with their heads held high, maybe one of them, grateful my Aliyah allowed them to be born on Israeli ground, not in cursed and blood-soaked Poland, maybe one of them comes in at night and in gratitude fills my fridge. I've got a can of ground meat, eggs, a few tomatoes.

No, I'll eat after my workout.

So I put on a tracksuit, wrap my hands, carefully, slowly. I mean to jump rope to warm up, but I can't jump rope anymore, the rope wraps around my feet, so instead I do some running in place, then add alternating punches to make it a boxer's run.

My body isn't listening to me. I can see myself in the mirror. An old man. I look twenty years older. I'm sixty-eight, I look eighty-eight. I'm trying to do the boxer's run and I can't even look at it, my legs won't come off the floor, I'm flopping around in place like an old fart. I can barely raise my arms to shoulder height, in a pitiful, senile parody of what were once dynamic straights, hooks, and uppercuts, like someone cracking a whip.

In the mirror I see Jakub Szapiro working out fifty years ago, his quick, muscular legs running in place and his feet barely touching the floor, brushing it, bouncing right off it, his fists flying out in front of him and returning to his jaw, as though tugged by an invisible spring, he's one giant spring, tensed, flexible, and that's how he is later in the ring, his feet not still for a single second and his whole body moving in that secret, unfathomable choreography of his, head side to side, up and down, in a circle and in a triangle, complicated arrangements of his hands in his gloves, his feet, and his hips, nothing spontaneous, only hundreds of different memorized combinations of arrangements for his limbs, torso, and head, and seeking, seeking, seeking, seeking an opening between his opponent's fists, between the lines of punches and the planes of blocks and parries, and finding an opening; Jakub Szapiro knew better than anyone how to thrust his glove into that opening and make his opponent collapse to the ground, so Szapiro could light up a cigarette, because for some mysterious reason his lungs could work despite the tobacco smoke.

He was the only boxer I knew who could smoke the day before a fight or even the day of, and then despite everything not get winded.

I used to be like that too.

And now here I am in the mirror, an old geezer. Loose skin on flabby shoulders. Wobbly knees.

But no, I won't allow myself this. I pull myself together, another minute of the boxer's run, I try to pull my feet up off the floor, but it's like they're glued there. I try to throw punches, but I can't, I don't know how, I don't know how, but I try and finally I feel an awful pain in my rib cage and fall to the floor.

I regain consciousness an hour later. I'm not in pain anymore, I've just got a bruised hip. I crawl to the table, pull myself up on it, stand, remove my gloves. I fry myself an egg, slice some bread, try to eat, but I have no appetite. I make coffee, I return to my desk, its drawer no longer holds my handgun.

Magda took it for sure. Or Aviram. Or Yo'av. One of them took it. And my uniform too.

I pull the green cover off the typewriter. I want to write again.

I want to write about the start of the 1937–1938 academic year, about Moryc going to class.

◆ ◆ ◆

They came to the lecture hall mixed in among the crowd of Jewish students, even wearing student caps, and sat scattered around in the Jewish section. Neither the professor, who couldn't yet recognize his students' faces, nor the right-wing Christian students realized. Only Pantaleon got left in the hallway, because he was a head taller than the tallest Jewish student and would have attracted too much attention. Jakub brought fifteen people, there were seventy from the right-wing student groups, but the quality of combatants mattered more here than their number.

Moryc Szapiro was the last to enter, he closed the doors of the lecture hall, waited for the professor to take his place behind the lectern, then sat in a Christian seat.

"Sit where you goddamn belong, dirty kike," said the student sitting next to him in an elite fraternity cap.

Moryc smiled broadly at him.

"Get the hell over to the Jewish seats or I'll kick your ass over there," the fraternity boy said, rising to his feet.

"You'll really regret it," replied Moryc.

The fraternity boy slammed his fist into Moryc's ear. Moryc didn't duck, he wanted that first punch to land, but it hurt.

"Gentlemen, what's going on there?" asked the professor, indignant, from the majesty of his lectern.

"Some little Yid is sitting in the wrong seat!" someone shouted.

"Please watch your mouth . . . ," began the professor, but he didn't finish, because at that moment he noticed a bottle flying toward him, which Munja had thrown with characteristic skill. The professor ducked and hid behind his lectern.

And so it began.

The frat boy was trying to land a second hit on Moryc, but this time the younger Szapiro brother ducked effectively, grabbed the Pole by the wrist and arm, threw him to the ground, and twisted his arm behind his back.

The frat boy screamed a surrender, but Moryc didn't let him go until something crunched in the kid's shoulder and he fainted.

Then Jakub and his men, hidden in the Jewish section, got up and made for the Poles.

Jakub kicks the first one, a kid in a different fancy fraternity cap, in the stomach, then delivers an uppercut to the jaw, and the boy tumbles like a rag doll over the balcony railing of the Auditorium Maximum and falls to the lower level, crashing onto the desks and armrests, breaking both arms. Afterward they'll put those arms in casts, screwing the right one together, and for eight weeks his mother will have to wipe his ass like she used to way back when.

On the main floor of the lecture hall, Pantaleon Karpiński whacks the second one in the head with a loose, open palm and the boy goes limp like a leftover liverwurst skin and falls between two rows of seats, unconscious.

That's the first two.

"Violence! Call the police, the police!" wails Professor Paliński behind his lectern and curls up tight, because he can already see massive Pantaleon Karpiński heading his way, roaring and leaping over rows of seats like an Olympic hurdle jumper.

There's nothing more beautiful, thinks Pantaleon, than beating up someone like the professor, someone you can't beat up on a normal day. Where's the joy in thrashing a beggar or roughing up a Hasid who owes you money? But beating up someone in a morning coat and pince-nez, someone who lives in a house with a few servants and has manicured fingernails—that's a very rare pleasure, and there's even more joy in the anticipation.

◆ ◆ ◆

And now Pantaleon Karpiński stands on the lecture platform, gripping Professor Paliński by the hair and holding a revolver to his temple. The professor's pince-nez lies on the floor, smashed under Pantaleon's shoe.

The disorderly brawl shows no sign of stopping. People are fighting among seats and desks and Szapiro's people have the clear advantage, but it's hard to say they're beating the nationalist students, there are too many of them and new ones keep springing up in place of their fallen comrades.

Then Szapiro gives Pantaleon a signal and Pantaleon takes the barrel of the gun off the professor's temple, raises the gun over his head, and shoots into the high ceiling of the hall. The professor, convinced somewhat illogically he has heard the bang of a fatal shot, empties his bowels.

The tumult dies down.

"Now the professor will begin the lecture," says Pantaleon and returns the barrel of the revolver to the professor's temple.

"This is violence, assault," replies the professor in a weak voice, watching helplessly as a dark spot grows on his crotch. "I protest."

"Talk!" roars Pantaleon.

And in a trembling voice, the professor begins his lecture on Roman law.

"All right, students, sit down right where you are," says Szapiro, also holding a pistol in his hand. And Brownings, Walthers, and seven-shooters appear in many other hands.

The students sit down. Munja blocks the entrances to the hall with metal bars.

The students obediently listen to the lecture for fifteen minutes, clenching their fists and contemplating revenge, or, in the case of the more fainthearted ones, mentally reciting the Lord's Prayer, performing acts of contrition, and begging the Christian God to protect them from death.

After fifteen minutes the police burst into the lecture hall.

By sheer coincidence, just as the police are battering down the doors to the Auditorium Maximum, less than half a mile from the hall, Commander-in-Chief of the Armed Forces Marshal Edward Rydz-Śmigły and his right-hand man Colonel Adam Koc are leaving the Palace of the Council of Ministers after attending a stormy meeting of the Council's Presidium. Then, since the day is so beautiful, they make their way on foot to Simon & Stecki's restaurant, also nearby.

"Have you seen this, Marshal?" asks the colonel, passing Rydz-Śmigły the first page of the *Courier*.

"Fresh crayfish, lobsters, and oysters, starting today at Simon and Stecki's," reads the marshal out loud. "Well there you have it."

They could drop into the Bristol, but Simon & Stecki's is more discreet. Following at a polite distance are three armed and uniformed bodyguards. In their holsters, as per regulations, are Brownings: loaded and with the safeties off.

Attending the Presidium meeting earlier—in addition to the ministers, Prime Minister Sławoj Składkowski, the governors, and numerous assistants and secretaries—was President of the Republic Ignacy Mościcki himself.

During the meeting, Colonel Koc openly accused the governor of Silesia of sabotaging his efforts to expand the National Unity party. Colonel Koc also demanded the liquidation of the labor unions.

"Instead of unions, let us assemble trade corporations, as Dollfuss did in Austria and as Schuschnigg is continuing," he declaimed, gesturing like a priest giving a homily. "Let us liquidate all the political parties and integrate their structures into National Unity. Poland does not need political factionalism, Poland needs unity," he said, to the fury of the welfare, finance, and agriculture ministers, allies of the president known for their left-liberal views.

Now that the meeting is over, Rydz-Śmigły and Koc have matters to discuss, which the president, and especially the prime minister, should know nothing about, and their current location, a private dining room secluded from the other customers at Simon & Stecki's, is the perfect place for doing so.

The waiter pours shots of aged vodka and serves herring in olive oil, sardines, and steak tartare as appetizers.

The marshal waits for the waiter to go. He rubs his bald spot. The waiter leaves. Discretion is said to be a waiter's first virtue, but one never knows.

"Report," he commands.

"You've already heard some, sir."

"Report the rest. About the preparations for our purge, as the Soviets call it."

Koc drinks a shot of aged vodka, takes a bite of food, then stands to poke his head out the door of the private room.

"Don't let anyone in, Sergeant," he says to one of the bodyguards. "Until I say so. No one. Guns at the ready."

The guard nods, salutes, and takes his Browning HP out of his holster. The colonel returns to the table.

"Paciorski is taking direct command over the whole operation. Wenda will coordinate the strike. He has experience."

"He sure does!" agrees the marshal with a smile, recalling Colonel Wenda's perfect management of General Zagórski's "disappearance" ten years ago. He sips his vodka and picks at the steak tartare with his fork. "Well, precisely."

"And who'll see to the physical execution? Who will go up to the necessary people and pull the trigger?" asks the marshal, after swallowing some tartare.

"The Phalanx, meaning Piasecki's boys, first and foremost. They're already in Golędzinów district practicing shooting guns and throwing grenades." Koc has every answer prepared.

"Aren't we handing this Piasecki a dangerous tool?" asks the marshal, thinking his question remarkably insightful.

"Now we give, later we take away. We predict fifteen hundred targets, of whom the majority, well, it goes without saying. Some of the rest we'll lock up in Bereza, and a few of the most important in regular prison."

"Regular prison for who?"

"The president, first of all."

The marshal grins broadly. He couldn't think less of the president, after all.

"We'll also lock up Piłsudski's widow and his old close allies. We'll let the widow out later, if she promises to keep her trap shut. But you, Marshal, will be in Bucharest while all this is happening, along with Piasecki. Because we'll do all this the night of the twenty-fifth to the twenty-sixth."

"What about the prime minister?"

"We'll see about the prime minister. He might collaborate. He obviously won't stay PM, we'll put him in charge of some government department as a consolation prize. But not the police, obviously. Of course if he changes his mind, then, well . . . But he won't. He's not the type."

"What about that bastard of a welfare minister?"

The colonel gives a theatrical thumbs-down.

"Well that's splendid," says the marshal happily, only to turn worried. "But fifteen hundred, that's a lot . . ."

"It is, but that was the total when we counted them all," replies the colonel, refilling their vodka glasses. "We have to simultaneously wipe out the socialists, the communists, the old National Democrats, and plenty of our own men. That was the total."

"But isn't that too many? How many did Hitler knock out in '34?" says the marshal, concerned. "Are we exceeding that?"

"About a hundred, apparently. But he had the opposition sorted out already, all that was left was to sort out his own camp. While we, Marshal, have to install *Ordnung* simultaneously within the regime—over the left faction, the president's faction, and opponents of the National Unity project—plus outside the regime, over the Socialist Party and their thugs like that Kaplica from Kercelak, along with the National Democrats, the Peasants' Party, and the rest."

The marshal knocks back a glass.

"But fifteen hundred? How many people will we need for that?"

"Some five thousand," says the colonel, with distinct pride in his voice.

"Do we have structures for that?"

"We have men from Piasecki, first of all. Secondly, we've organized triads of trusted younger officers, up to the rank of captain, and if necessary each of those can split up, taking two verified sergeants or corporals each. Thirdly, we'll get the political police involved, though they won't be purging, just arresting. The arrested ones we'll probably gather up somewhere and purge all at once."

The marshal listens carefully, nods in acknowledgment, and this time refills the vodka glasses himself. They both drink, then spear trembling pieces of herring with their forks and take a bite.

"What about the meddlesome priests, Adam?" asks the marshal with his mouth full.

The colonel swallows his herring and gives a disdainful sigh.

"The primate will declare he condemns the crimes, they abhor violence, then they'll make a deal with us, because what choice have they got? Soon as they see how neatly we've tidied up they'll come around on their own, because some of them are good Poles, first of all, and second of all, they'll be terrified we might tidy them up too. And if we go after the Jews on top of it, I mean, all they'll do is applaud . . ."

"Ah, yes, the Yids, what about the Yids?" asks the marshal.

"I don't know about the Aguda, I don't get those Orthodox crazies. We're figuring them out. We'll have to knock out the Bund and the Poale Zion leadership just in case. We'll cut a deal with Betar, promise them training, weapons, a bon voyage and a kick in the ass, they can go to Palestine and tussle with the Arabs, or to Madagascar, so long as they go. Don't worry, Marshal. I'll keep a discreet eye on how our purge is getting along," assured Koc. "And you'll return from Romania to a new Poland. We'll liquidate the other political parties. Life will be based on two pillars: the National Unity party and the military, and they'll both converge in the person of the marshal. A united parliament will name you chief of state, one of the pantheon from Kościuszko down to Piłsudski."

"And how will we secure that constitutionally?" asks the marshal, his vanity tickled.

"We'll throw something together," said the colonel flippantly, pleased with himself. "Like they did with the Small Constitution in 1919. We'll still have to think about what to do with the Jews overall. I'm sure you've heard, Marshal, that starting this academic year, classroom ghettos have been implemented practically everywhere?"

"Sure have, of course," says the marshal.

"Nothing to fight for there. It's the will of the nation. We've already got admissions quotas here and there. Over two years we'll bring in a full ban on new Jewish students. We'll let current ones finish if they agree to emigrate, and the idea is by '42, '43 at the latest, there will be no Jewish students at any university in Poland. Starting next year we'll stop accepting Jewish draftees, push the officers into retirement, and slowly keep squeezing them tighter."

"And rather than drafting them?" asks the marshal.

"They'll pay a special military tax. At the moment we're aiming more for a poll tax on everyone of draft age, but some are saying better to tax them at the community level than wrestle every poor kike for a couple złotys. Then we'll take away Jewish doctors' licenses, and the same for the other professions in succession. We figure increasingly severe property expropriations from anyone who doesn't want to emigrate, through about 1945. We'll take their real estate anyway, we'll let them keep their movables if they leave the country on their own. And so on. Until we force all of them out of Poland. Or possibly make them assimilate."

"Assimilate?" says the marshal, surprised.

"A Polish language exam, baptism, et cetera," replies Koc. "We haven't worked out the details yet. But there are a few individuals it'd be worth keeping. We're working on it."

The marshal nods in a way that indicates the official part of their conversation has come to an end. At least that's how I imagine it. I have known many generals and every one of them could with just such a nod of the head make clear the official portion was over.

Koc rises and dismisses the bodyguard, they summon the waiter, eat lobsters, crayfish, and oysters, drink white wine, and finally the marshal demands some girls, and girls arrive.

◆　◆　◆

When the plainclothes police rushed into the Auditorium Maximum building, Szapiro called out the signal: "Everybody out!"

This had been arranged with the students beforehand, with the support of Moryc and the Jewish mutual aid organizations. So at that signal, all the Jewish students rose from their seats and started crowding toward the exits, causing as much havoc as possible in the process. In the confusion, the policemen couldn't tell us from the students, we were all in the same student caps, and we slipped out easily, scattering through the hallways of the university to take advantage of the confusion, leaving the building through different exits, and dispersing throughout the city.

Jakub and Pantaleon, with me following them like a shadow, ran up Traugutt Street and slowed, also ditching our student caps. We were passing the Czapski Palace when a Chevrolet Master raced out from Czacki Street and stopped, blocking the road, and Andrzej Ziembiński leaped from the car, pistol in hand. Someone must have phoned him about the brawl at the university.

He aimed for Pantaleon, who happened to be in front, and fired, but missed and struck the Wróblewski building a few hundred yards away, at 22 Krakowskie Przedmieście. The bullet chipped off a piece of stucco.

Ziembiński pulled the trigger again, but the second shot didn't go off—the hammer of the Spanish Astra caught the cartridge in the ejection port, and Ziembiński didn't have time to pull the hammer back and clear the lock. Pantaleon knocked the hand with the pistol upward and attacked. Ziembiński effectively dodged Pantaleon's wide flail as an expert boxer would probably have dealt with him if they were only boxing, but Pantaleon threw himself at Ziembiński and knocked him down like a wrestler, pinning him with his impressive weight, and started pummeling Ziembiński's head. The pistol fell from his hand.

"Let's take him!" shouted Jakub, but then someone else emerged from the car.

She looked to be about twenty-five, was tall and slim, but not particularly pretty. Maybe she was beautiful, it depended how you looked at her, but certainly not pretty. Her large eyes were extremely wide set, as though stretched toward her temples, and she looked a little like those slim, large-eyed women on American TV nowadays, though back then of course that would never have occurred to anyone. She wore her dark-brown, though not black, hair in fashionable waves, and had on slacks and a light pullover.

She picked up Ziembiński's pistol from the ground, efficiently reloaded it, removed the blockage, and aimed at Pantaleon and Jakub. "Leave him," she said.

Then Jakub looked at her and she looked at Jakub, and something happened that often did when girls looked at Jakub: she found him pleasing without even realizing, given she was aiming a pistol at him. But there was something about Jakub that made women start daydreaming about him the moment they laid eyes on him.

She was Andrzej Ziembiński's sister and her name was Anna. Which we didn't know then, but found out later.

"Go, all of you," she said.

Pantaleon put his hand in his pocket, seeking the grip of his revolver, but Jakub waved him off.

"We're going, no need to shoot, we're going," he said gently, and Anna found his voice pleasing. Still, she kept aiming the pistol at him.

Pantaleon released Ziembiński and got up, then we left, cautiously, and all the while Anna kept us in her sights, until Małachowski Square, where we ducked behind the Protestant church and out of her sight.

Then Anna helped her brother into the car, wiped the blood off him, and got in the driver's seat.

"Who was that?" she asked.

"A Jewish thug, Jakub Szapiro," responded her brother. "I fought him in the ring once and lost."

Meanwhile we made it back to Jakub's apartment with no trouble and didn't go out again that day. The boys had stayed home from school, they spent the whole day with Jakub and Emilia, playing cards and reading Makuszyński's *Satan from the Seventh Grade*, though Jakub grumbled they were always reading these Polish books, and not Yiddish ones. Then we listened to the radio.

On the radio, Professor Stępowski was giving a talk on the work of the mathematician Samuel Dickstein, there was a show for country youth, then at seven, a debut radio play by Elżbieta Szemplińska-Sobolewska called *The Palm Reader*, which everyone listened to in that rapt concentration that these days no one grants a radio playing in the background. After the radio play, Emilia switched over to the second program, which was playing recorded music.

For supper we had buttered bread, cheese, and tomatoes. We drank white wine. Jakub poured some for Daniel and Dawid too—one finger, diluted with water.

"What was all that for, Jakub? That bust-up at the university?" asked Emilia. "Just a matter of pride? No Pole was going to tell a Szapiro where to sit in a lecture?"

"Isn't that enough?" he replied. "What, should I let those bastards get away with anything, like last year?"

Emilia fell into thought for a moment. She took a sip of wine.

"That is enough," she acknowledged.

They went silent. He went silent because he wanted to prepare for what he had to say, he had to gather some strength in himself to say it out loud. She went silent because she knew he wanted to tell her something important.

"I wanted to tell you, you were right. Let's go, Emilia. To Palestine. In this country it'll be just like under Hitler before long. I know the Brits have Palestine closed off now, but Moryc will arrange it, through the organization. I'll join the Haganah. I'll do just what I do here, but for a greater cause than my own wallet."

She was silent for a moment. She gazed at her hands with her eyebrows raised, wise and strong.

"We're going to Palestine, boys," she said finally. "You've got to learn Hebrew. Like Uncle Moryc."

"Only I have to sort things out here first. Get money together. And then we'll leave. We won't be beggars there."

He refilled their glasses, hers and his.

"To Palestine," she said.

"To Palestine. To hell with Poland."

"I don't want to go to Palestine," said Daniel. "I don't have any friends there. And I hate Hebrew."

"Me neither," added Dawid. "It's far and there's nothing but sand, and Miss Chaja our Polish teacher isn't there. I don't want to go somewhere where there's no Miss Chaja."

They soothed them both, Jakub and Emilia, as you must soothe eight-year-olds in such situations; it's very difficult to comfort eight-year-olds, who are already smart enough to not take all their parents' words at face value.

Then they put the boys to bed, drank another bottle, and made love, and I spied on them, as Jakub's large, heavy body rested on Emilia's body, and Emilia looked over his shoulder and saw me, and knew I was watching. She wrapped her legs around his waist.

Then Jakub sensed me watching him. That's exactly how it seemed, he sensed me. He broke off, turned around, and sat on the bed.

"Who's there?" he asked into the darkness, groping for his pistol on the nightstand.

"No one's there, Jakub, come here," she said with the sweetest of voices, as though calming a skittish horse. Only women can speak with that voice, only wise women. "There's no one. Come here."

She laid a hand on his erection. He peered into the darkness for a moment, anxious, he was breathing quickly, yet then he returned to her, and I returned to my room and looked out the window at Litani, who was looking at me through the same window.

I am Jonah. Out of the depths have I called Thee, O Lord.

At that same time, in that same Nineveh, and under the sperm whale's same bloody gaze, in the thickets of Kępa Potocka park and by the light of a flashlight hung on a branch, Eduard Tyutchev was performing the final incisions on Lieutenant Jerzy Górski, separating Lieutenant Jerzy Górski's genitalia from the rest of Lieutenant Jerzy Górski's body. Lieutenant Jerzy Górski was still alive but sedated with a solid dose of morphine and alcohol, and felt no pain. The final three weeks of his miserable life he'd spent handcuffed to a radiator in the kitchen of Tyutchev's small apartment, where he'd been taken straight from Sobenski's snack bar and where Tyutchev treated him mostly indifferently, guarding Radziwiłek's future trump card.

And now the time had finally arrived to play it. Radziwiłek wanted the autopsy to show clearly a living man, not a corpse, had been tortured. Suffering and resultant martyrdom were important elements of this play. But the morphine and alcohol were Tyutchev's initiative. Both mercy and rationality had led him to give Górski vodka and inject him with morphine—he had no desire to struggle with a prisoner howling from torture or risk a passerby approaching, concerned by the screams.

On the other hand, Warsaw was known for having an intelligent populace, who, at the sound of screams coming from the bushes, would quicken their step rather than go poking around. One way or the other, Tyutchev had injected an entire vial into Górski. The lieutenant's suffering was of no use to him.

Meanwhile Jerzy Górski had another few minutes of unconscious life to go, though in reality he'd died long before.

He'd died at all of seventeen and the only thing left in him was the certainty he'd been betrayed. By his one-legged body, by Jewish Poland, by the entire female sex, which warmly bade him farewell as he headed for the front, bade him farewell, kissed him, waved handkerchiefs, promised much, even slipped a tongue into his ear after whispering those promises the day before he set off.

The female sex in the form of Second Lieutenant Jerzy Górski's fiancée placed a hand on his member when he was setting off for the front in a green British uniform, with a German saber and a Russian revolver at his side. And when First Lieutenant Jerzy Górski returned from the war the richer for medals and a promotion, but the poorer for a leg, the female sex lost all interest. His fiancée didn't wait out the war, and even before Górski lost his leg she married a certain affluent Jewish convert to Catholicism named Majewski, who owned three colonial stores and a 20 percent share in a brewery in Łódź, plus a car and two apartment houses in Warsaw, while below the belt he possessed two whole legs as well as a big, thick, circumcised penis, which he used to give the lieutenant's ex-fiancée a great deal of pleasure.

In those days Lieutenant Górski still deluded himself that as a wounded war hero he'd quickly find someone to console him from losing that Jewish whore, yet he soon discovered no one wanted a leg-less retired veteran with no money or job, whose capital of bitterness, fury, and resentment grew every day, no, every hour. Around the time Piłsudski and his leftist allies seized back power, this was compounded with something ordinary, and therefore completely black, because it was hopeless: despair.

Our mother, sister, and lover—and their father, brother, and lover—our black goddess with the fat body of the Venus of Willendorf and a giant maw, gaping ever wider like an anaconda's jaws, slowly swal-lowing us, from the feet up or the head down, but always completely.

Tyutchev took out *Podorozhnik* by Akhmatova and read as he waited for Górski to die. He too knew the taste of despair's toothy mouth, her black maw, but he had learned to make peace with it, allow her to swallow him without fighting back; he had melted into her and putrefied, and everything died in him that was not despair, and he became her avatar, an apathetic demigod treading lightly over the cob-blestones of Warsaw.

Once Górski had bled to death, Tyutchev returned the Akhmatova to his pocket and, per Radziwiłek's orders, stuffed dead Górski's genitalia—bloody and flabby after being severed—into his tooth-less mouth, then pulled two burlap sacks over the lieutenant's frail body, hoisted the bundle onto his back, and, groaning, carried it to Radziwiłek's rear-engine Mercedes, parked on Godowska Street. He dumped it into the front-facing trunk and drove to the corner of Krakowskie Przedmieście and Karowa Street, where he parked in front of the *Warsaw Courier* offices. He got out and looked around, it was three in the morning and the area was deserted. He hauled the bundle out of the trunk, set it down under a streetlamp, untied the sack, and pulled down the stiff burlap below the victim's shoulders, so his bloodied head was visible, then hung a small piece of paper around the victim's neck, reading, "With greetings to all anti-Semites on behalf of Polish socialists, Buddy Kaplica" and then got in the Mercedes and drove away. He stopped at the nearest phone booth and called Witold Sokoliński's apartment.

The journalist picked up immediately, he had a phone by the bed.

"Get to the newspaper office. Bring a photographer," he said and hung up.

Sokoliński sighed heavily, threw off the blanket, got up, and began to dress.

"And where're you off to?" growled his wife.

"Work."

She gave him a disdainful look.

"All these late-night phone calls mighta had me thinking you were seeing some whore at night, 'cept I know nobody'd put out for you for free and your broke ass couldn't pay for nothing."

"Why you got to talk to me like that?" said Witold, upset.

"'Cause it's true," snarled Mrs. Sokolińska, turning her face to the wall, and she was right.

Witold sighed again, put on his coat and hat, left the apartment, got on his bicycle, and slowly pedaled his way toward Krakowskie Przedmieście.

Litani gazed down with joy on the battered and desecrated corpse of Lieutenant Jerzy Górski.

There's something impossible about a sperm whale's body, its proportions and lines. When you look at a human skeleton, you see it corresponds more or less to a human body. But a sperm whale's skeleton suggests a completely different animal, looking more like a giant dolphin, an animal with a long, toothy beak. Nothing prefigures its huge, blunt head, full of transparent oil, which on contact with air turns milky white and resembles sperm.

So how could it hold a torch to the rounded, streamlined bodies of dolphins and orcas, which seem designed not by God or nature, but an ingenious engineer, a specialist in hydrodynamics and submarine vessels? A sperm whale is bizarre. It plows through ocean waters with its battering-ram head, runs rampant in them. Its disproportionately small jaw dangles underneath as though it belongs to a different animal.

Litani looks at me the way he looks at a squid he means to devour.

Sperm whales don't chew their prey or tear it apart, they suck it in, swallow it whole. Even ones with broken jaws can hunt successfully.

Giant squid defend themselves by enveloping that blunt head with their tentacles, squid beak versus whale jaw, tentacles able to carve deep into thick sperm whale skin.

Litani sings. He sees me with his song, not his eyes. Blind sperm whales hunt just as effectively as seeing ones; to hunt underwater, they need neither light nor vision, they see the world with their song, which bounces off squid or fish, returns to them, and reverberates in the bones of their skull through their spermaceti-filled head.

With that song, Litani touches something inside me I would rather remained hidden.

Yet all will be laid bare. Nothing will be concealed from his song and his burning gaze.

ה

HE

We set off for the snack bar on Leszno Street much earlier than usual, when it was still dark, before the first newspapers had arrived. There were three of us—Szapiro, Pantaleon, and me—and the city was asleep, dark, and deaf.

We sat at a table. Sobenski brewed fresh coffee and served warm, fresh-smelling savory and sweet stuffed pastries, plus boiled kiełbasa, bread, mustard, and hard-boiled eggs. Eating and drinking, we waited for the first newspapers.

The paperboy brought *ABC* and *Our Review* first.

Jakub read out *ABC*'s headline: "Extraordinary Attack by Jewish Gangsters."

"I beg your fucking pardon," grumbled Pantaleon. "I'm a good Pole, a Catholic, a proletarian, and a socialist. The gangsters are over in America."

"It gets better. This is fantastic. 'Evidently displeased by efforts to limit the Jewish mafia's influence at the university, armed thugs violated civilized morals, terrorized unarmed Christian students with revolvers, and impugned the dignity of a professor.'"

"What-ed his dignity?" asked Pantaleon, puzzled.

"Impugned. 'Only a belated and sluggish intervention by the police drove the criminals from the campus of Józef Piłsudski University. No one was arrested.' Pass me the *Review*."

I did. Jakub quickly flipped through the pages.

"Nothing?" he said, amazed. "Ah, no, here we go. A little paragraph. 'Clashes at Józef Piłsudski University over nationalist student groups' anti-Semitic policies.'"

"Was it worth it, Mr. Szapiro?" rumbled Pantaleon. "Buddy won't be happy."

"No, he won't. But I had to do something," replied Jakub.

Mr. Sobenski the snack bar owner emerged from behind the counter. He topped off our coffee and brought more pastries.

"I can understand that, Mr. Szapiro," said Pantaleon after a moment. "Sometimes you have to do something. I understand that."

"I mean, how can we let them get away with all this and not protest, Karpiński, where would that get us? What then? Getting locked up behind barbed wire? We've got to stand up for ourselves. Otherwise they'll think they can get away with anything. Then along'll come some little Polish Hitler and it'll be like under real Hitler. Nobody stood up to him either and you see for yourself what's going on over there."

"I hear they're locking people like me in hospitals and cutting them open alive to see what they've got inside. Scientists are."

"Vivisections?" said Szapiro, astonished. "On who?"

"Freaks, Mr. Szapiro. Degenerates. That's what a guy I knew back in the circus told me. Said they're doing research on degenerates like me. Experiments. Some pagan shit too, sacrifices. They don't respect God, Mr. Szapiro. Not mine or yours."

"I haven't got a God, Karpiński," Szapiro objected.

"Everyone's got a God, the one fate gave him. The Christian one, the Jewish one, or, I don't know, some Chinese or Negro one. And everyone owns the God fate's given them, the way humans own animals. So you can feed it or starve it. Love it and let it sleep by the fireplace like a gal with her favorite dog, or thrash it with a stick. Or cut its throat, gut it, skin it, eat its meat, and throw away the rest. And God can do that too, to the person fate gave Him to."

"That sure is some fairy tale, Karpiński . . . ," began Jakub, but he didn't finish, because the snack bar's door banged open and Buddy charged in, raging like a bull nipped by a horsefly.

His clothes were sloppy, an open shirt with no collar or tie, his jacket thrown over his shoulder. He clutched a newspaper in his hand.

"What in the name of fuck is this?" he roared.

"Buddy, I'll explain," began Jakub hurriedly. "I know I didn't ask permission. But we didn't have time. Was my brother supposed to sit at his desk like some second-class citizen?"

"Szapiro, do I look like I give a shit about some university?" Buddy snarled and threw the paper on the table. "What in the name of fuck is *this*?"

Two photos were reproduced on the first page of the *Warsaw Courier*. The first, very blurry, showed the corpse of Lieutenant Jerzy Górski. The second showed a card hung around dead Górski's neck. And an article by Witold Sokoliński.

"Jan Kaplica—the Jewish Bandits' Polish Kingpin."

"Radziwiłek took him the same day we brought him here, three weeks ago," Szapiro said. "I mean that Russki of his, Tyutchev, took him and I guess they kept him in Tyutchev's apartment, I wasn't interested, it wasn't my business."

"Not your business? Not your business? Well now we're in deep shit! Where's Radziwiłek?" demanded Buddy. "This is what he wanted Górski for!"

Szapiro glanced at Pantaleon. Now they understood.

"Sobenski, call Mr. Radziwiłek at home," ordered Jakub.

Everyone knew he wouldn't pick up.

Sobenski called. Radziwiłek didn't answer.

Now we knew. Now we understood. The world was turning, its hierarchies were under revision. What had gone up would come down. Buddy knew it too.

But he also knew nothing was set in stone yet, he could fight, and had to.

Then that same little urchin who'd once brought me the tickets to the Maccabi versus League boxing match raced into the snack bar.

"They're coming here, Buddy, they're coming!" he shouted, disheveled and sweaty from the run.

"Jesus's cock!" swore Kaplica. "Who's coming?"

"The Phalanx!"

"Where?"

"On Piłsudski Square now, heading for Tłomackie," gasped the boy.

"Lots?"

"A few hundred."

"Armed?"

"Sticks in their hands, guns in their pockets. They're shouting 'smash the Jew' and 'our great Poland, our great nation.'"

"Any cops?"

"None I saw."

Buddy seized the boy by the shoulder, leaned over him, and looked him dead in the eye, his face so close his mustache was touching the boy's freckled nose.

"Listen up, squirt," he said. "Get over to Kercelak on the double, to Choromańczyk's eatery, grab Mr. Choromańczyk, and tell him Kaplica says get everybody together who's up for a fist-, knife-, or gunfight— right away. Understand?"

The little urchin, used to being an errand boy, dashed off without question and at great speed.

How many more boys like him I'd see, in Warsaw and in Palestine, in the wars I fought or watched.

The nervous system of all a city's civil wars, street battles, revolutions, coups, and riots: ten- or fourteen-year-old boys who know the city like the back of their hand, inconspicuous enough to sneak past police checkpoints, smart, clever, weaving around corners with simple orders in their heads. Names, addresses, commands. Kill. Break his legs. Pay. Let him out. Catch him and bring him here.

He ran.

Szapiro was already behind the counter on the phone, dialing a number.

"Who you calling?" asked Kaplica.

I knew his gangster brain was working with all its computational might, like the electronic brain of a Soviet spaceship taking off.

"The Party. They gotta get their squads moving. In a sec I'll call the Maccabi . . . Hello? Hello, this is Szapiro, we're in a fix here."

Szapiro demanded the fastest possible mobilization of the Socialist Party's fighting squads, but Kaplica was no longer listening.

"All right. Choromańczyk will get the word out," replied Kaplica. He took the Browning from his pocket, checked the magazine, and reloaded it.

Pantaleon inspected the chambers in his seven-shooter.

"When you guys check your guns, I always wonder, didn't you check 'em in the morning?" asked Szapiro.

"What?" said Buddy, confused.

"I mean, when you put your heater in your pocket in the morning, Buddy, do you put it there not knowing if it's got bullets in it?"

"Whatcha getting at, Jakub?"

Szapiro waved his hand dismissively. He didn't check his gun, it was always loaded, he didn't have to check. If he fired it, he refilled the magazine. Simple.

"They didn't waste a second. The newspaper just came out," he said.

"They musta known in advance. It's all a setup. Gimme a city map!" demanded Kaplica. Sobenski brought one right away, they laid it out on the table.

"From Tłomackie they'll head for Wola district," said Buddy.

"Unless they get to work on our library and institute on Tłomackie. Or the Great Synagogue."

Buddy puzzled it over for a moment, staring at the map.

"Karpiński, what do you think?"

Pantaleon looked up at the ceiling, listening intently to the voice of his devil brother.

Pantaleon believed his devil brother's skinned-over eyes could see things impossible for human eyes. He felt his devil brother contorting his little face into a weeping grimace.

"They'll go to Kercelak."

"Down Leszno?"

"Down Leszno," replied Pantaleon with the certainty of an oracle.

Kaplica looked back at the map, jabbing his pudgy finger near the intersection of Leszno and Żelazna Streets.

"We set up a perimeter here. At Żelazna, by the Collegium school. One division waits by Ogrodowa Street, another on Nowolipie in front of the hospital. We hit their march bang in the middle, split 'em in two. By then Choromańczyk'll be there with his boys from Kercelak to hit 'em from that direction. The fuzz'll get 'em from behind. Done! Jakub, call the police!"

"We're not on the best of terms with the cops recently."

"Fine, call the PM. No, forget it, I'll call him myself. And you, Mr. Sobenski, grab some planks and board up your windows, I don't want 'em smashing up my spot. On the double! Help him out."

Sobenski got to work. He always had planks ready in the back room for occasions such as this. Szapiro, Pantaleon, and I went to help. The sun was starting to rise over Warsaw, and Litani was watching us with his song, watching with merciless eyes, he was bringing us under his control.

He didn't sing long. Not long. Wait another moment.

In the ocean sperm whales feed on squid. What did Litani live on, as he floated over Warsaw? Black milk.

Kaplica went out onto the street. His face was pale.

"Let's go," he said simply.

He got in his Chrysler and we got in Szapiro's Buick, with me in the back and Pantaleon next to Jakub.

"They said no," said Pantaleon.

"I think it was worse than that."

We set off. News got around fast, so the streets of the Jewish district were deserted. Businesses hadn't opened, many store owners had boarded up their windows like Sobenski.

This kind of news didn't surprise anybody here. The power of Warsaw's street brawls waxed and waned, sometimes there was even peace for a few years, like in the early twenties and thirties, but 1937 had been especially tumultuous, particularly compared to the fairly peaceful first half of the decade, and every prudent Warsaw store owner was prepared in case of a riot.

The streets echoed with the hurried banging of hammers. I watched them nailing up boards to defend their expensive plate-glass windows, rolling up signs if they were easy to detach, putting away flowerpots, benches, and anything else not bolted down, and doing so without fuss, just as though they were moving their belongings inside for hail or a thunderstorm.

We didn't drive far, we could have walked, but in situations like this it's common sense to have wheels on hand. We parked the cars on Wolność Street, in front of the Boarding House for Homeless Youth.

When we got out, I suddenly imagined my fate, Mojżesz Bernsztajn's fate, if Jakub Szapiro hadn't taken me under his wing but rather left me mercilessly on the streets of Warsaw, alone under Litani's burning gaze and cruel song.

Or if Jakub Szapiro had wanted to take me under his wing, had sent me a ticket for the Maccabi versus League match, but I'd torn it up or resold it, because what reason on earth would I, a Jewish boy from a religious family, have for going to a boxing match?

Meaning I don't leave, I stay with my mother and brother, I don't abandon them, and then what happens to us?

The landlord evicts us from our apartment: my mother, my brother, and me, because without a father who are we, a widow and two orphans. We roam from one reluctant relative to another—three people are too many to just take in.

I can't remember those relatives. But we had them, for sure, we had many relatives. And they all finally push us out. We end up on the street.

What happens to my mother and brother? I don't know.

Does my mother start whoring herself out? My mother, so pious and therefore stone-cold. Or does she just beg, like all the Jewish and Christian beggars who Warsaw showed its everyday, cruel face?

What about me? Maybe I end up on this same corner, in the Boarding House for Homeless Youth. I eat thin soup and get bullied by the Christian kids. They make me learn the Lord's Prayer, and cross myself, and kiss a crucifix. They dunk my head in the toilet. They rip out my peyos. They pull down my pants and laugh at my circumcised penis. They kick me in the balls. They punch me in the face and I don't know how to defend myself, because after all Jakub Szapiro hasn't taken me to the Stars' gym to train; I don't know how to hold my hands, how to dodge a blow, how to rotate under a clumsy sidewinder and then leap out from another direction and knock my tormentor to the ground with one punch where his jaw joins his skull, or further back, behind his ear.

And then what? A year later they kick me out of there, and the next year is 1939 and then what happens to me? I don't leave alone for Palestine before then, because how, with what money?

Jakub Szapiro slit Naum Bernsztajn's throat to save Moyshe Bernsztajn's life, so I could live, so I could become General Moshe Inbar, walk the path of battle, only to sit now at a typewriter, not leave home, simply exist, and write down my memories.

Saved by Jakub, I follow Buddy, Pantaleon, and Jakub himself, we run to the designated rendezvous point where Wolność, Nowolipie, Żelazna, and Żytnia Streets come together, in front of Saint Sophia's Hospital, which incidentally is a gynecological hospital.

Buddy soon gets winded, slows down, stops, leans against a fence, we wait for him. Jakub and Pantaleon are excited, relaxed, Jakub is hopping from one foot to the other, warming up his neck and shoulders as though prepping for a bout in the ring. Pantaleon stretches his joints out until they crack and runs a hand through his long hair, his fingers delicately touching his devil brother's face on the back of his head.

Buddy catches up to us, panting, out of breath, sweaty, pistol in hand.

"Hoo boy, gettin' too old for this, too old . . . ," he wheezes.

"There people are born," says Pantaleon, gesturing at the hospital, "but here we are solemnly gathered for death. Ours or our enemies'. Such is the order of things in this world. One is born. Another dies. Our Lord points His finger: this one is to be born, and this one is to die. People switch places. The one who is born takes the place of the one Our Lord's finger has marked for death."

Buddy and Szapiro aren't listening, only I am. Munja is smoking a cigarette and muttering something under his breath in a language I don't recognize.

Our people are slowly gathering. We're heading down Żelazna Street, toward Leszno, we can already hear the Phalanx but there are still only twenty-three of us, though we're the cream of the crop since the quickest to arrive weren't the workers but the gang's muscle boys, seasoned brawlers. They've pulled off their jackets and hung them on a fence, not worrying anyone will touch them, and have knuckle-dusters, cudgels, knives, and razors in their hands.

"Anybody with a gun raise your hand," says Kaplica.

About twelve hands go up. Revolvers, pistols, and two sawed-off shotguns.

"We shooting right away?" says Szapiro, double-checking.

I look at his hand with the dark-blue tattoo, squeezing the grip of his pistol, a two-edged sword, and the four Hebrew letters מוות, death.

"Yep. Before contact. The first round right into the crowd, 'cause if we shoot over their heads it'll just egg 'em on, they'll charge and swamp us, overwhelm us. But if we drop a couple, wounded and dead, the rest'll shit their pants and make a run for it. And then we can just shoot over their heads so not too many bite the dust. Any conscientious objectors?"

No one speaks up. Of course there are no conscientious objectors. After all, that familiar threat lurks in Buddy's voice, enough to put any conscience to rest.

"Good. That's fine. Heaters in hands and let's go. Pistols fire at twenty yards, shotguns at five. Clear?"

Guns no longer in pockets, guns in hands. We head off.

We move down Żelazna, a hundred yards.

We can already hear the noise of the Phalanx, they're approaching from the City Center. They're already close.

"Fifty yards," says Pantaleon, touching the face of his devil brother in a tender gesture.

"Where's the cops?" asks Szapiro quietly.

"Dunno," responds Buddy helplessly and for the first time Szapiro sees Buddy's unflagging confidence slip. "Let's go. Red banner high. Let's go. The police can suck it."

We're running. I remember it so clearly. Twenty yards separate us from the corner of Leszno, we're running, raised hands clutching guns, we dash around the corner, Szapiro's finger tenses on the trigger of his large Browning.

"Don't shoot!" screams Kaplica and tries to turn the whole gang back. "Cops!"

Policemen march slowly at the head of the Phalanx procession, wearing German helmets and trench armor, holding steel shields and pistols. They raise their pistols and open fire.

We have to instantly wheel around and flee, so we do wheel around and flee, our shoes slipping on the cobbles. Pantaleon turns back, but Szapiro grabs him by the shoulder and pulls, shooting blindly behind him in the direction of the nationalist protest, we run together. Police bullets whiz past our heads, close, as close as the narrow line between life and death.

That's something I've never been able to understand. How it is that you tilt your head two inches to the left and live, but tilt your head two inches to the right and the missile strikes the skull, blasts through it, destroys what lies within the frontal lobe, meaning the person, those secret sparks between neurons where the whole of us exists, since beyond that we don't exist at all?

Vladimir Demikhov grafted a puppy's head, shoulders, and front paws onto the neck of a German shepherd. This was some twenty years after we ran down Żelazna Street, fleeing Polish policemen in German helmets.

The two dog heads on one dog body behaved in a correlated way, but tried to bite one another. Pantaleon hated his devil brother, but at the same time they laughed together and died together.

Verily I say unto you, there is no such thing as man.

Two inches left, you live, two inches right, a corpse. You and your twin, two people. Fraternal twins, two people. Identical twins, two people. Siamese twins, held together by a patch of skin, two people.

Siamese twins with two heads, three arms, and the rest a common body, two people. But one head and two bodies—is that one person? And if the heads and brains are joined together, how many people is that?

Is Pantaleon one man or two? And how many of us are unaware we carry an absorbed brother or sister within us, now nothing but an internal cyst, yet a separate person when they began—and if they were then, are they still? And then how do we count them?

And given we can't figure out how many people are in one body, then there's no such thing as a person.

There's nothing but thinking meat and its various parts, there's no individual person. And without individuality there is no person. This makes more sense in Latin, because *persona* means a mask, from the Etruscan word *phersu*. A mask is something we stick on the thinking meat to represent this phantom individuality of ours, a *persona* is something unreal, not conjoined to the meat of the face.

Two inches left, you live, two inches right, you're a corpse.

"To the cars!" roared Kaplica. "Then to my place."

Then a police bullet hit him in the left forearm.

Two inches left, you live, two inches right, you're a corpse.

He stumbled, roared with pain, swore loudly, but kept running, covering a lot of ground on his short little legs.

That was the third bullet in the fifty-seven years of Kaplica's life that managed to penetrate his small and stout body.

The first had also been the last bullet in the cylinder of a Russian cop's revolver. It was an American revolver, a Smith & Wesson Russian, .45-caliber. The czarist cop was fat and a terrible shot, and the year was 1905, January, and there was a revolution going on. As Buddy—who was not yet Buddy but simply Jan Kaplica—fled Grzybowski Square, the cop fired six times and only the sixth bullet hit the then-young-and-slim revolutionary, tearing open the skin of his left thigh. Kaplica tumbled over onto the slick cobblestones, but as he looked behind him, he spotted the policeman desperately attempting to open his broken revolver to throw away the empty casings and reload. Jan Kaplica coolly aimed his Browning, fired, and struck the gendarme in the head.

That wasn't remotely the first person he'd killed, not even the first czarist policeman.

He'd killed his first person in 1897 at the age of seventeen, with his bare fists. The man had been dead forty years because he stole Buddy's shoes that day —an imprudent move, given he was younger, smaller, and weaker than Buddy. So he brought it on himself.

It was also on Grzybowski Square that Buddy had killed his first czarist policeman, in November 1904—two months before being shot—during the socialist guerrillas' first armed operation, which made him beam with pride to the end of his days and was a story he loved telling to anyone who'd listen.

His second bullet wound was the most serious and Kaplica had barely scraped through. It was in December 1922, in a street battle after Narutowicz was elected president. By then Buddy was Buddy, and a .30-caliber bullet from a Mauser pistol punctured his lung and they barely saved him. It was a young nationalist who shot him. A few seconds later, that young nationalist was shot by Jakub Szapiro.

As for the third bullet wound, neither Buddy nor Jakub punished the perpetrator on the spot. There was no time. We were fleeing.

We ran to the cars parked on Wolność Street.

"We'll take the long way around, through Wola, Ochota, and Rakowiec, not through the City Center," commanded Buddy, gripping his bloody shoulder. "And we'll split up."

Munja got in the driver's seat of the Chrysler. We got in Szapiro's Buick and set off, turning off Wolność Street onto Okopowa and then making an immediate right onto Żytnia, to avoid getting anywhere close to Leszno Street and Kercelak market, where the nationalist gangs, under police protection, now had free rein.

It later turned out Choromańczyk had managed to get fifty people together, but seeing the Phalanx's numerical advantage and the police clearly supporting them, which this part of the city hadn't seen since the bad old days before Piłsudski's coup, they realized it wasn't worth the risk and simply scattered throughout the whole district.

When the nationalists charged into Kercelak, with Ziembiński at their head, they found the marketplace empty.

The stalls were closed up, the sellers were gone. The nationalists only managed to lay hands on two Jewish traders who, heavily laden with goods, were too slow to evacuate. So they got a serious beating.

The first—the bucket seller Samuel Gerszom—the boys beat with their banner poles, breaking his hand and knocking out his two front teeth, while screaming this was for Lieutenant Górski. Gerszom hadn't managed to flee because he was lugging thirty buckets with him and, like Lieutenant Górski, was missing a leg, due to a streetcar accident years ago.

Samuel Gerszom didn't read newspapers and had never heard of Lieutenant Górski, nor did he understand Polish too well, but he accepted his fate and the thrashing he received, because in his wisdom he knew someone had to suffer in this world, and at this moment it had fallen to him.

When finally, after depriving him of his teeth, his money, and his goods, they left him in peace, he quietly thanked the Almighty with mute motions of his bloodied lips as he stealthily slipped out of Kercelak to his apartment on Gęsia Street.

The second was the tailor Józef Sztajgiec, who made alterations on the platform right in the middle of Kercelak. He would have escaped if he'd abandoned his sewing machine, his black-lacquered Singer, which he transported on a two-wheeled cart in a special case he'd custom-built himself out of thick, waxed cardboard, edged with thin brass sheeting. He would have escaped if he'd left behind his sewing machine, cart, and handmade case, yet Józef Sztajgiec couldn't abandon his Singer. The rest he could, but not the machine. Without the Singer Józef Sztajgiec would no longer be Józef Sztajgiec. He'd be just one of 350,000 Warsaw

Jews, meaning nobody. A pauper with no meaning in life, no vocation, no duty.

Even with the machine he was poor and without the machine he and his family would surely go hungry, yet more than that, the Singer sewing machine defined him, made him someone concrete, labeled: Józef Sztajgiec the tailor.

Józef Sztajgiec hadn't fled the moment he heard the cry go up that the thugs were on their way, because a customer was standing at his sewing machine with her husband's jacket. The husband was prospering, his prosperity had accumulated at the waistline, and the jacket had to be let out. The previous tailor had prudently left extra material for this in the seam running down the middle, it wasn't a difficult job. Józef was just finishing when the warning cry went up. But Józef didn't abandon his commission.

The brawlers Choromańczyk had summoned sped past, the stall-holders rushed to wrap up their goods, but Józef kept sewing, simultaneously assuring his client the job had to be done, the fuss was over nothing, no need to worry, ma'am. On the one hand he did think the job should be finished, on the other he didn't want to lose his promised two-złoty fee.

He finally returned the jacket, the woman chucked him five złotys, shouted he could keep the change, and made a run for it. Sztajgiec was thrilled at the extra earnings and set about packing up the machine and folding the wooden table it usually stood on. He still had to load all this onto the cart, so he ran over to where he stored it under the overhang of the roof of Choromańczyk's eatery, and that was where they attacked him first, though he got away. He wasn't an invalid like Gerszom. He wasn't a brawler either and didn't know how to fight, but he had fit legs and wasn't weighed down with fat, he could have fled into the alleys and lost his tormentors.

But he couldn't abandon his machine. He left the cart, grabbed just the case holding the Singer, but he couldn't escape. They attacked him on the corner of Chłodna Street, beat him unconscious, broke his nose, his jaw, and five ribs, leaving him with a concussion and an internal hemorrhage.

But most importantly, they took the Singer sewing machine. They didn't steal it, they wouldn't lower themselves to theft. They took the machine out of its cardboard case and smashed it on the pavement.

Then, full of righteous anger, they overturned a few hastily abandoned stalls and wandered aimlessly, pumped full of adrenaline, eager for a scuffle they could find no opponents for, just as enraged as they were disappointed.

They tried to burn down Choromańczyk's eatery but it had rained overnight and everything was too damp to catch fire.

Finally the police headed back to their barracks, and, deprived of their unexpected defenders, the Phalanx rightly felt uneasy and hurried off to friendlier neighborhoods.

Some good people bore Sztajgiec on a coat to the Jewish Hospital in Czyste district. When he regained consciousness, he asked about his machine.

"Who gives a damn about some machine, you've got a ruptured spleen and a massive internal hemorrhage!" replied the doctor, cruelly.

"What's an internal hemorrhage?" asked Sztajgiec, his voice weak, or at least so I was told.

"It means you're bleeding, but inside your body," said the doctor impatiently.

"You think I'm some kinda dope? Blood's s'posed to be inside your body, Doc!" said Sztajgiec with a laugh. Then he died. At least so I was told.

Meanwhile we pulled up to the backyard of Kaplica's house.

Kaplica's Chrysler was already there. A taxi with an open driving compartment arrived at the same time as us. The taxi driver was wearing a leather jacket and smoking a large, curved pipe, I remember it exactly, and a doctor got out of the car. I didn't know him, but he had a pointed goatee, round glasses, and a doctor's bag; he looked like a doctor, so he was a doctor.

We went inside along with him.

"In here!" shouted Kaplica.

He was sitting at the kitchen table in just his pants, blood was running from the fresh wound in his shoulder. A bottle of vodka stood on the table in front of him. He was smoking a cigarette.

Mrs. Kaplica was boiling some water. Her face bore the red mark of a fresh slap. The girls were gone. Munja was standing by the window with a pistol in his hand and doubt in his heart.

"Just grazed me," said Buddy. "Bullet kept going. Stitch it up, Doc. And you guys siddown, have a drink. We gotta talk this through."

I watched the doctor disinfect and clean the wound, the hooked needle piercing Kaplica's skin with no anesthetic and pulling surgical thread behind it.

How many times have they stitched me up? In all the wars here. After the Six-Day War, the Yom Kippur War, all of them. So many wounds, so many little holes from needles and surgical thread.

I get up from my typewriter, I walk to the bathroom, to the mirror, but I can't find the scars. They're lost in my aged, wrinkled skin, in the furrows and flakes. If scars can disappear, so can everything.

But I do remember the shrapnel on the Sinai, when I was on General Yoffe's staff. I think it was Yoffe. And I think it was his staff. Can't remember, it's been twenty years after all. The shrapnel left a wound on my ribs, not far from where the war left a blue, white, and red ribbon on my uniform.

But now I can't find the scar.

I can't find my own face. My face has gone missing somewhere between my eyes and the mirror—I stand in the bathroom with the light on and I don't see my own face, I only see a vague splotch amid the hair; I see everything individually, nose, eyes, what's left of my hair, sagging cheeks, large ears, bags under the eyes, gray stubble, but I don't see my face, I can't find my own face, I don't have a face.

So I leave the bathroom.

The toothy maw of the black Venus of Willendorf. She has no face or neck, just a head covered in grooves of hair, open jaws where her throat should be, her jaws are unexpected and black, and black and dark emerge from unexpectedness to swallow us up, choke and suffocate us.

I have to call Magda, my Magda, she's my only hope.

I haven't written about her, though she was part of all this after all, she was there the whole time, just outside the main course of events. She's my only link to those days.

I don't know why I've stopped writing about her. There was that last memory from the theater and then it's as if nothing came afterward, but something *did*, Magda Aszer, my Magda, the first and only woman of my life.

Not counting Emilia Szapiro. They were so alike, Magda and Emilia, new Jews, new women, the kind of Jewish women the world had never seen; athletic, confident, strong Jewish women like them later built our state, driving blunt tools into the dry and infertile land of our kibbutzim and moshavim. The land bore fruit, and their loins bore true Israelis, grown from the land of Israel: *sabras*.

They didn't shave their heads, they didn't believe in superstition, they lived.

But Emilia was different, totally different. I'll tell that story later.

I remember Magda watching the first time I went into the ring. I went in early, very early. I wasn't much good yet. My opponent was smaller and younger than me, my allies were the eyes of Magda Aszer, sitting by herself on the wooden bleachers. Apart from her, no one paid attention to the two skinny boys in the ring, not even Szapiro, who was jumping rope nearby to cool down after sparring.

The referee was my age, sweaty after his own training, equipped for the occasion with a gong and a stopwatch to measure the length of the rounds. He also couldn't have cared less about my first fight.

Only Magda Aszer cared, her eyes were fixed on me, my only allies.

I felt oddly confident. Maybe because my opponent was smaller and younger. Maybe because she was looking at me. Maybe because I hadn't yet encountered the black Venus of Willendorf or the sperm whale with the burning eyes.

The ref struck the gong, we touched gloves and started to fight, and two seconds in, I took a powerful left straight in the jaw and a right hook in the liver, knocking the wind out of me, and suddenly all my confidence evaporated, suddenly I saw this was like nothing I'd ever experienced. No one had ever fought me like this.

When we'd gotten into street fights with the boys from other heders and other courtyards, when we organized regular wars way back when on and around Broń Square, I'd always been able to run away somewhere, take shelter, hide.

Here in the ring I was roped in, and the only shelter was the gong, and she was watching.

So I had no choice but to fight and fight I did, though ten seconds in I knew I had no chance, this smaller, younger kid was better than me, like Szapiro was better than Ziembiński at my first boxing match.

My fists pounded air, because his head was never where it had been when I threw the punch. He snuck past my straights and under my hooks, then smashed through my guard with two lefts and I felt his punches like hammer blows against my head.

In the first round he gave me a black eye. In the second he gave me a nosebleed. In the third he left a large bruise on my left cheek, which stayed for a good two weeks while I watched each morning in the mirror as it spread and turned blue, then yellow.

There was no fourth round, we had only agreed to three. For three rounds I stayed on my feet with my head held high. I didn't turn my back in the ring, I kept moving and held my guard, that was all I could do.

I didn't land a single blow.

"I'm proud of you," said Magda, as I left the ring with wobbly legs and a beat-up face.

Or maybe it was someone else.

She wiped the blood from my nose, pressed ice to my puffy eyes. Szapiro didn't even glance at me, he was too wrapped up in himself, in front of the mirror, jabbing at the air with his frightening, loose punches, dodging an invisible opponent.

I get up from my typewriter. Now I have a thick stack of paper alongside it.

"Are you going to let me read that?" asks Magda.

I didn't know she was here. I turn around, surprised.

"Magda?"

"Don't call me that," she says, turns away, and leaves the room where I'm writing.

I follow her.

She's in the kitchen, placing eggs in the plastic tray in the fridge door. A package of gray toilet paper stands on the countertop.

"I stood in line for three hours. You should finally get out of this apartment, seriously."

I shrug.

The world outside has nothing interesting to offer. I go back to my room, where I write.

Magda leaves without saying goodbye, I hear her close the door behind her then turn the key in the lock. Could it be she's keeping me under lock and key? Could I be locked in?

But I can't check because I don't want to go outside. So what difference does it make? None.

I go back to writing.

"We gotta talk this through," said Kaplica and poured some vodkas, and I could see this was the first time Szapiro, Pantaleon, and Munja all heard helplessness and fear in Kaplica's voice.

"It's Radziwiłek behind this, so—" began Szapiro cautiously.

"Damn right it's Radziwiłek," interrupted Kaplica.

Munja suddenly stepped back from the window. He put his pistol away.

"I'm going now," he said. "I gotta get out of here."

All three turned to look at him—Kaplica, Szapiro, and Pantaleon— and they understood immediately and weren't even surprised. Munja shrugged helplessly.

"What can you do?" he added, clearly upset.

And he left by the back, garden door.

At the front door, someone rang the bell.

"Mother, go see who that is," Kaplica ordered his wife.

Maria Kaplica walked into the hall and peered through the window. Three unmarked cars stood in the driveway, with seven people next to them. Two uniformed police and four men in plainclothes, including Prosecutor Ziembiński and Lieutenant Czerwiński, both triumphant and happy.

"Cops're here," said Maria Kaplica.

Jan Kaplica fell into thought and scratched his stubbly cheek.

"You boys hit the road. They ain't gonna take you guys. No point putting up a fight. They can arrest me, you'll get me out quick. Look after the business and my family."

He threw his jacket over his shoulder, got up, and went to open the door. They bundled him off without a word. They didn't insult him by asking a lot of questions like "Are you Jan Kaplica?"

Only Czerwiński mumbled, "Ten years I've been waiting for this. And I lived to see the day."

Meanwhile we snuck out through the garden. Pointlessly, since if they'd wanted to stop us they'd just have put guards on all the exits. It was only Buddy they wanted. They drove away immediately.

Buddy already had a bad feeling from Czerwiński's smug expression, but we didn't know yet this was no ordinary arrest, he wasn't going to end up in one of Warsaw's many familiar lockups or even the jail on Daniłowiczowska Street.

But the paperwork already knew.

It was Radziwiłek and Piasecki who'd set it all in motion, but per their wishes, the paperwork showed no trace of them.

Bolesław Piasecki naturally had no significance in Warsaw's administrative hierarchy, but Piasecki and Prosecutor Ziembiński had spoken to Colonel Adam Koc, conveying Piasecki's idea to rid the gang-infested City Center of this proletarian pillar of the Socialist Party, and in the process ensure the absolute loyalty of Radziwiłek, who would step into his shoes.

Through the Rifleman's Association's structures and his own gang connections, Radziwiłek would nip in the bud any resistance from the working-class and criminal gangs of the City Center or Wola and Ochota districts, securing one of the key fronts for Koc and Rydz-Śmigły's plans.

Colonel Koc therefore submitted an official document, as leader of the National Unity party, to the regime-appointed mayor of Warsaw, Stefan Starzyński, drawing the mayor's attention to the substantial threat posed to public order by Jan Kaplica—alias "Buddy," former socialist guerrilla, Socialist Party member, and sympathizer of the Revolutionary Faction—who as such should be dispatched to the Bereza Kartuska Isolation Facility in a remote region two hundred miles to the east.

The document made its way to Starzyński's desk via courier shortly after Starzyński, himself a National Unity member, finished a phone conversation with Koc in which the colonel explained those aspects of the case that should not appear in the official paperwork.

The Revolutionary Faction Buddy supported was made up of breakaway Socialist Party members who consistently supported the regime—so they were not Bereza's typical clientele. But Koc explained why the situation was changing at this particular moment.

With the mayor of Warsaw's countersignature, the document next made its way to the Ministry of Internal Affairs, to the Political Department—marked with the Roman numeral I—and to the desk of that department's director.

The director received a phone call from Colonel Koc as well. It went without saying that the prime minister, minister of internal affairs, and former terrorist Sławoj Składkowski would have no desire to lock up Kaplica, an old comrade-in-arms from their golden days in the socialist guerrillas. So they would have to obtain Składkowski's signature by subterfuge.

They settled on a trick more or less as exceptionally refined as a schoolboy forging his parents' signature to get out of class, namely that the director of Department I would personally present the authorization to send Kaplica to the Bereza Kartuska Isolation Facility inside a thick folder stuffed with other documents. He simply politely indicated: please sign here, and here, and here—and voilà, Składkowski's countersignature was acquired.

After signing, Składkowski returned to his important duties, and the signed authorization traveled east by the highest priority mail to Brześć-on-the-Bug, seat of the examining magistrate in charge of the Facility. The examining magistrate in Brześć-on-the-Bug didn't want to live out his days as an examining magistrate in Brześć-on-the-Bug, so he fulfilled the ministry's expectations with tremendous zeal, and with that very zeal he signed the authorization to send a man completely unknown to him—Jan Kaplica, age fifty-seven—to Bereza Kartuska Isolation Facility, just as he signed every other authorization the moment it landed on his desk.

Meanwhile Jan Kaplica, alias "Buddy," was sitting in the very narrow back seat of a gray Polish police Fiat 508 with slightly rusty fenders. The Fiat was driving down Puławska Street and Buddy was calm, if slightly humiliated by having to ride in such a second-rate car.

Behind the wheel of the Fiat sat Senior Sergeant Ćwikła. Next to him was Officer Kulas.

"So where we headed, boys?" asked Buddy, to break the ice.

Senior Sergeant Ćwikła didn't respond. Senior Sergeant Ćwikła was silent because those were his orders, and Senior Sergeant Ćwikła valued his orders above all, which incidentally meant he'd attained the rank of senior sergeant particularly rapidly, despite his lack of either intellectual or spiritual qualifications.

Officer Kulas, on the other hand, was silent because he was sleeping, and he was sleeping because he knew they had a long road ahead of them.

The Fiat took Marszałkowska Street toward the City Center, because those were Sergeant Ćwikła's orders, and Buddy remained calm.

The Fiat turned onto Jerozolimskie Avenue, since that was where Sergeant Ćwikła turned the steering wheel, and Buddy wouldn't have worried if the little car had turned left, but the Polish Fiat 508 with Sergeant Ćwikła at the wheel turned right and Buddy became slightly concerned. The Fiat took the Poniatowski Bridge over the Vistula River and Buddy grew pensive as they drove down Washington Avenue.

But it was when the police Fiat left Warsaw, roaring briskly with two hundred horsepower along a paved road with an upgraded surface, in other words on the eastern highway toward Mińsk Mazowiecki, that Buddy understood where they were going.

And Buddy felt fear.

The Bereza Kartuska Isolation Facility had been set up three years earlier by the very director of the Internal Affairs political department who'd slipped Prime Minister Składkowski the authorization to inter

Buddy there. The idea to open the camp had belonged to then–Prime Minister Leon Kozłowski, and Piłsudski himself had applauded it.

Prime Minister Kozłowski had been very fond of the German reinterpretation two years prior of the concept of *Schutzhaft*, or protective custody, which allowed the police to inter persons suspected of threatening public order in a concentration camp, without any need to get judges involved. The renowned jurist Carl Schmitt advocated purifying the German legal system of foreign Jewish influence and letting judges be guided in their sentencing by the concept of *gesundes Volksempfinden*, the people's common sense.

At the time, Buddy had liked the idea a great deal.

"They'll finally lock up those Ukrainian separatist bastards!" he said in the summer of 1934, delightedly raising a glass of champagne at Ryfka's. "And the nationalists! And out there the police won't pussyfoot the fuck around! They'll kick their asses!"

It never occurred to him he'd end up in Bereza. He'd have sooner expected to see his own body floating down the Vistula than himself in the Isolation Facility.

Beyond Mińsk Mazowiecki, the paved road with the improved surface ended and Poland began. Officer Kulas took Sergeant Ćwikła's place at the wheel and they covered the thirty miles to Siedlce in two hours, bumping along over potholes. Buddy's wound was giving him trouble.

They stopped for gas in Międzyrzec. Buddy emptied his bladder onto the black earth, gazing out at the flat, plowed fields stretching to the horizon, then, at his escort's urging, he returned to the Fiat and they drove on, to Biała Podlaska; then came Brześć-on-the-Bug, Kobryń, and mud.

Twenty-five miles past Kobryń, and by then the next day, they reached Bereza.

The camp stood outside the town in redbrick barracks left over from the czar.

They stopped at the gate.

Sergeant Ćwikła approached the guard and started taking care of the formalities.

Buddy knew what awaited him. He'd heard firsthand stories about Bereza.

Buddy was afraid.

He'd seen people who'd left Bereza after the prescribed three months, he'd also seen ones who'd left after six.

The most hardened criminal would say he'd rather spend a year in the toughest prison than a month in Bereza.

There used to be a go-between in the City Center, he was called Abraham Bloch and he was just as friendly with the gangsters as with the cops; he felt equally at home at Fat Josek's as at the police station or one of the fancy coffeehouses. He was a bit of a fence, arranging various things for various people, and he had neither conscience nor scruples. He made most of his money selling small plots of land just outside Warsaw, he'd cook the books a little and even sell the same plot to multiple buyers, for a very reasonable price at that, well below market. But at a certain point his luck ran out, because one of his clients was the nephew of a department director in the Ministry of Internal Affairs, who didn't like being taken for a sucker and had no interest in a long, tedious lawsuit.

Bloch was splendid in his effeminate, Mediterranean beauty and looked like an Italian heartthrob, although he was actually solidly built and had broad, strong shoulders. He had an elegant bearing; he exuded confidence and good cheer; he was quick with his fists, his knife, and in love; he smelled of French perfumes and drove an elegant Lancia Farina. Women adored him and men envied him, whispering behind his back he was a parvenu and a pretty boy. But none of them dared say that to his face, for across the length and breadth of Warsaw, people told the story of how once at the Zodiak, an Uhlan second lieutenant by the name of Willemann had called Bloch a pretty boy and taunted him, saying, does this little Jew think if he gets a manicure and sprays on some Yardley cologne he can show up among sophisticated people and, what, nobody'll hear that Yiddish accent he's got? Like some peddler from Nalewki! First of all he oughta learn proper Polish, like a human being!

Bloch did not, in fact, speak the best Polish, making exclusive use of Yiddish in day-to-day life. He rose from his table without finishing his coffee, apologized to his lady companion, and approached the handsome officer in his handsome uniform. Bloch peered deep into the man's blue, Aryan eyes and saw in them the absolute certainty that no Warsaw Jew would dare disrespect the uniform of a Polish officer.

So Bloch grinned broadly, seized Willemann by his diagonal chest strap and saber, gave a yank, and dragged him out of the café into the street. The guests were too stunned to react, and Willemann got tangled up in his own feet and his scabbard belt. Once out on the street, Bloch sat on him and, with a couple of blows of his fist, deprived him first of his consciousness and then his sword and wallet. Then he took off, leaving the disgraced second lieutenant to the terrified waiters. He made up for abandoning his companion at the café and ruining the evening by sending his chauffeur for her and waiting at the door of her apartment with a massive bouquet of flowers. She didn't even pretend to be offended. The whole building could hear her cries of ecstasy until morning.

Bloch earned dual renown. First—he'd dared to do what many only dreamed, thumbing his nose at one of the masters of this country in which the whim of a wrathful God had condemned them to live. And second—he'd gotten away with it.

Selling the director's nephew a one-and-a-half-acre plot in Otwock was a different matter. The director's nephew didn't like seeing a sucker when he looked in the mirror, so on April 17, 1936, Abraham Bloch woke up not in the bed of one of his numerous lovers, but on the cement floor of a holding cell in Bereza, where he spent the first week of his stay sleeping in his underwear with no blanket or pallet, before being brought to the prisoners' cells. His first beating came on his very first day, after the first exercise period. Fighting back against cops was in Bloch's blood, and he didn't give a damn whether the policeman was in a Russian, German, or Polish uniform. So when the guard in Bereza told him to crawl through the thick layer of piss and shit covering the latrine floor, Bloch stood up to him.

That day they beat him unconscious, dunked his head into a bucket of liquid feces, and then sent him off to the barrack, not allowing him to wash his hands or face.

For a week, he rebelled; they beat him every single day, and he spent the whole time walking around smeared with shit.

After that week he stopped rebelling, but the Bereza cops were so used to giving him beatings that they kept at it. They knocked out one of his eyes and he ended up in the hospital in Kobryń for a week. When the week was through, he returned to Bereza minus an eye and they beat him again. He slopped shit out of the toilets with his bare hands, dug holes and filled them in again, drew water from the well only to pour it back in, and when his hands went numb after the hundredth bucket, they beat him.

He had another two stints in the hospital and three in solitary, where he received bread and water every other day. On top of that, every quarter hour during the day and every half hour at night, a guard would pound his truncheon on the door and the prisoner would have to report. If he didn't report, they went in and beat him, but the sleep deprivation was even more horrible. Bloch was released after three months exactly, in July.

He and Buddy knew each other well, Bloch used to hang out at Ryfka's, though I never saw him there, I only heard about it second-hand. He used to do a lot of business at Kercelak and had saved Buddy a tidy sum, so when Buddy learned they'd let Bloch out of Bereza and he was back in Warsaw, Kaplica told his men to find Bloch so he could pay him a courtesy visit and ask about everything, support him, and congratulate him on his release.

It took a few days to find Bloch. He was holed up in a tiny room east of the river, up in Pelcowizna district, and the watchman said he never so much as poked his nose out. He paid some kid to bring him food, vodka, and cigarettes.

Bloch didn't open the door without extended negotiations, and when Kaplica saw him, he understood why.

Abraham Bloch after Bereza was no longer the Abraham Bloch who didn't fear getting into a scrap with a cavalry officer. He wore a black eye patch, but instead of making him seem murderously debonair, he looked like a beggar. The starvation rations had left him emaciated, his hands shook, he was missing his front teeth, and his thick mop of black hair had gone thin and gray, as though he'd aged twenty years in three months.

Kaplica, genuinely upset, asked how he could help, what he could do, but Bloch only muttered he had atoned for his crimes and was asking for forgiveness. And to be left alone. When a streetcar bell rang outside the window, Bloch fell into his bed as though someone had given him an electric shock and he burst into tears.

"The worst part was they didn't let you take a shit," he jabbered after a while. "They did it on purpose. For days on end. And if someone finally went in his pants, they beat him and told him he had to walk around like that, with his pants full of shit. There was no way to wash them."

Buddy couldn't watch Bloch cry. He understood the man was already dead, so he left two hundred złotys on the table, gave fifty to the doorman, and told him to look after Mr. Bloch, then never thought of him again.

Not long later, Abraham Bloch hanged himself, because the department director's nephew was demanding a refund for the plot and threatening that if he didn't get his money back, Bloch would be sent to

Bereza again. Bloch had no money left, so he hanged himself with his own belt, since that was preferable to Bereza's isolation cells, beatings, and shit. And Abraham Bloch was no more.

Buddy, sitting in the back seat of the Fiat 508 at the gate of Bereza Kartuska Isolation Facility, remembered the tears streaming down the sunken cheeks of Abraham Bloch, a man who before Bereza hadn't been afraid to haul a uniformed Polish officer out of a restaurant and beat him up on the sidewalk, and after Bereza had trembled at the sound of a streetcar bell—and Buddy was afraid.

He remembered the word among the gangsters: better ten years in prison than three months in Bereza.

Sergeant Ćwikła was sorting out the formalities with the guard, who signed one document after another.

Meanwhile Officer Kulas turned around in the front seat.

"Buddy, we can't go in there, we're banned, we're here to keep law and order and I guess if they let us into a concentration camp we might lose respect for the order in this beloved homeland of ours."

"You a communist or what?" said Buddy, bridling.

"No way. I'm a decent Pole from a working-class family, a socialist same as you, that's why I'm telling you. When you're inside you wanna get a hold of Warden Kamala-Kurhański. And Mr. Buddy, tell him his aunt Adelajda sends her regards. Her address, and this is important 'cause it'll make an impression, is number two Rejtan Street, apartment one, first floor, with her dog, Reks."

Kaplica raised his eyebrows. He considered.

"I see you're hesitating, Buddy. Lemme explain. Back in '27 you helped out a poor old gal, a widow, Joanna Kulas she was called. She lived in Powiśle district, on Radna Street. You remember, Mr. Buddy?"

Kaplica's eyebrows were still raised, but he added a shrug of the shoulders.

"A lotta people got helped, a lotta people got hurt," he said, which was true.

"Joanna Kulas got helped, and we ain't forgotten, Mr. Buddy, sir. She was hungry and abandoned. You fed her, got her a roof over her head. You even found a penny for shoes and elementary school books for me, 'cause she was my ma. And you helped a lotta others, Mr. Buddy. The people of the capital remember. We couldn't stop this or warn you, it came from too high up and too quick, but we ain't forgotten. Adelajda Fuks is Kamala-Kurhański's aunt, a widow. When you tell him what you got to say, Kamala's gonna get a fright and call his aunt Adelajda. But Aunt Adelajda ain't gonna answer. This one tough guy's gonna answer, a bruiser I picked up a couple days ago carrying dough from a speakeasy and I let him walk free if he swore to do what I said. And y'see how quick he's gonna make it up to me? Kamala's probably gonna put out an alarm, he'll call, but by the time the cops show up there ain't gonna be no bruiser or Aunt Adelajda in the apartment. We'll hold her in our hideout until they let you outta this camp."

Buddy grinned broadly, overjoyed.

"Swell! Now that's just swell! You got a thousand złotys from me, sonny boy, soon as I get outta this dump. After I do, come see me before dawn at the snack bar on Leszno and that thousand is yours."

"Thanks a bunch, Mr. Buddy. Good folks're good to good folks. Best of luck. Hang in there."

Sergeant Ćwikła returned to the car.

"Out," he said sharply.

Buddy got out and sighed deeply. He thought how far he was from Warsaw. He didn't like getting away from Warsaw. Outside Warsaw he felt naked. Except for Łódź—where he often went on business, never spent the night, and which he considered a distant suburb of the capital—he'd been out of the city twice.

Once in 1928 he, the girls, and his wife had taken a vacation to the mountain resort of Zakopane. The food in the boardinghouse had been awful, the company unbelievably stupid, because they were all overeducated, snooty, cocksucking intellectuals. Of all the smart and dumb people in the world, the dumbest of the dumb are always intellectuals.

By the end of the trip, Buddy couldn't hold back when over breakfast, some clerk from Bydgoszcz with a high tenor voice started pontificating for the seventh time about the need to categorically oppose the Teutonic element with all the nation's power, both spiritual and material. Hearing this yet again, Buddy got up, begging his wife's and daughters' pardon. The women rushed to their room to hurriedly pack their bags. They knew there was no arguing with Buddy when he took that tone, so they abandoned their unfinished meal without a backward glance and threw themselves into following their master and father's command. Meanwhile Buddy approached the Bydgoszcz pontificator and socked him in the back of the head so hard that the man's face plopped into his plate of cold, oversalted scrambled eggs. Next, to emphasize the strength of his argument, Buddy yanked the chair out from underneath this tribune of the Polish cause and broke it over the man's shoulders, whereupon he bowed, left the boardinghouse, and asked for his car to be brought.

After a few minutes two farmers came at him, brothers, real highlanders, furious at him for beating up boardinghouse guests who were paying good money. They brandished their shepherd's axes and fists, spurring each other on with energetic vulgarities. Kaplica pulled out his pistol and said if there was anything in the world he hated more than fascists and Russkies it was sheep-fucking highlanders, and if they so much as opened their mouths again he'd happily shoot them dead on the spot. Seeing his revolver, the farmers politely made their apologies, Buddy got into his car—at the time he was driving a then-new Polish CWS T-1 with an open-top body—and, checking his wife and daughters had packed fully, he set off for the capital, swearing he'd never willingly cross the city limits again.

Yet cross them he did, going a year later to the Universal National Exhibition in Poznań, a trip he regretted almost the instant it began, loathing the difficulties of travel; still, that trip passed without any drama.

And this was the third time.

"Forward," ordered Sergeant Ćwikła and Buddy took a deep breath into his barrel chest, as though expecting that inside the barbed wire of the camp there wouldn't be much air to breathe.

They set off.

Sergeant Ćwikła led Kaplica to the guardhouse, then left the entrance to the Isolation Facility with relief.

"Family name?" The guard at the desk wore round wire-rim glasses and looked like a kindly postmaster.

"Kaplica."

"Given names?"

"Jan Jerzy."

"Father's name?"

"Jan."

"Mother's name?"

"Katarzyna."

"Date and place of birth?"

"December twenty-third, year of our Lord 1888, in Warsaw."

"Religion?"

"Not religious."

"Religion!" repeated the guard forcefully.

Buddy considered for a moment.

"Roman Catholic," he finally replied, so as not to be mistaken for a Jew.

"Hand over your personal items," ordered the guard.

Buddy sighed and dug all the odds and ends out of his pockets: his wallet, his cigarette case, the lighter with the tax sticker, a pocketknife, a comb, mustache wax. The guard sorted it all carefully and made a list.

"Shoelaces, tie, and suspenders."

Kaplica sighed a second time, bent over, and started undoing his shoes. He was struggling, the laces were tangled up.

The kick in the ass caught him by surprise, he lost his balance and hit his head on the floor, blood poured down his face.

"Pick up the fucking pace, you filthy crud, hurry it up, this isn't a fucking vacation!" screamed the guard who looked like a postmaster.

Buddy got up off the floor, spat out blood from his split lip, then gave the guard a hard right hook to the temple, shattering his glasses and knocking him out at the same time. He roared in pain at his wounded shoulder, but the dull thud of the unconscious policeman hitting the floor was music to his ears. Kaplica was now alone with the unconscious guard in the otherwise empty guardroom. His eyes landed on the policeman's belt and the holstered seven-shooter. Tempting.

He knew if he did something like that, then every crook from Wilno to Sosnowiec, from Lwów to Kalisz, the length and breadth of old Poland would sing ballads about him. They'd raise glasses to him in the dives of the Northern District and Praga, and tell the story a thousand times over of Buddy in Bereza, when he knocked out a guard, took his revolver, and perished in a beautiful, one-sided, heroic battle with the cops, taking a dozen down with him.

He wouldn't take down a dozen. It was impossible to reload a seven-shooter that quickly, you couldn't just tilt the cylinder to one side like in the new Smith & Wesson revolvers and eject all the used cartridges with the press of a button, nor could you break open the whole gun like the British Webleys, which ejected their used cartridges automatically when the gun was cracked open. With a seven-shooter you had to knock out every leftover cartridge one by one through a narrow opening, each time giving the cylinder a one-seventh turn, and then slide the new bullets in one by one. You couldn't do it quickly, especially when someone was shooting at you.

Maybe he'd take down five. The thieves' ballad would make five into fifty, including the police chief himself. Eternal glory.

He gazed at the holster. Tempting.

The guard who looked like a postmaster was starting to regain consciousness. Buddy knew it was now or never. The final seconds. A beautiful, heroic gangster's death or the humiliation and torture of Bereza?

But he wanted to see his daughters again, he wanted to eat crayfish with dill at the Pod Ryjkiem delicatessen, sip coffee and sink his teeth into a stuffed pastry at his snack bar on Leszno, drink vodka at Glajszmitka's, eat tripe at Fat Josek's, and sauerkraut stew at Choromańczyk's in Kercelak market, and he also longed to taste a girlish body at Ryfka's, revel in her virginal bashfulness as his bristly mustache brushed her young skin, and break through that bashfulness, and afterward enjoy the warmth of his family in hearth and home, listen to his daughters sing "The Warszawianka 1905," accompanying themselves on the piano, and be glad he'd spent so much money sending them to those piano lessons. It was worth staying alive. Or at least trying to.

He sat down in a chair. The policeman regained consciousness. It took him a moment to collect himself and understand what had happened. Buddy sat there calmly. It occurred to him there was no point pulling out his shoelaces anymore.

"Help!" roared the policeman, unbuttoning the top of his holster. It was over. He'd chosen life.

A moment later, three men were beating him up. Kaplica curled up on the floor, knees to his chin, arms around his head, they gave him a savage working-over. Two of them calm, methodical, the third furious over his smashed glasses and embarrassed at being knocked out cold. The other two had to hold him back so he didn't accidentally kill Buddy. They did break his ribs, knock out his two front teeth, and damage his kidneys. The wound on his left arm opened up again and bled copiously. They finally let up, long after he'd lost consciousness.

They brought him to the infirmary passed out on a stretcher. There Buddy was examined by a field medic, butcher, and alcoholic by the name of Bakalarczyk, who lacked even a passing acquaintance with the study of medicine, though he was known throughout the Brześć counterintelligence division for being able to drink anyone, even a Bolshevik, under the table. The field medic cursorily dressed Kaplica's wounded arm and pronounced his opinion that, to the best of his knowledge, the prisoner was fit for solitary confinement. Kaplica was revived with ammonia, stripped naked, and led to the isolation cells in a brick building at the center of the camp.

He could barely stay upright, so two policemen led him and he somehow walked, wobbling on muddy legs, bloodied, his only clothing the bandage on his left arm; his mighty privates dangled beneath his large belly, and one policeman, himself very modest in that department, kept sneaking jealous glances at them.

They threw Buddy into a windowless cell dug deep into the earth, where it was bitingly cold despite the unusually warm October. It was furnished only with a single stone bench, with no sleeping pallet or anything else. The floor was covered in an inch or so of frigid water. Despite the cold it stank mightily, shit was floating in the water because the latrines for prisoners in solitary were usually leaky. The guards also went straight into the usual routine.

Every fifteen minutes a policeman pounded on the door of Buddy's cell. He'd been instructed that every time they pounded he had to answer with a thunderous "Here!" This procedure was aimed exclusively at his own well-being: this was how the guards would make sure he was alive.

During the day he was required to stand, sitting was forbidden. So he leaned on the cold, moldy wall, found a patch of floor slightly higher than the rest, where the water was maybe half an inch, and stood there, answered "Here," shook with fever, and thought about young girls' bodies, breasts not yet in full bloom, the taste of vodka and strong beer, the sauerkraut stew at Choromańczyk's, and the champagne at Ryfka's, and though his entire now-aged body was telling him that he'd die here, that he was too old, too fat, too weak for this concentration camp, too weak to survive here, he kept telling himself: "I'll get out." I'll get out. He'd finally face Kamala-Kurhański and give him the message about Aunt Adelajda. As long as that crook was waiting in her apartment for the chief's phone call, as long as he hadn't given up.

Knock-knock.

"Here!"

He passed out three times, the knocking startled him awake. In the evening they allowed him to lie down. Reporting every fifteen minutes was still required. He didn't hear the seventh knock, he'd fallen asleep. They came inside, putting galoshes on first, and whipped Kaplica with a chain.

Knock-knock.

"Here."

Knock-knock.

"Here."

Knock-knock.

"Buddy Kaplica here, you fucking sons of bitches!"

They beat him again, but he didn't regret it.

"You think you're gonna get out of here? You raised your hand to a police officer, that's like raising your hand to Poland, you miserable louse. You won't be the first one to bite the dust in here, disgusting crud," the policeman who looked like a postmaster hissed in battered Kaplica's ear.

"I was shooting Russkies for Poland while you were still hanging out of your father's cock," spat Kaplica.

Another thrashing, on the back with a chain.

He thought he wouldn't live through the night, but he did. His left arm was in horrible pain, he was coughing, his nose was running, he was so feverish he could barely stand, he was hallucinating too, and yet in the morning, when they told him to get up, he did.

Knock-knock.

"Here!"

Knock-knock.

"Here!"

◆ ◆ ◆

We, meanwhile, remained orphaned in Warsaw, without Buddy.

We returned to the Szapiros' apartment in silence. Jakub told Pantaleon to come with us and stand guard.

So Pantaleon took a stool from the kitchen, set it up in the main stairwell at the entrance to the Szapiros' apartment, put his seven-shooter in his pocket and a sawed-off shotgun loaded with buckshot on his lap, and sat.

We went to sleep, safe. Jakub and Emilia whispered for a long time in the dark.

Pantaleon had no fear of dozing off. His devil brother wouldn't let him.

Pantaleon and his devil brother whispered for a long time in the dark.

You should kill his kids. Two sons like two loaded barrels, you go inside, into their room, their wealthy room, your kids don't get an ounce of this wealth and how does this Jew live? He lives like a lord, go inside two barrels two heads two shots then your pistol and into his room shoot him rape his woman then kill her. Go, go, go, Pantaleon, go.

"Shut up, devil," Pantaleon would say loudly. "In the name of the Father, and of the Son, and of the Holy Ghost I command you, shut up, devil."

On his left shoulder and upper back he had a patch of skin completely covered in scars. He had no sensation there and believed that part of his body belonged to his devil brother, that his devil brother could feel that part of his skin.

Go now go two kids in the head two barrels and dead.

"Silence, demon," said Pantaleon loudly and took a razor from his pocket, reached his right hand over his shoulder, and dragged the razor along his skin, cutting deep, yet another line in the network of long scars.

The devil brother howled in Pantaleon's head, opening wide its silent and blind lips hidden beneath his hair, then merely whimpered, like a buzzing in his ear.

Pantaleon remained motionless on the stool, feeling the blood dripping down his shoulder, and he sat that way until morning, until Jakub came out and relieved him from his vigil and asked him to join them for breakfast. Jakub didn't ask about the dried blood on Pantaleon's shirt, he knew.

The six of us ate breakfast together, Emilia, the boys, Jakub, Pantaleon, and me.

"He's not in Warsaw," said Jakub. "I called around. He's not anywhere. The folks in the ministry still won't talk to me."

"They took him to Bereza," said Emilia. "That's the simplest answer."

"What's Bereza?" asked Daniel Szapiro.

"A concentration camp," responded his father.

"What's concentration?" asked the boy.

"It's a sort of prison where they lock people up without trial. The Germans have one in Dachau. They lock people up to scare them, they hold them for a while and break them. And based on that one in Dachau, the Poles built their own in Bereza."

"But they're not gonna lock us up there?"

"No. Because we're leaving for Palestine."

259

"I don't wanna go to Palestine!"

Jakub smiled at Emilia. She smiled back.

"We have to work it out with Moryc," said Jakub. "Set a date. Next spring, maybe. Or maybe the end of this year. And we'll go. I'll just get some more dough together. And we'll go. Actually this year's probably better."

We talked about it all day and went to sleep with thoughts of Palestine. I dreamed of the white buildings of Tel Aviv, which I'd seen in pictures and at the movies, I dreamed of palm trees and sand.

The next day the three of us sat at the bar at Ryfka's, Jakub, Pantaleon, and me. Jakub was drinking vodka and Pantaleon, tea, while Ryfka polished her nails behind the bar. On the bar top lay the latest *Warsaw Courier*, open to page six, where amid ads showing Chevrolet Master Sedans, Fuchs gourmet chocolate, a mouse that didn't know where to hide since the house had switched to Tungsram Krypton light bulbs, and Maciejewski Brothers coats, there was a short article penned by Witold Sokoliński: "Warsaw bandit finally caught. Jan Kaplica in Bereza Kartuska Isolation Facility. Capital sighs with relief."

It was late afternoon, getting on into evening—that undefined time between five and seven. There were no customers yet, the place was closed for the moment, the girls were just starting to do themselves up, so we sat alone, not speaking much.

Jakub read Sokoliński's article a third time.

"That weasel, that jumped-up weasel," he swore under his breath, furious and helpless.

When Munja and Tyutchev came into the salon it took a moment for anyone to notice, since their presence at Ryfka's was as natural as syphilis in a whore. Munja even had his own key.

It took Szapiro two seconds to register, then he reached for his gun.

"Hang on," said Ryfka, who could see more and thought a little faster.

Munja and Tyutchev raised their hands, which held no weapons.

"The Doctor wants to know if we can talk without guns or knives," said Munja. "For everyone's benefit."

Szapiro scratched his stubbly chin.

"We can always talk," he finally responded.

"*Ladno.* You all give your word of honor," demanded Tyutchev. "No shooting."

They agreed. Munja stayed upstairs, Tyutchev ran downstairs, then returned with Radziwiłek.

He looked better than ever. He was wearing a new Rifleman's Association uniform and a round officer's cap, he was clean-shaven and smelled of English cologne.

"Good day, all ladies and gentlemen here," he declared, removing his hat and placing it under his arm in a military gesture. His bald head glistened as though polished.

Szapiro slid off the stool, stood across from Radziwiłek, one force facing another: Jakub in an undershirt that revealed his boxer's shoulders and upper arms and was tucked into his high-waisted pants, Radziwiłek in his uniform and glistening boots; both men the same height; Radziwiłek slim, Jakub heavy and broad-shouldered; both Jews, but Jakub with a distinctly Mediterranean beauty, Radziwiłek none at all.

"Fact is we gotta look after Kercelak market," said the Doctor. "And nobody do that better than you, Mr. Szapiro."

"I work for Buddy," replied Jakub.

"Mr. Szapiro. You know sometimes is change. World change. Was czar, now czar *nyet*. Was no Poland, now is. Was Buddy, now is not. Change is good. Gotta love change. Gotta adapt to change."

Szapiro was silent.

"Gonna be like it was, Mr. Szapiro. How much money you keep for yourself, what you collect for Kaplica?"

"Seven percent," replied the boxer.

"So now you keep two times. Fourteen."

Jakub shook his head and frowned.

"Fifteen," said Radziwiłek.

Jakub calmly calculated. He recognized the anger flowing in his veins, but if he hadn't learned to master that anger he'd have been dead long ago. That was the source of his strength, in controlling his anger like a cart driver controls a horse, not letting it rule him.

So he thought. Palestine. Palestine. Palestine. He needed money. War with Radziwiłek would be costly. And hard to win. At least open war. It was easy to take a stand and fight. To fight and win was harder, and Jakub hated losing and never fought a war he didn't expect to win. There was no dignity in picking a fight when you were going to lose it.

"Fine," he finally replied. "But on one condition."

"I am all hearing," said the Doctor glowingly.

"We say 'all ears,' 'I'm all ears.'"

"What ears? What are you talking, Mr. Szapiro?"

"Forget it. My condition is you don't lay a finger on Kasia. Or any of Ryfka's girls. Better we don't see each other here at all."

"Mr. Szapiro." Radziwiłek smiled and shrugged, his arms wide. "Plenty of fish in the sea! I gladly give word! My foot not set in here! We got deal! Drink! Miss Ryfka, pour everyone vodka and I change location in a sec."

Ryfka poured the drinks, everyone had one, even Pantaleon.

"But by me is also one condition," said Radziwiłek, wiping his mouth. "Miss Ryfka not have variety. Now we sell more things at Miss Ryfka's. Tyutchev, give her."

The Russian went up to the bar and lay down two small packets.

"This cocaine, this heroin. Fifty gram each. Miss Ryfka, you sell as much as you want. You pay me one thousand złoty for cocaine and one thousand seven hundred for heroin. Together is two thousand seven hundred Polish złoty."

"Buddy would never agree to this," said Ryfka.

"You right, Miss Ryfka, and maybe that exactly why Buddy sits now in Bereza but we sit here."

"For the love of Jesus," noted Pantaleon grimly, "on the market a gram of cocaine goes for eighteen złotys and heroin for thirty. It doesn't add up."

"But Miss Ryfka have wonderful client! Wealthy client! Miss Ryfka sell one for twenty-five per gram, other for forty-two per gram, and Miss Ryfka have profit."

"I haven't got that much cash. I can take it on consignment," said Ryfka.

"Consignment is okay, but tomorrow Tyutchev come get money." The Doctor smiled.

"That's not how consignment works," protested Jakub in feeble anger.

The Doctor gave an innocent shrug. He didn't have to make threats, everyone here was very familiar with the etiquette of these conversations, there was no need for the threats to be out loud.

"And therefore, as Englishman say, from now on is *business as usual*," declared the Doctor. He bowed and left, Tyutchev following right behind him.

Munja hesitated for a moment, leaning on the bar.

"Scram," growled Pantaleon, whose categories of loyalty were very simple. "Or I'll send ya out the window."

Munja preferred the stairs, so he hurried out without a word, his eyes down.

The four of us were left, including Ryfka. Not long until opening time.

"So that's it?" she asked. "You're gonna work for him?"

"Officially, at least. We're leaving for Palestine anyway. With Moryc. I need money. I gotta sell my apartment, but if I don't find a buyer I'll leave without selling."

Ryfka froze, a glass and dishrag in her hands. Jakub turned to look at her and understood. Along with that understanding came shame— how could he be so stupid and so insensitive to say it so simply, so simply—that they were leaving.

"You two are leaving," she said finally and Jakub understood that "two" hurt her just as much as the fact that Jakub would be disappearing from her life.

"You can come too," he said, only to realize immediately this was cruelty and idiocy combined.

She sniffed and Jakub saw she wanted to cry, but also knew she wouldn't. Not Ryfka.

"You gotta spring Buddy from Bereza first, Jakub. You can't leave me alone with Radziwiłek. What am I supposed to do with these powders? I mean, it's not gonna be easy to sell this stuff."

"Miss Ryfka's right, wise words," said Pantaleon, feeling his devil brother tingling. "Being alone with the Doctor is a curse."

"Okay, I'm listening, you two got any ideas how to spring someone from Bereza?"

"You gotta get to whoever in this country decides who gets locked up there and who gets let out," said Ryfka matter-of-factly, almost banally. "The other option's to get together every tough in Warsaw, Łódź, and Lublin, load 'em into trucks, which you'd have to steal from somebody first, go halfway across Poland, and drive into the camp, pistols and shotguns blazing, shoot the cops, let out the prisoners, and then I dunno what, run over the border to the Reds?"

Szapiro gave a dismissive wave of his hand, though he did smile. Ryfka went quiet, there was really no point wasting her breath.

The girls came out of their rooms, all done up for work, drifted into their armchairs around the room, and took on languorous, spoiled poses and jaded expressions, because that was what the clients liked most. Next Bykow arrived, put on his work tuxedo with the cream-colored jacket, ate the dinner he was entitled to, fussed a little about the meat being stringy, then sat down at the piano. His fingers danced briefly over the keys, then he started to play quietly. The first customers had also arrived and the girls went to work, while Jakub stayed at the bar, drinking a little and thinking.

Ryfka held her tongue, not even so much offended as wounded, painfully wounded, but he wasn't able to truly hurt her. She loved him, after all, and he knew that and loved her too, though differently now, not as she wished he would. But she had accepted that, because she was a master at accepting reality.

She wondered where to get the money for Radziwiłek and quickly let go of her ire and again accepted the reality—it was obvious she had to earn it, she had to sell the drugs.

And suddenly Ryfka's went quiet. First the hushed chatter of initial negotiations between the girls and their customers ceased, then Bykow stopped playing, breaking off after the first bars of a popular tune, and silence fell.

There was a woman standing in the doorway. That didn't bode well, because it couldn't possibly bode well. Women looking for work never took the main entrance into Ryfka's, the only women who did were hunting after their husbands. Even then it was only the ones who were smart enough to work out the address—no minor matter given their husbands were hardly eager to share the information and Ryfka didn't advertise her presence with a sign or even a visiting card on the door, not to mention everything took place here very discreetly, at least when Radziwiłek wasn't firing his pistol at her terrified customers, and even the piano was muffled.

"A tsure of maa kop, nukh ayne iz gyekime' farn man iyo' . . . ,"[29] Ryfka hissed under her breath.

Only then did Jakub turn around.

---

29 Just what I needed, another one come looking for her husband.

In the door to Ryfka Kij's brothel stood Anna Ziembińska, looking as though she owned this place, the building, the neighborhood, the southern City Center, all of Warsaw even, from Bielany to Mokotów, from Ochota to Targówek. She was wearing a low-cut dress drawn together on her left hip in an asymmetrical drape and made of material neither Ryfka nor Jakub had ever seen, a mesh that would be seethrough if it weren't filled out by strings of crystals, glistening black lacquer, and cubic zirconia.

Anna went up to the bar, audacious, confident, beautiful.

The moment Ryfka laid eyes on Ziembińska in all her splendor, she understood immediately women in dresses like that didn't come to luxurious brothels in search of wayward husbands.

She wondered what this lady could be looking for, then glanced at Jakub and answered her own question: the only person a lady in a dress like that might be looking for at Ryfka's was Jakub Szapiro, sitting at the bar in a sleeveless undershirt tucked into high-waisted gaberdine pants, hunched over his fifth vodka.

Ryfka took another look at Anna, who gave her a kindly smile, revealing white, wolfish teeth, and felt very old, ugly, and used up. She understood that in any conflict with this tall, young Polish woman, whose dress probably cost around five thousand złotys, she'd lose, lose right away, at the very moment the confrontation began.

Jakub looked at Anna and only then recognized her.

"What d'you want?" he growled, and to Ryfka the authentic aversion in his voice was like the most beautiful music, like the singing of angels.

"I thought I might join you for a glass of champagne, Mr. Szapiro," said Anna.

Szapiro turned on his barstool to face Ziembińska and eyed her up and down for a moment, looking weary and sick of women.

"So you think you can just turn up here, you stupid Polish whore?" he said quietly, his voice very calm.

Anna kept smiling, but Ryfka knew Jakub's words had had the intended effect—of a slap in the face. She also knew he'd done that in part for her, for Ryfka, he'd done it because he still loved her and didn't want this Christian woman's advantage to be so visible, so painful. Ryfka knew men better than anything else.

For a woman like Anna, life had given her no reason to be used to someone speaking to her that way. Unlike Ryfka. Men had spoken to Ryfka every way imaginable since her breasts started growing when she was thirteen, because before then most men had barely registered her existence.

She was born in 1908, but by 1937 she looked much older than twenty-nine. What I'm about to write she told me once when we were alone together, back that August. Jakub had left me at Ryfka's and gone to Kercelak on his own to sort out a loan Buddy was supposed to give Choromańczyk, naturally at usurious interest.

Ryfka came from Łódź, she didn't know her father, her mother was Jewish, unemployed, and from the very bottom of the Łódź lumpenproletariat. She maintained Ryfka's father was a great lord, a German baron, his family too wealthy and important to support a bastard daughter. The first years of Ryfka's life were those of a single mother and daughter in a Łódź Jewish household, but by the end of the war she was living on the street. She spoke a mix of Polish and Yiddish, she didn't yet know how to separate the languages. She learned later.

It was Buddy who brought her from the streets of Łódź to Warsaw, in 1922. First he had her to himself, keeping her in a small room in a cheap rented apartment in Koło district, where she gave herself to him with total indifference. She was glad to have a roof over her head, warm meals, and dresses to wear instead of rags. Besides, Buddy even gave her money, Polish marks at that time, which she saved up very prudently but which by 1923 had lost all their value to hyperinflation.

Two years later he handed her over to a good brothel in the southern City Center. She only worked there for six months and remained under

Buddy's care, so she didn't have it hard. She saved up all over again, this time exchanging her złotys for dollars at Kercelak, and accumulated 120 of those dollars, though she lost it all when she went straight from the brothel to the women's prison on Dzielna Street, nicknamed "Serbia." Within fifteen minutes of Ryfka being escorted from the brothel by the brave policemen, the other girls had stolen everything.

She ended up in Serbia because she'd killed a trick. She'd killed him with a Spanish fold-up knife she'd stolen from a previous connoisseur of her body and she'd kept it in her bed ever since, just for such an occasion. This trick had wanted to stick an empty wine bottle in her ass and see if he could get the whole thing in. Maybe he could have, but he didn't get the chance to find out, because that was a boundary Ryfka had no desire to cross, so she plunged the knife into his neck, then into his chest to be sure, then cut off his genitals. In death the trick orphaned five children, and they wasted away along with their mother, and no one wept for them except their mother, and she didn't live long. The little youngsters disappeared, dispersed into the streets and alleyways of Wola and Muranów districts, and nothing remained of them, all because of that one bottle.

While Ryfka was awaiting trial, Buddy dutifully paid off the judge and prosecutor. She only got four years and served two, enjoying a reputation as a powerful woman and the universal respect of her fellow prisoners, which nevertheless she had to constantly reinforce with her fists, and she did, because she had the hard fists of a street kid. She also had a few prison romances, which cheered her up and brought a welcome change from the boredom of incarceration, but also confirmed Ryfka's belief that love required a cock, even though cocks were unfortunately attached to representatives of the male sex.

They released her under strange circumstances just after Piłsudski's return to power. In the confusion following the coup, Buddy whispered a word here and there, greased some palms here and there, and Ryfka was out, and as she left Serbia, she knew she'd never go back to prostitution, though she didn't know what else she could do with herself, but that was also the day she met Jakub.

She met him when Buddy invited everyone to the Bristol to celebrate the release of his Ryfka, who he'd always had a soft spot for and indulged. Jakub had been discharged in 1923 with the rank of platoon sergeant, then joined Buddy the year before the coup, while Ryfka was still in prison. Listless after leaving the barracks, Jakub joined the boxing section of Maccabi Warsaw, which had only been active for a year. He quickly showed himself to be an exceptionally talented and committed competitor. Buddy had an interest in boxing. He saw Jakub training, approached him, and immediately recognized him as a street boy, a tough—they talked about prison, the war, and then Buddy offered him a job. Jakub was clever, strong, a good shot, and totally loyal. By the time Ryfka got out of prison, Jakub had already become Buddy's right-hand man.

Ryfka arrived at the Bristol with a certain journalist who'd been courting her. Jakub was standing with Munja and a couple others, already drunk. He'd just returned from the seaside resort of Sopot, where he'd broken up with a certain neurotic young lady, and was telling everyone he'd had enough of women. The journalist wanted to show off to Ryfka that he knew someone as remarkable as Szapiro, so almost forcibly introduced them, saying Ryfka wanted badly to meet Mr. Szapiro, which she immediately hotly contradicted, exclaiming she hadn't wanted to at all.

Szapiro struck up a conversation and they talked for a long time. An hour later, Jakub finally suggested they leave the party—and they did, walking slowly and drunkenly to the building on the corner of Wilcza and Emilia Plater Streets where Szapiro lived at the time. Ryfka was wearing a long flower-print dress and Jakub was very careful not to step on it when it got tangled around her feet.

She didn't go inside with him and he didn't invite her. They sat on the steps and talked. Finally she got up and gave him her address and telephone number, saying if he wanted to join her for breakfast to give her a call.

He did. They went to an ordinary stall by the river for breakfast, and the woman surprised him with her appetite.

After two years in prison Ryfka had the feeling that life had passed her by and she really needed a man—a big, strong, handsome man— and Jakub was just that. Meanwhile Jakub needed a woman he could talk to like a man—and Ryfka was just that. Experienced and intelligent beyond her years, she understood what mattered to Jakub like no woman before or since.

For the next four days they didn't part even for a moment. The first day they spent in a hotel room at the Bristol, drinking champagne, snorting cocaine, making love, ordering food, drinking again, sleeping a little, making love, and sleeping again. Then they went dancing for a few hours in second-rate dives, because that was where they felt most comfortable, then ate tripe with the Jewish cart drivers at Glajszmitka's on the corner of Dzika and Okopowa Streets, drinking one large shot of vodka after another and chowing down on "Catholics," as we called pickled herrings back then.

Jakub didn't yet have his apartment at 40 Nalewki Street, he was living in one hurriedly and briefly rented room after another, at that moment one at the corner of Emilia Plater and Wilcza; he was prince of the nomads with all his possessions in a canvas sack and his pockets stuffed with cash. He hadn't met Emilia yet, had no children, was twenty-six, and liked having fun much more than he would eleven years later. In those days he tore around Warsaw in an open-topped green Austro-Daimler and they drove that green Daimler up to Bielany district, he taught Ryfka to shoot in the park, then they drove to the Pod Ryjkiem delicatessen on Marszałkowska Street to eat crayfish boiled with dill by the dozen—which Pod Ryjkiem always served in late spring and early summer—and to wash those red crayfish down with white Austrian wine.

Then they headed for Berlin, because Ryfka said she'd like to. She'd never been abroad. They drove for three days, but they got there, and Berlin in 1926 was beautiful.

They listened to jazz at an outdoor concert in the Tiergarten. Jakub didn't care for the jazz, so they drank champagne and schnapps, danced in a working-class dance hall whose walls were decorated with colored tinsel, they ate and made love in the best hotels, then drove three days back in the Austro-Daimler, which broke down in Poznań, so they went the rest of the way by train. Jakub never went back for the Daimler, some kraut probably drove it until it fell apart, or the Poles finally confiscated it, or the Nazis, when the war came thirteen years later. On the train, the conductor caught them having sex in a first-class compartment, Jakub tossed him fifty złotys without leaving Ryfka's body, and the conductor went off pleased for the money; he didn't trouble the loving couple any more.

For a year they were joined at the hip. Ryfka often put on men's clothes and carried a knife and pistol in her pocket, just like Szapiro. She shot, punched, swore, drank, snorted cocaine, and in the evenings put on her best dress and danced at Oaza with Jakub and neither he nor she needed anything more from life and demanded nothing more of it.

When the year was over, they'd worn themselves out. After quitting training in 1925, Jakub returned to it and needed a more stable and regular lifestyle. Ryfka wanted to have fun. Jakub didn't. Ryfka said she was leaving for Berlin. She had plenty of her own money. Jakub refused to go with her and stayed in Warsaw. She said he shouldn't write or call unless he wanted to come. He didn't. He was taking care of Moryc, who was growing up, in Warsaw—he needed to look after him.

When she left, he felt empty inside. He suddenly understood how much he needed her, how much she'd given him, and how lonely he was without her. She was the only one he could talk to about what mattered to him, who understood his life and at the same time was interested in it, even more than her own. He kept no secrets from her and trusted her mysterious wisdom.

She returned from Berlin six months later and told him in those six months she'd had several men and none of them was one one-hundredth the man he was. Jakub said he loved her and didn't even want to look at another woman.

They moved in together, a small apartment in Wola district.

Then Ryfka started drinking. In fact Ryfka was drinking the same as always, but Jakub was drinking much less, since he was training seriously and had had enough of underworld life by then, and Ryfka's apocalyptic drinking started to bother him.

The fights they had were infamous all over the Jewish district.

Ryfka would shoot her pistol at Jakub. She once blasted the hat off his head—accidentally, because she was aiming lower. But she'd wipe the blood off him after a boxing match and was the loudest to cheer when he knocked out an opponent.

Jakub threw a dresser full of her clothes out the window, without opening the window, and the whole window frame went flying out along with the dresser and the glass, and everything lay on the pavement for three days, no one dared touch it because every crook in Wola district knew who the stuff belonged to. Then Jakub quit training and they spent three days in the apartment, naked—they drank, snorted cocaine, made love, and fought.

Ryfka smashed several bottles over Jakub's head. Jakub never hit her, just grabbed her arms when she tried to punch him and laughed when she roared with impotent rage. Then she'd try to play the good housewife but get nowhere; she didn't know how to cook or clean and after a few attempts she dropped it.

In those days Jakub started reading more, partly so he wouldn't fall too far behind his younger brother. He also came to see that, though it had nothing to do with reading, he wanted to have children.

"I can't have children. When I was in the brothel something broke inside me down there and I can't," Ryfka told him then, and two days later Jakub met Emilia Kahan. It was the middle of 1928.

Emilia came from a good, secular, somewhat assimilated family. Her father was a lawyer and a socialist, her mother a refined lady who shared her husband's views. They'd raised their daughter in a leftist spirit as well, so Emilia was always drawn to the lower classes, particularly if they were personified by a boxer's handsome, powerful, two-hundred-pound body, clothed in the finest suits and coats from Zaremba's, driving beautiful cars, and besides that criminally charming, warm, sincere, and glowing with an uncertain quality that made every woman feel safe with Jakub. And they all were.

When he left, Ryfka said she'd slice Emilia's face with a razor. Jakub answered if he ever saw Ryfka near his fiancée he'd kill her and throw her body in the Vistula. And she should imagine the eels and lampreys eating out her eyes, slithering through her dead eyes—through her mouth, ass, pussy—into her body and eating her from the inside.

"You never bought me a ring," said Ryfka and decided not to get anywhere near Emilia, because she didn't want eels and lampreys eating her from the inside, and she'd long since learned to take Jakub's threats seriously.

"You don't buy a ring for a barren whore," hissed Jakub, then left and never returned to her again.

She didn't resent that, at the end of the day she was a whore and she was barren, he hadn't said anything false. The only thing she did resent was him leaving. She never forgave him for that.

A year later Emilia bore twins. They didn't have a wedding, they didn't need a wedding, they simply lived together. The thought of standing under a chuppah made Jakub feel sick. Emilia didn't care, what difference did that make? All she cared about was having a family.

When Emilia had the boys, Jakub, with her knowledge though without her approval, gave Ryfka ten thousand złotys to start up a business. Just like that. He'd stolen the ten thousand specially for her from the state lottery ticket office on Koszykowa Street, in broad daylight, tearing out the safe with chains hooked to a truck, loading it into the back, and driving off. Inside it held twenty thousand złotys, ten thousand he divvied up among his cronies and ten thousand he kept for himself, just to give to Ryfka.

She accepted it, though she didn't think she would.

"She got a ring from you and sons from your loins, so I've got a right to the money and the business I'll start with it," she said.

Jakub was happy with Emilia. For a few years. He enjoyed a quiet life. The street didn't sing songs about them, the street kept singing songs about Jakub and Ryfka, about the lovers shooting revolvers at one another, the love between a bandit and a whore. The street didn't care about the love between a bandit and a lawyer's daughter.

Ryfka was unhappy without Jakub, but happy for the money and the position she rose to from owning her own business, one lovingly guarded by Kaplica and located from the start in the soaring apartment house on Pius XI Street.

After nine years of unformalized but real marriage, Jakub was still with Emilia and the kids, while Ryfka was without Jakub but with her brothel. Yet neither was happy any longer, Ryfka since the beginning, Jakub for some while.

Jakub understood there was no such thing as happiness and often wondered what might have happened if he'd gone off to Berlin with Ryfka back then. They would have had to keep going in 1933, to America, but they could have gone to America, he'd have been free with Ryfka, he could have done anything with Ryfka, but now, with Daniel and Dawid, he could do very little, because these two little eight-year-old lives weighed on his mind, heart, and conscience.

Ryfka was worn out. From the day-to-day routine, from wrangling with drunken customers and finicky girls, but above all worn out from what she'd seen over those nine years, and what she'd seen was her small but perfectly formed little business sucking girls dry, one after the other, wringing them out like dishrags; she'd seen them rotting from within, peddling their youth and beauty for next to nothing, and only a fraction of that cheap price remaining for them, a fraction of what that beauty generated, because the remainder went toward rent, expenses, Ryfka's pay, Buddy's share, bribes for the police, toward everything but them. Every single girl was a fool, completely convinced they'd find someone at Ryfka's, an officer in a handsome uniform, a doctor, or an heir, who'd fall in love with her, like in the romance novels they devoured, and pull her out of the brothel, out of her trade, make her his wife, get her pregnant, and shower her with gifts and everything a girl needs in life. Of course some johns did fall in love, they kept coming, spending their last penny, even getting girls pregnant, then when they went totally broke you'd have to kick them to the curb and get the girls scraped out, and the men would stand out on the street wailing, the poor saps, and then they'd get over it, because people always do, and Ryfka knew better than anyone you don't buy a ring for a whore. Whores got champagne in good times, a slap when they mouthed off, an abortion when expecting, and boredom and loneliness in old age. A life like a dime novel on the consequences of moral decline. Ryfka sometimes read books like that and was amazed how well their authors described the consequences of street life, yet without understanding it at all or even knowing it.

Some of her girls she ran into later, on the street, because there was no getting ahead in this business, some ended up begging and died of poverty and neglect—Ryfka hated seeing that and it wore her out even more.

Meanwhile for Jakub, being with Emilia wasn't the problem. The problem was with himself. The problem was the stability and peace he'd worked so hard to build because he was smart and knew anything else would be the end of him, he'd founder in vodka or his obsessions like so many others he knew and saw foundering. So the problem was the stability. For a soldier, a gangster, and a boxer—because he was all those at once, used to knives and guns, to fists and that extraordinary elation that came with winning, to that emotion, incomparable with anything, even an orgasm, that washed over a person when he saw his opponent laid out on the mat after a brief fight—for someone like that, building a stable and peaceful life was much harder than for a lawyer, a shop assistant, or a bookkeeper. But he built such a life anyway. And now he missed that wild life with Ryfka, and she knew he did, though he never revealed his feelings to her, because he missed it but couldn't throw away his stability after taking responsibility for his sons, for Daniel and Dawid, even though no one had ever taken any responsibility for him.

Maybe that was the very reason.

◆ ◆ ◆

I look at my hands on the keyboard of my typewriter. I examine my right hand. On my wrinkled skin, between the liver spots, I can make out traces of navy-blue ink, but not on the skin—I haven't gotten dirty—in the skin, beneath the slightly peeling surface, like a tattoo, and the ink is arranged in the same pattern Jakub Szapiro had on his hand, a sword and death and I don't remember when I would have gotten that tattoo.

But it doesn't matter. What matters is writing. Only the past matters.

I feel like I've disappeared in these memories. There is no Moyshe Bernsztajn, there's no Moyshe, there's no Mojżesz, there's no Moshe Inbar, only Jakub, Jakub, Jakub, Jakub.

◆ ◆ ◆

I think it was Ryfka he did it for. And I think he loved no other woman the way he loved her, back then, through that beautiful year of 1926 and even a little afterward, though not after that. After that he might have even loved Emilia more than he used to love Ryfka, after all she was the mother of his sons, after all he bought her a ring, after all she was a good, smart, and pretty woman he'd decided to spend his whole life with, but he didn't love her like he loved Ryfka in the summer of 1926, in Warsaw, in Berlin, in Zakopane, on the beach in Sopot. He never loved any woman that way again, not like that.

And he did it for her. It was for her that in the summer of 1937 he called Anna Ziembińska a stupid Polish whore, of which only the adjective *Polish* was correct. He did it because he knew that Ryfka, in her twenties hairstyle and somewhat unfashionable dress, wilted at the sight of her, had no chance against her.

Ziembińska stood, elbow on the bar, seeming neither shocked nor offended. She seemed to be analyzing what had happened, what was happening. And after a few seconds, glancing at Ryfka and inspecting Szapiro's slightly drunken eyes, she seemed to understand everything as well.

She gave a slight, indulgent smile.

"You're not that stupid, Mr. Szapiro," she said.

Jakub turned away from her, downed his glass of vodka, drew a pack of Gitanes from his pocket, and lit one.

"If you ever feel like coming to see me sometime, give me a call. Maybe we'll meet again," said Anna and she placed a calling card on the bar.

The pianist started playing. Jakub still had the lighter in his hand, he reached for the calling card, lit it, and tossed it in the ashtray. Anna smiled again, turned around, and walked out, slowly, unhurriedly, her hips swaying very gently, then she left without saying goodbye, as though no one in Ryfka's brothel was worth saying goodbye to.

"Di bist a nar, an idyot biste, Szapiro,"[30] said Ryfka.

---

30 You're a fool, an idiot, Szapiro.

"Obe farvues?"[31]

"You were s'posed to go see her!" she said, switching to Polish. "Charm her, feel her up, she'd fall in love with you and your cock in a heartbeat and you'd have her."

"Don't need her."

"What a dummy you are, Szapiro. Yes you do! She's Ziembiński's sister and old Ziembiński's daughter, isn't she? With her on your side, it'd be open season on them. Any dame in love with you'd betray not just Poland, the holy Catholic faith, and her moral principles, but also her father, brother, mother, and her whole shitty, Christian, upper-class clan."

Jakub was silent for a moment, drinking.

"Maybe you're right," he finally said, convinced.

"Who gives a rat's ass, since you, aza nar, hot fabrant deym bilyetl,"[32] she laughed.

He sighed deeply, releasing a puff of blue smoke, and watched it curl in the light of the bar's light bulbs.

"I memorized the phone number," he finally admitted.

Ryfka abruptly turned her back to him and busied herself with putting away the glasses. She didn't want him to see right then she'd somehow gotten teary-eyed.

The burning gaze of the sperm whale and the black mouth of the terrifying Venus of Willendorf had reached her too.

They kept drinking. An hour later, she placed the telephone on the bar for him.

"Call her."

"What are you doing this for, Ryfka?"

"I'm doing it for myself. And for you."

He called.

---

31 How do you mean?

32 . . . fool that you are, burned her card.

ו

VAV

He lay in bed with her after it was over, in the best room in a quiet hotel on Wierzbowa Street, and he didn't wonder what he'd come here for, why he'd called her earlier without explaining himself or apologizing in any way for how he'd treated her at Ryfka's, though she hadn't expected either explanations or apologies.

Now she lay beside him, naked, resting her head on her hand, observing him as he, naked too, smoked his Gitane.

"Does your wife know?" she asked with a broad, insolent grin, and Jakub thought she hated him, but she was pretty fond of him and he was pretty fond of how her body tasted.

She was different from Jewish girls, he thought, and then it occurred to him she was also totally different from Christian girls, who after all he'd had plenty of, so it was likely a factor of class, as Moryc would put it, rather than ethnicity.

Even her body was somehow of a different class. Emilia came from a good family, she had an athletic body, even after the boys were born, because she was an enthusiastic sportswoman too, but Anna was different. She didn't play any sports, he was sure of that and certainly knew what he was talking about; she had almost no muscles, the only thing separating her bones and skin was a thin and, he thought, remarkably sexy and feminine layer of fat. Only her backside and hips were muscular. He wondered why for a moment, then realized she rode horses. That would suit her, horseback riding, a woman of her class could do that. Horses or tennis, but she lacked the shoulders or biceps of a tennis player.

"Well come on now, does your wife know?" she pressed him.

"Give it a rest," he replied. "Emilia's not my wife, she's my woman. And we're not going to talk about her, slut."

"Come on, I know you're not just here for fun. You want something from me, Jakub. That's why you called."

"What then?" he lied, though he knew it sounded awkward.

"You think I'm some kind of fool?"

"No, you're a Polish whore who wanted a taste of circumcised dick."

"Well then thank God you said 'whore,' Jakub. I wouldn't stand for being called a fool. Give me a smoke."

He did. They smoked together. He wondered why he was treating her this way and couldn't come up with a decent answer. She made him feel simultaneous attraction and disgust, authentic disgust, but he was beginning to understand his disgust wasn't directed at her personally, at her herself, but at what she represented, or maybe rather symbolized.

This was their first encounter, a few days after she'd come to Ryfka's. He'd decided to get right into questioning her then never sleep with her again, but found he couldn't formulate a single question, so he just lay beside her on the sweat-soaked sheets, smelling of sex, expensive perfume, and the cigarette ashes that sometimes dropped off before making it to the ashtray.

Suddenly he got up, stubbed out his cigarette, pulled on his underwear and pants, put on his shoes without bothering with his socks, threw on his shirt, grabbed his jacket and tie, and strode out of the room without a word.

She smiled to herself.

He returned ten seconds later, furious and embarrassed in a strange way she found charming, then reached into the drawer of the hotel desk, took out his pistol, and strode out again.

"Goodbye, Jakub," she said to the closed door. She knew she'd see him again.

I was waiting for him downstairs, in the Buick, I think so, that's how I remember it, but maybe I was at home, with Emilia and the boys?

A few days flew by as though nothing had changed. In fact, maybe not much had changed. Practically nothing. We went to Kercelak to collect money, everyone was relieved Jakub was there, no one was especially troubled Buddy was gone. Radziwiłek was not well liked on the market square but everyone knew somebody had to be in charge and as long as the enforcing arm of this gangster government was someone as respected and popular as Szapiro, it was fine for him to report to a lunatic like Radziwiłek.

Prospective buyers came frequently to the apartment at 40 Nalewki Street to take a look at the building, but no one offered what Jakub thought of as a good deal.

Moryc came over often and they talked about Palestine.

"Let's take a plane," said Jakub at one point.

"You know how much that costs?" asked Moryc.

"Yeah. I want to pay. I want to fly away from this country the way a bird flies away from the earth. You understand?"

Moryc didn't understand, but he didn't protest.

"Okay, Jakub, we'll fly to Thessaloniki, there's still a ship from there. I've already written to the Haganah folks in Jaffa to request false papers so the Brits don't arrest us. We can wait in Thessaloniki. Or sail to Beirut and wait there."

"And how's things at school, Moryc?"

"Going smoothly. We sit in the Jewish section."

Jakub banged his fist on the table, suddenly incensed.

"Jakub, I just want to get school over with before we go. I've got two classes left to take, a little studying, then I'm done, that's all. That's why we're leaving. To a place where no damn Polack is going to stick us in a segregated classroom or tell us how many of us can study in a department so those tawny-haired intellectual aces of theirs can study on their own. We've already showed them we won't take it lying down. Now I just want to graduate. That's all. Let's leave it be. And then just get out of this cursed country."

"You see Ziembiński around? On campus?"

"Sure."

"You maybe know where he lives?"

"No. At his parents' still, that's all I know. But if you need me to I can find out."

"Do. And careful around him."

Moryc lifted up his shirt to show the grip of a pistol, then left. Emilia put the boys to bed and sat down at the table with Jakub.

"You got some new girlfriend?" she asked. "I can see it in your eyes. You do."

"Leave me be."

She left him be, she always did. She knew who she was bound to.

That's how she'd put it to me once when Jakub was away, the boys were at school, we were alone in the apartment, or maybe she said it when Jakub was there?

But she said it. She was looking out the window at the street, at the bustling storekeepers, at the men walking by in frock coats and yarmulkes, or the rarer ones in hats and suits, at the women in wigs and at the women in dresses.

"At the end of the day, I know who I married," she said to herself. "Every girl here wanted him and he wanted me, but I do know who I married. I'm a modern girl, I don't get worked up about him going to bed with someone else from time to time. So long as he loves me. And he does. Me and the boys. That's enough for me. No girl's had that with him, not even Ryfka."

She knew about Ryfka. They didn't like one another and Emilia scorned her somewhat. Emilia was a modern woman, a Jewish suffragette and socialist, but she had two children and on some subconscious level had to look down on that old flame of Jakub's, the childless, barren, shared hero of many street tales. At the same time she feared her—even though she was much prettier, younger, and smarter than Ryfka.

Maybe Emilia Szapiro, née Kahan, could sense on some level the very thing Ryfka considered her dearest, most cherished, and most beautiful memory, the thing she thought of on lonely nights: having something with Jakub no other woman had ever had, which he could share with no other, certainly not that daddy's-girl Emilia, because a pampered lawyer's daughter could never understand him, not the way Ryfka did, not the way one child of the street understands another, not the way you understand one another only when you've both eked out the cruelest, purely biological form of existence, when you had to take everything, *everything* from the world by tooth and claw, and then fight to keep it.

Jakub had been through that and Ryfka had too, which was why they could love each other in a way impossible for anyone from a home where they listened to music on the turntable, where everyone played the piano, with electrically lit dining rooms, with housekeepers, where the salon smelled of Father's expensive tobacco, and where in the evening they read books together or talked about the Jewish question, socialism, spiritual progress, and the achievements of science.

Homes like that are warm and comfortable, but in a home like that something inside you dies, or maybe something inside you is stunted, that something they both had, the something at the root of their savage, animal, bodily love, which Jakub certainly did not experience with Emilia.

Maybe Emilia Szapiro, née Kahan, somehow could sense all this—and there was a lot she knew, after all, because of the songs sung on the streets about Jakub and Ryfka fighting and carrying on. Maybe that was the reason she put up with all of Jakub's flings—because none of the girls was Ryfka. Every girl who blushingly slipped into his dressing room after a boxing match and who Jakub fucked wherever, however, still dripping with sweat, each one was a slap in Ryfka's face, because those girls, somehow, lessened Ryfka. But Emilia's status they couldn't touch.

"All that will end when we leave for Palestine," she said to herself, still looking down at the street. "In Palestine they won't have all the whoring we've got here."

Then she thought about the kibbutzim and decided they weren't going to live on a kibbutz. Wives were supposedly shared on the kibbutzim, so would she have to share Jakub as well? So no kibbutz. Maybe a moshav if they had to. In Palestine she shouldn't share Jakub anymore. Not with anyone. She'd sell the building, Jakub would squeeze as much money as he could out of the whole neighborhood, and her socialist, engaged parents would turn a blind eye as usual rather than think about where their daughter's money was coming from. Jakub would convert the money he'd squeezed out of the neighborhood into gold or dollars, they'd use it to buy a house in Tel Aviv, and live. There would be palm trees, and sea, and oranges, and it would be warm and they'd be at home. Jakub felt their home was here, on Nalewki, and she might have felt that too, but she wasn't blinded by what blinded Jakub, his strong fists, the pistol in his pocket, his powerful friends. Blinded by his own power, Jakub couldn't see they weren't at home here, maybe they'd never been at home here, being driven every hundred-odd years hither and thither across Europe. No, power didn't blind her, Emilia could see: they weren't at home here. The Poles wouldn't let them be at home here. When the Polish procession marched down Tłomackie Street for Corpus Christi, even though no Pole lived there, the Poles still marched as though they were at home there. They marched that way on purpose, to remind Warsaw's Jews: You are not at home here, not even in your neighborhoods, not even on your squares, in front of your synagogues. This is a Catholic country, all this is ours, and you are here only by our mercy.

Which can run out.

Evening fell over our Jewish city, and over our Jewish city a sperm whale floated with burning eyes. Droshkies, taxis, sometimes a car went driving by, people walked by and Litani's gaze fell on them, and they couldn't feel him, couldn't see him, but more important than their blindness was that Litani saw them, opened and closed his jaws, and started to sing, and I saw them vanish into his maw, one by one, Litani sucking them in, drawing them in, and I knew nothing on earth was equal to his power, nothing could oppose it, there was no power on earth stronger than Litani's power and the burning gaze of his small eyes hidden in thick skin. There was no sound louder than the silent song he used to find his victims, to devour them, suck them in.

Emilia couldn't see the sperm whale, but she sensed him, she was at the window a long time, watching the constant traffic on Nalewki Street and wondering if she'd miss this. Then she turned around, saw Dawid and Daniel at the table, reading a book in Polish and a book in Yiddish, respectively, by the light of an electric lamp, and she realized she wouldn't miss this at all. She wondered where Jakub was, if he'd gone out to his new girl, and she figured that must be it, he probably had.

Or gone out on darker business.

Meanwhile Jakub hadn't gone to Anna's, though they'd arranged to meet later.

Jakub had gone out on darker business.

Jakub's darker business required a visit to the Palace of the Council of Ministers, though how could his business compare to the dark business of the government men inside?

He slowly meandered his way through town to make sure he wasn't being followed. He'd put on his best suit; he showed his identification at the entrance, and walked through three antechambers to reach the office of Secretary Litwińczuk. He waited his turn at the door and was finally invited inside.

"I want to speak to the prime minister," he said, without so much as a greeting.

Litwińczuk, bald, obese, and every inch the government official, raised his hand in a gesture indicating he was focused on a document he was just reading and nothing could bring him to interrupt this extremely important activity. Szapiro understood this meant their relationship had made a 180-degree turn. Before Buddy's arrest, Litwińczuk would have leaped up from his desk, asked him to take a seat, and offered a coffee or something stronger.

Szapiro had left his gun in the car; he wondered for a second if he should hurt Litwińczuk with his bare hands, but quickly rejected the thought. The prime minister's secretary kept studying the document, reveling in this tiny humiliation of a man whose very existence humiliated Litwińczuk. The secretary hated Szapiro and always had. He hated him because Szapiro was a Jew, that first and foremost, and no Jew should be so strong, so handsome, so well dressed, and so luxuriously motorized, he hated him because he physically feared him, and also because women loved Szapiro while Litwińczuk had to pay for love in cold, hard cash or with the help of the church's sacramental bond.

But now he had the chance to get even. He wasn't reading anything important, of course, he was staring blankly at an irrelevant report and waiting. He knew why Szapiro had come to his office, he knew Buddy had been sent to Bereza, and he knew if Szapiro got the chance to talk to the prime minister he could get Kaplica out of Bereza. Meanwhile, though he had nothing to do with the marshal and Colonel Koc's plans, the thought of old Buddy locked up in the Isolation Facility made Litwińczuk very happy, for personal reasons.

Jakub stared at Litwińczuk's bald spot as he continued to read and decided he had no use for the humiliation of a refusal, the only possible outcome here.

He turned on his heel and left. Litwińczuk was very disappointed.

He would be even more disappointed if he knew Szapiro went straight from his office to meet a woman who was not only beautiful, but whom Litwińczuk had met a few times in social settings.

Jakub had arranged to meet Anna in a Warsaw better than his Warsaw of Nalewki and Kercelak, in a Warsaw of Anna's standard, in a Warsaw that lay, in fact, on a different continent than Jakub's Warsaw, a Warsaw almost in Europe, to which Nalewki and Kercelak with their Asian aroma and noise obviously did not belong.

He already knew where she lived, Moryc had called and given him the address, but they arranged to meet at the Taubenhaus building on the corner of Matejka Street and Ujazdowskie Avenue, in those small patches of Warsaw elegance, where elegant gentlemen in suits and uniforms promenaded down the sidewalks with elegant women, and the cars belonged not only to gangsters and boxers extorting protection money but to the higher rank of officials, engineers, writers, or actors. For instance, the famous comedian Adolf Dymsza drove his Lancia Farina down Ujazdowskie Avenue, President Mościcki drove the king of Romania down Ujazdowskie Avenue in his Cadillac 370, while two miles away were the slums of impoverished Polish and Jewish neighborhoods, spawning all their offspring: every Jakub, Mojżesz, Kaplica, Pantaleon, Ryfka of this city.

Szapiro let her wait for him, and she waited, obediently and even without anger, as though this was part of the ritual of their affair. She waited, elegantly dressed, hair styled, wearing a light fall jacket and red pumps, men were looking at her, and it pleased her to be waiting for a man for the first time in her life, a man who'd told her to wait for him.

He picked her up in his elegant brown Buick, which attracted attention even on Ujazdowskie Avenue in the evening, though of course not so much as Kaplica's red Chrysler, now uselessly dormant in the garage at Buddy's house on Domaniewska Street.

She got in.

"Are we going to a hotel?" she asked.

"Not wasting a hotel on you," he replied.

She smiled.

They drove under the Poniatowski Bridge, turned off the Kościuszko Embankment past the cross-city rail bridge, looped back, and parked under the first span of the Poniatowski. Jakub turned off the engine, without a word unbuttoned his pants, and she without a word bent over his crotch.

In some ways he was helpless against her. He now saw that the worse he treated her the more she enjoyed all this, and that a dependency, a weakness, was beginning to germinate in him, not her.

After a while they moved onto the back seat. He placed a lit flashlight on the front seat, it shone on the ceiling liner of the car, throwing irregular shadows onto their bodies. He wanted to be able to see her.

Another fifteen minutes later, they sat side by side, out of breath and soaked in sweat, she completely naked with tousled hair, Jakub in unbuttoned pants and a shirt, both smoking Jakub's cigarettes, Anna didn't have her own.

"All right, so what do you want from me?" she asked, breaking the silence. They hadn't spoken a word since she'd gotten into his car on Ujazdowskie.

For a moment, Jakub wondered what he did want from her. Why the two of them were writhing around in a car under a bridge, why with her in particular, why this at all. He'd kept away from women for a long time—not counting the rare sessions with Ryfka's girls, because with them it was obviously different. He didn't fall in love, didn't seduce or let himself be seduced, even though the girls flocked to him.

Ryfka had left a large hole in him that Emilia couldn't possibly fill, but she could make it scar over somehow, heal it partway, she and the boys. So what was he doing in a car with Anna Ziembińska, Prosecutor Ziembiński's daughter, Andrzej Ziembiński's sister, why?

He remembered what Ryfka said and he tried to accept that explanation, but he knew that was only the most superficial truth, and so at its heart not the truth. He knew he was just pretending not to know, he knew he was kidding himself.

"I need some dirt on your father or your brother. And I thought if I made it with you you'd help me out."

She started laughing. She laughed, choked, covered her mouth with her hands. Naked, still covered in saliva, sweat, and sperm and completely shameless, she laughed so infectiously he started laughing along with her.

"Such insight into female psychology! What a pleasant surprise from a boxer!"

He shrugged.

She turned serious.

"You're an idiot."

He shrugged again, even rolled his eyes, didn't look at her, stared straight ahead into the cloud of smoke slowly drifting out through the Buick's slightly open window.

"It's true, you're really stupid. What if it was them that sent me? My dad or Andrzej? Did you think about that?"

He hadn't. He remained silent.

"All right, listen up. I hate my father. I'm meeting you a second time because I like you, because I like the taste of your come, but the other reason I like you is my father thinks you're an enemy. His own personally and also an enemy of the Polish nation. He thinks every Jew is an enemy of the Polish nation, but you in particular. And I hate my father. And I'd like you to help me hurt him."

He'd never met a woman like this. He never had any interest in silly girls comfortably and deeply rooted in the patriarchy, meaning the majority of the female population. You could never call Ryfka a liberated woman, because Ryfka had never needed to liberate herself from anything. Her entire wild nature made her free, she'd grown up on the street like it was the jungle, her freedom was a wolf's freedom, not a woman's. She'd never learned any convention to liberate herself from. Emilia was a liberated woman, a true socialist, people even called her a "Jewish Krzywicka." The feminist campaigner Irena Krzywicka was Jewish herself, of course, but in the eyes of both religious and secular Jews, assimilationists like her had renounced their Jewishness and so were left somewhere in the middle, belonging to no one, no longer Jewish but not yet Polish. In any case, Emilia's liberation was tasteful, not embarrassing but shaped by good breeding, and they had a great love life, but there was no corruption in her.

Maybe he needed corruption. Polish, not Jewish, corruption.

Suddenly he understood. He turned to look at her. She was sitting next to him, naked, half-reclined, resting her long legs on the back of the driver's seat, making no effort to cover any of her nakedness, and that was just what she was, corrupt. And that corruption excited and attracted him. And that was why he was sitting with her here, in a car under a bridge.

"First swear to me you won't move against my brother."

"How the hell am I supposed to swear that? Look, I'm a Jewish socialist in a gang, he's a Piasecki guy, a Phalanx guy, a National Radical, a little Polish Hitler. Come on, we shoot guns at each other!" said Jakub and swiftly recognized that if he'd been here only, or at least primarily, for the reasons Ryfka had given him, he'd have sworn to anything without a second thought, sworn to join the Nazi Party or to buy her the Free City of Danzig, whatever would get him the result he wanted. Anna knew that too.

"I know," she replied, turning toward him, cuddling up against his shirt, and staining it with smeared mascara. "But I love him. Like no one else on earth. So either lie or think up a way I can hurt that bastard without harming Andrzej."

"I'll be no threat to him unless he attacks me," Jakub promised, terrified to realize it was an honest promise.

"He will."

"Well dammit, if he attacks me I'll defend myself, but I won't go to your house with Pantaleon, I won't drag your brother out of bed, I won't take him out of Warsaw in my car, I won't cut his throat, I won't cut him into chunks, and I won't throw the chunks into the clay ponds."

She went silent for a moment. She was looking him over carefully. He couldn't make out her eyes in the weakening glow of the flashlight and couldn't remember what color they were. But he could see she was thinking for the first time about who he really was.

Ryfka had known who he was from the beginning and didn't forget it for a moment. Emilia knew, sort of. Sort of, because she knew her husband was a gangster and she definitely realized he killed people, but what would she do if she'd seen how he killed Naum Bernsztajn?

"You've done something like that?" she asked finally.

"None of your business."

She kissed him. He could see she was aroused.

"My father is a monster. He's never hit me, but he killed my mother."

"How's that?"

"Her whole life he beat her, for everything. Usually with this sort of riding crop. Four years ago she finally decided to leave him, after twenty years of torment. He was furious and shoved her when she was standing on the stairs. She fell, broke her spine, and died."

"And no one charged him?" Jakub asked very foolishly.

She gave him a pitying look.

"Well, right," he said, coming to his senses.

"He's the one who does the charging, no one charges him. The police said Mama tripped, it was an unfortunate accident."

He only nodded.

"You deal with prostitutes, right? Do they pay you?"

"Are you asking if I'm a pimp?" He smiled. "I used to be. A long time ago. Just after the war. Not for a long while now, though. I've got a different job."

"But in that brothel back there, I mean, you know the prostitutes, right?"

"They all pay Buddy. I mean, not now, 'cause Buddy's in Bereza. But they pay. And I know them."

"Well listen. My father goes to one of those, in Wola district. They call her Madame de Potocki, but she's not a de Potocki any more than I'm the duchess of York. This tall, large woman. You know her?"

"I do."

"I made myself a spare key to Dad's office. He's got a lovely collection of photos of women beating and torturing men. Some of them are even hot. My guess is that's what he goes to her for."

Jakub considered for a moment. He knew de Potocki. She paid Buddy fifty złotys on the first Friday of every month. Anna was right, she was no de Potocki, she was really called Aniela Kuznik, she was apparently born in Harbin like Munja Weber, she'd adopted her refined manner and noble last name because from 1910 on she served in the best homes of the old empire, in Petersburg first, then in Warsaw from 1913 on. She was a quick-witted and sharp-eyed woman with a natural talent for acting, so she had no problem soaking up the language and manners of her masters and mistresses.

Right after the war she'd been in service to a certain government minister's family where, at the master of the house's urging, she handled not only cooking and cleaning, but also flogging that same master of the house, plus other activities related to flogging. Having not the slightest attraction to men herself, she wouldn't let him touch her, which couldn't have suited him better, and in return he paid her far, far more than her housekeeper's salary.

Having thus uncovered a marvelous source of profit less fatiguing than housekeeping, she quit the latter after a few years and rented an apartment in Wola district, where she lived and received a few choice, wealthy clients. She was forty-three. No client saw her naked, she allowed no one to touch her, and she didn't consider herself a prostitute and neither did her carefully selected clients. Outside work she maintained no relations with men, but from time to time yet another young girl would move in and Kuznik would have a torrid romance with her, then the girl would move out happy and a few hundred złotys the richer, leaving Kuznik alone with a broken heart and a depleted account at the Postal Savings Bank.

She mended her heart and her wallet by thrashing the pale, plump bottoms of Warsaw's titans of the bar, industry, politics, and culture until they bled. She also managed to graduate from teachers' college, and Jakub vaguely remembered that last he'd heard she really meant to become a teacher, so had moved out of her old, crappy little apartment and into a fairly spacious one in a teachers' residence on Bem Street.

"Will you do something with that?" asked Anna.

"Sure."

"I just want him to know it's because of me. Tell him."

"Sure."

"You know where I live?"

"Yeah. Up in Żoliborz district. Five Koźmian Street."

"How?"

"I gotta know certain things. It's my business."

He kissed her and pressed her to him. Anna knew she'd won.

Litani floated over the bridge, up high, gazing down at them, and loved them, loved the city that had begotten them. He loved the plots they dreamed up as if they'd live forever, he loved their fantasies and plans. He sang his hunting song of love.

"Are you still writing that?" asked Magda.

I spun around. She'd given me a start. I didn't know when she came in. I looked at her. She was so old now, so very old. Her face covered in a web of deep wrinkles. Skin drooping under her chin. Her hands creased and covered in liver spots. My Magda, so old.

I pulled the sheet from the typewriter and lay it on the pile of typed pages, facedown, so she couldn't read it.

"I'm writing."

"How come?"

"'Cause what am I supposed to do since they threw me out of Aman?"

"What on earth have you made up?"

"I don't understand."

"What's Aman?"

I didn't understand.

"What do you mean?" I asked, surprised.

"Come on, what's Aman? What on earth are you talking about?"

"Well, I served . . . Intelligence . . . Come on, you know. Why are you acting like this, Magda?"

"I'm not Magda. Who on earth is Magda?"

I went silent. I was suddenly very sad.

"Can we stop already?" she asked. "Quit playing this game? Can we forget this fairy tale you've made up now, Jakub? Who is Magda?"

Jakub? Jakub? Jakub?

I look at my hands. On the right one, the tattoo is completely faded. Faded, but it's still visible.

"I'm not Jakub," I say, but I say it without conviction.

"Then who are you?"

"I'm Moyshe Bernsztajn," I almost whisper, I want to believe it so much.

"Who?" says Magda, confused.

"Moyshe Bernsztajn. The son of Naum Bernsztajn."

"You mean that poor man you killed in '37? For owing Kaplica money?"

I say nothing.

"No, *he* was called Naum. I get it. You're imagining you're his son? Do you not remember, do you really not remember what happened to that boy?"

I say nothing, because what am I meant to say? I'm disappearing. *Go away,* I think. *Go away.*

"Go away," I whisper, as quietly as possible. "Go."

I close my eyes and wait for her to leave. I go back to writing.

I remember what happened to Moyshe Bernsztajn.

◆ ◆ ◆

Jakub drove out from under the Poniatowski Bridge. He didn't wait for Anna to get dressed, but she didn't protest, she liked being naked. She dressed as they drove and it started to rain. Despite the rain he dropped her off at Three Crosses Square, they parted without saying goodbye.

Jakub Szapiro thought it was best to part without saying goodbye because he knew only two types of goodbyes: ones that hurt—like saying goodbye to Anna, whom he didn't want to part from—and ones that made him happy—when he didn't want to waste another moment in company that revolted him. In both cases it was best to just turn on your heels and walk away.

He wanted to go straight to Aniela Kuznik's, but decided to stop on the way and sate his hunger at Handszer's New Metropol on Tłomackie Street. He drove up Nowy Świat and Krakowskie Przedmieście, turned left onto Trębacka, then Wierzbowa and Teatralny Square—where the city ceased pretending to be the European metropolis it had never been—meaning by Bielańska Street he already felt at home, and by Tłomackie he simply was home, like an heir on his estate.

He parked in front of the bar, got out, and went inside, where it was nearly empty. Handszer was already clearing the tables and grew worried when he spotted Szapiro, knowing if he was here he couldn't close the bar on time at ten o'clock, meaning he definitely had another fine coming if the police happened to turn up, and they had it in for him because there'd been complaints, so they probably would turn up.

He sighed and mentally prayed to an undefined absolute—for he was a deist—and pleaded for there to be no fighting, at least.

Jakub ordered pickled herring and a small bottle, ate, and sipped at the warm vodka. He didn't notice someone was watching him through the front window of the bar. That I was watching him.

He finished his food and wanted to pay, but Handszer objected, so he left without paying and then I threw myself on him—having hidden beforehand behind the trunk of his Buick, which I'd never been inside—I threw myself on him, hungry and freezing and weakened, I threw myself on him with a knife, meaning to stab him in the back, but at the last moment I slipped and jabbed the short blade of my penny knife into Jakub's buttock.

Mojżesz Bernsztajn jabbed the short blade into my buttock.

Jakub Szapiro did not take Moyshe under his wing.

I wanted to, I wanted to save that poor Jewish boy I'd seen twice in my life, once when I took away his father, and second when I was at the theater with Emilia and he was there, with Magda Aszer, with Magda, whom I knew only by sight, from the Maccabi swimming pool, where I sometimes swam too, figuring swimming was a good all-around exercise to help build up a boxer's biological efficiency.

Magda Aszer from the Maccabi pool.

Jakub Szapiro swam in that same pool, in that same Vistula water. Jakub Szapiro killed my father, Naum Bernsztajn, dismembered his body, drove it from one clay pond to another and allowed me, my mother, and my brother to waste away, evicted from our apartment, without the means to live.

My mother died a month after my father's death. Of anxiety, of poverty, but above all of pneumonia. My brother ended up in a Jewish orphanage and his fate after that is unknown to me, but what could it have been?

I meanwhile didn't let myself get locked up in an orphanage. I ran away. I lived on the streets, I slept wherever I could, I begged. I didn't sleep in a warm bed in Jakub's apartment. I didn't enjoy his wife Emilia's warm body. I often peeked in their window at night, saw their dark silhouettes in the bright square windows. I watched her coming out with her sons, taking them for walks in the Saxon Gardens or the Krasiński Gardens, taking them for ice cream, sometimes I even followed them and brooded, wondering whether I could kill her.

All the while Litani, the old sperm whale, floated over me, floated over us all, calm, patient, and indifferently cruel.

My clothes turned to rags. Jakub never took me to Zaremba's to dress me up in a handsome suit. The only suits he got made at Zaremba's were for himself.

I didn't leave for Palestine. I didn't serve in the Palmach or the Haganah, I didn't take the last name Inbar, I didn't have sons with Magda Aszer, I didn't become a general, nothing happened, or everything happened in theory, just not to me, to someone else, someone else had sons, was a general, served, and got decorated and wounded, but for me nothing, nothing, not a thing.

As I stood at the window of the Metropol I wasn't waiting Jakub out, I was standing there because I just wanted to feast my eyes, if nothing else, on the sight of food, steaming tripe on plates, juicy gefilte fish, challah, schnitzels, and Catholic herrings. And when I saw him, I thought this might be my only chance. I had a fever, I was sick, and I knew I might die soon, of pneumonia, just like my mother. I didn't want to die without avenging my father, whom no one had even said Kaddish for, a thing I couldn't do now because I knew God didn't exist, my father didn't exist, and there was no point throwing words out into the void.

I lay in wait behind the Buick. I wanted to kill Jakub Szapiro, the gangster and Maccabi Warsaw boxer, but I only managed to shallowly jab the short blade of a knife I'd stolen in Kercelak market into Jakub's buttock.

Jakub roared when my knife pierced him, swung around, and practically instinctually smashed his fist into my temple, with all the force of a heavyweight boxer. I immediately lost consciousness and flew backward like I'd been hit by a hammer, already engulfed in darkness, the back of my head struck the curb, blood flooded my brain, and I died—Mojżesz Bernsztajn, age seventeen, of the Jewish faith, born in Warsaw in 1920, son of Naum Bernsztajn, died of hitting his head on the curb on Tłomackie Street in front of the Metropol bar, he died hungry and sick, and alone, barely nicking the man who'd orphaned him.

He didn't take his last year of high school. He didn't graduate or pass the exams to study medicine at Józef Piłsudski University. He didn't sit in a classroom ghetto, he didn't end up within the walls of a worse ghetto. He didn't die of typhus, or in an uprising, or of hunger, or in a gas chamber. He died because he hit his head on the curb.

Behind the car, Jakub swore, pulled out his pistol, and looked around, expecting another attack to follow. When after a few minutes nothing had happened, he finally took a look at the boy who'd attacked him with the knife, recognized me, and understood. He touched my neck, there was no pulse, he swore silently.

He remembered me, he'd remember my face forever.

He put away his pistol, touched his slightly bleeding buttock, and could tell he needed to go have the wound dressed. He opened the trunk, tossed Mojżesz Bernsztajn's nearly weightless body inside, pulled out some rags to lay on the driver's seat to keep the blood off the upholstery, got in, and wondered for a moment whether to go to the hospital or the Vistula first.

He chose the Vistula, that good river. He drove through Muranów district toward Gdański Station and turned off Zakroczymska Street and drove out onto the bridge by the Citadel.

Litani rose and fell lazily in the air over the bridge, singing.

Jakub stopped in the middle of the bridge, got out of the car limping and bleeding, lifted my starved, lukewarm body out of the trunk, wrapped his arms around me, kissed my cold forehead, threw me over the barrier, and what a moment before had been Mojżesz Bernsztajn fell through the air, struck the surface of the water, and sank into the black current. Jakub leaned over the barrier. Though he was only superficially wounded, his buttock still pulsed with pain. Jakub wept.

The sperm whale dove down to the Vistula, dove into its waters, singing, he saw me with his song and swallowed me up, and I settled in his belly, and God did not speak unto the fish to vomit me out after three days; I did not spend three days after being vomited out walking the streets of Warsaw calling for repentance, Mayor Starzyński did not shed his suits or put on penitential garb, Jews and Poles—rich and poor, men and women, children and youths, blind and seeing, law-abiding and criminals—did not pour ashes on their heads, did not fast, did not perform penance.

That is why God showed no mercy on that cursed city.

But Jakub wept.

Jakub peered into the black current of the Vistula, that good river. Litani sang.

Blood from the pierced skin of Jakub's buttock dribbled down his leg.

Jakub took a deep breath and thought for a moment how the life he led was utterly unbearable. Then Jakub remembered who he was.

"I am Jakub Szapiro," he said out loud into the darkness. No one answered.

He carefully hobbled to the car, got in, and thought that maybe that was enough for today after all. He drove home. He didn't leave his car at the Dynasy garage. He parked right in front of his building, climbed the stairs, wincing with every step, asked Emilia to call a doctor, got out a large bottle of vodka, and lay down in bed.

He'd drunk half the vodka before the doctor arrived. Once there, he examined Jakub and said in his opinion the wound was shallow and clean and would heal up shortly, snickering a little at its unfortunate location, then he cleaned and disinfected the wound, put in four stitches, told him not to strain them, collected his ten złotys, and left.

Jakub was furious at his carelessness. Things could already have been moving forward, he could have spoken to Kuznik by now if he hadn't let his guard slip. Thanks to that slip, Buddy had to spend one more night in Bereza. And who knew how someone his age could handle the torments of that place?

He finished the bottle and fell into a heavy, alcohol-induced dream, thinking of my skinny body sinking into that good river, of my body in the maw of the sperm whale, of the whale's belly, my skin soaking in Biblical digestive juices, my frail muscles, my insides becoming the whale's insides, my body flowing in the current of that good river north past Kępa Potocka Park, Pelcowizna district, Bielany district, and floating away, away from this cursed city.

Emilia sat down on the bed next to Jakub, stroked his hair and his hard shoulders, and thought how this man in the bed had taken her whole life and there was no chance of getting it back.

Buddy was waiting too. He'd lost his sense of time, he'd stopped counting the quarter hours the knocking marked off. It was completely dark in his cell, the only thing distinguishing day from night was being forced to stand during the day. And every fifteen minutes, knocking. Knocking. Knocking.

"Here!"

Sometimes they knocked more often anyway. He could feel infection setting into the wound on his arm.

"I got a wound on my arm and it's oozing pus," he said when the guard opened the door to present Kaplica his dinner: bread and a glass of water.

"You ain't gonna be the first bastard to croak in here," replied the guard, backing it up with a kick and slamming the door.

Knocking.

"Here."

They took him out after three days, once he'd stopped answering and didn't regain consciousness even after they beat him. Naked on a stretcher, soiled with his own excrement, they carried him to the hospital. Blood and pus were dripping from the bullet wound on his forearm, the arm was swollen and red.

At the camp hospital, Bakalarczyk the field medic examined Buddy's forearm and admitted this case exceeded his otherwise very limited competence. He ordered them to transport Kaplica to the hospital in Kobryń.

Kobryń was forty miles west of Bereza. Kaplica didn't regain consciousness at the camp infirmary and didn't regain it when he was loaded into a narrow peasant's wagon hitched to a skinny nag, nor did he regain it for a single moment of the long journey over the muddy and bumpy terrain of Polesia province. His forearm reeked.

The doctor at the hospital in Kobryń—a real one this time, with a medical degree unlike Bakalarczyk—examined Buddy and had no doubt they needed to remove the arm.

He wondered if he could leave the elbow, but after carefully investigating Buddy's condition he determined he couldn't risk it. He moved to amputate quickly due to the state the patient was in, but the procedure itself he performed carefully and artfully.

Buddy regained consciousness a few hours later. He looked down at the stump of his left arm and felt very old, very weak, defeated, broken inside. He thought of all his triumphs and those triumphs' victims, the people whose bodies had floated down the Vistula, the graves dug under cover of darkness in the forests outside Warsaw, the people whose wives or daughters had to be raped before they'd finally pay up, he thought of the victims and for the first time thought of them differently.

Jan Kaplica only valued winners. He had no respect for the defeated and he himself never forgave weakness. But now he lay with a fever and missing an arm and was in no way winning, and he found it hard to forgive himself.

He only spent two days in his hospital bed; forty-eight hours later Commandant Kamala-Kurhański barged into Kobryń hospital, banging the door open.

"I hear we got a faker hanging out in here!" he roared, until he was obligingly shown Kaplica's bed.

Two policemen accompanied Kamala-Kurhański. They stood over Buddy's sickbed, the timid doctor behind them.

"See, I'm faking so hard I got 'em to hack off my arm," said Buddy, his voice still feeble, and he lifted the stump, still wrapped tightly in bandages.

"Get him out of here," ordered the commandant.

"Commandant, sir, he's not well enough yet, it's only two days since the amputation," the doctor protested.

"Silence!" snarled Kamala-Kurhański. "We'll put him in our infirmary for a week then he'll do as long as it takes in the hole. That'll teach this filthy scum to run his mouth."

"Everyone out, only the commandant stays," ordered Buddy in a voice weakened, but accustomed to giving orders, and that voice still contained such conviction his order would be carried out that the policemen and doctor's first instinct was to head for the exit.

"Who you think you're talking to, you human shit stain?" Kamala-Kurhański's roar of amazement stopped them in their tracks.

"Kamala, you got an aunt in Warsaw," whispered Buddy. "At number two Rejtan Street, apartment one, first floor, with a dog, name of Reks. And your aunt goes by Adelajda. You oughta give her a call, Commandant, but she ain't gonna answer 'cause she's tied to a chair and pissing herself like us guys in that hole of yours. But she's got a heavy sitting with her, a real sharp operator, and it's him who's gonna pick up the phone."

Kamala-Kurhański stared at Kaplica, and said nothing, and went pale. He didn't move or speak for a few seconds, then suddenly dashed out, slamming the door behind him.

Meanwhile in Warsaw, in Jakub's home on Nalewki, the master of the house rose very early, before the morning urged him up, rose from his own, warm bed in his own, warm apartment where his own wife made him coffee and fried him some eggs. He looked at his penny knife–sliced backside in the mirror and happily noted it was healing up well, the wound wasn't messy, there was no pus.

Then he remembered, I remembered, my skinny body striking the black surface of the water of that good river.

He shaved, looked himself in the eye, and searched his face for a trace of all those murdered people. He found none. Only young Moyshe Bernsztajn had left something in him, some trace. How light his body had been when he threw it over the bridge railing. Maybe ninety pounds. How light, just skin and bones.

He left himself a small mustache, a little strip over his lip, shaved down from the top. He figured that would look better.

"Mustache?" asked Emilia when he sat down to breakfast.

"Screw the mustache," he muttered to himself.

"What did Daddy say?" asked Dawid.

"Forget it, kiddo. Jakub, I've got a buyer for the building."

"How much is he offering?"

"Eighty thousand złotys."

"If he makes it twenty thousand dollars the building is his. But we're not moving out until we leave. You mind arranging it?"

"He's not going to want to talk to me. Far as he's concerned, you're the partner to talk to here, not a woman."

"The building's in your name. Tell him you're Jakub Szapiro's wife and he'd really rather talk to you than to me. 'Cause with me he'll get a different talk."

She smiled again.

"I'll sort it out tomorrow," she said, grateful.

"I don't want to move away," whispered Daniel, but his parents didn't pay attention.

"You're going to have to sign everything afterward though," she said. "Some bills of exchange, I don't know, I'm not sure how it works."

"I will. See to that twenty thousand from the building. That'll be our future. I've got another fifty set aside. With seventy thousand dollars we can land on our feet, even in Palestine. We can land comfortably on our feet."

Someone knocked at the door, in a code they'd set long ago with their loved ones. Four knocks, a pause, two, pause, three. Emilia opened the door, Moryc was standing in the stairwell.

"Join us for breakfast?" she asked.

"Fuck it," he said, sitting down at the table with the whole Szapiro family.

"Moryc! The kids!" hissed Emilia.

"Fuck what?" asked Jakub. Emilia just rolled her eyes.

"Everything. Fuck it. I don't want to graduate. Apparently that coup's a sure thing now. If they pull it off, we might end up like Germany."

"You sure?"

"Yeah, we've got informants in the government."

"Who?"

"You gone soft in the head?" said Moryc with a laugh. "Why should I tell you?"

"Because we're leaving."

"So it's no difference to you. Let's get out of here as fast as we can."

"We gotta leave anyway. Coup or no coup."

"You got it. I had a response from Palestine. They're sorting us out a spot on the ship from Thessaloniki to Jaffa."

"I know, you told us at the airport. But I asked around and apparently you can fly straight to Palestine, to Lydda. You can buy a ticket for it. From here you fly to Lwów, then Cernăuţi, Bucharest, Sofia, Thessaloniki, Athens, and finally Lydda. Some ten, twelve hours including refueling stops and we're in Palestine."

"There might be issues with legalizing ourselves once we're there. Passport control and so on. I'm sure that's why the organization suggests taking the ship from Thessaloniki. But how much would a ticket like that cost?"

"Fourteen hundred."

Moryc whistled through his teeth.

"I haven't got that much. I haven't even got half, not even a quarter of what I'd need for a ticket for me and Zosia."

"I do."

The Zionist true believer had to stop and think for a moment whether he'd take money from a criminal, even if that criminal was his brother. So he considered and decided he would, though he'd known that full well before he even stopped to think.

"For a ticket to Palestine I'll have it from you. Emilia was saying yesterday you've got a buyer for the building?"

Jakub nodded, then rose, leaving the kitchen without a word. He went into the living room and returned after a moment, handing Moryc a wad of bills.

"Here's ten thousand. Enough for a ticket for everyone and some additional costs. Sort it out."

"When for?"

"As soon as possible."

Moryc pocketed the money. It occurred to him he'd never in his life held even a tenth of that sum in cash, and was struck that the thought didn't particularly impress him. He ate some eggs and a slice of buttered bread, washed it down with coffee, and left.

He got on the A streetcar, rode to Okęcie Airport, and bought six plane tickets to Thessaloniki for October 21. He could have bought them just as well in the City Center, but he only realized that by the time he'd gotten to the ticket desk at the airport.

Jakub finished his coffee, put on a jacket and tie, went outside, got in his car, slowly settling onto his hurting buttock, and drove to Madame de Potocki's.

She lived in Wola district, by the train tracks, in a teacher's residence by the elementary school building on the corner of Bem and Siedmiogrodzka Streets. Of course the administration at the school where she'd been teaching early learning since September didn't know her main occupation. The doorman at the teachers' residence had swiftly cottoned on and was amply bribed with a promise of a monthly cut. The elegant guests in the stairways of the four-story teachers' residence roused no suspicions, while the doors and walls of Madame de Potocki's study were padded with a thick layer of muffling upholstery, so the cries of the flogged stayed where they should.

He had to ring the bell three times before she opened the door. When she did finally open the door, still on the chain, she recognized him immediately.

"But *dengi* not till last day of month," she said with a distinct Russian accent, not opening the door completely and considering a greeting superfluous.

When she was playing the role of de Potocki, she spoke wonderful Polish, Russian, or French, as the client wished, but as Aniela Kuznik she spoke like Aniela Kuznik, a little boorishly and with a Russian accent.

"I'm not here for money. I got a proposition. Let me in."

"I got customer."

"I'll wait."

She gave it some thought, then took the door off the chain. She offered him a seat. She was exceptionally well built, of Jakub's height and not much slimmer. She wore a silk, patterned dressing gown that fit her ample body so tightly she looked like a large, upholstered piece of Louis Philippe furniture. But she had stockings on her legs and elegant shoes on her feet.

"You have to wait, it take a while longer."

He sat down, hissing with pain.

Madame de Potocki eyed him up.

"But you sure you not come for session?"

"Session?" He didn't understand.

"*Nu*, you got ass spanked? And you want more? Someone recommend? Wife not want beat you?"

"I . . . ?" He didn't understand for a moment. "Oh, no, not like that, some boy stuck me with a knife," he said with a grin.

"Boy? With knife?" she said, even more surprised.

"No! I mean yes, but no, on the street, he attacked me!"

"No matter, wife, boy. I no care," she said with a wave of her hand. "Wait here."

She threw off the dressing gown. Underneath she wore a corset, a string of pearls, a garter belt. Nothing else. In gear like that, she didn't look like a piece of furniture anymore. She went back to her study, closing the door behind her. Even through the padded doors he could hear the blows and screams. After fifteen minutes the door opened and out walked a fully dressed, portly older gentleman, who, pretending not to notice Jakub, gave Madame a silent bow and departed.

Madame de Potocki wrapped herself in her dressing gown, kicked off her elegant shoes, swapped them for soft slippers, and now as Aniela Kuznik invited Jakub into the kitchen and sat him down at the table. She fired up a Tula samovar: she took embers from the kitchen oven and poured them in the central pipe that heated the water. She already had tea concentrate brewed in the teapot on top of the samovar.

"Well now, what proposition you have, *molodets*?" she finally asked after a long while, filling some delicate glasses with hot water from the samovar.

"Prosecutor Ziembiński comes to see you, right?"

She didn't respond. Silent, she gently touched the glasses of hot tea, but she didn't drink, she stared at them with eyes seemingly of iron. He understood.

"I know you don't want to talk."

"My clients powerful, important people. They pay me a lot of *dengi*. They pay so I whip bare bottoms but they also pay so I keep trap shut."

"I need to take a picture of him. While you're seeing to him here. I'll pay, I'll pay well."

"Enough for nice coffin?"

He thought it over silently for a moment.

"I've got to have something on him. Otherwise I can't get to the PM. I need to get to the PM. Buddy won't survive Bereza. He's too old."

"So why the hell I should help you? Did Buddy ever help me? Or you?"

"We'll owe you."

"And when I call in debt, how they will kill me?"

"They won't kill you. No one will help him. There must be something you want. Something you need. I'll give it to you."

"You take sugar?"

He shook his head. She added three spoonfuls to her tea and stirred carefully, elegantly, not knocking the spoon against the glass.

"Is something I want. I want Marysia should love me. But Marysia loved me as long as I paid. I was stupid and want test if she love me or my *dengi*. And I test, because I stupid. And turn out she not love me, only *dengi*. I test, now I know. But I love her. But I would like that Marysia loves me. Can you give me that, Szapiro? You have that for me?" she asked.

"That's the commodity everyone wants most in the world," he replied.

"Sure is."

"I'll get Buddy out of Bereza one way or the other. But afterward we'll remember who refused to help us. You don't want us to remember you that way."

"Listen here, Szapiro. Minister lick my boot, I whip butt of one police lieutenant, another I piss in mouth, you think they not do what I say? If I promise I let them kiss my ass?"

"You don't need a war with us."

"I risk it. I need war with them even less."

Aniela Kuznik impressed Jakub. He didn't say anything more. He finished his tea, got up, took his hat from the stand, and left without saying goodbye. He knocked on the door of the watchman's apartment on the first floor. He asked where the nearest telephone was and the watchman indicated a telephone booth in the entryway, which Jakub had previously overlooked.

"Great," he said. "How much do you earn, fella?"

"Twenty-five złotys a week, boss, plus whatever I get from tips," replied the guard eagerly, smelling a windfall.

Jakub pulled a thick wad of bills out of his pocket and counted out five hundreds. The doorman's face lit up with greed.

"A certain man's gonna visit Madame de Potocki."

"A lotta men visit."

"Name of Ziembiński."

"I ain't no fool, boss. I don't ask nobody for a name."

"A prosecutor."

"Ain't written on his forehead."

"Tall, gray hair, skinny, with a mustache. Real gent."

The watchman's first virtue was his memory for faces. His second was a talent for forgetting them. His third was how easily he could bring back what he'd forgotten when a banknote changed hands.

"I seen him."

"How long does he visit de Potocki for?"

"'Bout two hours, always."

Jakub pressed the rest of the hundreds into the man's hand, thinking how the money he'd saved was going up in smoke.

"You'll get that much again if you call right after he goes into de Potocki's. Here's the number. Ask for Miss Ryfka, say the pork delivery's arrived."

"Consider it done, boss, but what does a Ryfka want with pork?"

"She's an atheist."

The doorman touched his cap with two fingers, a military gesture.

"Yes sir, boss."

Jakub sighed, walked outside, got in his car, and drove to Ryfka's.

"Mustache?" she asked when he walked into the salon.

"Screw the mustache," he replied gloomily.

"Screw it," she agreed. "You want a girl?"

"Don't want any of 'em," he said dismissively.

Ryfka thought about Anna and turned somber, suspecting that for now Jakub only wanted that Polack.

"Vodka?"

"Yeah."

He drank, but not a lot, just three shots. He called home and asked Emilia to send a change of underwear, which it hurt Ryfka to hear though she didn't show her hurt in any way, she was too smart and too tired to show hurt. Jakub made a second call to Pantaleon, who soon arrived.

Later came the girls, the pianist, the customers, everyone, the ordinary day-to-day of Ryfka Kij's den.

"What now?" asked Ryfka.

"We wait."

So they waited.

They waited two days, but the call finally came, it came when Buddy was still in the darkness of solitary confinement in Bereza, being eaten up by simultaneous boredom and anxiety. But finally the watchman at the teachers' residence on Bem Street spotted what he was meant to spot, picked up the receiver in the telephone booth, and called the number Jakub had given him.

"Two of 'em showed up, Ziembiński and some baldy. They're just heading upstairs," he whispered into the receiver after Ryfka passed Szapiro the phone.

This whole time, Jakub and Pantaleon had been waiting at the ready at Ryfka's, not even drinking too much. When the watchman reported, Szapiro called Emilia and asked her to pack up right away, take the boys and the money from selling the building and go to the Francuski, a little hotel downtown at 112 Marszałkowska Street. The Stylowy movie theater was in the same building, she could even take the boys to three screenings a day, tell them it was a vacation, in any case they were to stay there until he gave word and not show their faces on the street.

Emilia didn't object. Emilia never objected. At the apartment they had a special fund prepared for such occasions, five thousand złotys and a thousand dollars that Jakub never touched, meaning this time she wouldn't have to dip into the twenty thousand dollars from the building, so she and the boys packed in fifteen minutes, she took the money, a few books for herself and a few for the boys, and took a taxi to the Francuski, where she checked in under a false name and with a false ID. The receptionist gave her a suspicious look, but she met that gaze, met it with no trouble, she felt Jakub's strength behind her.

Emilia's appearance was entirely Aryan, so her false ID featured the Polish name Maria Anna Szczerbicka, religion: Roman Catholic. Jakub had the same kind, under the name Piotr Szczerbicki, but he never used it, he was too proud of being Jakub Szapiro to ever pretend to be someone of no renown and no name, let alone a Pole.

In the hotel room, she gave a złoty to the bellboy who'd brought up her spartan luggage, placed the slightly frightened boys in armchairs, gave them books, sat down on the bed, and took a moment to try and answer her own question about the beginning of the long chain of events that had led her to this room. When had it begun? Why? Why had she always agreed to the next link? Why hadn't she left him? Taken the boys?

One doesn't leave Jakub Szapiro, she told herself, but she couldn't believe it.

She got up and hugged the boys tight, surprising them with this unexpected affection. She did her best to hold back tears, but she burst out in a silent sob.

"Don't you want to go to Palestine either, Mama?" asked Daniel. "Is that why you're crying?"

"I'm not crying," she replied.

Pantaleon and Jakub had brought an ordinary gun, plus Karpiński's sawed-off shotgun, a camera, and two powerful crowbars. They put all this in the trunk. Pantaleon climbed in on the passenger side and Jakub stood for a moment over the open trunk, thinking, then closed the lid and admitted there was no other life he'd want, no other life he was suited for.

But then he thought of Palestine. Would he have to work for a living there? Would they pay him to run around with a revolver, shooting at whoever needed shooting at over there?

There was no Anna in Palestine. He surprised himself with that thought. In Palestine there was no Anna, in Palestine there was a new life, there were Emilia and a lot of other women, but there was no Anna.

He couldn't believe his own thoughts, but those were his thoughts.

He sat down behind the wheel, lit a cigarette, and drove to Wola district, to Bem Street, to the teachers' residence.

The doorman was waiting outside. Not for Jakub, of course, but for the five hundred złotys he'd been promised. Which he got.

"And if there happened to be another hundred coming, I'd be happy to report I've got keys to every apartment, boss," he said, pocketing the money.

There happened to be another hundred, the crowbars stayed in the trunk, Pantaleon and Szapiro stood at the door to Madame de Potocki's apartment with a full set of keys. Jakub opened the door as quietly as he could, entered, and pulled his gun from his pocket.

Jakub indicated the padded door to Madame's study. He counted to three on his fingers, they pushed the door open, and burst in.

Inside, Prosecutor Jerzy Ziembiński was kneeling. He was naked, he had his wrists tied to his ankles, and he was blindfolded. Between Prosecutor Ziembiński's thighs was Sokoliński the journalist's head, and Prosecutor Ziembiński's small penis was placed in the journalist's mouth.

Sokoliński was also naked and hog-tied with a narrow cord, his hands pinned to the sides of his soft, plump body.

Madame de Potocki, in stockings and a corset with a switch in her hand, sat in a chair with legs shaped like curved scissors, forming a rounded X like a curule seat.

"What's going on?" asked Prosecutor Ziembiński, terrified, when he heard someone entering the room.

"Afternoon," said Szapiro. "Please hold still."

"Oh shit," said Sokoliński, releasing Prosecutor Ziembiński's penis from his mouth.

"Sodom and Gomorrah," moaned Pantaleon. "Abomination and ignominy. God is watching you! Have you no shame?"

De Potocki said nothing. She was too smart to scream or protest.

"Pantaleon, take that off his eyes."

"But it's so revolting, Szapiro," replied Karpiński.

Szapiro took out his pocketknife, opened it, and cut off the blindfold on the prosecutor's head.

"Two birds with one stone, Szapiro," said the giant. "But it's hard to look at people being so filthy."

"You think? Fantastic. Hold still now, gentlemen," said Szapiro cheerfully and opened the shutter on the Leica Model D. "I didn't expect such strong material. Madame, please continue with the gentlemen as you usually would, we're only here to document."

Sokoliński, de Potocki, and Ziembiński said nothing. A variety of threats ran through Ziembiński's mind but there was none he could convincingly make while kneeling naked with his wrists tied to his ankles.

De Potocki hesitated.

"Don't do this," grumbled Ziembiński helplessly.

Madame got up and slapped him in the face.

"You'll rot in prison," said the prosecutor.

Madame's switch went to work, Ziembiński howled.

"I can't watch this, Mr. Szapiro," Pantaleon said miserably. "It's wrong, no Christian should watch a dame whipping a guy, not even a fascist bastard, not even one that on top of being a fascist is a prosecutor too. And even whipping a hack journalist, it's not right, even if the hack's the lowest son of a bitch on this earth and doesn't deserve to shine a whore's shoes. But it's not right. This shouldn't happen, it's not the order of the world, Szapiro."

He spoke and felt the face of his devil brother moving, heard him whispering inside his skull. Kill her kill. Rape her rape. Kill her kill.

He punished his devil brother for those words.

"You don't have to look. Wait in the other room," replied Szapiro.

He did. Fifteen minutes was all Jakub needed. Madame continued, the prosecutor and journalist did what they had to in this situation, while Szapiro snapped photos and marveled at Madame de Potocki's ingenuity. He chose his shots very carefully so there would be a lot of photographs with the gentlemen appearing separately, to ensure he could blackmail one without burning the other.

"I'm going to make ten prints of each," said Jakub, once they'd finished. "And I'll hide them in different places. And now, Madame, take Mr. Sokoliński and get out of here, I've got to have a chat with the prosecutor."

Opening the door, he called Karpiński.

"Keep an eye on them, don't let them out yet."

He went back to Madame's study. Ziembiński lay, bruised and bound, on the floor.

"You'd better shoot me now, kike, because I intend to devote the rest of my life to destroying you." Ziembiński gasped.

Jakub remembered Anna's wish.

"You know how I found you here?"

Ziembiński didn't respond.

"Anna told me."

"Which Anna, Jew?"

"Your daughter. She told me you come here. She copied the key to your office and saw the pictures. She knows all about you, queer."

"I'm no queer," snarled Ziembiński.

"I don't know what your definition of a queer is, Mr. Ziembiński, but no more than fifteen minutes ago I saw your prick in that scribbler's mouth, so how about we stick to the facts."

"What do you want?"

"You're gonna bring me to the PM. Tomorrow."

"What for?"

"None of your goddamn business."

"He can't tomorrow."

"That's too bad because tomorrow I'll have the prints," hissed Jakub. "And if you force my hand, I'll make sure every politician, every journalist, every judge and lawyer in Warsaw gets a look at these photos. Now you're gonna wait here with Pantaleon and I'll get these photos developed and printed, and when everything's ready and safe, I'll let you know. If anything happens to me, these photos are getting sent out, that clear? Understand?"

"I understand," Ziembiński finally grunted in reply.

"You got a gun on you?"

"In my pants pocket."

Szapiro ran his hands over Ziembiński's suit, which was carefully hung up in the study, and found a small, nickel-plated Baby Browning, pulled out the magazine, fished out the bullets, pocketed them, and replaced the gun. In a jacket pocket he found a secretary wallet, and inside, a few sheets of office paper folded in thirds. He unfolded them and had a look. The pages showed a long list of names, typed on carbon paper, with notes by each one. A couple were crossed out, others were marked with a few words in pencil. Jakub put the list in his pocket.

"I'll come here tomorrow morning, you get on the phone and set up the meeting, 'cause we'll go straight from here to the PM's."

"And if he refuses to see me?"

"It's your job to make sure he doesn't. Sort it out. I'm only interested in one outcome."

He left the study.

"Mr. Sokoliński, you and me are gonna talk in the future," he cheerfully announced to the journalist, who was sitting unhappily on the floor, already dressed.

"And what about me, Szapiro?" asked Aniela Kuznik, wrapped in her silk dressing gown.

"They won't do anything to you."

"They will. Even if not now, he not forget this. And he come back for me when you stop caring. Which you will."

Jakub knew she was right. He wondered if he could help her in some way and after a moment realized he couldn't. He shrugged. It wouldn't be his concern anymore.

Kuznik nodded.

"You all the same. All of you," she said.

"All people are the same, ma'am. That is how Our Lord made us," replied Pantaleon. "There are no good people. Only evil ones. Everyone is evil. You're very evil as well."

Kuznik glowered hatefully at Pantaleon.

"Keep this merry band here overnight," Jakub ordered him, and left.

It was raining. He turned his face to the rain.

"I hate this city. I hate this country," he said out loud.

He got into the car.

Palestine, he thought. *Have to go to Palestine. Everything will be different there. I hate Poland. Have to go to Palestine.*

Yet for now he only went to a friendly photo store on Nalewki Street. He left the 35-mm roll of film, paid a hundred złotys for developing it, for ten prints of every photo, and for discretion, then drove to the snack bar on Leszno Street for lunch, but instead of eating he drank a bottle of vodka.

Palestine. Have to go to Palestine.

Anna, he thought, sitting at the table.

"I've got to see her," he said.

"Who's that, Mr. Szapiro?" asked Sobenski obligingly.

"Got any cocaine?"

Sobenski brought it immediately. Jakub snorted some, didn't say thank you because he didn't have to thank anyone for anything, took a small amount of it with him, drank a coffee and his last shot of vodka, put on his coat, and walked out, climbed into his car, and without a moment's thought simply drove up to Anna's in Żoliborz district, drunk and high.

He had to see her.

ז

ZAYIN

At that very moment, Colonel Adam Koc was crossing the Vistula in his government Cadillac, going east over the bridge by the Citadel, then exiting onto Modlińska Street and heading north for Golędzinów, to the barracks of the State Police Reserve Divisions in the former Fort Śliwicki. In these unstable times, this unit was the pride and joy of Prime Minister Sławoj Składkowski, who personally oversaw its organization, training, and equipment, correctly wagering violence was the most reliable method of quelling social unrest.

In the courtyard of the fort, training exercises were underway.

But it wasn't policemen training. There were, of course, ten policemen in navy-blue uniforms in the courtyard, but for the moment they were acting as instructors. The ones gathered for training were over a hundred young and middle-aged men in boots, dark jodhpurs, and light-colored uniform shirts with diagonal chest straps. Phalanx men, under the command of Andrzej Ziembiński. Some, including Ziembiński, wore holsters on their belts at their left hip.

They started with ordinary warm-ups, leg swings, deep knee bends, standing squat-thrusts, forward bends. They did the exercises determinedly, with no grumbling.

Koc got out of his car and a policeman with a lieutenant's three stars on his sleeves ran up to him, saluted, and with all a martinet's insincerity expressed his gratitude for the colonel deigning to honor the trainees with his presence. Koc told them to continue.

After the warm-up, the policemen divided the Phalanx volunteers into ten groups of a dozen or so each, and each group in turn went into the barracks armory to get weapons. They brought out rifles, revolvers, and machine pistols, laid them out on previously prepared tables, then set up targets by an earthen rampart.

The policemen started with theory. First they showed how to work a Mannlicher rifle, which differed from the Phalanx men's familiar Mosins and Mausers in that its bolt didn't rotate, you simply pulled back and pushed forward to put a cartridge in the chamber. The instructor explained how to load the gun, how to unload it, briefly presented the theory of aiming, then moved on to a Nagant system revolver, loading, unloading, shooting stance; finally came time for the machine pistols. First the Suomi, caliber 9 mm with a drum magazine, then the Thompson, an American gun with fat, American .45 ammunition, thicker than the German ammunition by two and a half millimeters. Theory, meaning disassembly and reassembly, loading, shooting position, aiming, and so forth.

The machine pistols particularly interested Colonel Koc, not even the guns themselves so much as the doctrine of using them to quell street demonstrations, because they had been purchased expressly for that purpose. He asked the martinet lieutenant about his experience suppressing demonstrations, but the policeman couldn't praise the automatic weapons.

"First of all, Colonel, rifle bullets penetrate too far. You usually shoot at a protest from distances between three hundred and a hundred fifty feet, the bullets often pass clean through, they ricochet dangerously. For street distances, pistol ammunition works perfectly. As you know, sir, because you've surely read about street battles in Colonel Rowecki's book, the first salvo always has to be into the crowd, then only the second one in the air, but the psychological effect of machine-gun fire from several barrels is also much stronger than even one salvo from a whole company."

Andrzej Ziembiński came up to Koc in his Phalanx uniform, a Thompson in his hand.

"Colonel, we're getting some resistance here from the policemen, and I would really encourage handing out to our groups . . ."

Koc placed a finger to his lips. Secret! Ziembiński bit his tongue and they went off alone, stepping away from the rest of the training participants.

"Please forgive me, I'm not accustomed to . . . ," explained Ziembiński. "The policemen are hesitating to hand out these machine pistols to us. They've got fifty on-site here, I'd really like to encourage them to give one each to the primary strike groups we're sending into areas of anticipated resistance."

"We'll arrange it."

Ziembiński saluted and immediately felt inappropriate giving a military salute, faced with Koc's colonel's uniform and his chest hung with ribbons. The colonel gave no indication that it upset him to any degree. But naturally he was furious.

The shooting began. The Phalanx men knew how to handle rifles and revolvers, so they took to practice happily. The policemen moved on to tactical training: firing while moving, using a bayonet, firing from cover.

Colonel Koc felt everything was going to plan. The Phalanx men might lack experience, but they made up for it in ideological zeal, devotion to the cause, and aggression. The colonel found this entirely satisfactory. Earlier he'd been at the training sessions for officers chosen for the coup, temporarily quartered in the barracks of the Twenty-First Infantry Division, the "Children of Warsaw," the same division Jakub Szapiro had been in seventeen years earlier, fighting the Bolsheviks.

Trusted, true-believing lieutenants and second lieutenants led by trusted, true-believing captains were getting used to working together in strike triads; trusted, true-believing majors wove a complex system to govern this organization, whose unique goal was to project power to the elites of the Republic who were undermining it. For the purification of Poland. For Great Poland.

The Phalanx men were plunging their bayonets into straw-stuffed mannequins and blasting holes in targets with rounds from police Suomis and Thompsons.

"There's our new Poland being born, Sergeant," he said to his driver, who was already in the Cadillac.

"Yes sir, Colonel," replied the driver, thinking his wife was right, they really ought to emigrate to America. Time to get the hell out of Poland.

Meanwhile Jakub was driving to Żoliborz district and also thinking about emigrating, to Palestine. He had to get the hell out of Poland. Leave, build a Jewish homeland, become a new Jew, a new man, a Maccabee. Moryc was buying the tickets. They were leaving, flying away. Flying to Palestine.

But meanwhile he turned onto Koźmian and looked for number five.

He finally found it.

The Ziembińskis lived in a sumptuous city villa, with a portico supported by four plump columns, a large arched French window opening onto a small balcony on the roof of the portico, and a multilayered red-shingled roof.

Szapiro reached for the packet of cocaine, snorted a little, got out of the Buick, hopped over the low, gated fence, walked up to the door, and rang the bell.

A man who wasn't Andrzej Ziembiński opened the door. The man was wearing a silk smoking jacket and a cravat, was distinctly younger than Jakub, and had manicured hands and hair combed with Brilliantine.

"And who the fuck are you?" asked Szapiro, high on the cocaine, and then he noticed Anna.

She was standing back in the hallway in an elegant, modest peignoir and a mismatched shawl to protect her shoulders from the cold.

"This is my fiancé," she said simply.

Szapiro felt fire in his guts. A sudden wave of jealousy. Though maybe it was just the cocaine that burned like that.

"Now look here, what's the meaning of this . . . ," began the man in the smoking jacket. Jakub hit him. The punch was strong and well aimed and the man in the smoking jacket fell, unconscious. Jakub stepped over him and approached Anna.

"You really think violence is the solution?" she asked.

"There's no problem violence can't solve."

"What are you doing here?"

"I came to see you."

"My fiancé doesn't like that."

"Do you?"

"Of course I do."

Jakub turned around, seized the still-unconscious fiancé by his collar, dragged him onto the portico, closed the door behind him, and closed the latch. He went back to Anna, turned her around, lifted off her peignoir, and unbuttoned his fly. Anna leaned over a small console table in the hallway, jostling some porcelain knickknacks.

"Spank me," she said.

He spanked her once, twice, she had soft, muscular buttocks, and then he grabbed her hard by the waist and did what he'd come to do. After a moment they moved to the floor, with Anna on top of him.

But he didn't finish, because the door smashed open and there stood Andrzej Ziembiński, in his Phalanx uniform, with a gun in his hand.

"What in the name of fuck is going on?" he roared.

When he drove up to the house and saw his bloodied future brother-in-law, he immediately realized it could be a political attack. The door was locked, but only with a latch, so he broke it down. He'd expected to find Szapiro or one of his people in the house, he'd wanted to save his sister and didn't expect he'd find her furiously riding the bucking Jewish boxer, with one hand on his chest and the other in his mouth.

He lowered his gun.

Szapiro leaped up, throwing Anna off him, which was a mistake, since Ziembiński wouldn't have fired at him while Anna was sitting on his dick.

"Don't shoot!" she screamed.

He shot but missed because Jakub got tangled up in his own pants and fell flat on his ass. Yet as he fell he managed to get his little Browning out of his jacket pocket and aim at Ziembiński, aware there was no bullet in the chamber.

"Don't shoot!" Anna screamed a second time.

He didn't. They had their guns pointed at one another, Ziembiński in his uniform, Jakub on his back on the floor, his pants around his ankles and his circumcised privates protruding absurdly from between the tails of his shirt.

Anna stood between them, disheveled, her peignoir torn at the breast.

"Put your guns away," she requested.

They both lowered their pistols. Jakub rose, pulling up his pants with one hand. Behind Ziembiński, Anna's fiancé was getting to his feet.

"What's going on here?"

"She's fucking this Jew," said Andrzej grimly.

The fiancé dropped to his knees, looking like he'd taken another right straight to the jaw.

"I knew it . . ."

"As if you two give a shit who I'm fucking!" she screamed, furious.

"I love you," whispered her fiancé in a voice so forlorn it made Jakub button up his pants in disgust.

"Goodbye, all," Jakub said and headed for the door, slowly, not taking his eyes off Ziembiński.

"You'll regret this," snarled Anna's brother.

Szapiro grinned.

"Did you inherit your daddy's proclivities?"

"What?"

"Bet you did. In which case, Mr. Ziembiński, fuck you in the ass."

The only reason Ziembiński didn't shoot was because he didn't understand what Szapiro meant. By the time it hit him, Szapiro was already in the car with the engine running and it was too late to shoot. Jakub meanwhile leaned over to the passenger side and cranked the window down.

"You coming?" he called.

She grabbed her coat from the rack, pulled it on, and, still barefoot but clutching a bottle of cognac she'd grabbed somewhere, she made for Jakub's Buick. Andrzej seized her by the arm, she slapped him in the face with an open palm, and he released her. Her fiancé was on his knees, crying.

"Give it a rest, you pathetic fucking moron," snarled Ziembiński.

Getting no answer from his would-be brother-in-law, Ziembiński shoved him out the broken-down door. He went up to his bedroom to remove his Phalanx uniform and put on a civilian suit, then in his suit, with his gun, he went out into the nocturnal city, with a very concrete plan.

Jakub was moving, from Koźmian Street he turned left on Camaldolese Street, which ran along the Vistula, and drove in silence. Anna was silent too. She took a large swig of cognac and passed him the bottle; he took a swig too. They drove north as far as the former Camaldolese monastery on the Warsaw city limits.

"Wołodyjowski's monastery," she said out of nowhere.

"Whose?"

"You know, Wołodyjowski. When he became a Camaldolese monk, it was here."

"But who's Wołodyjowski?"

She looked at him carefully, to see if he was joking. He wasn't.

"You know, from Sienkiewicz's *Trilogy*, Colonel Wołodyjowski. I can't believe you don't know, everyone's read the *Trilogy*."

"Dunno it." He shrugged. "I've heard of Sienkiewicz, he's one of your writers, but I haven't read him, not my thing."

She stared at him openmouthed and fascinated.

"That's amazing. Incredible and amazing. Now I like you even more."

Jakub was being a little coy because he knew she'd enjoy that, he knew the name Wołodyjowski was from some important book the Poles had, but that was all he knew on the subject. So his coyness wasn't exaggerated.

"What's the story with the fiancé?"

"No story, what story should there be? I'm supposed to marry him."

"You sleep with him?"

She started laughing, very loudly, as though she'd just heard the best joke and couldn't stop. She doubled over with laughter.

"No, not with *him*," she finally choked out. "We're waiting until the wedding for that."

He looked at her in fury and disbelief.

"Seriously. Ignacy is very religious."

He believed her and knew that in any other circumstance this was grotesque enough to make him burst out laughing too, but at that moment he couldn't.

"But with other guys?" he continued, himself terrified of his own words and what they implied.

"Of course with other guys. Like you. I love fucking, what can I do."

Past the monastery they turned off the paved road onto a dirt one, into the brush. His hands clenched the steering wheel. He didn't understand what was happening inside him. He was sometimes jealous of women. He was madly jealous of Ryfka, and she'd been happy to toy with that jealousy when they were still together, marking the true end of their love as when she could go around with a man in public without the man losing a couple teeth and getting a broken nose or arm in the process, as had happened before whenever Ryfka had enlisted someone for the purpose of thumbing her nose at Jakub.

Emilia, who suppressed her own jealousy, didn't allow Jakub to be jealous of her. She flirted with men, but he doubted she'd sleep with them, because who would be bold enough to sleep with the wife of Jakub Szapiro? But one way or the other she hated feeling jealous and she knew how to put her fears to rest before they got out of control.

But for Jakub—here, now, when it came to this strange Polish woman—something flared up inside him, in his stomach, flared up and turned his mind to who might claim his rights to a woman he seemingly had no connection to beyond physical relations.

"I love fucking," she'd said, and he imagined someone else doing what he did with her and it was like an artillery grenade exploding in his brain, he went white with rage, then after the rage came helplessness. Showing jealousy like that meant showing a great weakness, which Szapiro wouldn't allow himself in front of a woman.

He knew no feeling worse than helplessness. He hadn't felt helpless twenty years before in Czerwoniak prison in Łomża, where he was beaten and starved and tortured, and where he lost sixty-five pounds, leaving him ninety-nine pounds soaking wet and made up of nothing but anger and loose, dry skin over bones. He hadn't been helpless in the trenches of Stryj, standing against the Bolsheviks' cavalry charges with his last four bullets in his Mosin, and what was worse, totally unconvinced he was fighting for the right cause, that he shouldn't be on the other side of the front. Because why defend Poland with all its feudal lords and Jew-hating when in the Soviet Union a Jew could be anyone he wanted—a commissar, an officer, a minister, whatever they called it over there. In the Soviet Union a Jew could be a man everyone feared, like Trotsky. Though for that matter they feared a Pole, Dzerzhinsky, even more.

So he'd been wavering, but not helpless. He hadn't been helpless in the ring or fleeing the police, or fighting in the street, or ever in love before then, but he was helpless against her words, the way a person is helpless against a hurricane, an avalanche, a flood.

He stopped the car.

She leaned over to his fly, undid the single button he'd fastened, took him in her mouth, and when he was ready, climbed on top of him. He grabbed her by the throat. She didn't protest.

"My little boy is jealous." She laughed and slapped him in the face.

He slapped her back, she cried out with pleasure, she took his fingers in her mouth, she started to suck and move on top of him.

He couldn't finish, though she came several times, crying out and slapping him in the face. He let her. He didn't know why, or maybe he did, he was just surprised at himself—he let her do it because he'd let her do anything as long as he was inside her body. Maybe even as long as he hoped he'd be inside her body again. Afterward they sat next to one another in silence, gazing at the black outlines of the trees against the dark-gray, cloudy sky, drinking cognac, and once they'd finished that, vodka, which he had a few bottles of in the back seat. Anna was drinking a large amount and quickly, but she seemed just about sober until she suddenly opened the door, vomited, then crawled, mumbling something, onto the back seat, where she curled up into a ball, murmuring, "Take me home."

So he drove her back to the house with the broken-down door and woke her up—she got out, swaying, without saying goodbye. He wanted to kiss her but she pushed him away with a laugh, she reeked of vodka, meanwhile he was trembling so he snorted some cocaine again, that woke him up. He knew there was no going to sleep now. He waited until Anna had wobbled her way to the door, then set off and drove until morning through the feeble streetlights and rain of Warsaw.

He drove slowly, meandering through Żoliborz, Marymont, Koło, and Wola districts, he drove into the poor Jewish part of the City Center, from there to the wealthy Polish part of the City Center, then to the poor Polish one, then over the river to Praga and Grochów districts and back, to Nalewki Street, past his house, he drove up to the snack bar on Leszno and remembered his money and burst into solitary laughter at the thought.

He remembered the fifty thousand dollars he'd saved up the way he might remember a forgotten umbrella. He stopped, the snack bar was locked but he had his key, he unlocked the door, went into the kitchen, slid back a false tile on the stove, pulled out a package tied up tight with string and containing five hundred bills with Ben Franklin's portrait on them. He threw the package into the glove compartment next to his large Browning, which he usually kept in the glove compartment when he was driving, and moved on, leaving the snack bar unlocked. Now he was leaving everything behind him.

He drove down Tłomackie Street, then farther south, up to the hotel where Emilia was staying with the boys, up to Ryfka's brothel, but without going into either, without getting out of the car, he just drove, trembling and sensitive from the alcohol breaking down in his body and the cocaine he kept snorting in small amounts to keep himself going.

He stopped at a sausage stand and ate, not even really listening to the seller's nighttime story about how some hookers showed up wanting to eat for free, he wouldn't let them, then he let one because she worked him over with her mouth in a courtyard entryway, she got out my kiełbasa so she could eat another one, heh-heh, how the cops came, how a droshky driver was drunk, how some bruisers were sniffing around but they left, how he saw a grand lady riding all alone in the back of a gorgeous limousine. And so on. Jakub swallowed the last mouthful of frankfurter, took a bite of bread with mustard, and went back to his car. He turned the ignition and drove on. He laid his pistol on the seat next to him, then laid it on his lap, then held it in his right hand, then kept putting it under his chin, finger on the trigger, and wondering if the pistol would go off if the car went over a bump, then he remembered his sons and withdrew his hand, then put it back in position. Suddenly he had to slam on the brake, the Buick screeched to a halt. Jakub opened the door and vomited up the food he'd just eaten.

When the streetlamps went out and Warsaw glowed in the gray, feeble October sunlight refracted through the clouds, Jakub snorted one final, if generous, share of cocaine and drove to Bem Street, to the teachers' residence, and went to Madame de Potocki's apartment.

"Have we got a meeting?" he asked Ziembiński Senior.

Ziembiński only nodded.

"At the palace?"

"I couldn't manage it. Just an unofficial one. The PM will have breakfast at Simon & Stecki's, you can join him there."

"All right, let's go. Just one thing first."

He went up to Sokoliński. The reporter always looked depressed and suppressed, but at that moment he was a pathetic sight even by his usual standards.

"Mr. Sokoliński, is the *Courier* an anti-Semitic rag?"

"No, boss, I'm happy to report it is not," said Sokoliński, quaking with fear.

"Well then, Sokoliński, now I want you to write an article, once a week, denouncing anti-Semitism for what it is, the worst aberration of all. That clear?"

Sokoliński nodded eagerly.

"And if two weeks go by with no article, then we'll send out those lovely photographs everywhere we need to, that clear?"

"As day, yes sir. And I assure you, from the bottom of my heart, I loathe anti-Semitism, because . . ."

Szapiro stopped paying attention to him and ordered Pantaleon to release the hack, then go straight to Ryfka's and wait there for further instructions. All four of them went downstairs together. Pantaleon caught the streetcar and Sokoliński got on his bike, thinking he feared Szapiro less than going home and having to explain his all-night absence. Jakub and Ziembiński climbed into Jakub's Buick.

"Smells like you've been boozing in here all week," growled Ziembiński, channeling his helplessness into pointless remarks.

"Only since yesterday. Or for twenty years."

"And you want to talk to the prime minister in that condition?"

"You think it'd be more appropriate with a dick in my ass?"

Ziembiński jolted as though from an electric shock, then shut his mouth and turned to the window. He felt his defeat so severely, so painfully it felt like a nail hammered into his chest. As though this impudent Jewish thug had hammered a nail into his chest.

Jakub thought for a moment about his condition, pumped up on cocaine, poisoned by the products of the alcohol breaking down in his liver, but then remembered the list of names in his jacket pocket and felt more confident.

They pulled up to Simon & Stecki's. Ziembiński led Szapiro inside, feeling like he had a noose tight around his neck that nothing could loosen. This Jewish bandit held his civil death in his hand and wasn't hesitating for a moment, so Ziembiński had to either do favors for him or kill him, but killing him wasn't at all simple, because he'd have to kill the photos as well, an eventuality Szapiro had very effectively insured himself against.

The prime minister sat alone at a table in an empty room that had been cleared of customers. The waiters were bustling around urgently, while somber bodyguards stood at the door.

The prime minister, General Felicjan Sławoj Składkowski, was slim and of medium height, he combed his thinning gray hair back, and had a bushy mustache protruding under his nose and equally bushy eyebrows, making him somewhat resemble Marshal Piłsudski, whom he'd modeled himself on his entire life, though naturally without any delusion of being his equal. His face wore the grimness of a man perfectly aware he'd achieved immortality when his campaign to improve rural hygiene had led country folk to nickname their new government-built outhouses *Sławojki*, after him.

Składkowski had stuffed a large linen napkin into his uniform collar with its general's braiding, and was just attempting to eat an entire poached egg he'd speared on the end of his fork.

"Prosecutor!" he said cheerfully at the sight of Ziembiński, and the yolk dribbled onto his napkin. "Have a seat, gentlemen, join me."

Ziembiński greeted him sourly, embarrassed. The prime minister swallowed the egg, then speared another on his fork. The yolk ran out all over his plate. Składkowski frowned, displeased, and soaked it up with a slice of bread. Jakub was feeling confident thanks to the cocaine. He shook the head of government's hand and introduced himself.

"With your permission, General, I'll excuse myself, Mr. Szapiro has a matter to discuss with y-you . . . ," stammered Ziembiński and felt his face burning with shame. "I'll leave you both to it."

"Hang on," mumbled the general, his mouth full of food, but Ziembiński bowed and made his escape, and the waiter looked after him in surprise, having just brought a place setting for him.

The prosecutor stepped outside, breathed in the fresh air, and quickly remembered the noose around his neck. He meant to go home, but he went to Saint Anne's first, sat in a pew, and attempted to apologize to God for his numerous sins, before deciding there was no point screwing around. He remembered the copy of the proscription list in his jacket pocket, he reached into his wallet, but the list was gone. He realized Szapiro must have taken it, leaving him, as a final humiliation, his favorite nickel-plated FN .25-caliber pistol, but unloaded.

Szapiro, the Jewish crook who now, thanks to him, was breakfasting with the prime minister.

He stepped out of the church into the rain, caught a taxi, went home to Żoliborz district, and discovered the broken-down door. He went into the house. His daughter lay half-naked on the floor in the foyer, covered with her coat. She was sleeping, snoring gently and, with all her girlish charm, filling the hallway with the stench of stale alcohol. At the end of the hallway, he could see a hole in the English paneling covering the wall that, as a criminal prosecutor who knew his stuff, he recognized instantly as a bullet hole.

His life was falling apart around him, he thought, all just because his daughter hated him.

Or because nothing turned him on more than being humiliated and degraded at the feet of an imperious woman. Only Madame de Potocki made Prosecutor Ziembiński's penis respond according to its purpose, with ordinary whores the prosecutor's body remained dormant.

And did that mean he served Poland any worse than a man who fulfilled his sexual needs in another way?

He passed his daughter without waking her, went upstairs to his study, sat down at his large ebony desk—black as his sins—and opened the locked bottom drawer. He pulled out a file of erotic photographs of fantasies that could have come from the stories of Baron von Sacher-Masoch, and looked through them without any arousal, only with the nostalgia we sometimes feel looking at photos of good times so irrevocably gone by that even the memories they've left behind seem false. He threw the photos into the wastepaper basket and set them alight. They twisted in the flame, blackened, and burned out.

He thought of the other papers he should burn and glanced at the armored, fireproof cabinet holding them. He thought of the human lives he'd witnessed and reflected, of the human weaknesses, errors, and baseness those documents showed, of the human hopes and fears those documents prompted, of the authority they gave him, enormous authority over so many powerful people, though not powerful enough to tear off the noose that uneducated simpleton of a boxer had tied around his neck.

He whispered the old fraternity toast under his breath: "God be with us, to hell with them." But it no longer gave him the internal sense of his choices being the right ones, the way it used to.

"To hell with all of you," he wrote on a piece of office paper, then reached into his drawer for the box of .25-caliber ammunition, loaded one into the magazine, cocked the pistol, then immediately, without hesitation, placed it to his temple and fired—immediately, to escape fear, to escape anything that might make him hesitate, make him go soft, make his hand tremble, stop him from pulling that small metal plate that, by moving a bar releasing a hammer hidden under a firing pin, would decide his life and death.

So he fired immediately, to escape his doubts. And he succeeded, he escaped.

Over the Vistula River, Litani dove down to Żoliborz district, nearly touching the ground, peered one burning eye into the window of the Ziembińskis' house, saw the prosecutor's body, opened his maw and sang, and saw Ziembiński with that song.

The shot woke Anna. She opened her eyes and for a moment didn't know where she was, who she was, or the situation she found herself in; then one by one she recognized the house, herself, and a situation that was embarrassing, to put it mildly. Her mouth was completely dry, she had a splitting headache, but she remembered a shot had awakened her, that part wasn't a dream, and a shot was something you had to investigate even with a horrific hangover. Danger. She got to her feet. She was still drunk, the hangover notwithstanding. She remembered the shot had come from upstairs, so she went up on wobbling feet, saw the door to her father's study open, and entered. Jerzy Ziembiński was in his chair, his head blown open and resting on his desk, his arms hanging limply to the ground. On the wall, on the floor: blood.

Anna vomited up bile from her empty stomach.

"Well now, what's all this about, Mr. Szapiro?" said the prime minister in the meantime, taking a bite of toast and sipping his coffee. "Have something to eat."

Szapiro peered at his breakfast. He poked a trembling poached egg with his fork until it finally broke open and the yolk spilled out on the plate. He didn't feel like eating.

"Mind if I smoke?" he asked.

"Be my guest."

He lit a cigarette, took a drag. The cigarette tasted good, but at the same time summoned up the slightest shadow of boredom, somewhere in the pit of his stomach.

"Now, what is it?"

"You guys put Kaplica in Bereza."

Składkowski looked amazed.

"What do you mean put him there? Who did? Buddy Kaplica? In Bereza? For that banditry of his? The protection money from Kercelak?"

"I don't know what for, General."

"What else would it be for . . . ? An old rebel who fought right under Piłsudski and he's in Bereza, for something stupid like Jews paying him? It doesn't make sense."

"You're the prime minister here, General."

Składkowski looked even more distressed.

"I don't even know anymore. I suppose I must have signed it."

"You obviously did, General."

"They must have slipped it onto my desk."

"That's what's gonna happen from now on. They're gonna stick our guys in Bereza. Except the ones they mow down in the coup."

"Come now, you're just repeating silly rumors," the prime minister said dismissively.

Szapiro pulled out the target list he'd taken from Ziembiński, laid it on the table next to the coffee cups, dishes of jelly and butter, the basket of bread, and the plate of cold cuts and sausage. Składkowski wiped his fingers on his napkin, put on his glasses, and looked the list over.

"What is this?"

"A proscription list. Make sure to read the notes written in pencil."

"Aleksandra Piłsudska, internment, if she shows resistance—on the spot. Sławek, propose honorable suicide. If he refuses—on the spot. Mościcki—on the spot. Prystor—on the spot," Składkowski read out loud.

"You're on the list too, General. Back page."

"Składkowski. Forced written declaration supporting the coup. In case of refusal—on the spot," read the prime minister. "Where did you get this?"

"I took it off Ziembiński. I squeezed him. That's why he brought me here."

"How did you squeeze him?"

"That's my business."

Składkowski pondered.

"And what does this have to do with Kaplica being in Bereza?"

"Radziwiłek's taken control of the Northern District. Replacing Kaplica. He made an agreement with Piasecki and Koc, promised no trouble between the Jewish workers and the Polish ones on the night of the coup. No street battles like in twenty-six, nobody's gonna hurt them. With Kaplica in Bereza they're safe. The street won't rise up. But if Kaplica comes back, no coup will get through. Not with our folks on the streets. I mean, we've been whipping fascists much as we like, for years."

"Well that's true, and I get that. But why do you care about this?"

"Because I owe Kaplica, first of all. Second of all, how do you think life's gonna be for us in a country where Piasecki's in charge? Like under Hitler, right? Or worse. Because the Germans, they're a cultured nation, you know?"

"Piasecki was in Bereza too, as it happens, in thirty-four. And they somehow didn't beat this fascist nonsense out of him out there. At any rate, I'll call Kamala-Kurhański in a moment and bring Kaplica back to Warsaw," resolved Składkowski. "I'll send a car for him specially."

"To Bereza? Just let him out discreetly, General. I'll send one of my men in Kaplica's car. Safer that way. You got too many enemies."

"I do?"

"In the ministry. Somebody slipped those documents onto your desk."

"Indeed. Very well. But give me a card or something. I've got to be able to get in touch with you."

"I'm sure you've got Ryfka Kij's phone number, General."

"What's that supposed to mean?"

"We know you've been there, General. Just gotta call. I'll be there, by the phone."

The prime minister stroked his mustache and said nothing.

Szapiro got up without having eaten and bowed awkwardly; the prime minister rose and offered Jakub a butter-smeared hand. He had egg yolk in his mustache.

Szapiro went back to his car and felt horribly, enormously tired. So he drove to Ryfka's.

◆ ◆ ◆

Everyone's dead, but I'm alive.

◆ ◆ ◆

Climbing the stairs to Ryfka's, Jakub has to rest every few steps. He thinks about all the fights in his life, about those moments when he sees his opponent running out of breath, then Jakub dips into his reserves of energy, left, left, break through his guard, push him onto the ropes, right, he's still blocking, so go down, right hook to his liver, it lands painfully, so his opponent instinctively lowers his guard, then another left in the ribs, the spleen, and expelling what's left of the air from his lungs, his opponent's guard is low now, Jakub's back and stomach muscles still have reserves, they twist, hips, back, finally a fist in a short arc and Jakub finishes with a right hook to the jaw, it's over.

And now he can't get up the stairs, his lungs are wheezing.

Too many cigarettes. No gym in a long time.

He's done with boxing, done with fighting, that's for sure.

He finally got to the right floor and pressed the door handle, the door was locked. He knocked. Pantaleon opened the door with the sawed-off shotgun in his hand.

"Closed today?" asked Szapiro.

"I thought that was best," answered Ryfka.

She wasn't standing behind the bar, she sat in an armchair smoking a slim cigarette and drinking cognac.

"I gotta rest. Pantaleon, take Kaplica's car and drive to Bereza Kartuska. You know where it is?"

"Out past Kobryń, right, Mr. Szapiro?"

"You'll find it on a map. Ask for Buddy at the guardhouse there, they should hand him over. I talked to the PM. Anything fishy goes down, find a phone and call here."

"Then God willing, Mr. Szapiro, I'll get on the road."

"Bring somebody else to help drive, don't stop except to tank up. Bring Buddy back here fast as you can."

"I'd take Munja . . . but I can't."

"No, you can't. Get moving. I gotta rest. Need to sleep this off."

Pantaleon put on his coat and newsboy cap and went outside, leaving the shotgun on the bar. He quickly caught a taxi and asked to go to Kaplica's house in Mokotów district. Despite the long route the driver didn't want payment.

"You ride free with me, boss, every time!" he said, and bowed, his respect just as authentic as the fear he made no effort to conceal. To

Pantaleon, both sentiments were simply the tribute he deserved, just as pleasant as they were self-evident.

He knocked on Kaplica's door. His daughter opened it, they greeted one another politely and she invited him inside, where Maria Kaplica sat in the kitchen; despite many years of wealth she still hadn't gotten used to the living room.

"Mr. Karpiński . . . Well he got what was coming to him, they took my man away to die."

"I gotta take the car, Mrs. Kaplica. I'm bringing him home, Mrs. Kaplica."

"You go ahead, I ain't got no use for it, them automobiles don't mean nothing to me."

Her older daughter handed him the keys. He bowed deeply, respectfully, walked out, got in the Chrysler, and started heading east.

In the meantime, Ryfka was now standing behind the bar.

"Moryc was here," she said. "He left an envelope for you."

"I'm sure you opened it, so quit pretending you don't know what's inside."

"Plane tickets. For you, for your lovely wife, and sweet little kiddies. For tomorrow morning. Twenty-four hours."

"Give it a goddamn rest, Ryfka. I need to sleep."

"I'll give you some valerian drops."

She did, Jakub put the tickets in his jacket pocket, slipped his gun under the pillow, took the drops, went to one of the rooms, lay down, and went to sleep. He dreamed he was fighting in the ring with a huge, fat boxer, two heads taller than him and weighing maybe 450 pounds, covered in mounds of fat. Jakub was punching him with all his might, but his fat cushioned the strongest blows, the gigantic fat boxer roared with laughter and then transformed into the Venus of Willendorf, enormous and faceless, yet endowed with a vast black maw.

Litani floated in the night sky over the ring, his burning eyes like a plane's navigation lights.

Jakub screamed, still asleep, but screamed nonetheless.

A while later, someone else knocked at the front door. Ryfka picked up the shotgun, looked through the judas hole, and hesitated, wondering if she should open the door.

"I hear someone in there," said Anna. "Let me in."

Ryfka took a deep breath, turned the key in the lock, pulled back the sturdy bolt, and opened the door, resolving to throw this miserable bitch out on her ass, but she wasn't going to hide behind a locked door, she'd do it face-to-face, she could afford to. There was no way some snot-nosed, fancy-ass Polack was better than Ryfka Kij, parentage unknown.

Anna stood trembling in the stairwell in a torn peignoir with her coat wrapped around her. She was hungover, makeup was streaked down her face, she stank of stale alcohol and vomit. Ryfka's heart softened. She stepped out of the way and gestured for her to come in.

"Need money for the droshky driver," said Anna in a weak voice.

"And I'm supposed to pay?" said Ryfka, bridling.

"I didn't bring any money, my father shot himself . . ."

Ryfka sighed. She felt like pushing this insolent brat down the stairs, but she thought of Jakub asleep in the room nearby, then sat Anna in one of the chairs where the girls usually waited for tricks, went downstairs, paid for the droshky, and came back up.

Anna was still sitting where Ryfka had left her and still looked like she'd been through all the plagues of Egypt. Ryfka took her by the arm and numbly led her to the girls' bathroom. She sat her on a stool, filled the tub, poured in bath salts, stood Anna up, and undressed her. Anna allowed her to do all this. Ryfka helped the girl get into the bath then returned to the salon, took a large swig of cognac, put on water for coffee, and made the girl breakfast—eggs, bread, coffee, fruit preserves.

"Why am I doing this?" she asked herself, genuinely surprised. After all she couldn't stand this Polish whore.

"For Jakub, dummy. Because he'd want you to." She answered her own question, out loud once again.

She brought the girl's breakfast to the bathroom.

Meanwhile Jan Kaplica, alias "Buddy," got no breakfast that day. He stood on the parade ground of the Bereza Kartuska Isolation Facility. He was standing in nothing but his undershorts, barefoot, with the stump of his left arm wrapped in already-soiled bandages. It was raining. He was shivering with cold. Other prisoners stood in two even rows alongside Kaplica: Ukrainian activists, communists, a few nationalists, a few obstreperous leftist journalists, some speculators, a few Bundists, all in only their undershorts as well, all imprisoned not by courts but by bureaucrats.

Kamala-Kurhański was addressing the assembly.

"This individual here, a certain Kaplica, a Warsaw hoodlum, a communist piece of shit, imagined he could blackmail me, Commandant Inspector Józef Kamala-Kurhański. So this certain Kaplica sent one of his thugs to the apartment of my aunt Adelajda, a resident of Warsaw. And he wanted to blackmail me, saying if we didn't treat him well here, he'd hurt my aunt. Can you imagine that, you scum, you bastards, you human weasels?"

The camp's prisoners said nothing.

"I asked you a question!" roared Kamala-Kurhański.

Silence again. A few policemen set on the ranks of prisoners with their batons. The prisoners started screaming that no, they couldn't imagine it.

"Well then I'm thrilled that you cruds gathered here can't imagine anything so unbelievable. Because Kamala-Kurhański can't be blackmailed, you hear that, you bastards? Can't be done!"

The policemen moved toward the ranks of prisoners.

"We hear you, Commandant!" cried the prisoners.

"And do you know why, you human shit stains?"

"No we don't!"

"Because I don't give a wet shit if my aunt Adelajda lives or dies! As far as I'm concerned Aunt Adelajda can float down the Slavic Vistula all the way to the Free City of Danzig! I don't give a fuck about Aunt

Adelajda! The only thing I give a fuck about is our beloved homeland, which wants to stamp out human shit stains like you! And I'll beat you bastards straight! You've got my word as a police officer, you rats! Down!"

The prisoners threw themselves on the muddy ground. Kaplica too, though with one weakened arm he couldn't do it as quickly as he should. One policeman helped him out by knocking his feet out from under him with a baton. As he fell, Kaplica caught himself with the fresh stump, roared in pain, and passed out. They beat him awake. Blood was seeping through the bandages.

"Up."

He got to his feet, like the others.

Next Kamala-Kurhański ordered them to crawl in the mud, then dig ditches and fill them right back in. A policeman handed Kaplica a shovel. Kaplica, barely able to stand, showed him his stump. The policeman punched him in the face, Kaplica fell facedown in the mud.

"Leave him alone, murderer!" cried one of the prisoners, a young man who looked about twenty. "He's an old man! With an amputated arm."

They beat the boy too.

"Beat me, you pricks," Buddy managed to groan, lying on the ground. "Leave the boy. I'm a better Pole than all of you put together but I'm an old crook and I got blood on my hands."

The policeman kicked Kaplica in the ribs.

"Go ahead, kick me. I'm the only one who should be here. Not them boys. I'm guilty. They're innocent."

"You're gonna dig with your hand, scum," ordered the policeman.

"Halt!" roared Kamala-Kurhański. "Can't you see Mr. Kaplica is indisposed? We'll find him an easier job than digging. The shithole needs emptying!"

The prisoners carried waste from Bereza's latrines to a large pit at the edge of the camp. From time to time the pit had to be emptied out into a horse-drawn tank by the men, standing knee-deep or even waist-deep in rotting excrement, using buckets.

The policemen led Kaplica to the workstation, then pushed him into the pit and threw him a bucket.

"Fuck you all in the ass," said Buddy. "Buddy Kaplica ain't gonna slop out shit."

So he got a beating, they broke a couple of his ribs, then they threw him naked—because his undershorts tore while they were beating him with batons—and covered in excrement into solitary.

Knock-knock.

"Here."

Knock-knock.

"Here."

Knock-knock.

◆ ◆ ◆

Everyone's dead, but I'm alive.

She's alive too, but I don't know who she is.

I'm sitting at the window. I take a bite of buttered bread. I bite into the bread with toothless gums. I don't know where my dentures are. I look at the streets of Tel Aviv.

The Arab boy with the cart, the old furniture on the cart. Or styled to look old, the bentwood legs and the striped upholstery on armchairs and couches stacked up.

I've seen him here before. Nothing changes.

Cars. A yellow Fiat, a white Peugeot, a yellow Mercedes. I can almost hear their horns.

By the newsstand a religious Jew in a black frock coat is smoking a cigarette, waiting for something. He looks like Naum Bernsztajn, his body chopped up like a rooster for kappores. A girl in a green uniform passes him, she has a black rifle on her back. Blond hair.

I don't know if she's beautiful or not, she has her back turned to me. I can almost see her hips sway. I can almost see her walking.

Silence. The window doesn't let any sound through.

"I can't remember anything, I don't know what happened afterward, not a thing."

"You gonna keep pretending you don't know who I am?" she asks. She's sitting in a chair next to me. She's old, very old.

"I remembered the Magda you were talking about. Magda Aszer, right? There was a girl like that, pretty good-looking. You even slept with her, like you did all the good-looking girls in our neighborhood. You got it into your head that poor boy you killed was dating Magda Aszer, right? That he made Aliyah with her?"

I'm not listening. I don't answer.

"Idiot," she snorts.

"When did we leave Warsaw?" I ask.

She looks at me, her steely eyes like the mouths of guns. As if she has something to tell me. But she doesn't speak. She only shrugs and turns away. She puts a lump of yellow cheese and some aspic wrapped clumsily in grease-stained paper into the fridge. She puts a semistale loaf of bread in the breadbox.

I look at the thick stack of pages next to the typewriter. I'm finished writing.

What comes next shouldn't be written down.

"I don't know how we got to Tel Aviv," I say, my voice trembling.

She looks at me. I still have a boxer's wide shoulders, though the rest of me's gone flabby like an old buzzard, bald head, baggy skin under my chin, hands covered in liver spots. On my right hand the now barely visible Hebrew letters: מוות, *mem, vav, vav,* and *tav,* death, death, death, death.

"You've been imagining you're someone else and somewhere else, is that it?"

The Arab boy with the cart, old furniture on the cart. Or styled to look old, bentwood legs and striped upholstery on armchairs and couches piled high. A picture clipped from the newspaper, set in a leftover frame from a religious painting and hung on the wall.

"You're Jakub Szapiro. And you're here. You're eighty-eight years old. And you're here with me."

Suddenly I know. I've known all along, but now suddenly I know, like someone's switched on a light in a dark room, and suddenly everything I had only known I can now suddenly see.

Ryfka. It's her. Why Ryfka? Where is Emilia? I look at the wall.

Ryfka rises with a grunt and pulls open the dusty curtains. We live high up, on the eighth floor. Gray apartment buildings, small houses, a large pond. The pond has ducks swimming in it. A few cars are parked out on the street. Two little Fiats, an old Warszawa, a Škoda. In pastel colors. Farther along, some trees, a church.

The locals call the pond "Morocco." That I know. It's mainly miners living in the apartment building, they speak strange Polish, like some kind of slang, sometimes I hear it through the door, but I never see them. I haven't left this apartment in ten years.

"We're not in Tel Aviv," I say, I don't know why.

"You were the king of Warsaw. For two years."

I know I was, a twenty-three-month reign, yet I remember nothing.

"And then?"

"Come on, what do you think?"

Then there's a black hole. Nothing. Void.

"Emilia was too weak. For the ghetto. Such a little lady. She had no chance."

"Shut up," I whisper, though I'd like to scream.

"You shut up, Jakub. I've held my tongue for too long. I've held my tongue for this whole fucking Polish life. I've played along with your circus. You had Polish papers, remember?"

I don't remember anything.

"You don't want to remember. But you were too well known, the great Jakub Szapiro, the big man, you had to get out of Warsaw but you were too proud for that. You got ratted out and ended up in the ghetto like everyone else. You remember the ghetto?"

I don't remember anything.

"The great gangster Jakub Szapiro in the police cap and armband of the *Jüdische Ordnungsdienst*. A fat, drunken pig with a truncheon at your belt. Remember?"

I don't remember anything. I struggle to lift my hands and cover my ears. But I can hear everything.

"You do, you do. You're just pretending you don't. It was me who got us out of the ghetto, me! Did you forget that too?"

"Quiet, please, be quiet," I whisper.

"I won't be quiet. I've been quiet too long. I'm the one who saved us, you son of a bitch. You were too drunk to do it. And too fat. Too sluggish. I took what was left of your money and bought our way out. Remember? In '42, back before the *Grossaktion*."

Suddenly a thought appears, a terrible thought explodes in my head, burns, pulses with blinding white light.

"Where are the boys?" I ask.

Ryfka starts to laugh.

"Where the fuck do you think?" she cries. "Same place as everybody!"

Why am I alive? Why is she alive? I don't uncover my ears, but I can still hear everything.

"I didn't want them," she says. "I didn't want Emilia. I only wanted you. And there was only enough money and gold for the two of us, understand? They got left behind."

Daniel. Dawid. I remember their little bodies. White burning light explodes under my skull, flows into my stomach, twists my insides. Daniel. Dawid.

We're at the beach on the Vistula River. I don't know what year it is. They're maybe seven, maybe eight. They're up to their knees in the water, bathed in the harsh July sun. It's hot out. They're splashing, shouting. I'm lying on my back, on a towel, I can feel drops of water drying on my skin. Daniel runs up to me, shouts "Dad!" and throws himself onto me, wet and cold, and lies on top of me, so wet and cold, goose bumps making the little transparent hairs on his body stand up. I can wrap the fingers of one hand around his tiny arms. Daniel cuddles me and I stroke his wet hair. Dawid, jealous for fatherly love, runs up a moment later, I cuddle him too, their skin touches my skin, they're both lying on top of me, then we start play wrestling, the boys try to defeat me, they're sitting on my arms and shouting for me to give up, I give up, I'm defeated. I've never loved anyone so much and I never will, not before, not after, I love them with a love that could have saved them, but didn't.

◆　◆　◆

Moryc left Jakub's and Emilia's plane tickets to Thessaloniki at Ryfka's and went to his own modest apartment, where Zosia was waiting for him. He showed her their tickets. She held them a long time, studying them, the way a pious Jew studies Torah.

"We're going," she finally said. "We're going."

She embraced him. She kissed him. They went to bed and made love, thinking of their new life, then lay there smoking cigarettes, then got out of bed and didn't get dressed, they ate dinner naked, then went back to bed and made love again. The tickets lay on the nightstand, and Moryc and Zosia cuddled and talked.

They talked in hushed tones, as though it were a secret. They told each other everything they knew and thought they knew about life in Palestine, they talked about it expecting hardship, but above all full of hope. They talked about the children they'd have once they were there.

Zosia was particularly excited to imagine flying in a plane and kept asking Moryc if he knew what kind they'd be taking. Moryc answered probably a Lockheed Electra, but he wasn't sure.

Then they fell asleep in one another's arms, but soon they were awakened by the bang of the door bursting open.

Moryc woke up a half second too late. He reached for his gun, grabbed it, but didn't manage to get a shot off, because two bullets from Andrzej Ziembiński's Astra struck him in the chest and another in the forehead. That bullet, a .30-caliber like the previous two, obliterated the frontal lobes of Moryc Szapiro's brain and Moryc Szapiro was no more, and Moryc Szapiro didn't even know what had happened, the last thing he felt was fear, and fear isn't knowledge, it's bodily reflex. But once Moryc Szapiro was gone, it was as though he had never been. Those who remembered him remained, and I remember him, my brother Moryc, but my memory of Moryc is me, not Moryc. Moryc existed, but he disappeared, and when he disappeared, he disappeared completely. As if he'd never been. Nothing remained, only a body, but a body will disappear too before long; it started disappearing when it died, because a body is an arrangement of matter, not matter itself, and that arrangement ends with death. From nothing to nothing.

Zosia screamed, but briefly, because a fourth bullet hit her in the forehead and Zosia also disappeared in a fraction of a second, before she could really understand what had happened, what was happening, and why she wasn't taking a plane to Thessaloniki. And there was no more Zosia Beylin, who never managed to become Zosia Szapiro, or adopt a new name in Palestine.

"Andrzej, you didn't say the girl too . . . She was so pretty," said one of Ziembiński's men quietly.

The man had a name and his own story but that doesn't matter. What matters is from the moment they killed Zosia Beylin, he never stopped thinking of her and thought of her for decades to come, and then he died.

"She coulda kept her trap shut. Let's get outta here," replied Ziembiński, peering at the bodies. He felt satisfaction, burning satisfaction from revenge taken. He went up to the nightstand, took the tickets, inspected them, and put them in his pocket.

They left.

And I slept. I slept all day, I slept as they killed my brother, I slept badly. And it was only Ryfka who woke me up.

"Moryc is dead," she said simply.

I looked at her, I didn't understand, and then I did.

"How?" I finally choked out.

"Ziembiński. Shot. Zosia too. This morning."

"And I was asleep."

"You were asleep," she said without a shadow of pity. "That Polish whore of yours is here. She got here an hour after you did, hungover, barely alive. She's sleeping. Old Ziembiński's shot himself."

I sat up in bed and stayed there, slumped, in my shorts and undershirt, I looked at her and felt those words sinking into me, boring deep tunnels inside me. Moryc. Zosia. Dead. Tickets. Palestine. They won't go. Ziembiński. My jaw and throat hurt, my nose was stuffed up.

I remember I stood up, I stood up but it didn't feel like me standing up, it felt like someone else doing it.

He got up, I got up, Jakub got up, not saying a word, he pulled on his pants, pulled his suspenders over his shoulders, slipped on his shoes. Moryc. Dead.

"I gotta make a call," he said with a voice she'd never heard from him, seemingly lifeless.

He went to the empty salon, picked up the phone, called the Francuski, asked them to bring Emilia to the phone. He waited, pressing the receiver to his ear, losing himself in the sound, while a blazing white light pulsed in his head. Ryfka gave him aspirin and a glass of water.

"Emilia? Pack up yourself and the boys. I'm coming to get you. Yeah. We're going to the airport. Yeah. You got the money from the building? Yeah. We're flying out early tomorrow morning, to Thessaloniki. Don't tell the boys or they'll lose it. We'll wait overnight at the airport. No. No, Emilia. Moryc is dead. I know. I haven't got time for this. Tough. Yes. I'm coming for you."

He hung up. There was hope.

"You're going, just like that?" she asked. "To Palestine? And who're you gonna be there? A normal Jew? You gonna be a storekeeper?"

"Fuck off."

"You gotta find Ziembiński. You gotta kill him."

"I don't have to do anything. I don't want to kill anybody anymore. Not in this city at least. I need to get out of this cursed city. And take the boys. Far away. Far from Poland. Where there is no Poland and never will be."

"And you're going to let him just get away with this?"

"You got a gun, Ryfka?"

"Yeah."

"Then go kill him yourself. You know how to pull a trigger too."

"He was your brother."

"He's gone now. I won't bring him back from the dead."

"Say Kaddish over his grave. And kill Ziembiński."

"I don't give a shit about Kaddish, Ryfka. The rabbi can say it if he wants. There is no God. There's no anything. No miracles are gonna bring Moryc back to life. Moryc is gone."

I was calm, Jakub was completely calm, he didn't raise his voice, he spoke colorlessly, like a radio announcer.

"You got a clean shirt?" he asked.

She had a few in her wardrobe, always ready if he needed them, in two different sizes. For Jakub and for Kaplica.

"You want blue, white, or checkered?"

"Whatever."

She looked at his suit, at the ties hanging in the wardrobe, and handed him a blue shirt and a claret-colored Italian tie. For a moment she felt normal, as though this was all as usual. He got dressed and put on the tie. His suit, gray English gabardine, was a little crumpled but he didn't care anymore. He'd need new threads in Palestine anyway. Moryc said nobody wore suits there, pants and a shirt were fine. But then where would he keep his pistol? Maybe his pants pocket, but that was uncomfortable.

Moryc. Dead. Moryc is gone. Jakub feels nothing.

"Vues vet zaan mit iyo'?"[33] asked Ryfka after a moment.

He felt something for the first time since waking up.

He thought about her, tasting her skin, entering her, filling her up. Moryc. Dead.

Tickets. Palestine.

"Vus i' mit iyo'?"[34] he replied flatly.

"Come on, you fell in love with her, Jakub. Don't I know that? You think I'm blind? Why d'you think I let her in here, into my place? For you."

He looked at her, calm, seemingly detached from reality, looked at her and said nothing. She waited that silence out.

"So what?" he finally asked.

"Are you leaving her? Are you leaving her to go to Palestine?"

"Ryfka, are you asking me if I can be a man? Ryfka, you know better than anyone else I can be a man. In vi azo' kien akh zaan a mantsbil!"[35]

She didn't respond. She knew he was right. She knew he could and how he could. She understood her last chance of holding him here with her—even with his Emilia and the kids—had slipped away. She knew he was going now. Knew he'd disappear from her life. But she couldn't go with him. She couldn't leave Warsaw.

"Don't you want to see her?" she asked, feeling like she was pulling her own guts out of her stomach. That bottle of wine her trick had wanted to stick in her ass, the one she went to prison in Siberia for, suddenly seemed like nothing much compared to what was happening to her now. That sucker she'd stabbed with a knife. But she wouldn't do anything bad to Jakub. She couldn't. She'd have liked to, but she couldn't.

---

33   And her?
34   What about her?
35   And how I can be a man!

But she'd hit her target.

"Where is she?"

"In Kasia's room. Sleeping."

He went to her. She really was sleeping, curled up in a peculiar ball, naked and with the sheets only covering her from the waist down—her white skin, her hair scattered and tousled, her long fingers, her slender body. He wanted to lie down beside her. Undress. Kiss her neck, like she loved most, run his tongue over her, keep kissing her, and then hold her down under all his weight, penetrate her, put her fingers in his mouth.

He turned away, left the room, and quietly closed the door behind him. Ryfka stood in the salon.

"You leaving?" she asked.

He shrugged, went out into the stairwell, and ran down the stairs, leaving her behind him, as if she'd disappeared, as if she'd never existed.

He thought about being together in Berlin. About how they could have gone to New York, he'd even had an in, Radziwiłek was in contact with Meyer Lansky, who was looking for strong Jewish men. Jakub would have been ideal, because he didn't know anyone there, he'd have been in Lansky's hands, meaning absolutely loyal. So he'd have had the same job as in Warsaw, the same gorgeous cars and suits. He could even have boxed. Maybe could have only boxed? Another few years and he'd have managed. He'd have picked up the language somehow.

Language skills weren't what mattered in his line of work, anyway. He could get by even without the language, all he needed were fists and courage.

There was no New York. There was Palestine. Good thing too. As far as he could get from Warsaw, as far as possible from this cursed, musty city that stank of mud, shit, garlic, and incense. As far as he could get.

He walked outside, got in his Buick, and looked at his watch. He still had plenty of time. He was surprised to find he'd suddenly caught his breath again, as though the cigarettes, the cocaine he'd snorted, and the alcohol he'd drunk had disappeared. A new life. A new life.

Then Kaplica's red Chrysler turned onto Pius XI Street. Jakub leaped from his car and ran up to it.

Pantaleon turned off the engine and got out. It looked like he'd been turned off as well, like he'd run out of the fuel that had powered him until now.

"Buddy's dead, Mr. Szapiro," he said.

Jakub spotted, I spotted Kaplica's body on the back seat of the car. His bare, dirty feet stuck out from under Pantaleon's coat.

"They handed him over to me as soon as I arrived. I drove nonstop. He was already barely alive. I wanted to take him to the hospital but he told me to drive to Warsaw."

"You drove there and back without stopping for the night?"

"I slept, and my brother stayed up and watched the road through my eyes."

"Did you take something?"

"A little vodka for strength and some powder not to fall asleep. Buddy recorded a message for you on the Dictaphone, Mr. Szapiro."

"What?" he said, not understanding.

"On that diabolical machine for recording voices, Mr. Szapiro. You saw it. In the car. Go ahead and listen."

Szapiro got in the Chrysler. The interior reeked horribly of shit. Kaplica's corpse lay on the bench of the back seat, so Jakub sat on one of the folding seats.

"You drove the whole way in this stench?"

"You can always withstand a stench, Mr. Szapiro, the Good Lord has given us that much strength. A stench is nothing. A stench isn't a wound, a stench isn't an illness, a stench isn't despair. You can withstand it."

The wax cylinder was already in the Dictaphone. Jakub pulled the funnel-shaped Bakelite microphone/speaker off its hook, moved the needle to the start of the cylinder, flicked the switch from DICTATE to LISTEN, and switched on the power.

"No one's ever recorded me before but now I'm going to talk and I'll be recorded on this machine. My name is Jakub Szapiro, I'm a boxer in Warsaw, I'm thirty-seven, I was born on May 12, 1900, in Warsaw, and I've lived here my whole life long. My mother's name was Dora, my father was called Yankyev . . ." The machine spoke in Jakub's voice and cut off, staticky.

I remembered us recording that, driving with Kaplica to the Metropol after the fight, so recently, Munja was driving, then I beat up Singer the journalist at the bar, Sokoliński watched it, then we drove to Ryfka's, same as always, Buddy, Munja, and me.

"Kuba, it's me, Buddy." Kaplica's voice resonated in the speaker, weak and rustling. "By the time you hear this I ain't gonna be alive anymore, kind of a voice from beyond, like a ghost. I'm dying. I'm weak and I'm dying. I was a bad man. A great sinner. I hurt a lotta people. But now it's your turn. You're gonna be king of this city, but remember . . ."

Jakub turned off the Dictaphone.

"Buddy was still talking," said Pantaleon.

"I don't need to hear any more of that. We gotta carry him up to Ryfka's. Then you gotta hide our wheels."

"Yes, boss."

"I'm not your boss, Pantaleon. Not anymore. By tomorrow morning I'll be gone. I'm flying to Palestine."

"Yes, boss."

Pantaleon pulled his coat off Kaplica, spread it out on the sidewalk, then effortlessly pulled Kaplica's body out of the Chrysler and onto the coat. Jakub noticed the stump of an arm wrapped in a filthy bandage. Such is the fall of kingdoms and the end of kings.

They carried Kaplica's body on the coat up to Ryfka's door, Jakub knocked, Ryfka opened it after a moment, though without removing the chain.

"You still here?" she said, surprised. She wasn't supposed to ever see him again, but here she was seeing him again fifteen minutes later, like teenage lovers who break up and swear eternal love three times in a day.

"Open up," ordered Jakub.

She did. She laid eyes on Buddy's corpse. She understood.

"So Buddy made it back from Bereza . . . Pick him up."

They did.

"Put him here, I wanna look him over."

She stood over the body and remembered him taking her off the streets of Łódź, twelve years old, locking her up in a little room in Koło district, him coming to see her, twelve years old, and doing what he did to her, twelve years old, and then handing her over to the brothel.

"You're lying there, and I'm standing here, you son of a bitch. Look what you've come to."

She spat, the saliva landed on Buddy's filthy dead face. Pantaleon crossed himself piously, as though it wasn't Ryfka's spit but holy water from a priest's aspergillum, blessing Kaplica's corpse.

"Take him into one of the rooms," ordered Ryfka.

They did.

Jakub glanced at the clock. There was still time.

"Pantaleon, you gotta kill Radziwiłek," he said.

"Yes, boss."

"Can you find him?"

"If you tell me to, I'll find him."

"Ryfka, give him a call, tell him you've got his drug money. Make sure he comes himself."

"He's not an idiot, Jakub. He'll send Tyutchev or Munja, or even better some barefoot little shrimp."

She was right. Pantaleon turned the cylinder of his seven-shooter seven times, checking if all the chambers were loaded, which Jakub found so hilarious he almost laughed out loud, and sensed this was the last time he'd make fun of his comrade for checking his gun. Karpiński also took a large butcher knife from Ryfka's kitchen and the keys to the Chrysler, then went out.

He set off into the nocturnal city. His devil brother was whispering away, but Pantaleon didn't listen. He was exhausted but at the same time hopped up on the cocaine, the trip, and the voice of his devil brother, and excited envisioning what he had to do.

Upstairs, Jakub hugged Ryfka, clumsily, awkwardly, and she didn't want him to hug her either, she didn't return the embrace.

"You'll have peace. Pantaleon will find him and kill him."

"You should go with him."

"I've had enough of killing now. Pantaleon can handle it."

She wriggled out of his arms. She didn't want this.

"And what then?"

"Pantaleon is staying. He'll take Buddy's place."

"You know as well as I do Pantaleon won't take Buddy's place. You might. He can't. Somebody else'll come along. Pantaleon'll roll over for anyone with enough power. Some Pole, God forbid."

"Buddy was a Pole too."

"The hell he was. Buddy was a normal person, like us."

Jakub thought about the inevitable violence. Pantaleon would kill Radziwiłek. Radziwiłek would kill Pantaleon. Blood would flow. Happy Litani would sing, and see people with his song.

Then Anna came into the salon, sleepy, wrapped in someone else's very immodest peignoir, which Jakub and Ryfka both immediately recognized as one of Kasia's working outfits.

"If you're looking for work, by any chance, I got a job for you," Ryfka said, with clearly audible satisfaction.

Anna shrugged and went up to Jakub, who was sitting at the bar. She rested a hand on his back.

"Get me out of here. Let's go somewhere. Please."

Szapiro glanced at his watch.

"In eight hours I'm flying out of Okęcie Airport. I'm going to Palestine and never coming back. So I can't take you anywhere."

She wrinkled her nose as though about to burst into tears, but she didn't.

"That's enough. Get me out of here."

Jakub looked at Ryfka. Ryfka had turned her back to him. She didn't want him to see her crying. Jakub went up to her, mindful he was now seeing her for the last time. He laid a hand on her shoulder.

"Goodbye, Ryfka. I'll always love you and remember you," he whispered and was so embarrassed at his saccharine tone it made his guts twist. He'd wanted to say something so badly that he'd said the stupidest thing possible.

"Go to hell, Jakub. I curse you, your Jewish wife, your Jewish children, your Polish whore, your fucking Palestine, and your brother's memory. I curse you."

He turned away, took Anna by the hand, and they left. That curse hung over his head, hung over my head, for ever and ever, until the end of time, until never. I curse you, your Jewish wife, your Jewish children, your Polish whore. For ever and ever. White, burning, pulsing light in my head, it burns, as if meant to burn through my skull, through my skin and hair, as if I was meant to disappear, to incinerate in that white flame.

Out the windows, over Pius XI Street, Litani swam through the air, excited and agitated. He was singing.

Andrzej Ziembiński left Moryc's apartment satisfied and happy, but feeling like his work was not yet done. He got into his Chevrolet Master, went to Oaza for a drink, drank for a long time, talked to the whores, and finally took one to a room for an hour, but he'd drunk too much to get it up, so they simply lay in each other's arms, and the hooker told him her clichéd life story, not sparing a single tragic lumpenproletarian twist or turn, nor an entire family tree's worth of Hanias, Kasias, Stanisławs, Janeks, and Krzysztofs, a full cast of characters whose stories didn't interest even the street balladeers singing of Jakub and Ryfka's love. Finally, weary, he fell asleep.

No one sang ballads of Colonel Koc. Colonel Koc was anything but fascinating and at that very moment was thinking how he was an uninteresting, boring, uncharismatic martinet. He thought this as he drove to a meeting with Marshal Rydz-Śmigły, who'd summoned him urgently. He was sad. But he still hoped the new Poland the marshal wanted to create would give him hope for a better life. A truer life. One he wished to devote completely to the glory of Poland.

He reached the palace, presented himself in the antechamber, his trepidation mounting; finally he was called, he entered, clicked his heels, stood at attention. Alongside the marshal sat the prime minister, whose presence at the meeting startled Koc slightly. He was not offered a seat.

"Well, look who it is," growled the marshal.

Koc sniffed nervously. Prime Minister Składkowski said nothing.

"I've just found out from the prime minister that someone around here is thinking of staging a coup!" roared the marshal. "Whoever's spreading these rumors, Colonel, deserves to get court-martialed for treason! I hope you've got nothing to do with this!"

Koc quickly gathered his thoughts.

"Marshal, I never—"

"Silence, Colonel! You are responsible for this! Morally, and legally, and generally, and before the homeland, and, well . . . Responsible!"

"Yes sir!"

"You will resign the National Unity leadership! You're as suited to it as a lump of shit is to dinner! And no more cozying up to those Phalanx punks! Do I make myself clear?"

"Yes sir!" cried Koc and even from a few yards away could practically feel the flecks of spittle flying out of the marshal's mouth with each exclamation striking his face.

Prime Minister Składkowksi stood up.

"Is it true training sessions are being held in Golędzinów district with those hoodlums?"

"General, I can report that is not the case!" said Koc, marveling that the prime minister would ask such a question, being, as he was, simultaneously minister of internal affairs and therefore head of the State Police, which had jurisdiction over the Golędzinów barracks.

"Now scram," snarled Rydz-Śmigły.

Koc fled the marshal's office and felt unadulterated, concentrated hatred, the worst kind of hatred, because it was powerless.

A second later, the marshal's office door opened a crack and Rydz-Śmigły peeked through, then came out into the hallway.

"What in the name of almighty fuck is going on?" he snapped quietly. "The PM came to me with our proscription list!"

"I apologize, Marshal."

"Don't give me apologies, just make absolutely fucking sure they tidy up out there and ship them all off to Bereza on the double."

"The Phalanx men?"

"No, the parish priests. Yes the fucking Phalanx men!"

"All of them?"

"Well how many are out there?"

"One hundred fifty."

"No, lock up about thirty, the rest'll get scared and go to ground."

"But won't that have to go through the ministry?"

"Like hell it will. Call Biernacki, tell him we're sending a transport, and then go to Golędzinów and tell the policemen to arrest those little shits, stick them all on a bus under escort, and get Biernacki to instruct Kamala to hold them a couple months."

"No documents?"

"No, none, there can't be a paper trail."

"Yes sir. Piasecki too?"

"No, leave Piasecki. Why should they bust a gut over him?"

"Yes sir."

"Now don't worry, Adam, it'll be fine," said the marshal, suddenly taking a milder tone and even giving Colonel Koc a pat on the shoulder. "Once I take the presidency, I'll give you Internal Affairs and we'll tidy up anyway. Just got to be a little patient. Then in 1940 we can start everything our way. Good and quickly seldom meet. All right?"

"Yes sir."

"Off you go."

Koc drove straight to Golędzinów. He thought hard how Poland would change in three years when the marshal seized the presidency. How they'd put everything in order. Everything. How the nation would unite and, being united, move in one direction, devoting all efforts to greatness.

At Golędzinów he required no documents or authorizations. He knew perfectly well that in Poland a uniform, epaulettes, and a name got you further than bureaucracy. The police sergeant simply couldn't conceive of refusing an order from Colonel Koc—who after all, was Colonel Koc—and carried it out unquestioningly, even though Koc had no authority to issue it. Piasecki's men were arrested without great resistance, nothing got broken but a few ribs and two fingers, plus a couple knocked-out teeth.

When, four days later, thirty terrified Phalanx men entered the gears of Kamala-Kurhański's machine, the commandant wasn't pleased. He preferred Jews and communists as prisoners. But he was a Polish officer and to him an order meant duty, and his duty was a matter of honor. And since his orders were clear, he went to work on Piasecki's boys with absolute dedication and professionalism.

Less than three years later, the Gestapo arrested Kamala-Kurhański, then under an alias, and sent him on one of the first transports to Auschwitz. That same transport held communists being sent to the camp, many of whom had done a few rounds in Bereza. They recognized him the very first day. And they ripped him apart. It was fun for the German guards to watch. There was nothing left of Kamala-Kurhański, not even anything to bury—he was torn to shreds under the fingernails of men he used to torment. There's no meaning in that, it's just what happened. It didn't take Pantaleon long to find Radziwiłek. There was no meaning in that either, it was just a thing that happened.

Radziwiłek was drinking at Glajszmitka's, drinking like a man who had the city—meaning the world—at his feet. He didn't notice Kaplica's Imperial with Pantaleon behind the wheel coming down Okopowa Street, but Pantaleon spotted Radziwiłek leaning on the counter in his Rifleman's Association uniform, with Munja and Tyutchev beside him. Pantaleon turned onto Dzika Street and parked the Chrysler farther along, in front of the Circus—as the homeless shelter the Albertines ran was known. He recalled spending three months there in 1924, after escaping the real circus, and getting thrown out because he broke a monk's arm, nose, and three ribs when the monk tried to exorcise his devil brother.

Pantaleon smiled at the memory.

He put his revolver in one coat pocket and the knife in the other, climbed out, walked up to Glajszmitka's, and waited. The bar had no toilets. If you had to go you went into the courtyard entryway next door, and it was there Pantaleon waited, concealed in a recess in the wall. It stank horribly, but a stench never bothered Pantaleon.

Munja came first. Once he'd unbuttoned his pants and fished out his dick to piss, Pantaleon snuck up behind him, covered his mouth with his left hand, and with the right stabbed the knife into his kidney, yanked it out, stabbed again, yanked, stabbed. The pain of a blade puncturing the kidneys, destroying the ganglia and arteries inside, is paralyzing in the literal sense, Pantaleon's large hand on Munja's mouth was only there to hold him in place. Pantaleon's left arm and the blade driven between his ribs sent Munja to his knees, then Pantaleon once again yanked out the knife and, making with a long, quick cut, sliced through his throat, severing arteries, veins, esophagus, and larynx, cutting so deep the blade ground against Munja's spine. And he didn't let go.

"So this is how it ends, comrade, with me slitting your throat like a pig, not you slitting mine," he whispered in his ear. "How lucky for you this suffering redeems all your sins, your blood has washed your sins clean, comrade, and so you die innocent."

Within a few seconds Munja was dead. Out of Christian charity and respect for the deceased, Pantaleon put Munja's penis back in his pants, dragged his corpse into the courtyard, hid it behind a wooden chicken coop, and returned to his hiding place.

He hadn't expected Radziwiłek to follow Munja, but that was what happened. The Doctor, probably without noticing Munja's disappearance, came out to pee, but once he'd unbuttoned his uniform trousers he felt a greater need, so he pulled them and his underwear down and worked his way into a squat, propping himself up with one hand on the wall. Pantaleon was just about to make his move when someone came into the entryway.

"Fuck off, I'm shitting here!" shouted Radziwiłek.

"Munja *ne vernulsya*," said Tyutchev.

"Probably went home. Now scram!"

Tyutchev returned to the bar and kept drinking alone, reading his poetry.

Pantaleon had no intention of showing the Doctor the mercy he'd offered Munja. Pantaleon and his devil brother remembered too clearly all the cruelties the Doctor had committed against them.

Radziwiłek died slowly, not far from Munja's body, his pants still down, since Pantaleon didn't pull them up, recalling Ryfka's girls and what they'd suffered at Radziwiłek's hands. At the end, he showed still-living Radziwiłek his own severed genitals, then killed him, wiped his hands on his uniform, took the Doctor's pistol, and went into Glajszmitka's. He walked up to the bar and stopped beside Tyutchev.

Tyutchev looked up from his book at Pantaleon, noticed the blood on his clothes, moved as though to pull his pistol out of his pocket, but froze, knowing he wouldn't make it in time.

"Forget it," murmured Pantaleon. "They're finished. I got nothing against you."

He'd made up his mind to spare Tyutchev.

"You can be with us."

Tyutchev shook his head in disbelief, ordered a tea, and went back to his reading.

Pantaleon figured today he deserved it, so he allowed himself two shots of vodka, had a little herring, and went home without going back for Kaplica's Chrysler, since he lived nearby on the corner of Miła and Lubecki Streets. The light in his apartment window told him his wife wasn't asleep yet. The thought pleased him.

Unfortunately she was furious when he got home, saying she didn't know where he'd been the last couple days, that he never drank when she first married him but now he constantly reeked of booze. Pantaleon wasn't in the mood for a lecture, so he seized her by the scruff of the neck and hauled her into the kitchen, laid her on the table, then, slightly drunk, fumbled with his belt.

Pantaleon Karpiński's wife knew what she was in for. A beating—a long, hard beating until she bled, until her skin broke, until he wore himself out. Then maybe, even worse, he'd move on to his painful idea of lovemaking.

She got to her feet and looked at him.

"My mama once said no matter how bad you were, at least you don't drink. But now you're a damn drunk like all the others."

Pantaleon didn't listen to what she was saying, because he thought listening to women made even less sense than listening to birds singing. So Pantaleon Karpiński's wife grabbed a kitchen knife and plunged it into Pantaleon's throat, hitting her target dead-on.

As he gazed at the growing puddle of blood on the floor, still standing and clutching his throat with both hands, he thought it must be divine justice for him to die the same way he'd just killed two men.

"Only the devil will judge us," wheezed his devil brother through Pantaleon's mouth, and then Pantaleon died.

When he collapsed facedown on the floor, Pantaleon Karpiński's wife parted the long hair combed down over the face of his devil brother. His blind mouth was moving. She drove the knife into him, once, twice, over and over again she stabbed the devil brother's face on the back of Pantaleon Karpiński's head, to make sure they were both dead. Then she pulled herself together, washed the blood off, and dug through his pockets for his wallet. When she found it, she was thrilled it was so plentifully full, then hit the town to celebrate this incredible night and to relive the days before the war when she'd been pretty and young, and the men had looked at her greedily.

She didn't relive those days in the end, because they were long ago and not entirely true, but the fun she had that one last time belonged only to her and to those she paid so plentifully with Pantaleon's money. She even found an admirer of her sixty-year-old, corpulent body, who pleasured her tremendously on a bench in a secluded spot on Muranów Square.

Then, early in the morning, she stumbled back toward the apartment on Miła Street, where Pantaleon rested as peacefully as only the dead can. The only people still out at this hour on Miła Street weren't so much suspicious as obviously immoral, but Mrs. Karpińska felt invincible, at least so long as word hadn't yet gotten out about her husband's death.

Litani floated above Miła Street, and as Mrs. Karpińska was passing the corner of Zamenhof Street, the sperm whale with the burning eyes swept down into the canyon of four-story apartment houses, opened his cetacean maw as wide as he could, scooped up plump Mrs. Karpińska, sucked her in, swallowed her, digested her, and then spewed her out in a cloud of brown excrement floating in the air, just as he will swallow all of us and shit us out.

Litani was also watching somewhere else, as Anna and Jakub got into Jakub's Buick, as we got in, as we drove to the Ziembińskis' house.

"My father shot himself," says Anna. "And Andrzej's going to kill me."

Jakub says nothing. I say nothing. I can feel something is breaking inside me, and I know I have to hurry before it breaks completely. I know inside she's saying more. I know inside, in my head, she's still saying: *Don't leave me. Stay with me. Send them to Palestine and stay with me.* But she won't say that out loud.

I park in front of the Ziembińskis' house and we go inside.

"He's still up there, lying on his desk with a hole in his head." Anna points to the stairs going up.

I don't know what she expects me to tell her. That I don't care her father's dead? That theoretically I'm glad? She doesn't look shocked either. She kisses me and reaches for my fly, I'd like to refuse her, but I can't.

"Stay with me," she whispers once I'm inside her. She whispers so quietly I can't hear it.

She puts my fingers in her mouth.

I break away from her and button my pants. She sits half-naked in the hallway on a secretary table, whose drawers probably hold lint brushes, or shoe polish, or a sewing kit, or something equally trifling and unnecessary. She looks at me. She doesn't speak. *Don't leave me,* says her silence. *Don't go away.* A silence louder than any scream.

I turn away and start to go. I want to stay with her. I want that more than anything else in the world.

I want. I go. Step by step, as if I were just learning to walk. I go. I want to turn back, but it's too late. There's no going back now.

I leave the Ziembińskis'. In front of the house sits Andrzej Ziembiński's Chevrolet, in front of the Chevrolet stands Ziembiński, a pistol in his hand.

Where's my gun?

The small, flat Colt I always have on me is lying under the pillow in the room at Ryfka's.

I didn't bring my gun, why didn't I bring my gun?

The large Browning is in the glove compartment next to the bundle of five hundred hundred-dollar bills. Both guns are fully loaded, my guns always have a full magazine and an empty chamber. And I haven't got either one on me.

Ziembiński looks at me but he doesn't raise the hand with the pistol in it. So I walk toward the car, calmly but confidently, I walk and my pulse is pounding like I've just left the ring after a second round of heavy sparring. I walk. His eyes follow me blankly. I walk past him, he doesn't shoot me in the face, maybe he'll shoot me in the back, but he doesn't. I simply walk past him.

"I shot your brother. And his whore. And now I'm going to shoot your whore," he says behind me, but he doesn't shoot. I don't turn around.

I get in the car.

Ziembiński isn't looking at me. He's walking to the house.

I can reach for the pistol inside the glove compartment. Get out and shoot him before he makes it inside for her.

I have three seconds to do it. I can make it. I won't miss. But if I kill him, I'll go to her. And if I see her again, I won't go to the airport. I'll stay with her. I should save her life and kill her brother, but I won't.

I turn the ignition and time seems to slow down, I clearly hear the crankshaft turn, the cylinders move, and the spark plugs suddenly light, the engine start. Ready. Right then I know the moment I could have saved her has passed. Andrzej Ziembiński walks into his house.

I can't drive off. I know it's already too late, I won't make it, still I should try, maybe he's hesitating, maybe he hasn't pulled the trigger yet, it can't be easy firing a gun at your own sister. I should get out of the car, run for the house, kill him.

But I don't want to kill anymore. I sit in the car.

A shot. And another. Now I know. I let him do it. I let him do it so I could escape Warsaw.

Suddenly calm, I drive away.

Ziembiński will die too, as everyone does. He'll hide out for two years in a boardinghouse in Otwock on his father's money, he won't fight in September '39 because a wanted man can't be called up, later some old friends will help him join the Confederation of the Nation, a small, far-right resistance group where he'll write to the "Youth of the Empire" under a pseudonym, meticulously drawing little maps of a Slavic empire to be founded on the ruins of the old world. While serving in their Cadre Strike Battalions, he'll shoot a few Germans and *Volksdeutsche*. After 1945, he'll reject Piasecki's reconciliation with the communist authorities and keep fighting in the resistance. He'll shoot two Reds. In 1947 he'll get caught and after a long, torture-filled investigation and a short trial, they'll shoot him in Mokotów Prison and throw his body, disguised in a Wehrmacht uniform, into an unmarked grave along with many others.

But he'll live another ten years. I let him. So I could escape Warsaw.

I drive on, I don't recognize the streets, I don't notice the people, the other cars, I just change gears, work the gas and the brake, sometimes I turn, sometimes I drive straight through an intersection. I have no thoughts.

At some point I realize I'm passing the Francuski Hotel. I look at my watch and suddenly come to my senses, suddenly come back to reality. Our plane is leaving in forty-five minutes.

Forty-five minutes. I can make it.

I brake hard, the Buick dances on the cobblestones, I leap out of the car and run up to get Emilia and the boys, they're frightened of me, all three of them are frightened of me, there's no time to pack, I'm yelling, you're drunk, who cares, come on, Emilia grabs some bags and Daniel's hand, I take Dawid, the boys take the large teddy bears I'd brought them back once from some trip, the boys were still really little then, and now they're screaming, we don't want to go to Palestine, we don't want to go, it occurs to me without Moryc I've got no contacts there, but come on, I have seventy thousand dollars, that's enough to buy yourself a good life, we'll get as far as Lydda at least, we're in the car, Jerozolimskie Avenue, Grójecka Street, the straight-eight engine's cylinders roar and howl as I step on the gas, we zoom down Grójecka doing sixty, eighty.

I reach into the back, take the boys' teddy bears, they protest, I hand the bears to Emilia, I take my knife out of my pocket, I hand it to her too.

"Cut them open and hide the money inside. Take out two thousand dollars for expenses, keep it on hand. You got a needle and thread?"

She does, in her wallet, needle's already threaded. As always. We drive. Keep an eye out. Airport. Emilia sews the stuffed animals back up and the boys get them back. The pistol stays in the glove compartment. We get out. I leave the keys on the seat. I don't lock the car. I'm not going to need it anymore.

But I'm sure no one will touch it for a long time anyway, they'll be afraid to, everyone knows it's my Buick.

Why can I remember so little?

I remember we made it in time. That's important. We're on time.

Passport control, we show our real documents, the tickets are real too, Jakub Szapiro, Emilia Kahan, is this your wife? No, but the children are ours.

The boys have already forgotten they didn't want to leave, they're excited, an elegant, if somewhat short and plump, Lockheed Electra stands on the tarmac, silver and shining like a mirror, two engines, a twin tail, the staff lets us approach, we approach, it says LOT POLISH AIRLINES over the windows, the tail fin shows a horizontal crane in a circle, we wait for them to open the doors, standing in front of the plane I hug them, I hug the boys, I hug Emilia, they open the doors and invite us in, we squeeze through the small entrance, inside are ten seats in two rows, each seat by a window, with a narrow aisle down the middle, the pilot greets us.

They ask for passengers Moryc Szapiro and Zosia Beylin, no, Captain, Moryc and Zosia won't be flying to Palestine, the boys ask where Uncle Moryc is, I don't answer, Emilia says nothing either.

We sit in front, the seats are very comfortable, the boys are thrilled they've got their own seats like grown-ups and can see what's happening in the cockpit. There are three more passengers behind us, all men, in coats and hats, they're saying something in French. We get in our seats, the plane shudders as the engines start and the propellers vroom to life, we taxi onto the runway and take off, I'm flying in a plane for the first and last time, Emilia is scared, I'm not, the boys are squealing, the runway falls away under our wheels, the plane lifts off from the ground, I hear the landing gear retract, and Warsaw suddenly appears beneath us.

Split by the stripe of the Vistula, joined together by four bridges, Mokotów, Ochota, Saska, the oval of the racetracks, the flat squares of Lindley's Waterworks, and beyond, my homeland, my kingdom of the Northern District, a kingdom I am abandoning for the sands and palms of Eretz Yisrael, though I believe neither in God, nor in the book, nor in our blood.

I look down. I see Tłomackie. I see Kercelak. The lines of streets, Leszno, Chłodna, Miła, I don't know which is which, but I know they're there, I know everyone who walks their cobblestones, and everyone surely knows me, on those streets I am Jakub Szapiro, policemen doff their caps to me, girls smile, observant Jews indignantly avert their eyes, the fascists and market sellers fear me, I am Jakub Szapiro.

Be king of this city, says Buddy's voice humming through the Dictaphone. *Be king of this city. Behold your kingdom.*

"We're turning around," I say.

"What?" says Emilia, stunned.

"I gotta stay. Go with the boys. I'll join you later."

"You're drunk. You've lost your mind."

"We're turning around!" I bellow. "Captain! Land, please! Excuse me! Please land the plane!"

I unbuckle my seat belt, the plane is still gaining altitude, so the path to the cockpit is difficult, I have to practically climb, I grab the walls of the narrow passageway.

"Sit down, sir!" screams the pilot. "Sit down, dammit!"

"Captain, please land, I can't leave Warsaw. Please land! I remembered something!"

"Sit down!"

"Jakub, sit down!" shouts Emilia.

The boys are crying. The three gentlemen passengers are shouting in Polish and French for me to calm down. But I won't calm down.

The other pilot unbuckles his seat belt, gets up, and seizes me by the arm, holding on to the seat back with the other.

"Calm down, please, take your seat."

"I can't leave, I can't!" I cry.

"Please, sir, you can disembark in Lwów if you have to, we'll be there in two hours."

"Land the plane! Land the plane!" I shout.

The pilot turns around, holding on with one hand.

"Staś, land her, we can't fly with this lunatic, it's dangerous with him panicking, we gotta land," he shouts to his commander, who agrees with a nod of his head. "We're landing, did you hear that, sir? Now sit down."

"Fucking Yid," swears the commander under his breath. "Maniac!"

I sit down. Fucking Yid. I sit down. Emilia looks at me, terrified. She doesn't say anything.

"We're not going to Palestine?" asks Daniel.

"You're going, I'll catch up with you later," I say, although I know Emilia won't go without me.

"We're staying!" says Dawid happily, because he knows it too.

Both the boys are happy.

If I'd taken Bernsztajn under my wing all those years ago, if he'd been with me that day, I'd have told him to stay on the plane. He'd have flown to Palestine. He'd have always said the Kaddish Yatom on Naum Bernsztajn's Yahrzeit. He'd have fought in all those wars of Moshe Inbar's, the ones I've read about in the local paper and seen on television my whole life. If I'd taken him in back then.

My sons would have fought in them too. If I hadn't gotten off the plane.

But I didn't take him. And I did get off. Naum Bernsztajn's body chopped up like a rooster for kappores.

The Lockheed banks and lowers its altitude. We're approaching for landing.

I am Jakub Szapiro. Not time to abdicate yet.

I am king of this city.

I close my eyes.

The two Pratt & Whitney radial engines turn the two propellers. Each propeller has two arms. The propellers spin in the air and pull the Lockheed's silver, glistening fuselage behind them. The pilot presses the appropriate control switch and the wheels emerge from their niches in the engine pods.

Warsaw is beneath us. We come in for landing. Then the plane takes off again, this time without us, the pilot plots a course southeast, to Lwów, where the first stopover is planned. Then Cernăuți, Bucharest, Sofia, and Thessaloniki, then Athens, then Lydda. But I am staying. Emilia is staying and the boys are staying, their little boyish bodies, their wet, cold skin on the hot sand on the Vistula riverbank. I am staying to reign and my reign will last twenty-three months, then I will lose everything.

The boys' little bodies, their skinny arms and legs, their tiny fingers. They are granted death, I am condemned to life.

"When are you coming back, Dad?" asks Dawid four years later, much more grown up, as I leave the apartment in a Jewish policeman's cap and armband, I'm leaving drunk and don't yet know I'm seeing him for the last time, and later on the other side I'll still hope I can get them out of there, that I can get them in time, and then Ryfka and I stand in a Polish crowd on the Polish side of the wall, me no longer wearing a Jewish policeman's cap or armband or a star on my chest, I'm wearing a hat, I've got false documents, and a mustache and glasses; Ryfka holds me by the hand and we watch as on the other side of the wall Nalewki, Tłomackie, and Miła burn, our whole world with all the people in it, and I know I didn't get them in time. I think of the plane that left Okęcie Airport and landed six stops later in Lydda.

Small, boyish bodies, arms so skinny I could close the fingers of one hand around them, wet, cold skin on the hot sand by the Vistula River. To atone for Naum Bernsztajn's body, their bodies were chopped up for kappores.

And now we're still over Warsaw. Over Nalewki, Tłomackie, over Miła Street, over Gęsia Street and Kercelak market, over my kingdom. The Lockheed hangs over the city as though it's lost all its speed, like a child's model on a string suspended over a desk.

I look out the window of the plane and I see the gray head of a sperm whale. His eyes are burning.

He looks at me, opens his toothy maw, and sings his hunting song.

Berlin—Pilchowice
April 2015–June 2016

ACKNOWLEDGMENTS

Special thanks to Piotr Paziński, for scholarly advice on details of Jewish history and society; Ewa Geller, for translations of dialogue into Yiddish; and Sebastian Schulman, for his help preparing the Yiddish texts for the English edition.

ABOUT THE AUTHOR

Photo © Zuza Krajewska

Szczepan Twardoch is the author of the bestselling novels *Morphine*, *Drach*, and *The King of Warsaw*. He is the recipient of numerous honors for his work, including the Brücke Berlin Preis, Le Prix du Livre Européen, and Nike Literary Award: Audience Award. Rights to his novels have been sold in over a dozen countries. *The King of Warsaw* is the first of his books to be translated into English. A TV series based on the novel is being produced by Canal+. He lives in Pilchowice, Upper Silesia. For more information, visit www.szczepantwardoch.pl/en/home.

ABOUT THE TRANSLATOR

Photo © 2016 Julia Sanches

Sean Gasper Bye is a translator of Polish literature, including books by Lidia Ostałowska, Filip Springer, and Małgorzata Szejnert. A native of Bucks County, Pennsylvania, he studied modern languages at University College London and international studies at the School of Oriental and African Studies. He spent five years as Literature and Humanities Curator at the Polish Cultural Institute New York. He is a winner of the *Asymptote* Close Approximations prize and a recipient of a National Endowment for the Arts translation fellowship.